ENDEAVOR'S
run

BOOK 1 IN THE HOPE PROPHECY SERIES

TOBIN MARKS

Boyle
&
Dalton

Book Design & Production:
Boyle & Dalton
www.BoyleandDalton.com

Copyright © 2022 by
Tobin Marks
LCCN: 2021924891

Paperback ISBN: 978-1-63337-581-9
E-Book ISBN: 978-1-63337-582-6

Printed in the United States of America
1 3 5 7 9 10 8 6 4 2

PRAISE FOR ENDEAVOR'S RUN

"Tobin Marks has created a masterpiece. Not only has he created a magical world on a different planet in space, but he has a constructed some fantastic characters. This is the second book I have read from this author, and I'm completely blown away. This story was full of suspense, action, fantasy, family craziness, and a bit of magic. It's a fantastic mashup of science fiction, fantasy, and adventure."

—Madison Degraffenreid, the Chapter Goddess

"Wow, that was one hell of a ride! This book managed to break my heart at times and make me laugh out loud at others. It has action, mystery, humour, adventure, prophecies, dragons, spaceships, psychic powers, sword fights, and aliens. Whew! This was an awesome combination."

—May, Goodreads reviewer

"Tobin Marks has mastered the art of transition and engages the reader at every point of the story. The science mixed with the fantasy aspect is impressively intelligent and incredibly entertaining."

—Katie, Goodreads reviewer

"This book offers emotional character interaction and intensive action scenes. It masterfully creates scientific technology. At times I felt as though I was in a virtual reality with the characters and scenes. *Endeavor's Run* is carefully crafted to combine the human spirit and science fiction."

—Patricia Cifra, Goodreads reviewer

"First let me say one thing…DRAGONS!!!"

—Karen, Goodreads reviewer

"This book is mind blowing! The plot is absolutely incredible. Marks' way of describing scenes, technical details and world building is just amazing."

—Shuchi Vyaz, Goodreads reviewer

"The story is beyond great, the character development is unmatched (so many great details), and I cannot wait to see what is ahead in the remaining books of this trilogy."

—Matt, Goodreads reviewer

"*Endeavor's Run* is so very well done. Sci-fi here and fantasy there. This is the first installment and I have to say, I can't wait to read all of them. Solid plot and solider (that's not a word) writing. Solid work, Mr. Marks."

—Daft Scholar, Goodreads reviewer

"What a fantastic read! Marks crams so much world building and character growth into his pages that at times it can be hard to keep up. I found that this book was the perfect blend of science fiction and fantasy. You've got starships with virtual reality decks that let the main character run and fight wherever he pleases, in spite of being in the blackness of space. You've got astral projection and telekinesis. You've even got dragons. You can't go wrong with dragons!"

—M.J. Falke, Goodreads reviewer

FOR ANYA, BRITT, LORRAINE(S)
WITH INSPIRED LOVE

NORTHERN OCEAN

Fire Bay

Rond'r
Mountain

North Pole

Sanctuary
of the
Final Order

Drakon Rus

Valley
of Towers

Split
Mountain

Spiral River

Troytown

Rodina's Loir

Hidden Trail

Spine

Crystal River

Cambia

Magellan's
Fist

Northern
Continent

N

NORTHERN OCEAN

PROLOGUE

MESSAGE SENT
AQUEOUS—ORBIT DAY 11 - AD 2110

There were no victors nor vanquished in the eternal war between land and sea, but it was a perpetually bloody conflict that had inflicted countless casualties.

Always on the same man.

For millennia, a wall of giant crystal shards had stood their unyielding vigil at the battle line: a small stretch of coastline on the watery world of Aqueous. Century after century these stone sentinels had held firm against the ocean's relentless assault. Murderous waves broke against the jagged columns, and died in a frothy spray, giving life to the warm swash that gently caressed the unconscious man bleeding out at the water's edge. Crimson rivulets of his blood turned pink as they diluted and soaked into the wet sand.

Though the Earthling had only moments to live, fate decreed that he would not die alone. A giant dragon towered over him and spewed a white-hot jet of flame that blasted a dozen meters in the air. After a few seconds the flame died out and the dragon craned its long muscular neck downward until its open mouth hovered a mere meter over the unmoving man. Steam rose off the viscous red liquid that dripped from the dragon's carnassial teeth and bathed the man just as its jaws were about to engulf him.

But there was a third being present as well, someone who had watched this enduring spectacle countless times.

The constant witness.

Looking down from her disembodied state, the woman was unable to tear her eyes away from what the dragon was doing to the man. This was a recurring scene, one she'd seen many times throughout her life, more than any other vision, but it had never been like this before—never this vivid nor palpable.

She watched transfixed as the dragon suddenly tensed. Its quick movement flicked tiny droplets of water off its golden hide, and it lifted its gaping, red-drenched maw away from the dying man. The creature seemed to sense her presence and slowly turned its reptilian head until it faced her. Its eyes, green with red viper pupils, narrowed with recognition as they bored directly into hers. The woman was shocked beyond comprehension; how could it possibly know she was there?

This too had never happened before.

A voice—she was certain it came from the dragon—strong and resolute, suddenly entered her head. *"It is time, Mother. You must hurry. Everything depends on your message."* Its fierce unblinking gaze lingered a moment before turning back to the blood-stained sand, and then, with unexpected gentleness, the dragon picked up the mortally wounded man, leapt into the air, and flew toward the human colony.

"Mother?" Why did it call her that? Time for what? What could that possibly mean? The dragon's words, especially its tone, sounded literal, but that was impossible. The bond between mother and child was the strongest among all life forms in the universe, and like the injured man, the woman was a human born on Earth.

But this was not Earth.

Even more disturbing than the dragon's words was the voice it used to speak them, a voice she found hauntingly familiar.

Because it was her own.

Dr. Nadezhda Yanbeyeva gasped for breath as she bolted awake, heart pounding, and kicked off the clammy sheets that clung to her legs. Nadya gripped the edge of her bunk and shook her head to clear it from the fog of sleep.

How could she possibly interpret this?

How was it that an entity from a vision so far in the future could acknowledge her?

It took a moment, but as her mind became focused, an unsettling clarity slowly replaced her confusion, and the dragon's words began to make sense. "*It is time.*" If taken at face value they could only mean one thing: a warning. "*You must hurry.*" Nadya groaned as understanding swept over her. She pushed a sweat-darkened blond tendril away from her face and scrambled out of bed. In her rush to don her uniform, a slight moan escaped her throat because she knew the dragon's warning meant that there was little time left to carry out the most important moment of her life: the event she had been born for. Nadya hurried to begin the process that would result in a man of her bloodline leading humanity during their most desperate hour.

One thousand years in the future.

An hour later she and her husband, Sasha, were in the tiny launch bay control room preparing a drone for its return mission to Earth. The Earth they alone knew no longer existed.

With his back against the wall, Sasha had squeezed in next to the small console and retrieved the override program he'd buried deep in the starship's database. After a couple minutes he glanced down at his wife seated in the cramped launch room's only chair. "Tell me more about this dream," he asked, and then dropped his voice. "Sorry, you know I meant '*vision*'."

Ignoring his entreaty, she pushed to complete the task—her task. "Later, Sasha," she insisted, "we must launch now!"

"All right, Nadya, but I still can't access the catapult system. My override is limited," he told her as he finalized the drone's flight plan. "You do realize that without the catapult, the drone's small EMD will take almost one hundred years to reach Earth," he explained while initiating the launch sequence. "And besides, your message isn't uploaded yet."

"It doesn't matter. I'll upload it after it's too late to retrieve. Now launch!"

He tapped on the Nav-Screen. An electronic alarm sounded just as the airlock doors opened, and the drone was flung into space. "It's away, Nadya," said the worried man. "I hope we don't end up in the brig."

"Hush, Moozh, while I send the message."

"Captain Troy," yelled the starship's navigation officer from across the arkship's bridge, "a communication drone has just launched."

"What? I haven't authorized this!" The captain jumped out of his control chair and ran over to the navigation console. "How was it accessed?"

"Sir, there seems to be a remote override installed from the launch bay itself."

"Retrieve it now!"

The navigation officer frantically tapped his keyboard for a few seconds, then stopped, turned, and told his captain, "I can't, sir. The override has locked out this console."

"Damn it to hell," growled the captain of the *Magellan II*. "Can you at least access the message it's carrying?"

"Yes, sir. I still have telemetry function." A slight frown creased the officer's brow. "That's odd. There's no message aboard—wait! A message is being uploaded now."

"Cut it off. Cut it the hell off now!"

"Nadya, the bridge cut off your feed." Sasha looked over at his wife, even more worried than before. "I don't think all of it made it."

"I know, but hopefully it was enough. God help them all if it wasn't."

CHAPTER 1

DARK DRAGONS
CAMBRIA—AQUEOUS - AD 3087

Four dragon riders approached the Cambrian province in the pitch-black dead of night. No starlight ever penetrated the mass of clouds that shrouded every square meter of land on Aqueous, and they had to rely on dead reckoning to find their target. But these were elite riders, the army's covert mission experts—the Dark Dragons.

They knew exactly where to go.

A few electric lights glowed in Cambria, so when the riders were close enough to the city, they adjusted their heading and silently glided to their destination. As they approached their target, a large three-story residence, two of the riders remained aloft and kept watch circling the house while the other two landed on a large balcony, only meters from their objective.

The riders were armed only with combat daggers tightly secured to their flat black flight suits. The dragons had been muzzled, and their feet bound with soft cotton cloth.

After quietly dismounting, the two riders approached each other. "It's the second door on the left," the officer in charge whispered. "Here's the blanket, so wrap him up nice and warm like, and be quick about it."

The other rider looked down at the blanket and seethed. "I didn't sign up with the Dark Dragons to kidnap babies from their cribs."

At six centimeters under two meters, the young soldier stood half a head taller than his superior officer. The older man had to reach up to grab him by the nape of his collar to draw him in uncomfortably close.

"Great fucking time to bring this up, Moroz. But since we're already here, allow me to refresh your memory. He may be a bastard, but that's the Tsar's son, not to mention your cousin in there," he hissed menacingly. "And in case you forgot," he sneered, "he's also your family's oh so almighty seventh-generation male. All this was made clear to you before we left Drakon Rus." Standing on his tiptoes, the officer jerked the young man so close they were practically nose-to-nose. "Now go carry out your fucking orders."

The young dragon rider clenched his jaw. After a moment's hesitation, he grabbed the blanket, turned, and quietly slipped through the balcony door. Light-footed, he moved across the nursery to the object of their assignment. He could hear the infant's soft breathing and was tempted to make a loud noise just to compromise the mission. But Moroz knew that to do so would end his career, and he would be in disgrace. Despite his misgivings, he allowed his training to take over and crept forward.

The baby was about six months old, with light tufts of fine blond hair, and smelled of baby powder. He was asleep on his back, so it was easy for the strapping young officer to reach down and gently scoop him up without waking him. Carefully wrapping the infant in the warm blanket, the dragon rider quickly returned to the balcony.

Quietly taking the baby with them, the two riders mounted their dragons and were airborne in seconds. No alarm had been raised, and the boy was still asleep. Soon the four riders were far from the baby's home—a home he would not see again for almost eighteen years.

A home he would one day try to destroy.

CHAPTER 2

THE PATH
KORYAK ENCLAVE—EARTH - AD 3097

At 06:59 GMT on 7 July, AD 2100, the nations of the Earth committed suicide. The blue planet's death was an apocalyptic cataclysm known to the few survivors as World War Extinction. Arsenals of ultra-advanced, hyper-fast weapons systems took less than one day to reduce the world's teeming population from eleven billion to slightly more than one million souls. The face of the planet became a hellish inferno as radioactivity destroyed almost all life on its surface. Every major city was turned into a smoldering ruin with many nothing more than blast craters. Not a single national government remained as the era of nation-states came to a burning end. Small pockets of humanity managed to survive only by taking shelter in deep underground bunkers scattered throughout the planet. The subsequent generations forced into this subterranean existence called it the Enclave Era of mankind.

Without competing national interests, Earth became a planet devoid of war. It took over two hundred years, the longest period of peace in mankind's short violent history, but the handful of surviving enclaves eventually emerged from their bunkers and rebuilt a new planet— one free from the political and religious divisions that had destroyed the old.

But survival was never an assured thing.

Almost one thousand years after that planet-killing war, humanity suffered another extinction-level event. It came in the form of a prolific pandemic called the Omsk hemorrhagic fever. The outbreak devastated one of the planet's most advanced surviving enclaves and its surrounding region. It was the most lethal tragedy since WWX, and, like that war, it killed indiscriminately, quickly, and without mercy.

That year, a hot, wet summer created the perfect breeding conditions for a long-forgotten but virulent mutated virus. The hosts were the bacteria-ridden ticks that accompanied an explosion in the rodent population. In late summer, the plague appeared without warning and swept through northeast Siberia with deadly effect. Nothing since the war had wiped out so many so fast.

The first day, five severely dehydrated patients arrived at the hospital with its symptoms, and within twenty-four hours all of them were dead. Swollen glands, weeping pustules, and destroyed immune systems had ravaged their bodies. The next day, more than two hundred of the afflicted overwhelmed the hospital's ability to cope. By day twenty, the stricken numbered in the tens of thousands.

Even at ten years of age, Alex Porter knew his mother was too young to die. Her hair showed not one sign of gray. Dr. Nadya Porter had spent days on end in the most contaminated wards of the hospital fighting to save as many lives as she could. If not for her selfless dedication, entire families would have perished.

Ultimately, she was unable to save herself, and forty-nine days after the plague first appeared in Koryak, it appeared in the young boy's mother. Thirty-six hours later, she lay in her own hospital's hospice, only moments from death.

Alex fought the urge to disobey the strict orders he'd been given. He'd been barred from seeing his mother as she lay dying. He was even banned from touching the door latch to her room—her death room. But his resentment festered and eventually he abandoned all sense of obedience. Alex stood up and defiantly stalked to the hospice door. A shock of light brown hair hung limply over his forehead as he glared down at the object of his anger. Just as his hand reached out for that forbidden latch, he felt footsteps approach from the other side of the door. He stepped back and looked down at his feet. He didn't even notice it open but was suddenly aware of someone standing very close to him. He soon felt a doctor's arms reach out and gently hold him. The grieving boy couldn't see which doctor it was.

Tears blurred his vision as he buried his face in the doctor's coat, soiled with days of thankless toil. "I wanna see my mom. I-I just need to see her one last time. Can't you please let me in for a minute? It'll only be for one minute. I won't get sick—she wouldn't let that happen to me. I know she wouldn't."

Through the deluge of tears he heard the gentle voice of his mother and realized that it was her arms he felt around him. "It's all right, Alex. I'm with you now."

He looked up, wiped the tears away, and threw his arms around her. "But, Mama, they said you were too sick to leave the bed. They said you would d-die soon." A fresh sob gripped him once again. "C-can we just go home? Please, Mama, can we j-just go home now?"

She brushed his hair back and kissed the top of his forehead. Her voice was so calm, so reassuring. "Never forget what I've taught you, and lead your own children there when their time comes, but until then you must walk the Path on your own." She continued in her soothing voice, "Alex, *you* are the family's seventh-generation male, and the reason for my being." With a gentle finger, she tilted his chin upward. "For it is you who will save the human race from another destruction. You, my darling son, are their only hope."

"Mama, please don't talk like that," begged Alex. "Don't talk like you're going to l-leave me." He didn't care about any of that family legacy stuff. Not so long ago he liked hearing her tell him those things, but not now. Nothing mattered now except the burning need not to let her go. But even though he had so many questions, he could think of only one. "B-but why, Mama, why did you go to those dangerous places where everyone was dying? Why did *you* go, Mama, why?"

Her last words would remain ingrained in his soul for the rest of his life. As the last of her strength failed and life finally slipped away, she could barely whisper. "Because, my son, it was *my* life's Path."

The warmth of her arms disappeared, and once more Alex stood alone.

Inside the hospice room the heart monitor became a steady shrill. It was a hideous sound, the harbinger that announced her death—his mother's death—the death of the most important person in his young life. Through the fog of grief, Alex understood that she had made one final astral projection to spend her last moments with him. He also knew that he would never see her again.

The heart monitor suddenly let out an electronic screech and went silent as every light for hundreds of kilometers sparked and blew out. Alex felt a jolt of electricity surge through his body the instant everything went dark.

Light had fled from Koryak.

CHAPTER 3

MESSAGE RECEIVED
OLYMPUS MONS—MARS - AD 3097

The lieutenant's footfalls echoed loudly throughout the long empty hall as she anxiously approached the little-used archive room. Housed deep in Interstellar Fleet Command's underground labyrinth at Olympus Mons, the drab archival office had smooth cement walls, a heavily scuffed floor, and an ancient steel desk. It was chilly, uninviting, and held mankind's possibly most significant historical artifact. Authenticating that artifact was the most important errand of the young officer's short career. Maybe the most important errand of any IFC career ever.

The message received a week earlier by the deep-space communications department, her department, had thrown the top brass of the IFC into the biggest uproar in their long history, and it was now her responsibility to verify its authenticity.

The knife-edge creases of her impeccable dark blue uniform barely made a sound on Second Lieutenant Lan Ni's trim frame as she approached her destination. Lan had made her way down from the upper level where her department sat atop the main support base for all humanities interstellar missions. It had a population of over thirty thousand service men and women who lived and worked in the fifty-seven-story complex that covered over a thousand hectares. Thirty-two of those levels lay beneath the Martian surface.

The underground base she headed into contained twenty massive, hundred-meter-deep, launch-ready chambers that housed a fleet of small support ships called Orbital Vehicle Atmospheric Landers, or OVALs. Powered by two fusion engines, they shuttled passengers and cargo from the surface of Mars to a fleet of orbiting transports that regularly traveled back and forth to the home planet of Earth.

But the main mission of these support craft was to fly their sorties high above the Martian atmosphere to service the pride of the IFC—a fleet of starships capable of reaching far beyond the confines of Earth's solar system. The fleet's home base was a massive spaceport orbiting Mars called Port Apollo. It was here that starships were built, docked, and awaited orders for their primary mission, the exploration of interstellar space, finally giving human beings the ability to reach other star systems well within a human lifetime. They were humanity's first real step toward colonizing the galaxy.

Then that message arrived.

The contents of which altered the entire perspective on human colonization. An ancient message from a thousand-year-old starship many believed was nothing more than a child's fairytale, a message that changed everything.

The archive was a sparsely manned department, and, at the moment, it was manned by a thoroughly bored noncom whose wrinkled uniform suggested it was a rare day when he had an officer standing in front of his desk. The balding archivist remained seated when the superior officer entered the room, but if Lieutenant Ni noticed this slight breach of protocol, she ignored it and got right to the point.

"Sergeant, I need your help."

"That so? What can I do for you, Lieutenant?" responded the elderly sergeant as he fastened the top button on his shirt.

"Just a moment." Ni made a fist with her left hand and raised it sternum high. A small sensor resembling a jewel on her multifaceted officer's ring server interfaced with the personal computer implanted in her optic nerve. After making a positive retinal scan, a holographic image of her home page appeared in front of her. She used two slender fingers on her right hand to touch a couple of tabs on her virtual screen, which interfaced with the sergeant's archive computer. With her index finger, she slid a file from her screen to his. "I need this transmission code authentication, and I need it now."

The old sergeant opened the very official-looking file, and then glanced over the rim of his glasses in bemused silence. After an uncomfortable moment scrutinizing the young officer for any sign of subterfuge, he finally asked, "With all due respect, Lieutenant, is this some kind of joke?"

"Sergeant, I assure you that this request came straight from the top." Ni set both her hands on the edge of the old, steel desk, leaned across it, and stressed, "I need access, and I need it now."

Adopting a half grimace, the sergeant arched a brow, typed in the call sign authentication code for the name request, and hit enter. He looked at the screen, frowned, and then turned to Ni. "Well, that turned up nothing, Lieutenant. Where do you want to go from here?"

"Make an archive-wide search for any file that refers to the *Magellan II*."

"All right, Lieutenant, whatever you want." The old sergeant typed in the search request. After several seconds of watching a blinking light on the monitor, a series of unrecognizable code sequences came up on the screen. "Well, that would have been too easy," groused the archivist, reading the screen response: "File not found."

Lieutenant Ni set her jaw. "I see, but I really don't want to hear you tell me that this is the end of the road. Am I understood?"

He frowned, closed one eye, scratched his temple, and then expanded his search into a rarely accessed area of archival history. "Understood, ma'am, and we're not quite at the end of the road yet." He leaned forward and squinted at his screen.

Ni crossed her arms as she stood back. "Where will you look now?"

The sergeant began typing again. "There's an old database that I can link with the mainframe," he mumbled without looking up. "It's hundreds of years old, and our last chance at finding your request. I've only accessed it a few times ever, but it might have something related to this." He clicked on the file request still open at the top of his screen.

The sergeant's deep search soon paid off as something unusual popped up. His unenthusiastic demeanor changed to one of amused tolerance as he asked the lieutenant, "Did you happen to bring a HAZMAT to wear over your nice uniform, ma'am?"

"No, I didn't. Why?"

"Because, Lieutenant, where you're going hasn't been visited for ages—maybe decades, maybe longer." A grin spread across the archivist's face.

Ni gave the older man a suspicious glance. "You'll to have to show me, Sergeant. Don't even think about trying to get out of this."

"Oh, I'll be with you, ma'am, every step of the way. That I will," he said. "Except there's only room for one person on top of the ladder, and these old bones just can't make that climb anymore. That part you'll have to do on your own."

"Ladder?"

"Well, ma'am, that deep in the artifact chamber ain't accessible to the grav-lifts." He adopted a look of sympathy. "And apparently there's something way back there, dunno what exactly, but it looks like there's one item that refers to the *Magellan II*."

"Just what are you getting at, Sergeant?"

"Take a look here." Ni leaned over and studied the ancient ledger entry. "According to this," he said, glancing back at the screen, "there aren't any electronic files, but there seems to be something stored in the archive chamber. Looks to be a physical item that was placed there hundreds of years ago, and most likely stored in some kind of sealed container," he mumbled. "There's no record of it ever being retrieved, so I'm guessing it's still there, and probably hasn't been opened in all that time. It's been buried somewhere deep and dark."

Ni scrutinized the screen while the old sergeant just shrugged and said, "This ain't gonna be no walk in the park, ma'am."

"Do you know where this archived box is, Sergeant?"

"Yes, ma'am. I reckon so, anyway. The computer says it's file AAA 001." He sounded less than confident.

"And that would be found—where exactly?"

"It looks to be the first file, as in the very first file. Our best chance of finding it is in the dungeon."

"The dungeon, Sergeant. Really?"

"Yep, the deepest, oldest deck at Olympus Mons. Hell, I've never even been down there. Don't know if anyone has for generations." The lieutenant's clenched jaw told him he was about to make his first trip. "But let's go see what we can dig up. This way, ma'am."

He led her through an access door at the back of his office and into a cavernous, well-lit storage room. There they picked up a grav-lift and hovered past massive storage shelves for three hundred meters to the rear of the artifact chamber. The old sergeant got out, walked to an unremarkable steel door, tapped an ancient scroll lock, and held the door open for her. Inside was a large elevator. They took it down three flights and entered a long, dark, six-meter-tall corridor lined with old shelves. He flipped a large breaker switch across from the elevator and waited as a dozen rows of lights popped on. The hall intersected six other corridors the same size and length. "Told ya," muttered the sergeant.

"What is all this?" asked Ni as she took in shelf after shelf of stored artifacts.

"Just the stuff the museums don't want," said the sergeant with a shrug, "or know about."

Twenty minutes later they arrived at another steel door. This one was unlocked, but it screeched in protest when the sergeant shoved it open. They stepped inside and onto a pitch-black spiral staircase.

"It's freezing in here," Ni complained.

"Yeah, maintenance don't get down here much," he grumped and flipped the switch on and off several times. "Damn lights." They turned their torches on, gripped the handrails, and made their way down two flights of the creaky old stairs. At the bottom they found a hundred-meter corridor. They entered and made their way to the far end. Its walls were naked rock, and it was even colder than at the top of the stairs.

It had obviously not been visited in multiple decades, maybe longer, and as the archivist had said, the shelves had built-in ladders every five meters. The lieutenant's torchlight finally revealed a barely discernible AAA written on a plaque on the top shelf. She blew warm air into her cupped hands, rubbed them together, and started climbing. Once reaching the top shelf, four meters above the floor, her torchlight lit up an object far in the back about three meters away: a small, forty-centimeter-long, crust-laden, metal box. She crawled across the filthy shelf to reach it.

The engraved word on the box was not completely legible, but after brushing at it with the sleeve of her uniform, a word slowly emerged: *MAGELLAN II*.

She grabbed the box, but at first it wouldn't budge. It had been sitting there so long that, even though it was stainless steel, some corrosion and hundreds of years of frozen dust had melded the box to the shelf. She braced her back against the hard rock, placed her feet against the old box, and kicked as hard as she could. After a couple of strong wallops, the box broke free, slid across the frozen metal shelf, and fell to the floor with a loud metallic clang.

The old sergeant yelped in surprise, shined his torch up to the shelf, and then called out, "Are you okay up there, Lieutenant?"

"No worse for wear," came the sheepish answer. "Are you all right?"

"Pretty sure it missed me by at least a meter, ma'am. I'd stepped back some when I heard you kicking the crap out of something." He shined his light on the beat-up box and said, "Can't say that what's inside that box is all right, though."

"The latches are completely corroded shut. Let's take it up front to open it," said Ni as she climbed down and tried to brush off her filthy uniform.

They took the ancient box up to the front office, but first stopped by a maintenance locker where the sergeant picked up a small handheld laser cutter and a pry bar. It took him several minutes of awkward labor and a few choice cuss words, but when he finally managed to pry it open, they found little material. Inside were some old, yellowed plasticized printout schematics and a small plastic box that contained some small, strange-looking, metal-and-plastic sticks.

"What the hell are these things, Sergeant?" Ni asked. "Any ideas?"

"Aw crap, ma'am. Yeah, I know what they are," the sergeant said unenthusiastically. "They're called USB drives and were used to store data several hundred years ago. I've got an old adapter around here somewhere. I'll go try to find it."

After he left, Ni held up the plasticized hard copy of the ship's schematic, shook her head, and muttered to herself, "This thing was absolutely enormous. Our biggest ships aren't even a tenth this size today. Maybe the legends are true after all."

The sergeant returned holding a small device of a type that Ni had never seen before. "I haven't used one of these for years, ma'am, but we find these old memory sticks from time to time, so this might work."

"Let's give it a go, Sergeant." She watched intently as the old adapter was connected to his computer. The device powered up, and the USB drive was inserted. Ancient files began filling the archivist's screen.

He selected a file titled "Communications" and hit enter. As soon as the file opened, the old sergeant scrunched forward, squinted, and muttered, "This subfile looks interesting."

"Open it, Sergeant."

As soon as he clicked on it, the file blinked out but reappeared a couple seconds later, only to disappear a second time. The sergeant frantically hit the icon over and over until the file opened, and then stayed open. The sergeant blew out a sigh. "Well, I'll be damned. There it is, ma'am."

The lieutenant didn't even realize that she'd been holding her breath until a gasp escaped her lungs. She looked over the file, smiled for the first time that day, and said, "Transfer it to my computer, then put the drive back in the case and give it to me."

"Ma'am, I'm not authorized to give out any archive material without written authorization," protested the sergeant.

"Do you honestly think that anybody's going to come down here looking for this material in the next few hundred years, Sergeant?"

"I reckon not, but I still need that authorization. I really don't want my pension fucked up because I failed to follow one of the most adhered-to rules, ma'am."

An irritated groan escaped the lieutenant's throat as she tapped one finger against her pant leg, and finally said, "Fair enough, Sergeant, you make the call and I'll get you that authorization, but I need to take this entire cache with me right now. Any problems with that?"

"None that I care to say, ma'am."

CHAPTER 4

A LONG NAP
OLYMPUS MONS—MARS

Lan Ni took the ancient case to her office to study before she submitted the report to her superior. Located two floors below the top of the base, it was far more comfortable than the archive had been, with carpeted floors, pseudo-wood paneling, and large, auto-dimming windows through which the slow transformation of the red planet was in full view. After two hours of going over the schematics and communication transcripts, she practically ran up to her department's headquarters. The officer in charge of deep-space transmissions was wearing out his own carpet, anxiously pacing and waiting for the information held in her hand.

"Did you get it, Lieutenant? Your uniform looks like you crawled through hell and back to find it."

"Funny you should say that, sir. Did you know this base has a dungeon?"

"Of course." He shrugged, ignored her scowl, and asked, "Well, did you find it?"

"Hmm, yes, sir. Don't ask me how, but a few physical items were actually archived." A slight frown creased her brow. "But there's something rather strange about these transcripts."

Twenty years her senior, the salt-and-pepper-haired officer was anxious to get started. "Let's get this checked out first, then we'll go over these 'strange things.'" Lieutenant Commander Anthony Bennett's optic computer received the file. He tapped a few keys on his virtual board, and the object of all their present anxiety popped up on his screen. "Damn, this is an ancient file," he muttered as he compared the files and correlated the two codes. "It's a match, Lan. Goodness knows how, but it's a match." He leaned back in his chair and smiled, but after a glance at the lieutenant's face his smile evaporated. "So, other than this being an almost thousand-year-old transmission, what's so strange?"

"That's just it, sir, it's not a thousand years old. After I authenticated the transmission code, all the other transmission's sensor data opened up."

"And?" he grumbled.

"Sir, they used spectral Ka frequencies back then, and all their transmissions had to be exactly linear."

"I know that, Ni, so what's your point?"

"This transmission is three point seven degrees off, which means it couldn't have come from Kepler 3211. In fact, it would miss by almost two light-years. I also played around with the transmission speeds and found something rather odd." She paused to bring up her screen.

"You've still got my attention, Ni. Go ahead, keep ruining my day."

"Look here, sir." She pointed at a graph on the screen. "When we play the transmission at normal speed, the frequency waves are normal, but watch this." She touched a couple tabs on her virtual screen and continued, "When I slow the transmission down, the frequency waves become much larger. If it came from deep space, they wouldn't change."

"What are you saying, Lieutenant? That this message has been faked?"

"Not necessarily, but it's not what we initially thought it was."

"So, what's your professional opinion?"

"I'm not really sure." She bit her lower lip, then gave him a crooked grin. "But I know the exact coordinates of its origin."

"Let me guess, it's not from Kepler 3211."

"No, sir. In fact it originated only 153 billion kilometers from Mars."

"You're saying this came from the Oort cloud?" Wide-eyed, Bennett shook his head.

"Yes, sir, and I've pinpointed where in the Oort cloud to find it."

"What are you suggesting?" Bennett asked.

"I'm suggesting that you authorize a ship to investigate, because that's the only way we can genuinely authenticate this message."

"All right. I'll arrange it, Lieutenant, but I want you aboard. Understood?"

"Yes, sir." She smiled at the opportunity to go into deep space. "I was hoping you'd say that."

Ten days later, after Lieutenant Ni had completed her mission to the far edge of the solar system, the two officers were looking at a relic from another era. It was like nothing they had ever seen before, and it lay in pieces at one of the huge facility's maintenance labs.

"Looks like you found some new toys, Lan, but was your trip worth it?" Commander Bennett frowned as he picked up an unfamiliar piece of equipment.

"It answered some of my concerns, like why the transmission wasn't linear from Kepler 3211," she explained. "The small asteroid it was attached to had drifted. But it also raised a lot of new questions I doubt we'll ever have the answers to."

"What new questions?" He set the component back down. "I need answers, not more unknowns."

"I understand." Ni moved to an ancient computer screen inside the six-meter-long craft. "Take a look at this, sir." He glanced at her, confused, then looked down at the program she had brought up on the screen. "It's basically an alarm clock," she told him. "One set for a nine-hundred-year wake-up."

"That's a long nap, Ni."

She moved around to the other side of the craft. "I've no doubt that this communication drone is from the *Magellan II.* The code authentication proves that. But the message was not sent to us from Kepler 3211. It was sent from this drone that's been parked in the Oort cloud for nine centuries."

"But why did it wait so long to transmit its message?"

"Because that's when the alarm clock was set for, sir."

"That's no answer, Ni."

"That's my point, sir, and only one of *many* unanswerable questions."

"If you can't give me a definitive answer, just give me your opinion."

She took a deep breath as tiny creases found their way to the smooth skin at the edge of her eyes. "Fine, here's my take. Whoever sent this drone purposely programmed it to do exactly what it's done."

"But why?" he pressed.

"That's just one of the answers I don't have."

"Dare I ask," he folded his arms, "what's another one?"

She glanced back at her commanding officer and stifled a frown. "I was able to download the drone's mission functions from the moment it was programmed to return to Earth. The message we received wasn't uploaded into its memory until after its launch."

"That doesn't make any sense. Why would they launch a communication drone without a message? Did they forget, and only later remember the message?"

"Highly unlikely, sir, but I have another theory," said Ni.

The commander spread his hands in a questioning gesture and Ni continued with her rationale. "Sir, I think that both the drone and the message were sent clandestinely to the edge of the solar system, where the drone powered down, then waited for the alarm to go off, before sending us that message one thousand years in their future."

"Okay, that's plausible—barely," admitted Bennett, "but why would they say they've established a colony before the ship had even left orbit?"

"That's the real mystery, Commander. Perhaps the sender was a visionary?"

"Let's try to be serious, shall we?"

"I am being—um." Ni closed her mouth, smoothed down the front of her uniform, and asked, "What do we do now, sir?"

"Now, Lieutenant? Now you go pack a bag because we're taking a trip over to IFC headquarters at Tharsis Rise to hand-carry this to the admiral who dropped this bucket of shit in our laps." The commander turned back to his screen and continued, "This whole mess is sure to stir up a shitstorm, and I'll need a shit shield to deflect some of the bigger pieces." He arched one brow and grinned at the lieutenant.

CHAPTER 5

POTENTIALLY OMINOUS
THARSIS RISE—MARS

The next day, the two communication officers took the maglev train for the 1,232-kilometer trip from their operations base on the 21,287-meter volcano of Olympus Mons, the tallest in the solar system, to the massive city of Tharsis Montes. With 167,000 people, it housed the largest population on Mars. Its terraforming complex dwarfed the city built to support it.

Wearing their dress whites, both officers stood at parade rest in the office of Admiral Rex Ryland. At forty-one, the admiral was young for an officer of his rank and built like a tree stump with arms. His office was large, plush, with a real wooden desk, and had one entire wall filled with scale replicas of the various starships under his command. He scrutinized the code authentication report that had been transferred to his OC and shook his head in disbelief. "You're sure this is legitimate, Commander? Because if I go upstairs with this, and it turns out to be some elaborate hoax, then all our asses will be sporting a new hole."

Bennett's voice sounded confident, but the slight twitch in his left eye lessened the impact of his words. "Everything about the drone had checked out and, based on those criteria, we just couldn't dismiss it. We believe the drone came from the *Magellan II*, but the legitimacy of the message is in question."

"Understood. So how *do* we explain why an ancient communication drone slept for the better part of a millennium before it woke up to transmit a message?" The admiral directed his next question to Ni. "And what the hell does any of this have to do with that blackout in eastern Siberia?"

Tilting his head in her direction, Bennett shared a glance with Ni indicating she had his permission to answer the question.

"It's all very strange, Admiral," Ni explained. "The message arrived at the exact instant the blackout occurred." She folded her hands in front of her as she went on. "It just seems odd to me that one thousand years ago a message was sent with an exact time and date to transmit, and when it finally does, a massive blackout occurs exactly where the purported author of the message originated from."

"So, you're sure this doctor was from there?" asked Ryland.

"Sir, the drone not only carried the message," Ni explained, "but the entire ship's log, including a full crew manifest, complete with points of origin. I have no reason to doubt its merit."

"Well, I guess we can't just ask them, can we?" mused the admiral.

Bennett quickly gave Ni another nod, and she steered the topic away from the unanswerable blackout anomaly to outline the best evidence they did have the answers to. "Sir, we did a molecular analysis on the craft, and it's pre-WWX. We believe that the drone is the real deal."

"While that is significant, it's not proof enough," countered the admiral. "I need more than that. What else have you got?"

"There's this, sir." She transferred the drone's analysis transcripts to his optic computer. After a minute of studying them, he looked up at her and nodded. She concluded, "The drone was assembled by JPL in old Pasadena and, as you can see, many of the components have serial numbers, construction dates, and even manufacturing locations. It's exactly what we'd expect from a craft built prior to WWX."

"So, you believe this to be legitimate, Lieutenant?"

"I believe the drone is, but why the message indicated that the colony was established when the *Magellan II* hadn't even landed yet is something I can't answer."

"My engineers tell me that there's no way the *Magellan II* was ever meant to land." The admiral looked up from his virtual screen and continued, "And that it would take months for the colonists to disembark via shuttle. In my mind, this gives the communication a little more credence. Wouldn't you say?"

Ni and Bennett glanced at each other and nodded.

"Good, then let's move on," Ryland said, and then summed up their report. "All right, just so I've got this straight: a communication drone is sent from an ancient starship on a hundred-year journey, with a message about an established colony, then powers down and waits for nine hundred more years, relatively close by, only to send an incomplete message?" Admiral Ryland turned his attention back to the commander.

"Exactly, sir." Bennett scrolled to the next page on the report. "And as you can see, the message referenced what has to be supernova DSN 2654b, which was first observed here only months ago, and created what the astronomy crew are now calling the Tiger Eye Nebula."

"The Tiger Eye Nebula?" quizzed the admiral. "What the hell is that?"

"I've got some friends over at astronomy that are calling it the Dragon Eye Nebula—because it's in the Draco constellation," Ni quietly mentioned to no one in particular.

Bennett ignored his junior officer's remark and explained to Ryland, "Sir, the Tiger Eye Nebula is a gas remnant that was instantaneously formed in the binary system Mu Draconis when the largest of the two stars went supernova." He glanced over at Ni and frowned. "The *Magellan II* was supposedly launched in early

AD 2100. This communication drone was launched in AD 2110, shortly after they arrived."

"Thanks, Commander," the admiral said, "but I know what the hell a nebula is."

"Right, well, sir, given that launch date, the light from that supernova event wouldn't have reached them for several more years," said Bennett.

"Are you sure about that?" asked Ryland.

"Yes, sir," answered Bennett. "The reference is strange. It just doesn't make sense."

"Tigers, dragons, whatever," blustered Ryland, "but what I need to know is how legitimate this thing really is, Commander. The nature of this whole message from Aqueous stinks to high heaven, but it's still possible."

"Aqueous, sir?" echoed Bennett.

"Yes, Commander, Aqueous. As you know, that's the name mentioned in the message your group picked up, and we've decided to go with that." He caught Ni's raised brows and switched back to the bigger issue. "Have you verified the distances from both Aqueous and this nebula?"

"Yes, sir," Ni answered, "and the math checks out."

"And do you have a credible explanation as to how they could have known about this nebula before the light even reached them, Lieutenant?" Ryland pressed the junior officer.

"No, sir," said a tight-lipped Ni.

Admiral Ryland ran his hands through his thick, black hair and looked up at the commander. "Okay, let's assume for a minute that this is a legitimate transmission from the *Magellan II*. It's still incomplete." He pointed at the actual message to make his point.

Bennett fidgeted uncomfortably. "Yes, sir, I agree. It's vague and ambiguous."

"It's also potentially ominous, Commander, and that's what has the top brass concerned. Now that you've verified the validity of the transmission codes, this takes on an entirely new emphasis—one that requires a response."

"A response, sir? I'm not sure I understand."

"You have to see this from Fleet Command's perspective, Bennett," replied Ryland. "The message says, and I quote: *'From Magellan II medical chief of staff, Doctor Nadezhda Yanbeyeva. Human colony has been established from original crew on Kepler 3211a, now known as Aqueous. Extensive primitive, but intelligent, indigenous life is found on planet. Aqueous is also protected by an advanced defensive system, but believe the present indigenous population is incapable of either creating or employing such technology. After the recent supernova, and the birth of the green nebula in the Draco constellation, we fully expect imminent inv—'*" He looked up from the report to the lieutenant commander to stress his point. "I believe your guys have established that the referenced Tiger Eye Nebula could only mean it was created from the supernova event, even if the math doesn't add up. I also, however regrettably, agree that this transmission was cut off during the last word. But what the hell does that word mean?" he asked rhetorically, and then answered his own question. "It could either mean *'invitation,'* which I highly doubt, or it could mean *'invasion,'* which not only seems likely but is what the IFC believes and is now preparing for."

"Preparing for, Admiral? Before I even had confirmation of the transmission codes?"

"Yes, Commander. As soon as you got this message, they began preparing for any eventuality, and as we speak, a starship is being provisioned for a deep-space mission to investigate."

"Sir, no deep-space mission is ever taken lightly, and one to this star system would be the farthest ever undertaken," said Bennett. "So by sending a starship, we're assuming that this message was, in fact, sent by the original colonists from the *Magellan II*. Am I right?"

"Yes, Bennett, that's almost a certainty," replied Ryland.

"If so, Admiral, allow me to play devil's advocate for a moment. Why did they wait so long to send us a message?"

"That specific question, Commander, is one of the mission's top directives."

Bennett dropped his voice slightly as he pointed out what he considered obvious. "Admiral, if all this is true, then wouldn't any invasion have long since happened?"

"True," replied Ryland, "but what if the human colony survived, and is still there?"

Trying hard to hide his incredulity, Bennett took a moment and a deep breath before speaking. "If you don't mind me asking, sir, what ship is being sent?"

The admiral turned to Lieutenant Ni and told her in no uncertain terms, "What you're about to hear goes no farther than this room. Am I clear?" Ni nodded, and Ryland walked over to the window and stared out at the millions of stars beyond the horizon. "Oh, for God's sake, Anthony, relax, would you? This has to stay between us for now. We're sending our newest, most advanced starship, the *Monarch*."

"Is that the three-hundred-meter monster being built at Port Apollo?"

Ryland pointed at one of the models on his wall, and then proudly explained, "Three hundred thirty meters, carries a crew of over sixty, two OVALs, and no, she's been finished for months and has just come back from her initial trial cruise." It was as if he was bragging about one of his kids. "She has the fastest EMD ever placed on a starship, with the first reliable electromagnetic push shield."

"What's that?" asked Bennett.

Ryland used his hands to describe the device. "It'll use the EMD to generate a gravitational push field that actually deflects space debris away from the ship while she's underway."

"Like a force field," muttered Bennett. "And you say she's ready now?"

"Ready and chomping at the bit. Her twin sister ship, the *Endeavor*, is being built as we speak. She should be ready in about fifteen months."

Ryland turned and stared out the window again as he confided in the two officers, "I'm not saying that I agree with all this silence about the mission, but the top brass wants this whole damn thing kept quiet for the time being."

Ni moved over to the shelf and studied the models before asking the inconvenient question. "Sir, if I may, why all this clandestine planning for what is sure to become one of the best-known missions in IFC history?"

Ryland exchanged glances with Bennett before answering Ni's question. "Because, Lieutenant, there's a theory that's gaining momentum that has caught the top brass's attention: that an advanced race of aliens is actually in control of that star system, and the IFC wants to find out for sure. This mission, to find the origin of the *Magellan II* message, is the perfect opportunity. The ostensible mission directive is to track down that mysterious message sent from a legendary starship that hasn't been heard from for a thousand years." He spread his hands out wide and went on, "Now, imagine what it would mean if we find a human colony alive and well? And in doing so we also happen to find an advanced alien race that has technology far more advanced than ours, then we really don't want to piss them off." The admiral sat and pointed at the message still on his screen. "And because of those three letters, '*inv*,' in that incomplete word—an incomplete word that the IFC simply can't ignore; an invasion of a possible human colony, even if it happened a millennium ago. Be it from the primitives, or from an advanced alien race."

"It just seems like a huge risk," said Bennett.

"Hence the secrecy," replied Ryland. "But aside from all that, there's keen interest to find this lost colony and see how humanity's fared a millennium removed from Earth."

CHAPTER 6

THE BRAVE THING
CAMBRIA—AQUEOUS

Two red-haired little girls sat quietly in the waiting room trying to be brave as they watched their distraught father pace back and forth. Sven Lawson nervously wrung his hands and gripped the sides of his head so that his thinning blond hair stuck out all askew. His unshaven face wore an anguished look, and he was barely able to hold back the tears.

He also failed at the brave thing.

The eight-year-old twins studied him for some sign of strength, some sign of hope, but try as he might, he was unable to find any to give them. Finally, one of the girls stood up and grabbed her father's hand. He stopped pacing as she held firm. "Daddy, please sit down. You're making yourself sad, and it hurts to see you sad. Look, it's making sissy cry." She glanced over at her sister who had tears streaming down her face.

Her own would come later.

"I know, Britt. You're right, sweetie," he barely managed to get out. He tried a weak smile, but it quivered and became a misshapen failure. "I'll sit, but only if you and Lorraine hold my hands—hold them tight."

"We will, Daddy." The steadiness in her voice belied the tears she, too, was fighting.

A young nurse approached the waiting room door and took a deep breath to muster her own courage. She stood silent for a moment, witness to the family's pain, before she lightly tapped on the door to get their attention. They looked up, hopefully expectant, but the nurse's face told them all they needed to know—hope was futile. "Councilor Lawson, Dr. Burt will be here in a minute. He needs to talk to you, alone would be best."

Britt jumped up, defiance blazing in her blue eyes. "Whatever he has to say he can say to all of us! She's my—" Britt glanced down at her sister "—our mommy too, you know." She plopped back down, crossed her little arms, and, with a pouting lip, glared at the nurse.

"I know, sweetheart. I'm so sorry. Here's the doctor now." The nurse quickly backed out of the waiting room and left the doctor to talk to the family.

Dr. Burt walked into the waiting room, took his hands out of the pockets of his smock, and placed them on his hips. He was a tall, prematurely graying man with stern, cold gray eyes. Especially when it concerned Sven Lawson. "We did all we could, Councilor," he said without so much as a greeting, "but the pathogens were just too strong, and she was so weak from all the exposure fighting this same epidemic." He gave Lawson a bitter scowl, and then lashed out with barely contained venom. "You should have stopped her from this—"

But Lawson had only heard one thing the doctor had said. Only one thing mattered. "You're saying she p-passed away, Doctor?"

"Yes, Lawson, she died about ten minutes ago."

Lorraine broke out in heavy sobs, but Britt jumped to the top of her chair, wagged a finger in the doctor's face, and yelled, "You could have saved her! My mommy was the best doctor at this hospital, better than you ever were, and she saved many people from this same sickness. They weren't any more sick than Mommy was!"

"Britt, please," begged her dad.

She turned back to her father. "Daddy, you know he let her die. You know his bad feelings about us."

The doctor's eyes flared with anger. "I don't have to stand here and take this from a little brat. You need to take your kids home, Lawson, then come back here and deal with the body. We can't have contaminated corpses lying around this hospital." He stepped up close to the grieving husband, and whispered menacingly, "Lawson, if you don't deal with her body, then I will." He practically spat out these last words, turned, and left the motherless family standing there.

"He could have saved Mommy, but he hates us, so he let her die."

"You know that's not right, Britt. Come on, let me take you girls home."

"Yes it is, and when *I'm* a doctor, I'll never let people die, just like Mommy never did." She looked up at her dad as her eyes began to glisten. "I swear I'll be the best doctor ever." She jumped off the chair and ran out the hospital door crying, "I will, I will, I will!"

Lorraine stood up, silently took her dad's hand, and held it to her wet cheek as they slowly followed her sister out the door.

CHAPTER 7

SINS OF THE FATHER
DRAKON RUS—AQUEOUS

The officer of the watch entered the opulent tapestry-adorned throne room, approached the Dragonhead Throne, dropped to his knees, and bowed his head in homage to his Tsar. He waited until given permission to speak.

Carved out of solid crystal and set inside the dragon's chasmal mouth, the seat of power was large, heavily cushioned, and occupied by the colony's tyrannical ruler. "Well, out with it, Lieutenant. You didn't come in here just to waste my time, did you?" growled the ever-impatient Tsar Yakov Yanbeyev. "Give me whatever your news is, and then get the hell out."

"Da, Excellency." The lieutenant kept his eyes locked on the floor and rose to one knee. "Sire, information has arrived from Cambria—"

The royal outburst was immediate. "What? Why the fuck do you think I care?" bellowed the Tsar. The skin around his thick neck turned as red as his tunic. "You disturbed my afternoon to bring me news from that shithole?"

The young officer stiffened and remained motionless for a moment before daring to continue. "Sire, our intelligence says that Dr. Susan Lawson has died."

A sneer of satisfaction quickly replaced the Tsar's tirade. "Go on," he said.

"Yes sir," responded the officer, his eyes still firmly cast down. "She died about two weeks ago from that flu epidemic that swept through Camb—the other colony."

"So, the ungrateful bitch is now a stinking corpse, huh?" The Tsar's sneer turned into a macabre smile as his demeanor quickly shifted. "Now that weak bastard won't have any reason to call out for his mommy anymore."

It was well known that the monarch's temper could shift violently, so the lieutenant stood and said nothing more. In a semblance of respect he kept his head down and backed out of the room.

"Sergei!" bellowed the Tsar. "Get your sorry ass in here this instant!"

"Da, my Tsar," the steward said as he cautiously approached the throne.

"Where's that little bastard?" It was the demand Sergei always dreaded.

"He's with his governess, sire, your sister," came the reluctant answer.

"For the life of me I see don't why she wastes her time with him," snarled the boy's father. "Bring him here, and don't dally this time. I mean it," he threatened.

"Da, my Tsar." The old steward backed away, distress etched on his face.

Five minutes later a scrawny, blond-haired ten-year-old boy was ushered into the throne room by his aunt. He trembled and stared down at the floor, fearing what was coming. His arms and throat showed recent signs of bruising. One of his green eyes was still swollen, with an ugly dark purple ring below it. He stood next to his aunt and tried to disappear behind her skirts.

Hiding never did him any good.

"Come here, boy," his father said evenly. It always started like this.

The little boy looked beseechingly up at his aunt and tried to take her hand as protection.

This never worked either.

"It's all right, Bayne," his aunt tried to reassure him. Her dark brown hair was showing streaks of gray, and she also wore royal red, but unlike her brother's finery, her floor-length dress was spun cotton. "I'm here."

"Who the hell do you think you're talking to, Oxana?" growled the now-angry Tsar. "Now shut the fuck up and send him over here, or I'll have you removed. Again."

Her reaction to her brother was swift. "He's just a little boy, Yakov."

This, too, never did any good.

"Sergei!" The steward instantly reappeared. "Remove this bitch from my sight."

"Da, my Tsar." Sergei gently touched Oxana's arm. The boy's aunt wrung her hands and hesitated a moment before she left.

Once they were alone, the Tsar's fingers drummed against the crystal fangs like the drumbeat of a dragon launch, his voice harsh and uncompromising. "I have something to tell you, and I don't want to shout, so get your ass over here!"

The boy hung his head and slowly shuffled over to his father's throne, unable to meet those angry eyes. He stopped and waited for the inevitable.

With unconcealed disgust, the Tsar looked down at the child and tactlessly told him the news. "That bitch who whelped you is dead, and since you can't possibly even remember her lying face, you will now stop crying for her every time your little feelings get hurt. Only babies do that. Do you hear me?" His voice began to rise.

"M-Mommy's dead? Nooo—"

"What, are you hard of hearing as well as weak?" The volume increased by the second. "I should have left you in Cambria."

"Mommy! I want my mom—"

The backhanded slap could be heard outside the throne room door. The boy flew two meters before hitting the hard crystal floor and lay still. "I told you to stop calling for her! She was as worthless as you are, you weak little bastard!"

The Tsar stood up from the dragon mouth and advanced on the trembling boy, now bleeding where his father's ring had left a deep gash on his cheek. The door burst open as Oxana flew into the room. She threw herself between the sobbing child and his tormentor.

"No more, Yakov! Please, no more," begged Oxana.

Several guards, including the Tsar's nephew, also rushed into the throne room. As soon as the Tsar saw his nephew, his royal ire boiled over. "Captain Moroz, if you value your mother's life, then remove her, and do it quickly."

The young officer gathered up his mother. He said nothing and kept his angry eyes from finding his uncle as he led her from the room.

A frantic seven-year-old girl raced into the room and threw herself on top of the boy to protect him. Her long black hair spread out like a protective veil over the boy's bleeding face.

This only infuriated the Tsar even more.

"Sergei! Take Princess Anya away, and make sure she's locked in her room."

"Da, my Tsar." The old man knelt down and whispered, "Come, Anya, you I will protect with my life."

"Daddy, please don't hurt him anymore," Anya begged her father. "He's my only brother!"

"Half-brother," their father corrected. "With the pedigree of a full-blooded bastard. You are not to go near him again." He looked menacingly at the steward. "If she does, it'll be you who pays the price."

Sergei cringed, but gently lifted the little girl from her half-brother. Blood had stained her fine blue dress where she had held Bayne's head close to her own. The steward tenderly wiped her tears away as he led the distraught princess out the door.

The Tsar reached down, grabbed the little boy by his arm, yanked him off the floor, and dragged his limp form from the throne room. Tsar Yakov was a big man, and his huge hand enveloped the boy's scrawny arm in a vise-like grip. He began stripping the child's tunic off until he wore nothing but a thin garment around his buttocks. "Weak bastards don't deserve to be dressed in such finery. Especially royal finery!" He dragged the whimpering boy along for several minutes until they reached the massive main gates leading to the launch terrace. A blood trail of small drops followed their path to the gates. He jerked the boy through an access door beside the gates, and threw him onto the terrace, outside the protection of the great hall.

And into a blizzard.

Frozen snow stung as it howled down from the mountain that towered over the cliff fortress. The monarch of the northern colony, and the absolute commander of a ten-thousand-strong army of dragon riders, had just thrown his only son onto the ice-encrusted terrace. "Maybe this will teach you to keep your fucking mouth shut about your whore of a mother." He turned and slammed the door shut, leaving the crushed little boy to grieve in silence.

In a few minutes he would be frozen to death.

Out of the driving snow a powerful roar sounded across the terrace, but the shivering boy was too cold to react. A second roar sounded, followed by a blast of heat directly over the top of the freezing child, instantly warming him. Hypothermia had already begun to set in, and the boy shivered uncontrollably, but the fire's warmth brought life back to his bruised, naked flesh. A huge warm wing draped over the boy and shielded him from the killing elements.

The access door flew open as dozens of crossbow-armed soldiers rushed onto the terrace, followed by their furious Tsar. As soon as he saw his son's protector, he flew into an uncontrollable rage. "Rodinya, you have no right to be here!"

"And what right do you have to torture an innocent child?" The golden dragon's words screamed into his skull.

Because of an ancestral link in their bloodline, the Tsar could hear her telepathic words, and what he heard pushed him to the brink. "He's my son, but no heir, and given that technicality, his life is completely at my suffrage."

"You will reap the torment you sow, Yakov, as will all those around you. Generations of your family will pay the blood price of your deranged hate. Are you that blind and ignorant?"

"I've had all the meddling from you I'm going to take," the Tsar threatened. "Leave now while you still can and never return, or I swear I will expend my entire army, both my dragon wings to destroy you. Am I clear?"

While the Tsar was distracted, facing off with the giant dragon, Oxana rushed onto the terrace, gathered the boy up in a blanket, and spirited him back inside the cavernous cliff city of Drakon Rus.

"It would indeed take both your wings, Yakov, but have no fear, you gloopi durak. I'll not return until after your death, and then only to piss on your sorry grave and join in the celebration!" With that, the thousand-year-old dragon leapt into the air and disappeared into the snowstorm.

Regretfully, she would be unable to make good on her promise.

CHAPTER 8

THE HOSHI KATANA
KYUSHU, JAPAN—EARTH

After his mother's death during the pandemic that had devastated his boyhood home, Alex moved to the Gaelic Enclave in the Scottish Highlands where his father had grown up. Even though Alex spoke fluent English, he was different from the local kids. His accent was odd, and he wore strange clothes. His first few years were lonely, but he made few attempts at finding friends. Then finally, five years after coming to Gaelic, he walked past the gymnasium at his school and heard the sounds of struggle and dedication. The sound compelled Alex, and as soon as he entered the gym and watched the practice, he knew that this was what would finally help him find a direction in his life. A life no longer dominated by solitude.

Already a competitive runner, Alex joined, and became totally immersed in the extreme discipline of martial arts. He could both channel his grief-stimulated frustrations and achieve the ever-elevating goals that the physicality of martial arts demanded of him. His natural athleticism and mental discipline ensured that as a young teenager he excelled, rising in rank and stature so that by the time he was eighteen, he had no local equal.

But it was only through long-distance running that he was able to access his family's Path—the ability to astral project.

During the grueling pain of running in the mountains, he could project his mind to another plane of existence with preternatural clarity. While his body was being pushed to its maximum pain threshold, his mind would go to another place where all physical pain was eliminated.

Many of the women from his mother's family back at the Koryak Enclave could slip into the out-of-body state by meditation alone, but not Alex. He had to achieve an extreme physical state of duress, change his body chemistry, and use the overt pain to achieve a condition where astral projection was possible, and then once achieved, the ability to go anywhere he wanted was within his grasp. It was a source of frustration to him that only pain, and not meditation, could produce these results.

Only pain allowed access to the Path.

Now at the cusp of manhood, and after his father's death, Alex was alone in the world, and uncertain just where his Path would lead him. But forever engraved on his soul were his mother's dying words and the dedication that she had given her life for. The clarity of that memory ensured that Alexander Preston Porter would never take a step back, and that he'd remain true to the Path no matter where it led.

Alex had contemplated doing many things with his life, and despite his family of physicians back in Koryak insisting he follow their legacy into the medical field, he knew it wasn't for him. The most compulsive motivation in his young life was an extension of his love for martial arts: the acquisition of a true Samurai katana sword. One day an opportunity presented itself, and he didn't hesitate to use it.

Alex entered the Edinburgh University School of Archeology. He had no interest in archeology, but intuitively knew that this was the only way to his Path. In his first year he'd conned his way onto an excavation team in the faraway, and still nuclear-hot, zone of the Fukuoka dig in Kyushu, Japan.

As the junior member of the archeology team, Alex was given all the crap jobs. One day, after being shunted off to the side, he left the dig site and explored on his own. There was one place of particular interest to him. Since it was over one hundred kilometers from Fukuoka, it had incurred relatively little damage during WWX. But there were no roads left to where Alex wanted to go.

On the southeast coast of the old Nagasaki prefecture sat the remains of a seventeenth-century castle. Like most of Japan, it lay in ruins, but had once housed the world's finest collection of samurai artifacts. It was also home to the mother of famed astrophysicist Dr. Hikaru Mizushima, the father of interstellar travel. Late in the twenty-first century, Mizushima had invented the Enhanced Magnetic Drive. His research facility in Fukuoka was the sole reason for the dig in the first place, but not the reason Alex was there.

The doctor's mother had lived alone near the castle after her retirement from their family's mega-corporation, Mizushima Industries. Her home was located at the foot of Mount Unzen in the beautiful seaside village of Shimabara, but close enough to the fast-paced city of Fukuoka so Hikaru could visit often. It was also where her son kept a strong steel safe containing his most prized possessions—his collection of museum-piece Samurai swords, including a famed katana.

To get there, Alex had to borrow, or steal as it was later alleged, a hover car and made the trip alone. Since no addresses remained in this long-deserted village, he had to use his powerful intuitive ability to find the ancient site, and still dug for hours through the ruins before he finally found the collapsed building that had once belonged to Dr. Mizushima's mother.

But the trip was worth the effort. Alex found exactly what had drawn him halfway around the world—a legendary sword made from the metal of a meteorite. From that point on, the Hoshi katana never left his possession.

After he returned to the dig's main camp, Alex was thoroughly reprimanded, thrown off the team, and sent home in disgrace. He couldn't have been happier.

CHAPTER 9

THE REAPING
DRAKON RUS—AQUEOUS

Another powerful cough painfully racked Tsar Yakov's body as a glob of something green, yellow, and bloody hacked up into his mouth. Through rheumy eyes he glowered at the group of nervous physicians fidgeting next to his royal bed and spit the bloody mess in their direction. It missed, but the message didn't. He suffered a dry swallow, and in a raspy voice swore at them, "You imbecile doctors are trying to kill me, and the next one of you morons who suggests transfusing me again I'll have dragged out to the stockade, and let the dragons transfuse him instead."

Yakov's suspicious glare turned to the other group of sycophantic vultures huddled near a heavily curtained window in his large, extravagantly decorated bedchamber. The stale air in the poorly lit room was ripe with a tinge of rot, and the few scented candles did little to mask the odor or light the gloom. The dull candlelight cast pale shadows across the room and barely lit the specters clustered at the window.

Dressed in long, black robes with matching skullcaps, the fidgeting group would occasionally cast a wary glance in their monarch's direction, but when the Tsar glowered back they quickly looked away. These were his ever-esteemed retinue of state, and he gave them the same message. "I should have the lot of you thrown off the terrace just to listen to your pathetic screams on the way down."

That thought brought on a small chuckle, which, in turn, brought on another wet coughing session. He wiped the bloody phlegm off his lips with the sleeve of his finely made bedclothes and mused loud enough so that everyone in the room could hear him, "I wonder if you can actually hear the screaming for the entire thousand-meter fall? Wouldn't it be entertaining to find out?"

No one dared utter a sound.

After yet another debilitating coughing spell, Yakov looked up and found the number one vulture standing next to his massive four-poster bed. The brazen insolence of the man, just standing there rubbing his chin with his hand—Yakov hated the presumptuousness of that pose, and he hated the man who donned it. "What do you want, blood sucker?"

"My Tsar, I beg your grace," said the robed man, "but you really must address the issue of succession and choose an heir."

"Can't wait for me to die, can you? The fucking lot of you are just counting down the minutes. But who knows," the Tsar wheezed false sincerity, "I might live another ten years."

"As we all so fervently wish, Your Excellency," lied the Minister of Royal Protocol, "but we must consider all the—um—possibilities, and the issue of succession is of prime importance."

"Do you honestly expect me to place a fourteen-year-old girl at the head of the dragon army?" spat the dying man. "Are you that fucking stupid?"

"There's always your nephew, Colonel Moroz, my—"

"Goddamn, you assholes!" blasted the Tsar. "That incompetent upstart is not of my loins and has risen farther than an insolent peasant deserves. He only made full bird because of my sister and will never become Tsar of Drakon Rus!" His screaming brought on another fit of uncontrollable coughing.

The black-clad minister glanced back at his minions who silently nodded their assent. The minister guardedly looked back at his monarch, bent stiffly at the waist, and spoke in a low clipped tone. "Your son is now of age, Excellency, and since he is a seventh-generation male—"

In an instant the Tsar's coughing fit turned into one of rage. His face went even redder than before. He managed to stop long enough to bellow at the minister. "If you dare to mention his fucking name I'll have you both thrown off the terrace—"

Another coughing fit raged out of his destroyed lungs so hard that he began choking on the bile it brought up. After a moment he was barely able to croak out, "Guards—"

As if on cue, the door to his bedchamber opened, but it wasn't his guards; it was his son. The son he had just threatened to throw off the terrace, the son who was now a tall eighteen-year-old young man, the son who wore a ragged scar on his cheek like a badge of honor.

It was anything but.

The young man wore a dapper high-collared royal red jacket trimmed in gold, and an impassive face. "Dying, are we, Papa? My, but that does look painful, hacking up all that thick blood and icky stuff. Oh, is that a piece of lung stuck to your sleeve?" Bayne's grim smile was pure hate. Even this hardened tyrant recoiled at the malevolence in his son's face.

As the young man stared down at his dying father, he spoke loud enough so that everyone else in the room could hear him. "It's time Papa and I have ourselves a little chat. Alone." He looked over his shoulder at the motionless group of doctors and ministers, who stood confused and frightened. "That means leave us. NOW!" he barked. The door to the chamber slammed shut on its own, and instantly burst open again.

No one had touched it.

Whispered rumors about Bayne's growing abilities had made their way to everyone in Drakon Rus, and the higher echelon of doctors and ministers had heard them all. Now they'd just witnessed the graphic truth of those rumors, and finally understood why his father hated him—feared him: Bayne was the most powerful Yanbeyev ever born.

They retreated en masse. As the last of them left, Bayne's white-haired aunt, Oxana, slipped into the room and stood near the door out of sight, just as it slammed shut again. The three Yanbeyev family members were now alone in the death room.

The reaping had come.

"I'll get right to the point, *dearest Papa*." Bayne's voice dripped with false sincerity. "You are going to name me as your successor. You remember: Tsar of Drakon Rus, and you will do so now. As your son, and the seventh-generation Yanbeyev, it is my right to rule. You know this, everyone knows this, and, furthermore, you will make this announcement in the next few minutes. While you still can. Is that understood?" he asked sweetly, and then added harshly, "Isn't this why you had me kidnapped from my mother?"

Shaking his head, the old man trembled in painful rage. His sagging jowls jiggled with every movement, and he could barely croak out the words. "N-never—you w-weak b-bastard—never!" Except for his screams, these were the Tsar's final words.

From deep in his throat Bayne chortled. He raised his hands palms forward, fingers splayed wide, and began kneading the air. Something made a squishy pop in his father's head as blood began to ooze out of the Tsar's nose, mouth, and ears. The old man's eyes filled with red viscous tears, as bloody shit ruptured out his bowels. Bayne's chortle became an outright titter as the torture continued. His fingers then curled into claws as if squeezing pus out of a large boil, and the stinking red spectacle on the bed went into convulsions.

And then the screaming began.

As soon as she realized what was happening Oxana rushed to the bed. "Stop, Bayne! I raised you to be a good man. Not this—"

"He beat that out of me, Aunty Ox," interrupted Bayne. "You know this," he growled, "you've witnessed this," but inwardly, he recoiled at her appeal for clemency. The memories of the gentleness with which she raised him—all her love, attention, and protection—came flooding back. She was the only one who ever showed him kindness, but not his father. Oh no, never his father. The endless years of torment, pain, and rejection were about to come to an end, and only one end was fitting. The tormentor had to die by the hand of the tormented. "Leave him to his fate."

It was a just reward.

"No, Bayne, you mustn't do this."

Bayne ignored her plea, pushed it out of his mind, and, just like his father before him, he would show no mercy. "Aunty Ox, stay out of this." He increased the intensity of suffering wrought on his father.

"I didn't lead you to the Path for this!" she screamed. "Please stop this, or you'll become no better than your father." She quickly moved between the father and son, shielding the Tsar with her body, as if to protect him, just as she had tried so many times to protect Bayne from this very man. But the force of Bayne's power hurtled her backward where she landed on top of her convulsing brother.

His aunt's plight took Bayne by surprise. He'd been inflicting maximum force at the object of his hate, but now his beloved aunt was in lethal danger. "Get away from him!" he yelled, but it was too late. Bayne snapped his hands closed as he tried to stop the destructive flow of power, but instead the force switched from expansion to contraction.

The crack of breaking bones mixing with hideous screams filled the bedchamber in a chorus of agony. The siblings' bodies contorted and crushed inward. Realizing his mistake, Bayne quickly flared his fists open, but the force of his power didn't change; it simply reversed its destructive Path yet again. Their crushed, tortured bodies convulsed and began bloating like a rapidly filling bladder.

Bayne's eyes grew wide with fear for his aunt, as he screamed in vain, "Nooo Aunty Ox. Get away from him!" He lunged, tried to save her, but it was too late. Her final agonizing scream only gurgled, cut off by fragments of her digestive tract that hemorrhaged into her esophagus. Both Oxana's and her brother's bodies inflated like balloons, and then erupted in a sticky red mist.

The force of the rupture swept the room with a pressure wave that drenched Bayne with bright speckles of red, white, and gray. There was nothing left of the brother and sister but a sheen of gore that glistened on the once-fine sheets and dripped throughout the room.

Bayne froze. Time seemed to stop. He squeezed his eyes shut and couldn't breathe for several agonizing moments. He shook out of his stupor when someone started to pound on the door. He finally attempted a gulp of air but gagged instead when the bile filled his throat, and he threw up on the floor. The pounding at the door became violently insistent. Bayne clasped his head with sticky, red hands, slowly opened his eyes, and cried out, "It wasn't supposed to be like this. W-why did you come in here? Why, Aunty Ox? Why?"

With a sharp crack the door splintered and crashed open. Colonel Vladimir Moroz burst into the room and stopped. His mouth fell agape and he couldn't breathe for several seconds. "What's happened in here?" Moroz barely managed to get out.

Bayne just sobbed.

Moroz's eyes darted around the room searching for his mother, but she was nowhere to be seen. "Where is she, Bayne? She was seen coming in here. She was heard screaming, and she did not come back out." His voice rose to a booming commander's tone. "I demand to know, Bayne. Where. Is. My. Mother?"

All the blood-soaked young man could do was shake his head and mutter over and over, "I d-didn't want th-this. I n-never would have h-hurt her. She was the only m-mother I ever knew." He fell to his knees and wailed in grief.

Colonel Moroz rushed over and angrily grabbed Bayne by his sticky wet collar and yanked him back to his feet. "What have you done?" he snarled in the young man's face. "She treated you like a son. She protected you when it could have cost her life, and you murdered her?"

Since that long ago night when he helped kidnap baby Bayne, Moroz had steadily risen in rank until he commanded one entire wing of the dragon rider army. None but his now dead uncle could question his orders. Inside the grisly death room, the colonel's voice filled with accusatory rage as he yelled out the door. "Guards!"

The room filled with armed guards who, upon seeing the appalling spectacle, lowered their pikes and advanced on the two men of royal blood standing next to the bed.

"Guards, arrest the prince!" Moroz ordered. "Bind his hands behind him and take him to solitary confinement. If he resists—kill him." The guards grabbed Bayne's limp form and dragged him whimpering from the room.

Moroz looked down at his hands, tacky with blood—his mother's blood—and closed them into fists. Still stunned, he sensed someone else in the room and turned to see the old steward standing aghast in the doorway. Both Sergei's hands covered his mouth, and his wide eyes and ashen face wore an expression of both horror and relief.

The dead Tsar's nephew walked over to the steward, and in a tone harsher than he intended, gave him the news. "Sergei, the Tsar is dead." Moroz made no mention of his mother. "I want you to go find Anya and have her meet me in the throne room at once." Before the steward turned to go, Moroz stopped him. "Sergei, explain nothing to her. Leave everything to me."

The elderly steward gasped and stumbled backward, shaking his head. Moroz blew out a shallow breath and softened his tone. "Fear not, old friend, and be gentle with her, because Princess Anya is now Tsarina of Drakon Rus."

CHAPTER 10

STRANDED
NORTH POLE—AQUEOUS

"*Monarch, OVAL Hammär!* Come in, *Monarch*. Do you copy?" The copilot tried every channel, but just like always, he couldn't raise their mother ship. "Bloody damn clouds anyhow," he swore. His pilot, Lieutenant Patti Hammär, fought to keep their shuttlecraft in the air.

She was about to lose the battle.

The storm over the north pole coalesced soon after they'd landed near the strange, cone-shaped mountain. Within minutes the wind buffeted their small craft so hard that Patti ordered an immediate launch. Shortly after they lifted off, they'd been hit by massive bursts of lightning that appeared out of nowhere. The lightning strikes had all but destroyed their avionics, and to make matters worse, the wind speed had now risen to near unmanageable levels. Turbulence pummeled their OVAL into an almost total loss of control.

OVAL Hammär was the last remaining shuttle from the *IFC Monarch,* and without it the starship's mission directive would be terminated. A week before, the only other shuttle had been lost without a trace while on a single craft reconnaissance to the strange parabolic mountain on the southern continent. Their present sortie had sent them to the top of the world, and over the towering snow-capped mountains that ringed the northern twin of that southern mountain.

At the moment it was in serious peril.

While its commander was well aware of the greater implications for the loss of her starship's last shuttle, surviving the next few minutes and saving her crew was all that mattered at the moment.

First Lieutenant Hammär was an excellent pilot, but her yoke vibrated uncontrollably in her hands, and she had almost no throttle response. Her long-range sensors had ceased functioning, and now it seemed that their communications were down as well.

She knew exactly what this meant.

After the first lightning strike had battered her craft, the optical computer implanted in her optic nerve ceased functioning. Without it there would be no outside communications because the two systems were fully integrated, and without her OC their over-the-horizon scanner was out as well. They were deaf, dumb, and blind.

And, at the moment, they were about to crash.

Her copilot was still yelling into the comms when Patti ordered him to cease and desist. "Dillon, for fuck's sake, you know we have zero comms below this cloud cover, so give it a rest and get your hands on the yoke. I need some help here."

"My stick feels loosey-goosey here!" called out the right seater after grabbing his yoke.

"Welcome to my world, Dillon."

"Seriously poor choice of words, Patti," quipped the usually unflappable right seater. "You gotta work on that bedside manner of yours—bleeding shit! That's the ground less than three hundred meters below us!"

"And coming up fast, gents." She made her decision in an instant. "Prepare to punch out," she yelled. "On my mark, three, two, punch it!" Both her copilot and rear gunner yanked their ejection handles and blew out of the stricken OVAL, but Patti's seat didn't fire. She was trapped inside her doomed craft and going down hard. She glanced out the windscreen an instant before her OVAL crashed and saw lightning strike both her ejected crewmates. They burst into flames and tumbled out of sight.

Patti screamed as another bolt of lightning hammered her OVAL just as it smashed into the ground. It blew a hole through the fuselage and slammed the craft into the planet's surface.

This was no ordinary lightning.

Her powerless craft impacted on the side of its hardened heat shield. It then careened across jagged rocks for several hundred meters before it finally came to a rest on a rocky shelf in a blaze of sparks and screeching metal.

Patti was stunned, battered, and bruised. Her fingers gingerly explored a sharp pain in the hairline above her right ear and found a blood-seeping contusion. She also thought she might have dislocated her left shoulder. Further examination revealed it to be sore, but still in its socket. Barely. Her left knee hurt like hell.

Then the reality of what had just happened hit her like a ton of bricks, and she cried, "Oh my God! I just killed my crew! How did they escape the crash and die, while I rode it down and lived?" A wave of optimism suddenly gripped her. "Maybe they did survive and need my help."

Patti tried to extract herself from her wrecked shuttle but found the hatch jammed shut. Unable to stand fully erect in the low overhead bulkhead, she painfully crawled through the detritus in the small cabin's rear and dug out a pulse rifle case. Sharp pain in her shoulder made even the simple task of opening the case a grueling ordeal. She fashioned a sling out of a lanyard, then used her one good arm to pull out the weapon and blew a hole in the hatch. The third shot finally blew it off its track, and she limped out to find her crew.

Her once-white flight suit was torn and bloodied in several places, and her badly bruised left knee made walking over the rubble-strewn crash path excruciatingly painful, but she used the pulse rifle as a cane, and pushed hard to find her crew. Patty limped through a bleak uneven landscape past piles of large crystal boulders half buried in loose sand. Few plants managed to cling to life in that fine shifting sand and even a slight breeze blew it in her eyes. Everything about this sector seemed barren and inhospitable. And to make matters worse the throbbing pain in her knee intensified with each step she took, but she refused to give up. She told herself over and over that they might have survived, and by the time light had started to fade from the northern sky she found them in a shallow ravine. Still strapped in their ejection seats, their charred bodies were in close proximity to each other, and over a thousand meters from the crash site.

Curling her hands into fists, she brought them up to the sides of her face. "I don't even have a tool to bury you with. I'm so sorry, my dear friends. Your deaths were so quick." Then a bleak thought threatened to overwhelm her as she whimpered, "Mine may take a bit longer."

As the last light of day faded, she lay down near her dead crewmates and curled up in a fetal position to keep warm. She tried to turn on her flight suit's temperature control, but it didn't work. The awful memory of how she had ordered them to their deaths plagued her every moment as she shivered on the frozen ground.

Patti tried to cry herself to sleep, but no sleep found her that frigid night. At least the lightning storm had run its course.

The next morning brought little relief as she ignored the pain, built up the courage to remove their scorched bodies from their ejection seats, and covered them with the crystal rocks that she found everywhere. Finally, looking down at their cairns, she cried a small prayer for them, and set out to find shelter. She decided to go back to her ship and wait for death. Her wreck was the *Monarch's* last shuttle.

There could be no rescue.

That morose idea abruptly ended when she spied the strangest sight of her life less than fifty meters away. A large flying reptile had landed close by, and it had seen her. But, even stranger, there was something rather human-shaped riding it. Soon two more of these flying riders landed next to the first one. The riders dismounted and walked toward her. They were obviously armed, but their weapons remained sheathed. She felt no threat as they approached, and her own weapon remained at her side.

When the riders were no more than three meters away, they pulled off their full-faced flight helmets. Patti was shocked to see human beings—two men and a woman. The woman stepped forward and with an unthreatening tone, spoke to her. Patti recognized the language as something similar to old Earth Russian, but she couldn't understand the words. "Do you speak English?" she asked hopefully.

The response was quick. "Are you hurt?" the rider asked as she looked back at her companions. They just shrugged.

Patti limped slightly forward and said, "I've got some minor injuries." She pointed to her knee. "I'm not hurt badly, but my two crew members were killed. Can you help me, please?"

A short discussion took place between the riders. Once it ended, the female rider stepped in close, concern evident in her voice, and said, "Come with us. We will take you to safety." Patti dropped the pulse rifle and winced in pain when the two men picked her up. They gently stretched her arms across their shoulders, carried her to one of the dragons, and placed her behind a saddle. The female dragon rider soon climbed up, took the reins, turned, and told Patti, "Hold my waist tightly during flight."

The riders took off and flew away from the cone-shaped mountain shadowing the wreck of her ship and the graves of her crew.

She had no idea what had happened to the *Monarch*, or the rest of the ship's company, but sometime during that dragon flight Patricia Oriel Hammär came to grips with the certainty that she would be stranded on this planet for the rest of her life.

CHAPTER 11

FOOD CHAIN
CHEYENNE MOUNTAIN—EARTH

A fter he returned from the wasteland of the Far East, Alex finished school, and began to travel. He looked for something to fill the void in his life, and after six months of aimlessly wandering he returned to Scotland. But his restlessness went unabated and within a few weeks that something manifested itself as an irresistible force pulling him in only one direction—Interstellar Fleet Command. He left Edinburgh, made his way to the Rocky Mountains, and applied his full abilities to the opportunities the IFC could offer.

And the IFC offered him the stars.

During his first year at the cadet academy near the Cheyenne Mountain Enclave, Alex met an overweight, introverted young genius named Basil Jonathon Hartley. They first met while Cadet Hartley was in the middle of losing an ass-kicking contest to a cadet named Dale Watson, an upperclassman known to bully anyone who couldn't fight back. While it was considered a breach of cadet conduct to intervene while an upperclassman taught a younger cadet his place in the food chain, Cadet Porter had seen enough.

Alex stepped in when the helpless cadet was unable to recover enough wind to get off the ground after a particularly vicious kick to his stomach. While the beaten boy lay on his side painfully emptying the remnants of his lunch on the ground, Watson skipped in and kicked him in the stomach again. Watson then danced back, performed a clumsy jig, and motioned for his victim to get up. At this point, Cadet Porter placed himself between Hartley and the still-dancing Watson.

The dance stopped. "What's this," sneered Watson, "you want your ass kicked too?"

"Of course not," declared Alex. "That's why I'm standing here."

"Huh? What's that supposed to mean?" His lip curled as his hands balled into fists. "What're you, some kind of smart-ass or something?"

"I'm not sure," said Alex with a shrug, "how many kinds are there?"

"Well, I'll tell ya this much, maggot," growled Watson, "there'll be one less in about ten seconds." He puffed his chest and strode forward.

Alex's face lost all expression. He breathed evenly through his nose, spread his feet, and slipped into a Shaolin Wushu stance.

Watson, who was half a head taller and twenty kilos heavier than Alex, hesitated for a moment, and then grinned, saying, "Well, well, look what we got here: a kung fu comedian. Now that is funny. I'm gonna enjoy this more than usual." He raised his fist. Watson's arm was still drawn back when the lightning-fast crescent kick made full contact with his lower jaw.

It was later determined that the loss of three teeth and the broken jaw suffered by Cadet Watson were the result of accidentally falling into some unfortunately placed granite benches. All the witnesses, including several upperclassmen, told the same story during the subsequent investigation. No one ever tried to teach Cadets Hartley or Porter their place in the food chain again.

The day after Alex first met Cadet Hartley, he found him sitting alone in the cafeteria eating lunch. Both of Hartley's light brown eyes were swollen with dark angry rings around them, and Alex could see purple lumps under the boy's closely cropped brown hair. Alex stood across from him holding his lunch tray and waited for an invite to sit. No invitation was forthcoming, so Alex set the tray on another table. The next day the same scenario played out again, and both cadets ate their lunches alone. On the third day, Alex pulled out a chair at the bruised cadet's table, set his tray down without an invitation and ate his lunch in silence.

The still black-and-blue cadet glowered at his unwanted table companion and testily asked him, "You don't take hints very well, do you?"

Alex just smiled, swallowed a bite from his sandwich, washed it down with some green tea, and casually said, "Guess not, but so far, the only *hint* I've heard is that you actually do know how to speak, gasp for air, and, of course, puke on the ground." He took another bite.

Cadet Hartley had learned condescension from his two athletically gifted but cerebrally average older brothers, and he hated it. "Why exactly are you here? Do you want thanks for the other day? Fine. Thanks."

"No thanks necessary. I'd just skipped a class and had nothing else to do."

"How noble of you."

Alex looked wide-eyed at the angry young man and said, "You really think so? Everyone always says that about me, but I don't know. It could be just a phase I'm going through. What do you think?"

"Oh, gimme a fucking break." Basil's ire started to rise. "All right, smart ass, just what is it that you want?"

Alex flashed his most sincere smile. "Well, now that you've asked, there is something I want."

"Yeah? I figured as much," snarled Basil. "So, what *do* you want?"

Alex steepled his hands, leaned his chin on his thumbs, and answered the harsh question with a soft voice. "I'd like a friend. I don't really have any. And since both of us always seem to eat our lunches alone, I thought maybe we could find common ground."

Basil was a local boy whose military family had come from the Cheyenne Mountain Enclave, and his father, a lieutenant colonel in the IFC, prized physical prowess above all else. Basil was anything but an example of physicality. Even when he scored the highest possible score on the IFC Academy entrance exam, his father barely recognized this extraordinary accomplishment. He felt like an outcast everywhere he went, especially in his own family.

None of his accomplishments ever mattered to anyone, not to his family, not to those few who feigned friendship. Everyone eventually, inevitably, cast him aside. Not once had anyone ever proved to be a *friend* past a final exam. Most never made it past the first test they needed to pass. Basil was intimately familiar with the only score that mattered; being friendless hurt, but it hurt less than being used and then thrown away. That hurt worst of all. Basil had seen it all before, and he had perfected a tried-and-true method for evening the scoreboard: never let anyone in.

But what Cadet Hartley couldn't know was that under this stubborn boy's smart-ass demeanor was an intuitive, altruistic nature, and Alex would use every fiber of it to tear off the coat of emotional armor that Basil had erected over a lifetime of failed trust. Alex looked across the table and smiled.

But Basil was ready for battle.

"I scored one hundred percent on the entrance exam." Basil scoffed at his unwelcome tablemate. "What common ground could we possibly have?"

Undeterred, Alex volleyed back. "That's really a fantastic score!

You beat me by two percent. I didn't think that was possible. I'm thoroughly impressed by your superiority."

As much as this goon's high score surprised Basil, he would never become the fat hanger-on kid for some smart, popular, handsome guy, and made his case crystal clear. "You say you don't have any friends? I find that hard to believe. I've seen the way the girl cadets fawn all over you, the way they act just to get your attention. Do you think I'm blind and stupid?"

Alex leaned back in his chair with a contemplative frown etched across his face. What he said next completely unnerved Basil. "And here I thought you were the undisputed genius in this academy. That's what everybody says, anyway, but that can't possibly be right. Not even close to being right. How could everyone be so utterly wrong about you?"

"Wh-what's that supposed to mean?"

Alex spread his palms out wide and said, "What do you mean, 'what do I mean?' You just said to a guy, who'd extended his hand in genuine friendship, that you don't want it because a few girls have shown some superficial attention, and therefore I must have a lot of friends." Alex shrugged nonchalantly, and then offered, "I have no alternative but to believe that your reputation as the smartest cadet in the history of the Interstellar Flight Command Academy is total bullshit."

Basil opened his mouth to counter, but he had nothing left in his quiver, so he shut it.

"Allow me to go one step further and conclude the following—and you really need to hear this because, Cadet Hartley," tapping his left palm with his right index finger, Alex bent slightly forward and said, "your statement—that because a girl flirts with you that makes her a friend—has got to be the stupidest thing I've ever heard."

Basil opened his mouth again, but for the first time ever, he couldn't think of an intelligent rebuttal. His mouth closed again for the second time.

Instead of becoming infuriated at his first-ever intellectual loss, Basil scrutinized Alex. No one had ever earned his respect before, and certainly no one had ever successfully bested him in a verbal contest.

Maybe this guy didn't just want to briefly use him for some test he needed to pass, and he really didn't seem the type to engage in fat-boy hazing. After all, he had voluntarily defended a perfect stranger and easily kicked the crap out of that Neanderthal upperclassman bully.

An epiphany began to take root in Basil's bitter soul: maybe there were people in the world who were worth a chance at friendship. He'd done the math all his life and was well aware that the hardest equation of all was the easiest to figure out—loneliness equaled unhappiness. As he looked across that cafeteria table, a life decision formed. Maybe it was time to take another chance.

———————————

Cadets Hartley and Porter soon became best friends, which proved to be mutually beneficial. The two constantly engaged in the verbal jousting that others found odd for friends, but Basil was never made to feel like the tag-along fat kid. He was treated with respect, and his opinions finally mattered to someone. The solid chip on his shoulder began to crumble away, and he learned a few positive social skills. He soon found out that there were others as genuine as Alex. At times he thought Alex might take some kind of credit for introducing him to a world without loneliness, but typical of Alex, he just brushed it off, saying, "It was always there inside you, Baseball. You just needed the puke kicked out of you before you could find it."

CHAPTER 12

PISSED OFF
IFC GALICIA—EARTH ORBIT

"Y ou can't die in a simulator," the flight instructor barked at the group of eight pilot candidates, "but you can down there." Commander Danea Mamakos jerked a thumb over her shoulder at the four-meter-wide view screen directly behind her. She studied the face of each trainee before saying to them, "Other than pissing me off, you will never do anything more dangerous than making an atmospheric drop." The beautiful blue curvature of Earth filled the view screen in the pilot ready room. The class was being held aboard the *IFC Galicia*, a two-hundred-meter supply ship orbiting above the blue planet. It was fat and ugly and austere, but it could transport a dozen OVALs in its hangar deck, which made it ideal for hands-on flight training. The cadets lovingly referred to the graceless old ship as Mama's Milk Cow.

And Mama had the patience of a rutting bull.

Commander Mamakos moved forward until her face was only centimeters from the student on the far-left end of the line. She stood a full head shorter than the candidate and jutted her chin up at him. "And nothing pisses me off more than one of my students burning up on a drop. So, Mr. Porter, I suggest you do your utmost to not piss me off today. Is that understood?"

With his eyes locked straight forward, Alex stood at a rigid parade rest and snapped out, "Yes, ma'am."

"We'll see," the commander said through gritted teeth. "What is the first rule of an atmospheric entry, Lieutenant?"

"Not pissing off the flight instructor, ma'am."

Mamakos stepped even closer. "Oh, you've already managed to do that, Mr. Porter," she hissed at him, "and it's only 06:00." Her dark brown eyes darted from Alex to the student next to him. "You and your buddy here may have the highest scores in the class, but I assure you that your wings solely depend on my largess. And at the moment I'm not feeling all that charitable." She looked back at Alex. "You need to keep it tight, Porter, starting with that smart mouth of yours. Got it?"

"Yes, ma'am."

Turning her attention to the student next to him, Commander Mamakos's voice dropped to a gear-grinding growl. "Mr. Hartley, do us all a favor and inform Mr. Porter what the first rule of making a drop is?"

"Yes, ma'am." Other than his lips, no other part of Lieutenant Hartley's body even twitched. "The first rule is full cognizance of all atmospheric conditions found in the immediate drop zone, ma'am."

"Starting where?"

"Ma'am?"

Mamakos sighed heavily and rubbed the bridge of her nose. "Where does the atmosphere begin, Mr. Hartley?"

"Oh that," replied Hartley. "At about one hundred kilometers; the Kármán line, ma'am."

"And directly below it?"

"The turbopause, ma'am."

"Well, it looks like you actually read your assignment, Mr. Hartley." She shifted her gaze and asked, "And what does that mean for us, Mr. Porter?"

Alex stiffened, hesitated a moment, and then answered. "That the gases are not well mixed in this section of the thermosphere, which causes inconsistent temperature fluctuations."

"Go on, Mr. Porter."

"Yes, ma'am. These fluctuations create unstable flow patterns beneath the reentry vehicle."

"Finally, Mr. Porter, somehow you've managed to answer back-to-back questions without inserting one of your shit-for-brains witticisms." Her eyes darted between Porter and Hartley, both of whom kept their mouths shut and their eyes straight forward. "See if you can manage a third; tell me why this is important, and how we deal with it."

"Heat correlation, ma'am," offered Alex, "affects our initial velocity and angle of descent."

"And why is this important?"

"So we don't burn up on reentry, ma'am, and piss off the flight instructor."

———————

Strapped in the copilot seat, Basil finished his precheck, pushed up his helmet visor, and chided his pilot. "Really? You just couldn't leave well enough alone, could you?"

"She seemed to take it in stride," Alex said. "We're here, aren't we?"

"Might I point out that the highest percentage of training accidents happen to the team that goes first."

"So, what's your point?"

Basil drew up his eyebrows. "We're first."

Alex glanced at his friend and shrugged. "That just means she has confidence in us."

"Outstanding. But just in case you're curious, my take differs somewhat from that stellar conclusion."

"Whatever, let's go prove her confidence in us to be well-founded." Alex hit the ship-to-base intercom. "And then when I'm done, you get to sit in the left seat, and try not to burn us up."

"If it's not already burnt to a crisp."

"Of course there's that," muttered Alex as he keyed his mic. "*Galicia,* Team Alpha in position. Do you copy?"

"Team Alpha, *Galicia.* We copy. Proceed as planned."

Alex clicked off the ship-to-base mic. "Time to put up or shut up."

"I should have gone into computer programming," moaned Basil, "or gone first."

"Oh ye of little faith. Are we all set to make the first drop?"

"All our parameters are green," reported the copilot, "but our flight path is suspect."

Lieutenant Porter guided his shuttle over the drop zone at Mach four while his copilot scanned the drop coordinates. "What makes you say that?"

Basil tapped his doppler radar screen and shook his head. "The temperature's a roiling witch's brew down there, Alex. Maybe we should abort."

"Abort, are you crazy?"

"Am I cra—" sputtered Basil. "Look, you're the one who—" He cut off his rejoinder and sighed. "Yeah, I must be."

"Great time for confessions," huffed Alex as he ramped up the fusion drive to push them out of orbit. "Now, let's go get our feet wet." Both men flipped their visors down and tightened their seat harnesses in the cramped cockpit. Alex engaged the forward thrusters, dropped their velocity, and pushed the OVAL's nose down to 42°. The shuttle skimmed along the top of the atmosphere for a few seconds, and then penetrated the Kármán line. Vibration hit them immediately, and within seconds, bone-jarring turbulence rocked the little craft.

"Engaging dampening control," reported Basil. The flight computer instantly began making synchronized thruster pulses to keep the OVAL on a steady trajectory, but the debilitating vibration only increased.

With his fists a white-knuckled vise on the yoke and his eyes darting between trim and airspeed, Alex called over to his copilot. "What's our temp, Baseball?"

"The heat deflector is blazing: about 1900° and climbing," reported Basil. "When we hit the mesosphere, we gotta slow down, or we really *will* piss Mama off."

Alex punched the nose thrusters and the OVAL began to slow, but the thrust pushed them into trim up and exposed more of their heat shield; the temperature spiked to 2500°.

"Alex, we're about ten seconds from one pissed-off commander."

"I only need seven," grunted Alex and yanked his yoke hard to starboard. A sudden impact accompanied by the sound of screeching metal wrenched the yoke from Alex's grip.

"What the hell was that?" yelped Basil.

"Thermal layer," replied Alex as he grabbed the yoke. "We're coming around."

"But it sounded like something got torn off the hull."

"Oh that," muttered Alex. "Hell if I know. Hang on." Then finally, protesting like an angry mule, the OVAL shuddered, gyrated, and made it through a wide sweeping turn. Their velocity dropped by almost one third. As they slowed, the thermal shield temperature stabilized, and then edged down. Ten minutes later they were skimming along five meters above the Baltic Sea. Alex grinned over at his partner. "Well, that oughta put Mama in a good mood."

Basil lifted his visor and said, "Well, that's one opinion, good old buddy of mine. Might I offer another?"

"Mmm—"

"Personally, I think she'll be pissed that we made it."

"Tell me more about these two, Danea," requested the tall starship captain as he read the evaluation report. "Their scores are off the charts."

The commander hesitated a moment while she took a deep breath and blew out a shallow sigh. "It's true they have some of the highest aptitude marks I've ever seen, sir."

"But?"

"But they have some personality quirks. Especially Lieutenant Porter."

"How so?"

"His mouth tends to overload his ass on occasion," offered Mamakos.

"And?"

"And, well, they went through the academy together," the flight instructor told him, "and are attached at the hip."

The captain shared a glance with the big commander who had accompanied him to the Olympus Mons flight school. "Interesting, but I think we can deal with that. Wouldn't you say, Gunnar?"

"It's what I live for, Captain."

Captain Richard Jennings nodded at his weapons officer, turned to the flight instructor, and asked, "So, what *is* your official recommendation, Danea?"

"I highly recommend them, sir. Without reservation."

Lieutenants Porter and Hartley graduated number one and two in their class respectively, and they received their pilot wings with honors. Together, they were invited to join a deep-space mission aboard the *IFC Endeavor*, commanded by a legendary starship captain, which they eagerly accepted.

It was rumored that *Endeavor* was heading out on a historic rescue mission into deep space. The parameters of the nine-year voyage included the farthest IFC mission to date, the possible discovery of a Class-M exoplanet, and, barring any major mishap during the flight, a probable promotion upon completion of the mission.

The Hoshi katana was returning to the stars.

CHAPTER 13

EXILE
DRAKON RUS—AQUEOUS

The throne room had undergone a drastic transformation in the first weeks of the young Tsarina's rule. Gone were all those musty old tapestries depicting all those glorious Drakon Rus victories in all those bloody wars with those disgusting Thith. And especially gone was that hideous dragonhead throne that had given the Tsarina nightmares since she was a little girl. In their place hung paintings of beautiful landscapes, and a comfortable, heavily cushioned seat, or throne as Anya must remember to call it. Those were about the only real rulings she'd made since becoming the monarch of humanity's northern colony. Now a real decision had to be made, and it was one she wanted no part of.

"It's your decision to make, Anya," said Vladimir Moroz, the bereaved son and close advisor to the Tsarina, "and as the first real decision of your reign, it must be decisive." The two cousins sat across from each other at a small ornate table set against the back wall of the throne room. Anya preferred the table to the throne whenever she could get away with it.

Still a young teenager, Anya had already reached her adult height of 163 centimeters and was fast approaching the raven-haired green-eyed beauty she would later become. "But how do I make a decision that will either kill my brother, or allow the murderer of the Tsar, not to mention your mother, go free? Please explain to me how I can reconcile all of that," she challenged her cousin.

"With all the aplomb and forbearance of your position as Tsarina—the last word in all matters of state." Vlad reached across the table and took her hands in a show of support.

Anya defiantly jerked her hands away and jumped to her feet. "Great! That's just great, Vlad. How's *that* supposed to help me?"

He frowned at her tantrum, sighed, and watched her rant. He'd seen it all before.

"I need help, Vlad. I need *your* help, the help of my closest advisor, and saying words like forbearance and aplomb—what the dragon ding-a-ling does that mean anyway?"

"Anya," he quietly warned.

She ignored his warning and glared at him. "I. Need. Your. Help," she insisted, then whirled around and stomped off.

"You mean you want me to make the decision for you," he yelled after her, "and I simply cannot do that. *You* are the Tsari—"

She stopped, whipped back around, and shouted, "YES, I know, the *Tsarina!* How could I forget?" She brought clenched fists up and covered both ears. "Two months ago, I was a fourteen-year-old schoolgirl who took dancing lessons." She dropped her hands, returned to the table, and sank back in her chair. "And now I decide who lives and who dies." Her eyes had lost their fury. "I never wanted any of this, you know. Never."

"I know, Anya, and for what it's worth, I feel bad about how this has all happened. But it has, and now we—you—must make some very unpleasant choices. I cannot make them for you. How would it look if word got out that I made the decisions for you?" His fingers lightly drummed the tabletop. "You cannot be seen as weak." Her sad frown and trembling lower lip finally tore at his resolve. He sighed in resignation and closed his eyes. Vlad's voice dropped to an almost whisper as he said, "Nevertheless, I will tell you what *I* would do if it were my decision."

This got her rapt attention. She leaned forward in her chair. "Yes? That's all I'm asking for, Vlad." She folded her hands and went silent.

He opened his eyes and said one word. "Exile."

"You mean it, Vlad? You would give Bayne life, and free of a cell?"

His answer was as unemotional as it was pragmatic. "It would be unwise for the new Tsarina to execute her own brother, and possible heir to the throne, as her first major act of state. Mercy is the best course of action," he told her, "because it will endear you to the people and, more importantly, prove to them that you are not your father."

"Yes," she somberly agreed, "*that* is important."

"All right then," he said thoughtfully, "I have a solution that takes care of two problems at once." He put his elbows on the table and steepled his large hands as he spoke. "We'll take the Earth woman to Cambria. She doesn't seem comfortable with us, and I think Cambria would be a much better home for her. Since Bayne is—was a dragon rider, I'll include him as part of her escort, and we'll have a tidy end to this messy affair."

"Escort?"

"Yes. I'll personally lead the group, to ostensibly drop this woman off, and when we get there we'll conveniently leave Bayne behind as well."

"So be it, and thank you for helping. It is a wise decision."

CHAPTER 14

A ROYAL INCONVENIENCE
DRAGON REST—AQUEOUS

For three days the small group of dragon riders had followed the tumbling river down a sweeping forested valley, and through several mountain passes, only to find themselves in yet another river-laden valley. They had left the cavernous cliff city of Drakon Rus early one morning about a month after Patti crash-landed and were now headed to what she understood was another human city. It was to be her new home.

At least she wouldn't need to learn a new language there.

Right before dark each evening they would land and set up camp in what she heard the riders call a dragon rest. It was obvious that these clearings had been used multiple times, maybe for hundreds of years, but they were not well maintained and had a rustic aura about them. Surrounded by the endless conifer forests that populated the valleys, the dragon rests were large enough to hold hundreds of dragons and their riders. The present one held only five, and one passenger.

Patti rubbed her aching butt, stretched her cramped legs, and tried walking out the soreness. After three days riding on the back of a dragon she was tired, sore, and still had no one to talk to. The lady dragon rider who she rode behind spoke minimally when they were on the ground, and nothing while they were airborne.

None of them had ever been rude to her, and they did see to her comfort, but the language barrier made talking difficult. The colonel spoke excellent English, but he rarely approached her. As for the others, except for a few questions about Earth, she was never included in any of their conversations.

Patti spent her evenings sitting quietly by the campfire. And as rare as a conversation with the other was, there were still only four out of the five dragon riders that had ever actually spoken to her. The fifth, a young man with a jagged scar on his cheek, was even more shunned than Patti. No one ever spoke to him either, or even approached him, and he made no attempt to interact with any of the others.

Sitting by the fire with only her thoughts for company, Patti studied the young man for several minutes. Like every night, he sat on his bedroll at the edge of camp with his back to the rest of the riders. He always sat stock-still, cross-legged, as if in meditation.

Once the crackle of the fire died down to an occasional pop, Patti's eyes grew heavy and she finally closed them. Suddenly, like a shout, a single word screamed into her head. *"Patricia!"* Her eyes snapped open and instantly caught the young man looking at her. His eyes were a vibrant green, and in the dimming firelight they seemed to almost glow.

Almost involuntarily, Patti stood up and walked over to where he looked up at her. Up close he seemed even younger than she had thought, maybe seventeen, or eighteen, a mere boy.

They stared at each other for several moments before he blinked and broke the silence. "Patricia," he finally said out loud.

"Call me Patti," she said. "And you are?"

"Bayne," he told her softly. "Bayne Yanbeyev."

"Ah, Bayne then. May I join you?"

His eyes darted to where the rest of the group sat and then back to Patti. "Please excuse my manners. Yes, of course."

She sat on a log across from him and took note of his wary glances over at the other riders. "Is there a reason you don't hang out with the others?"

"Yeah," he softly admitted, "there is."

"Am I out of place by asking why?"

He gulped, looked down, and spoke in an almost whisper. "I—uh am a pariah." He looked over at the group again, but this time his eyes were hard and defiant. "A royal inconvenience, truth be told."

This time Patti followed his gaze to the rest of the riders and saw that everyone was looking back at them.

"Royal, as in royalty?" She saw that the tall blond colonel had gotten up and now walked toward them. Pointing with her chin, she asked, "As in that Yanbeyev?"

"Yeah, he's my cousin," admitted Bayne, "but not a Yanbeyev. He's a Moroz. The Tsarina is my half-sister."

Patti wrinkled her brow and slightly shook her head. "I'm not sure I understand."

"Then allow me to clear things up for you, Madame Hammär," growled Colonel Vladimir Moroz as he joined the two. "The boy is under house arrest. For the moment that house consists of the dragon he's riding and the patch of dirt his bedroll sits on. But once we get to Cambria, he will be set free. However, until then he is to remain confined to his own thoughts. The terms of that confinement do not include conversations with women from Earth." Vlad moved closer to Patti, and said in a less harsh tone, "Please forgive my vitriol, my lady, but this man is a dangerous criminal."

"So, is it a crime here to be related to the ruler?" Patti asked.

"It is when you're the rightful heir," snapped Bayne, "and have had your throne stolen from you."

Vlad clenched his jaw and said nothing for a moment. When he did speak, the rage was barely under the surface. "You have just broken a term of your release. Speak again and I will invoke the alternative punishment." Vlad folded his arms and glowered at Bayne.

Bayne dropped his head and said nothing more.

Still glaring at the boy, Vlad's next words were to Patti. "To answer your question: no, in spite of what you must now believe, we are not so barbaric." Finally turning to her, he added, "This man is guilty of murder. Primarily regicide. So you see, my lady, we are also not so barbaric to allow one to earn the throne by murdering their father." He held out his hand.

"Oh," she said softly and took the offered hand. After regaining her feet, Patti looked down at the silent boy, now slumped over. His lank blond hair hung across his face.

"If you please, my lady," said Vlad as he led her away. "It would be best if you didn't speak to him again."

While they walked, Patti said in a hushed tone, "I'm a little confused here, Colonel. He's a prisoner now, but when we reach Cambria, you will free him? That sounds like exile."

"It is exactly that. On pain of death if he returns to Drakon Rus. You would be well advised to stay away from him once you reach your new home."

"But he's just a boy."

"Bayne is more than a boy, my lady, much more." Vlad's tone dropped to borderline anger. "He has the ability to kill in the most horrific manner imaginable. And do so with his mind."

Patti frowned dubiously and asked, "With his mind, Colonel?"

"He has already done so, Madame Hammär," he told her bitterly. "Do not let his boyish mien lure you into believing he is anything but pure evil."

"I wasn't defending him," Patti said evenly, "but it all seems so surreal."

"Just so."

They walked on in silence until they got to her bedroll. Patti hesitated a moment, and then asked, "Colonel, just one more thing: if Bayne's this powerful, why doesn't he use those powers and escape now?"

Vlad shot a quick glance across the campsite. Bayne sat slumped over with his back to them. "He might, but we are ready, and I don't think even he believes his powers are strong enough take us all down before one of us kills him. Goodnight, my lady."

CHAPTER 15

RETICENT
CAMBRIA—AQUEOUS

I n the 956 years that the governor's mansion had been the seat of power in the Cambrian colony, it had lost none of its grandeur. Eight fluted columns standing ten meters high supported the third-story balcony that spanned the building's thirty-meter façade. The mansion was separated into two main wings; one served as the governor's offices, while the other was his residence. Nestled in between the two wings and at the heart of the mansion sat a large, round ballroom framed on each side by grand sweeping staircases. The massive crystal chandelier that hung from ballroom's twelve-meter-high rotunda was at the exact center of the mansion. Dark wood paneling adorned its circular walls, while the floor was a highly polished travertine. The governor's ballroom was considered the most aesthetically appealing room in the entire colony.

Six people, four soldiers from the Governor's Guard and two civilians, entered the main entryway through tall wooden double doors, then marched through the vestibule and into the ballroom. The group stopped directly beneath the chandelier. Two of the group looked up and gawked at the room's splendor, while the officer in charge turned to the other three and told a huge hulk of a soldier, "Bull, you three are to remain here with the guests while I speak with the governor."

"Will do, sir," answered the big man.

The soldier stepped back, watched the officer disappear down a hallway, then turned and told the civilians, "Don't do nut'n stupid till the major gets back."

Grateful that everyone here seemed to speak English, Patti asked, "And then?"

"Guest he fergot to tell me," said the soldier. "Guest we find out together."

Governor Sven Lawson sat at his large executive desk working on a document. He kept his eyes trained on what he was writing when Major Garcia entered without knocking. "Morning, Billy," Lawson greeted the other man without looking up.

"Sven," said the major, "you're gonna want to come see this."

The governor stopped writing and looked up. "See what?"

"I have two rather unusual guests waiting in the rotunda."

The governor tapped his pen on the desk and said, "How exactly does this involve me?"

"One of them, a woman, claims to be from Earth."

The pen tapping stopped. "And the other?"

"A young man, about eighteen, and he claims to be your daughters' half-brother."

Clustered at one end of the large wooden dining table, the Lawson family sat with Bayne Yanbeyev, the newest member of their family. The boy sat with his hands folded in his lap, his head hung down, not once meeting any of their eyes. No one else spoke while the servants brought out the first course. The moment the door shut behind the last servant, one of the redheaded seventeen-year-old twins locked her blue eyes on the boy and demanded, "After, what, almost twenty years of zero contact from Drakon Rus, they suddenly unceremoniously drop you here unannounced?"

"Britt!" scolded her twin sister. "This isn't an interrogation. Pay no attention to her, Bayne. We're thrilled to have a brother, and such a handsome one at that."

"T-thank you," Bayne said softly. He finally looked up and met Lorraine's eyes. A crooked smile slowly found its way to his lips. "But, your sister's right—"

"*Our* sister," Lorraine stressed. "You're part of our family now."

Bayne opened his mouth to speak, but only managed to gulp air.

"It's okay, Bayne." Sven reached over and patted the boy's forearm. "We're not here to judge, but it is a fair question. You can tell us the reason, can't you?"

The boy looked down again and slightly nodded his head.

"Well?" pushed Britt and then shrugged when she got a withering look from Lorraine.

"I-I was banished for killing my father."

"You killed the Tsar?" Britt blurted out.

Again the boy nodded.

"Did you hear him, Dad?"

Sven placed his elbows on the table and leaned forward. "Yes, Britt, but now may not be the best time to discu—"

"He was an evil ruthless tyrant," interrupted Bayne.

"No argument there," agreed Sven.

Bayne dropped his eyes again as he continued. "He abused his power. He abused his subjects. He abused me." Bayne ran two fingers down the scar on his cheek and looked up, a defiant set to his eyes. "He gave me this the day he told me my mother—*our* mother—died."

"Oh, Bayne," gasped Lorraine, "you don't have to—"

"Not too long ago he was on his deathbed, and I—I eased his passing," confessed Bayne, "and they exiled me for it. Here. To you."

Major Guillermo Garcia lounged on the plush divan in Governor Lawson's wood-paneled office drinking a bourbon nightcap with his boss. He stuck a finger in his tumbler, swirled the ice, licked his finger, and said, "Something's just not adding up, Sven."

"Here, Billy." Lawson tossed Garcia a swizzle stick. "These work better than fingers."

"Oh, I thought those were straws they forgot to put the hole in."

"Of course you did. Now tell me why you think the math is bad."

Garcia set his drink on the coffee table and leaned back. "Think about it, Sven. If the boy really did perform euthanasia on the old bastard, then he'd be their Tsar right now, not a guest here in his—how do I say this—his stepfather's house?"

"Guardian, I guess," muttered Lawson. "Anyway, they're a monarchy where only the Grim Reaper gets a vote."

"From what I've heard, that's a pretty good description of the boy."

"Hearsay, Billy?" Lawson sighed, and then said, "Tell me more about the woman."

"Well see now, that's where the math gets kinda fuzzy." Garcia took a long drink. "First Lieutenant Patricia Hammär: That's the woman's name, by the way."

"I know that."

"She's my hearsay, Sven."

"Just go on."

"Right, well, it seems that she was told by some dragon-riding colonel that the boy butchered his pop with his mind."

"His mind?"

Garcia reached for the tumbler. "Said there was nothing left but a wet spot."

Lawson grimaced. "If this is true, then the boy lied to us."

"Murderers tend to do that on occasion."

"But she seemed fine with him during our first interview," said Lawson. "I mean, she was a little reticent. But who wouldn't be, stranded on an alien world?"

"Reticent?" The glass clinked when he drained the tumbler. "That's what we're calling it now?"

"Calling what?"

"Fear, Sven." Garcia looked over the rim of his empty glass. "That woman flew halfway across the galaxy, which, by the way, is a whole other bottle of bourbon we need to dive into, crashed on said alien world, hung out with an army of dragon riders, and then got deposited here."

"Why do I always seem to miss your point?"

"Well, could be any number of factors," answered Garcia. "But anyway, it seems to me that she's got to have a special kind of courage to do all that, and yet, here she is *reticent* of a scrawny eighteen-year-old boy."

"How did you get all this out of her?" Lawson asked as he filled both their tumblers again. "I spent an hour with her and the boy and saw none of what you're on about. Ice?"

"Always," said Garcia.

"Here you go," said Lawson as he dropped in more ice cubes.

Garcia's finger went back in the glass. "She told me all about it when I dropped her off at the library."

Lawson glanced down at the dry swizzle stick and grunted.

"The head librarian thought she could use her to fill in that omnipresent thousand-year gap we're all so shamelessly ignorant about."

"Gap," Lawson echoed thoughtfully. "Hmm, do you think she'll like it there?"

"Maybe," reflected Garcia, "it's a library; deathly quiet, full of books about dead people. What's not to love?"

"Cynic."

"That's the rumor," confessed Garcia. "Anyway, it'll keep her busy and put a roof over her head."

Lawson sighed softly. "Fine. Now the boy."

"Yeah, the boy." The old friends locked eyes from across the room. "You could very well have a cold-blooded killer living under your roof."

The governor followed the morning chatter to the kitchen and leaned against the china cabinet next to the pantry door. He said nothing as he watched his girls. Nothing in his life had ever given him more delight than being witness to these two vibrant young women as they moved into adulthood; nothing except for their long-dead mother. Like her, they were striking beauties with long red hair, deep blue eyes, and faces that could make an angel sing. Except for their personalities, the girls were almost indistinguishable from each other, but in that they were like night and day.

Sven Lawson would do anything to protect them.

Both girls were in their second semester of premed. They were chatting about the coming day when they finally noticed their dad standing behind the hutch.

"Taken to skulking around, Dad?" teased Britt.

"Dad doesn't skulk," corrected Lorraine, "he slinks."

Sven quietly moved into the kitchen and tore a hunk of bread off a fresh loaf on the counter. "I just came in to grab a bite," he lied.

"Uh-huh."

"Sure, Dad."

Reaching out to grab a plate from the hutch, Sven stopped and said over his shoulder, "Actually, there is something we need to talk about."

"Let me guess," said Britt. "It's Bayne, and there could be a problem there, Dad. Lorraine's been making kissy faces in the mirror lately."

"Shut up, lizard lips."

"Just say'n."

"Girls," Sven interjected, "listen, please." He turned to face them. "I've decided he can't stay here anymore."

The kitchen went silent.

Lorraine squinted her eyes and opened her palms. "But why, Dad? I don't understand."

"Because he's not the innocent boy he acts like," asserted Britt, "is he?"

"I'm not sure," said Sven, "and until I know more, I think it's best if he leaves."

"But where will he go?" asked Lorraine.

"Probably to prison," said a soft voice from behind the pantry door. "Isn't that right, Governor?" Bayne sauntered into the kitchen avoiding everyone's eyes. "You're going to throw me in prison, aren't you?"

Lorraine moved closer to her brother. "Dad, you're not seriously thinking about having him arrested, are you?"

"No, of course not," protested Sven. "That thought hasn't crossed my mind."

Britt leaned against the counter and folded her arms. "Then what are you planning, Dad?"

Everyone turned to the governor, who just shrugged and told them, "I'm not sure, but until I have a clearer picture," he turned to face Bayne, "I think it's best if you stay in the guard barracks."

"Why send me away at all?" Bayne's voice started to crack.

"Because your version of what happened at Drakon Rus doesn't add up," said Sven, "and another version does."

"All lies," whined Bayne.

"Be that as it may," Sven told him, "you need to go pack."

"Fine!" screeched the boy. He pushed off the cabinet, jutted his chin, and with shoulders thrown back, he half cursed, half cried, "You want to be rid of me. No problem, I'm out of here."

"But we're your only family," Lorraine protested.

"Not true, sister," countered Britt; "his other family got rid of him too."

"I have no fucking family!" Bayne shouted. His fists balled up at his sides. "And when I do get the throne that's rightfully mine, all those who could have been loyal to me will wish they had done so when they had the chance."

"You need to calm down, young man," Lawson said sternly.

"Shut up!" shouted Bayne. "Shut up, shut up, shut up."

"I've heard enough of this." The edge in Lawson's voice grew tense.

Bayne suddenly dropped his tone, twisted his face, and stepped in close to Lawson. "I don't have to listen to you, Governor," he sneered. "You're not even my family, but just like them, you're dead to me." His eyes darted around the kitchen, finally locking on Britt. His sneer became a snarl as he brought his fists chest level, splayed his fingers, kneaded the air, and growled, "You're all dead to me."

Both girls screamed as a powerful blast of wind swept the Lawsons off their feet and blew all the dinnerware off the cabinet shelves where it shattered on the floor. After a moment the tempest was over, and Bayne was gone.

CHAPTER 16

SHE'S HERE
DRAKON RUS—AQUEOUS

Two riders from a Dark Dragon patrol came hurtling through the giant main gate into Drakon Rus and made an abrupt landing inside the great hall. As soon as the groom grabbed the patrol leader's bridle, the officer pulled back on the reins. "Where's the colonel?" he demanded.

"Sir, I saw him in the stockade inspecting the young cadets about an hour ago," came the groom's quick response.

Without replying, the patrol leader yanked the bridle out of the man's hands and spurred his mount back into the air. He raced through the large hallway that connected the great hall to the massive stockade and spotted Colonel Vladimir Moroz lecturing a group of young men and women on the parade ground.

Moroz stopped talking when all his students quit paying attention to him. The colonel turned around to see what all the fuss was about just as the patrol leader hard landed his dragon in a cloud of dust, not four meters from where Moroz stood.

"Not exactly the type of maneuver I want these youngsters to see from a veteran, Pasha," commented the colonel. "A little unorthodox, isn't it?"

Without dismounting, or even acknowledging his commander's

93

comment, the dragon rider just blurted out, "*She's here, Colonel. My patrol was only a few minutes ahead of her.*"

Colonel Moroz flashed the cadets a don't-you-dare-pull-this-kind-of-stunt look and turned back to the dragon rider. "Who's here?" But the look on his patrolman's face told him all he needed to know. "Take over here, Lieutenant, and see if you can teach them proper landing techniques." Moroz sprinted out of the stockade and headed for the Tsarina's quarters.

The colonel pounded up the stairs leading to the royal apartment and burst into the outer office. He flashed Sergei a stern look, and the old man just threw up his hands and carped, "Why am I even here?"

Moroz bolted through the door and into Anya's apartment, yelling, "Anya!" as he rushed onto her balcony. "She's coming to—oh, I see, she's already here."

Wearing a warm, full-length red dress, Anya sat on a deeply cushioned divan on her large terrace. Lounging next to her was the massive golden dragon, Rodinya. The largest being on the planet's long neck was curled downward so that her smooth, three-meter, viper-shaped head was only a meter from where the Tsarina was seated.

Both women flashed annoyance at him.

Moroz ignored their scowl and since he also had the family's blood in his veins, he could talk with the giant dragon, and was suspicious of anything she had to say. "You," he said accusingly.

Rodinya snorted.

Anya's frown deepened.

Colonel Moroz locked eyes with the dragon and strode up to her. "You took your time getting here."

"*So what? I made a promise to the late Tsar.*" Moroz winced at the force with which the dragon's last word entered his mind. "*And however late, I meant to keep it. It's just too bad there was nothing left of him to bury.*"

I've been holding my bladder for days." The venom in her voice softened considerably. *"I'm truly sorry to hear about your mother, Vladimir. She was a noble woman."* Rodinya hesitated a moment before asking the indelicate question. *"And the boy?"*

"The boy is gone," came Vlad's calculated response.

"Gone?" Her eyes narrowed suspiciously. *"Gone where exactly?"*

"Exiled to Cambria. What did you expect from us—*exactly?*"

"Rodinya has come to show me something very important," Anya broke in, "and she was just about to explain when you barged in. I gather Sergei will be sulking for days?"

"Well, I didn't really mean to upset him," stammered Vlad. "It's just that when I heard *she* was coming—"

"Oh, lizard piss, Vladimir," snapped Rodinya, then turned back to Anya and said sweetly, *"And besides, I didn't come here to show you something. I came here to take you to get something."*

"What?" exclaimed the Tsarina.

"Not happening!" The colonel waved his hands back and forth as he confronted the fiercest creature on Aqueous.

"Oh, you'll have to come too, Vladimir. In fact, she'll need to ride one of your little dragons while I lead the way." A slight grin of recognition spread across her dragon features because she was just about to get her way. *"But of course, you'll need to lead the expedition."*

"Just what are you talking about, Rodinya?" Moroz demanded.

Rodinya yawned and blew a foul-smelling sigh in his direction.

Moroz squeezed his eyes shut and waved a hand in front of his face.

"Why do I have to go?" Anya was suddenly a young girl again. "And where are we going?"

"Wait, hang on, just wait a minute, I haven't agreed to any of this!" Moroz said.

"*Oh, but you will, Vladimir, you will,*" Rodinya told him. "*We're going to the Sanctuary of the Final Order.*"

"But why me?" asked Anya.

"*Because, my dear, the Order has been protecting something of extreme value for almost a thousand years.*" The giant dragon rested her head on the terrace next to the teenage girl. "*And all this time, they've been protecting it for you.*"

Anya glanced over at her cousin, and then looked back at Rodinya, who winked at her.

Only one more element of the prophecy needs to manifest itself. Rodinya kept this thought to herself. *And he will appear soon. He must appear soon.*

CHAPTER 17

LEFT THUMB
IFC ENDEAVOR—MISSION DAY 185

At over three hundred meters, Interstellar Fleet Command's newest and most advanced starship, the *IFC Endeavor*, was a thing of beauty. Except for her sister ship, the *IFC Monarch*, she was unlike any previous starship ever built by mankind. Her new delta configuration had a high-tech composite skin, few view ports, and though it was never meant to enter any planet's atmosphere, its smooth contour design dictated that it could. A twenty-meter-long blister, housing the bridge, protruded from her upper deck, and inside four much smaller blisters at the forecastle were the ship's only armaments, four pulse cannons. These were the only blemishes on the sleek, black, teardrop shape. Along the port side, two thirty-meter-wide bay doors sat seamlessly in the hull. Behind those large doors was the equally large docking bay housing the ship's two shuttlecraft.

At the rear of the superstructure hummed the heart of the ship: the Enhanced Magnetic Drive. It was the most advanced drive system yet developed by the IFC, and it could propel the starship up to three hundred light-years in only one solar year. For establishing orbit and making precise coordinate changes, the *Endeavor* used a fusion drive system located in the two decks directly below the EMD.

The crew's quarters were the most comfortable ever placed on a starship, and each of her sixty-two crew enjoyed their own cabin. Directly in the center of the ship was the holographic deck, a twelve-meter sphere where thousands of different program scenes could be projected with absolute realism. But the most popular spot on the ship was the galley. Early on during the design phase, creature comforts were given the utmost consideration, and the quality of the culinary experience was as good as most high-end hotels.

Lounging in a galley booth, the only two crew members not in suspended animation conducted their handover over lunch. Baseball had just pulled a pile of something yellow and steaming out of the microwave oven before sitting down with the starship's other pilot. "Want some of this, buddy?" he asked, shoving the large bowl toward Alex. "It'll only take a minute to print up some more."

"Ugh, I don't think so."

Baseball shrugged, dragged the bowl back, grabbed a spoon, and with a full mouth said to his tablemate, "Suit yourself, but this is the last meal you're gonna have for six months."

Alex grimaced and took a swig of green tea. "I'm pretty sure that somewhere in the regs it says something about mac and plastic being the last thing you want laying waste to your gut during the long sleep."

"Speaking of long sleeps, buddy," Baseball said in between bites, "the funniest thing happened during my last one."

Alex raised his mug to his lips and held it there. It failed to hide the smirk. "Oh really? That's nice."

"You might think so, but see, I woke up to find my left thumb jammed up my ass all the way to the metacarpophalangeal."

"So, what's the big deal? You're right-handed."

"There's supposed to be a rectal catheter up there."

"And?"

"Ya see, genius, the way it works is the catheter tube allows drainage, unlike a thumb that tends to act like a plug."

"Ew, I see." Alex wrinkled his nose. "And when you pulled it out all that, um, how can you talk about this while eating that?"

Baseball's light brown eyes squinted as he inspected the guilty thumb. "I scrubbed it like ten times." He shoved it in Alex's face and asked, "Do you think I got everything out from under the fingernail?"

"Get that thing away from me," Alex said, "I don't know where it's been!"

"Oh yes you do, Buster. And just remember that I've scored better grades than you on every single test we've ever taken."

"What's that supposed to mean?"

"Payback's a bitch."

"Well, that's a shitty attitude."

The next day Alex crawled into his life-support bed, complete with both catheters, and prepared for his extended downtime. Along with the ship's artificial intelligence system, Baseball would now have the helm for the next six months. It was mind-numbing boredom that Alex made more enjoyable on the holographic deck. There wasn't much for the human pilot to do, but being responsible for an entire ship's company was still a daunting task.

"Keep in mind that we're approaching the eighty-ninth quadrant, and that the next jump is four point six light-years into it."

"I know," Baseball groaned.

"SADI will do all the coordinate links."

"I know that. I helped write the program," muttered Baseball. He smiled and then told his friend, "I'm gonna start calling you Mother Porter."

"Don't."

"How about just Mother?"

"Look, I'm just trying to cover all the bases. It's a baseball thing."

"Whatever, let's get you prepped."

As Baseball prepared to seal the cryo-bed, and right before Alex succumbed to the physiology-slowing drugs dripping into his arm, he queried his friend. "So, exactly what are you going to do for the next six months?"

"Don't worry, buddy," Baseball reassured him, "all that talk about payback was just talk." He scratched his thumb. "Although it does still kind of itch."

Alex's vision faded, and his speech slurred. "Naw weally Bathba, wutchu—wazu—"

"What am *I* gonna do?" Baseball asked. "Oh, so now you're worried, but fret not, all I'm gonna do is work on a few software programs I've been tinkering with. Sleep tight."

CHAPTER 18

PROPHESY BOOK
SANCTUARY OF THE FINAL ORDER—AQUEOUS

A bone-chilling wind howled past the ice-encrusted main gate as it creaked open to the mammoth launch terrace. Standing fifteen meters tall, the thick wooden doors were all that protected the great hall from the blizzard raging outside. Deep thermal vents within the mountain warmed the cavernous fortress city but did little for the great hall once the main gates were open. Snow flurries, chased inside by the frigid air, swirled around the small squadron as they prepared to embark on the most unusual expedition to leave Drakon Rus in generations.

Heavily garbed in cold-weather flight suits, the travelers made ready next to one of the giant crystal columns that rose up to the hall's ceiling. The massive columns were set in four rows of ten that ran the length of the one-hundred-meter-long hall. There was enough space in between each column to allow a full-grown dragon to fly between them, and the great hall itself could hold hundreds of dragons and their riders at a time.

Today there were only three.

Led by Colonel Moroz and Tsarina Anya, the group was almost ready to depart. The largest member of the expedition had been ready for hours and stomped around impatient to get started. *"Not to push, or anything—"*

"Then don't," grumbled the colonel.

"—*but we really should leave before this blizzard gets any worse.*"

"Maybe this is a sign," snapped Moroz while trying to fit a cold-weather hood onto his protesting dragon, "that we should ignore your interference, and stay here."

"Vlad!" Anya scolded. "This is important to me. It'll define my reign."

A deep frown split her cousin's face. "Fairness and accountability will define your rule—ow!" He slapped his mount when it bit his thumb.

"*Ha! I bet that left a bad taste in its mouth.*"

Bristling, the colonel jabbed the sore thumb over his shoulder, saying, "And not her meddling." His mount head-butted him in the shoulder.

"*You should stop playing with your pet, Vladimir, and listen to your sovereign.*"

"Go jump off a cliff!"

"*I intend to.*"

"Seven Bells of Hell!" Anya bellowed, throwing her hands in the air. "If you don't stop your bickering, I'll go without you."

"*We need Vladimir too, Anya,*" Rodinya said.

"I meant both of you two," the Tsarina said, "children! Just listen to yourselves. I'm not behaving like a spoiled brat, and I'm younger than both of you," she glared at Rodinya, "by about a million years."

"*That was uncalled for.*"

"But fairly accurate," Vlad said just as his dragon jerked on the bridle and yanked him off his feet.

Anya tightened the last strap on her dragon, rolled her eyes, walked over, and placed a gentle hand on the neck of Vlad's unruly one. It calmed immediately. Vlad stood up and grunted. Placing her hands on her hips, she told him, "If you're done messing around, I'd like to get this parade started."

"I'm not messing—look, she's the one—" Moroz jutted his chin at Rodinya, "making them nervous."

Rodinya huffed a putrid breath in his direction.

"Stop doing that," hissed Moroz.

A low growl rumbled up from Rodinya's throat as she turned toward the gate. A moment later the sound of her heavy footfalls crunched towards the ice-encrusted terrace. She exited the main gates of Drakon Rus, snorted something about tiny dragons and their tinier children, trudged across the huge launch terrace, and then leapt off the cliff and into the storm.

———————

Early evening on the sixth day, just as the cold gray light of the omnipresent clouds slipped into shadow, the expedition's flight path began winding around scores of gigantic monolithic columns in the Valley of Towers. Hidden amongst these natural towers, and half their height, stood their destination. It was a squat tower unlike any of the others, and on its summit sat the Sanctuary of the Final Order. The sanctuary was manned by four dedicated anchorites and led by an elderly man whom Rodinya knew well.

"Good to see you again, Keeper Shaw," Rodinya greeted the sanctuary's leader, as she hovered for a landing.

Like all those who lived at the Sanctuary, the Keeper was of the blood and could speak with the ancient dragon. At seventy-two years, the Keeper had long, white hair, a longer white beard, and stood stooped in his floor-length coarse-spun robe. He moved with more of a shuffle than a walk as he approached the travelers. "Oh my, it's so good to see you again, my lady," Shaw affectionately greeted the dragon. "And is this who I think it is?" he asked as Anya dismounted her dragon, removed her riding helmet, and walked toward them.

"Yes, Keeper Shaw, she's the first Intended."

"And the second?" whispered Shaw. "What of him?"

Rodinya craned her neck downward until it enveloped both Keeper Shaw and the newly arrived Tsarina, and then answered his question, *"He'll be here soon."*

"Who will?" asked Anya.

"As with so many other things, Anya," Rodinya gently told her, *"that's why you're here: to learn your role."*

"My role?" exclaimed Anya. "I thought I came here to get something."

With a dip of his head, Keeper Shaw humbly said, "My Tsarina, there is something of immense value inside," he gestured his bone-thin arm toward a rustic wooden door built into the crystal rock, "the inner sanctum. If you please, allow me to show you the way."

"What valuable something?"

"Your prophecy book."

Anya stopped in her tracks and dropped her jaw. "My what?"

Shaw explained, "A millennium ago our ancestor, the Prophetess, wrote a series of prophecy books for specific individuals: the Intended."

"That's not what I've been taught," said Anya.

"You were taught wrong," confided Shaw in a hushed tone, "on purpose."

By then Moroz had arrived and stood just outside where Rodinya's coiled neck created a loose embrace. Keeper Shaw seemed slightly nervous about the colonel's inclusion. "The book is only for you, Tsarina," he said in a low tone as his eyes darted between Moroz and Anya.

"He's my cousin and closest advisor," said Anya.

"She doesn't leave my sight," Moroz sternly informed the group.

"Oh my," said the old man as he shot a desperate glance at Rodinya. "My lady?"

"It's all right, Keeper Shaw, Vladimir is only a tiny annoyance."

Shaw wrinkled his forehead and said, "Very well then, if you'll both follow me." Though Rodinya had to remain outside, she could still hear their words and their thoughts, and listened to everything.

Keeper Shaw guided the two cousins through the old weather-beaten door and into a wide circular room carved out of solid crystal. Its smooth polished walls sparkled in azure cobalt. A single lensed skylight shone down on the chamber's focal point that was placed at the exact center of the room. "This is the vestry, and that," Shaw's bony hand swept toward the illuminated wooden altar sitting directly beneath the shaft of light, "is the heart of the Sanctuary, and why you are here."

Atop the altar sat a meter tall crystal statue that refracted light in impossible angles of spectral hues. The effect mesmerized the newcomers, and no one spoke for a moment.

Anya finally broke the silence and asked in a hushed tone. "What is it?"

"The inner sanctum," Shaw said reverently.

"Well, that explains that," grumbled Moroz.

"Vlad, please," scolded Anya, and turned to the elderly man. "I'm not sure I understand."

"That's understandable," said Shaw. "You see, the sanctum holds two books."

"Prophecy books?" asked the wide-eyed Tsarina.

"Indeed."

"But how can you be sure that they're meant for me?

"I'm not," confessed Shaw, "but Rodinya is, and the book itself will confirm the validity of the Intended."

"You said 'books' earlier," Moroz pointed out. "And just who is this intended person?"

"Persons, and yes, there are two books. One for each of the Intended." Shaw gave Anya an affectionate smile. "The Tsarina is quite possibly the first."

"Possibly?" Moroz groused. "What's that supposed to mean? We came here based on the insistence of a flying lizard."

"I heard that."

"At your age?" mumbled Moroz.

"Grrrr—"

"If you please, Colonel," Shaw interjected, and gestured toward the sanctum, "gently remove the crystal statue of Rodinya and carefully set it down."

"How subtle. Figures it would be her," Vlad said, but he did as he was asked. Once the altar top was free of the heavy statue, a counterbalance released and a hidden panel slid open, revealing an inner chamber.

Shaw clapped his hands, bounced up and down on the balls of his feet, and with a barely restrained cackle said to no one in particular, "Oh my, what a day! This is the pinnacle of my life." He soon composed himself, tucked his long beard into his robe, reached inside the chamber, and lifted out a wooden box. Three metal bands wrapped around the box with an odd locking mechanism on the top of the center band. Carrying the fifty-centimeter box to a nearby bench, he carefully set it down. Shaw tried to sound solemn, but his eyes twinkled, giving his game away. "Come, Anya, only you can open this."

"How?"

"With a drop of your blood," he tapped a metal lock on the box, "smeared here."

Anya gave her cousin a wary glance, who shrugged and pulled out his dagger. "This should work."

"Ow," said Anya, wincing as he made a slight incision on her right thumb. "Was that really necessary?" she whined as a few drops of blood quickly beaded.

"How else was I supposed to draw blood?"

"Allow me to show you sometime."

"Hush, you two," ordered Anya, and then turned to Keeper Shaw. "And I just wipe it on that lock?"

"Yes, and make sure those two small holes are filled."

Carefully, Anya did as she was asked, and held her breath.

They all held their breaths.

Nothing happened.

"That went well," exhaled Moroz. He leaned toward his cousin, nodded at her blood-smeared thumb, and whispered, "Courtesy of a flying lizard."

"If patience is nourishment for the wise…"

Keeper Shaw looked stricken. "Oh my."

"What do we do now?" Anya sounded crestfallen.

"Now? Now we fly home," Moroz replied, "without the lizard."

"How much more so for the fool?"

At that moment the lock clicked open.

"Oh my."

CHAPTER 19

TRAINING DAY
IFC ENDEAVOR—MISSION DAY 1498

P ain. It was his companion, his competitor, and sometimes his friend. It kept him focused and molded his strength of character. Pain was both catalyst and a means to an end—the means he used to control his special ability.

And his only access to the Path.

It was a disciplined regimen of both physical and mental control, and it absorbed his entire being. He would become two entities, each with its own separate and unique abilities—each with the capacity to act autonomously of the other.

Only through pain could he astral project.

While Alex's incorporeal body dangled his feet in a babbling brook that ran through the forest glade near his boyhood home, his physical one splashed across a small creek that soon turned into a torrential stream that cascaded down a jagged alpine mountain before feeding its cold water into the Bavarian Salzach River. That he was also 998 light-years away from Earth, hurtling through the galaxy, was immaterial.

Alex knew he'd approached the end of his run when he heard the slight electronic warbling of SADI accompanied by a red blinking light that appeared in the midday sky. The light warned that he had only ninety seconds to go before he reached his goal. This prompted a signal in his mind; like a wisp of vapor, he evaporated from the glade and came hurtling back to his exhausted but still-running body on the mountain trail. It was time to push harder for the end-of-the-run kick. He picked up speed in an all-out sprint to today's final goal: timberline in the Berchtesgaden Alps.

With mere seconds to go, he broke out of the twisted firs and into the pristine clearing of a high alpine meadow, just as the feminine voice of SADI announced, "Time, Alex. You've made it to your goal at the top of the Übergossene Alm glacier in one hour, five minutes, and sixteen seconds. However, as usual, you need to replenish your body fluids immediately, or you will dehydrate, cramp, and possibly come down with hypoxemia. I've already prepared the electrolyte hydration drink in the galley. Please proceed there posthaste."

"Hypo what?"

"Altitude sickness, Alex. You remember—uncontrolled vomiting, severe headaches, and an inability to function beyond self-pity and crying for your mommy."

As if, thought Alex, barely able to catch his breath as he slowed down to a brisk walk. He held his hands high above his head to increase lung capacity and breathed in huge gulps of the high-altitude air in order to get the oxygen that his body so desperately needed. His white blood cell count would have more than tripled during the run but would drop just as fast as he recovered. But resting and recovery weren't in his plans. They never were. The second and even more grueling phase of his workout was about to begin, and nothing, especially his snippy electronic companion, was going to deter him.

"My mother was a neural surgeon, SADI, so it would only be natural for me to elicit her help while in a state of hypi—hypoxi—what you said. Remind me to remove the exaggeration bug from your protocol program. I wasn't crying. I was simply requesting some aspirin."

"And your mother."

"Whatever." He waved a hand above his head and asked, "So, are you ready to spool up the next program so I can finish my workout and take a shower? Come on, SADI, you know the drill. No recovery till after the fight, and that means now." It was his daily test of wills with the *Endeavor's* mainframe computer, officially known as the Systematic Artificial Direct Intelligence, a test that he almost always won.

SADI's female emotional response system usually made her assimilation with the human members of the crew easier to deal with. This was an essential element of her interaction protocols, but it had little effect on some of the more obstinate members of the crew like Alex.

Especially Alex.

"SADI, set up the program for today's opponent, and please make him more of a contest than the last one. I need to be able to hone my skill set, not just slaughter some poor palooka without breaking a sweat."

The AI gave him that exasperated feminine warble that always left Alex wondering who slipped the mothering inclination into her interaction software. Before complying with his order she demanded, "Why do you always finish an exhausting run and go straight into a potentially lethal fight without any recovery time?"

With an exaggerated sigh, Alex answered her question with one of his own. "Why do you always ask the same question every day at the same time, knowing you'll always get the same response?"

"Because you never answer my question. Lieutenant Porter, these programs were not developed for the type of training you insist on."

"Look, SADI, I'm the sole human member of this crew who happens to be awake right now. I have no one to talk to but you. Not that I'm complaining much, but in order for me to stay in both peak physical and mental condition, I need to keep the edge sharp, so to speak. And to do that, I engage in these harmless combat programs. If they were forbidden, they wouldn't be in your database, would they?"

Without acknowledging his question she curtly replied, "Since I cannot refuse access, then we will, as usual, proceed."

"Fair enough. So, what have you got for me today?"

After getting no response from SADI for several moments, Alex grew impatient. He was cooling off, his endorphins had begun to slip away, and he really needed to get to the next phase of his workout. "So—?"

SADI gave the monotone warble that typically signaled her frustration at having been thwarted yet again. "He'll be waiting for you in a moment."

CHAPTER 20

THE SPARTAN
IFC ENDEAVOR—MISSION DAY 1498

W hat so recently had been a high mountain trail blurred into a kaleidoscopic mist and then vanished altogether. Soon thousands of projector lenses embedded in the spherical enclosure of the *Endeavor*'s virtual reality deck rematerialized.

The virtual hologram created not only an illusion of the desired scene, but a physical one as well. So much so that the human participant could completely interact with the program, including sensations of touch. This was achieved by the instantaneous transmutation of molecules at the exact point of physical contact and was the main reason why Alex insisted on these combat programs.

Alex stood on one side of the holographic deck and said, "SADI, along with my katana and baldric, I want a combat tomahawk as backup, if you please." Turning to the center of the room, he casually asked, "So, who and what have you got for me today?" His gaze was, however, anything but casual. More akin to that of a predator as he mentally prepared himself for the coming battle.

SADI's now emotionless voice described the program she was spooling up. "Today you face a single Spartan hoplite from around BC 400. He'll be armed with a two-meter dory, a bronze shield, an iron short sword, and protected by light armor to enable quick mobility. This will consist of a hardened leather cuirass and greaves. He also has a full bronze helmet with side face shields. I gather you'll be armored in your usual T-shirt and running shoes?"

Ignoring her sarcasm, he focused on the impending fight. "Where will it take place?"

"At a Hellenic shrine on the Peloponnesian peninsula called the Menelaion, atop Therapne Mountain, about twenty-five kilometers southwest of Sparta. Your adversary is the shrine's guard, and he will be protecting the shrine with his life. Try not to lose yours."

The mist reappeared as the holographic deck blurred and shifted from the internal compartment of a starship to a warm Grecian summer day.

Alex adjusted his katana's baldric to an accessible position, tapped the tomahawk holstered at his waist, and reconnoitered the field of battle. It was a cloudless day, about 35°C, with a warm breeze that stirred rippling waves in the golden grass that covered the slope of the hill. Small dust devils kicked up in the treeless valley far below. Somewhere in the distance the low coo of a dove broke the tense silence.

Alex soon spotted the Hellenic era building—a small shrine about ten-by-ten meters. Its construction of limestone and marble was an aesthetic counterpoint to the dry plateau. The few oak trees surrounding the little temple did little to alter its contrast to the semiarid landscape. Stairs ascended to the center of the main deck where twelve Doric columns lined the building's periphery and supported a flat roof.

Inside stood a three-meter-tall bronze statue of a woman, whom Alex reckoned to be Athena or possibly Aphrodite. Short granite walls ran along each side of the structure, about one meter from the edge of the building. And standing on the statue's dais was a fit-looking warrior whose rapt attention was now focused directly on the approaching interloper.

"Halt, intruder," yelled the Spartan, "or I'll do it for you."

Alex understood nothing of what the guard had said, but figured it wasn't an amiable greeting. He was well aware that the hoplite would protect his charge to the death, and that there would be no quarter given and no end, save one—one of the combatants would not leave here alive.

The Spartan jumped down from the dais, stood at the top of the stairs, and placed his feet half a meter apart with the left foot slightly ahead. He lifted the round shield into what was both a defensive and an attack position with the two-meter dory placed on its top right edge. His dark eyes peered out from beneath the bronze helmet like a bird of prey and tracked the oncoming threat.

Opting not to meet his adversary head on, Alex shifted to his right, avoided the stairs, and began sprinting to gain momentum. He leapt to the top of the wall and ran parallel to the building's main deck. From the wall, Alex easily jumped to the shrine's raised deck, then slipped behind one of the columns and out of the immediate sight of the shrine's guard.

Alex's evasive move wouldn't last long, so he sprang up onto the dais and simultaneously, in one fluid movement, pulled the katana from its scabbard and positioned it in front of him. Crouched in the classic fighting stance, Alex only had a couple seconds before the warrior, who had followed the sound of his movement, slipped around the side of a column and confronted him head-on. Without hesitation the Spartan launched into a determined attack with his dory, the shield held up as protection.

It was an almost invulnerable fighting position.

With the dory protruding above his raised shield, the warrior lunged. He made a precise and well-aimed thrust toward Alex's exposed upper torso, and only a lightning-fast parry with the katana deflected the dory's bronze spearhead away from his chest. Even though it missed, the shield slammed into Alex and knocked him off balance. The Spartan immediately brought the dory back for another thrust, but Alex had quickly backed off and shifted tactics. After recovering from the body blow, he distanced himself by leaping back across the shrine deck to the top of the wall and ran toward the rear of the shrine. The Spartan followed with surprising speed.

When Alex reached the far end of the building, he leapt back across the gap between the wall and the deck, just a few meters ahead of the hard-charging Spartan, who now held the dory cocked above his head in a throwing position. But instead of throwing his primary weapon, he tracked Alex's leap back up to the deck and waited for the exact moment to strike. Quick as a viper, the hoplite grunted as he made an extended lunge to where he had anticipated Alex would land.

But Alex's planned leap had intersected one of the fluted columns where its base stuck out about ten centimeters. This small ledge provided enough of a toehold to plant the high-grip sole of his running shoe. Using his upward momentum, he launched his body. While at the apex of his leap, Alex twisted into a half gainer somersault. As he flew over the Spartan's head, he made a quick, downward slash at his opponent. The katana's razor-sharp blade sliced through the hardened leather protecting the Spartan's left shoulder and cut deep into his trapezium.

The Spartan's face twisted in agony as he screamed defiance at Alex, who gracefully landed on his feet two meters away. Blood poured down the warrior's left arm and spilled onto the tiled floor. In spite of his obvious pain, the warrior used his right arm to swing the dory in a wide arc. The heavy bronze tip caught Alex across his forehead with a bone-jarring impact.

"Argh!" howled Alex as the blow snapped his head back and knocked him off his feet. He landed hard on his back; his arms flailed out and banged a wrist against the sharp base of a column. The impact sprung his grip loose and sent the katana skittering across the floor.

Both combatants breathed heavily as they took a brief moment to assess their situations. While the Spartan had the more serious wound, he'd also retained possession of his primary weapon and soon recovered enough to make another thrust. As Alex scrambled to free the tomahawk, he simultaneously dove into a tumble and rolled away from the warrior's lunge. Fragments of granite flew as the spear tip clanged against the floor only millimeters from Alex's throat.

Alex's tumble placed him on the Spartan's flank while his momentum allowed him to roll into a kneeling position. With all his strength, he swept the tomahawk into a wide-leveraged strike. It hit his opponent in the unprotected back of his right calf, severing the fibula, before lodging itself in the back of the tibia.

The Spartan shrieked in pain as he hit the ground with a heavy thud, knocking the shield free of his grip. Even so traumatically injured, the Spartan spun away quick as a cat and crab-walked with the tomahawk still embedded in his lower leg. A hard tug proved that he was unable to wrench it free. The hoplite was bleeding severely, and seemingly unable to plant his feet, or even stand.

But he would never surrender.

Alex was now weaponless and warily kept his distance from his opponent. Even in a severely wounded state, his adversary was still in the fight, and still armed with his primary weapon. The blood pouring from Alex's forehead hampered his ability to see and gauge distance, and he couldn't close in for a kill without a weapon.

Groaning in agony, the Spartan had only one slim chance. As Alex began to edge closer to his katana, the Spartan used the dory as a crutch and made a heroic effort to stand. It took an agonizing moment, but once up on both feet he did the impossible by deftly twirling the dory above his head into a throwing position. Grimacing, a guttural cry erupted from the Spartan's throat as he planted his ruined leg, stepped into his throw, and flung the eight-kilogram dory with pinpoint accuracy, hitting Alex just below his right shoulder socket.

The impact spun Alex into the dais. He screamed in agony, grabbed the dory, and with a gut-wrenching tug, yanked it free. With little strength left, he dropped the heavy spear where it clattered loudly beside him. Alex clutched his severely wounded shoulder while blood poured between his fingers.

The Spartan still had one more weapon: his iron short sword. Dragging his useless leg behind him, he grabbed the sword's hilt. It made a metallic hiss as it was slowly pulled it out of its scabbard. The Spartan lurched forward and closed the distance. As he made his final approach, he used both hands to raise the sword above his head, screamed, and dove at Alex for the killing blow.

Even in the fog of pain, Alex saw that he'd landed close enough to his katana to grab the hilt. He barely managed to swing it into position just as the warrior made his diving lunge. The warrior's scream was abruptly cut off as the katana blade sliced through his heart and severed the spinal cord. An instant later the shrine filled with an agonizing howl as the dead Spartan landed on top of Alex. The impact sent waves of pain exploding through the victor's body.

Alex moaned loudly as he pushed the heavy Spartan off him just as the holograph switched off. In an instant, everything disappeared. Alex lay alone on the floor and gasped in pain. His wounds disappeared along with the rest of the program's projections, but the memory and emotional impact still lingered.

He heard SADI call out his name, but it seemed far away. "Alex! Alex, can you hear me? Please give some indication that you're hearing me."

Alex rolled over onto his back and grimaced. "Where the hell did you find that guy? He almost killed me."

A contrite SADI replied in a voice steeped in anxious concern, "You told me to find you a worthy opponent, so I chose the program with the highest level of difficulty. I'm so sorry, Alex. I never would have uploaded that program if I had known the severity of the outcome."

Alex's face brightened as he sat up. "You mean to tell me I just beat the baddest badass of them all?"

SADI went silent for a moment before she answered him. "Yes, Alex, you managed to defeat the most difficult level in the program." After a pause, the AI added, "You absolutely must adjust the way you use these martial training programs. They were never designed for a one-on-one, hand-to-hand street brawl, and certainly not for a man who has just expended a tremendous amount of energy running up a high-altitude mountain."

Exhaustion swept over Alex, and he lay flat on his back taking long deep breaths. He took SADI's gentle admonishment in stride, chuckled, and said, "Maybe tomorrow you could put me up against the little old lady in the wheelchair again."

That comment garnered no response except an exasperated electronic warbling. Alex figured he'd caused SADI enough trouble for the day. He finally stood up, shoulders sagged forward, and leaned against the curved wall of the holographic room. "SADI, the reason I always launch into these hand-to-hand battle programs after a run is because in real combat there is no respite from fatigue. There's only getting to the battle as fast as you can, and then joining in without hesitation. The better physically prepared you are to do that, the better your chances of survival."

SADI adopted her sternest schoolmarm voice. "I understand all that, Lieutenant, but just what battle do you think you're preparing for? We're heading for a possible Class-M habitable planet, 1,187 light-years from Earth to hopefully find a marooned starship. Even if we do find hostiles, we *will* try to avoid them. And if things get really bad, we'll use our pulse cannons, and then only to defend ourselves. Under no circumstances are we to initiate martial action. Ever. You are completely aware of the engagement rules. So why is it necessary to remind you of this?" When no answer came, SADI's voice rose in volume. "I refuse to be ignored this time, Lieutenant Porter, answer my question! In light of everything I've just said, yet again, what do you have to say for yourself?"

"There's another reason I engage in these fights to the death," he said quietly.

The volume of SADI's voice decreased as she pressed, "I'm waiting, Lieutenant."

"It—it's because I enjoy it."

"What exactly do you enjoy about killing your adversaries, Alex?"

His voice dropped to a mere whisper. "Just that—exactly that part."

"I'd suggest that you try to contain this bloodlust, Alex, because this will definitely reflect on your psychological profile, and hence your career."

"I see your point. I've seen your point all along, in fact. It's just that—that—"

Once again, he was unable to go on.

"It's what, Lieutenant?" The computer's passive voice became an emphatic warble.

"It's just that I need it so much," he confessed.

CHAPTER 21

WAKE-UP CALL
IFC ENDEAVOR—MISSION DAY 1512

Two weeks after the battle with the Spartan, Alex was awakened by the ship-wide alarm that signaled the end of his six-month shift. Since his was the last single-crew wake shift before the starship reached her destination, he had the arduous duty of waking the rest of the crew out of their suspended animation. The *Endeavor* was now 3.1 light-years from its mission objective, and a full crew complement was required for the starship's braking and subsequent orbital operation.

Alex spent the next several hours on the bridge, going over the reanimation procedures for multiple personnel. He'd woken up Lieutenant Hartley many times, but waking one person was far different than an entire ship's crew.

After reading the procedural guidelines, he leaned back, stretched, and quizzed SADI with some of his concerns. "Okay, so once I start the initial wake-up, how soon will it be before they can all talk to me?"

"As you will recall, Lieutenant Hartley became speech cognizant within seventeen point five hours. However, it will be different with each individual, and average speech cognizance usually manifests itself within the first eighteen to twenty hours. Before that, the core body temperature isn't high enough to engage in the motor skills needed to articulate a thought into words. Keep in mind that even though their vocal ability may not be available to them, their ability to reason is almost fully functional, and they will remember what you've said."

Alex blew out a slow raspberry and decided to just keep his opinions to himself. Of course, that didn't include Lieutenant Hartley, the prime perpetrator of the endless practical jokes that they both relished while the other one was in suspended animation.

First Lieutenant Basil "Baseball" Hartley was the only other helmsman aboard. During Baseball's last wake shift, and prior to the one he just finished, Alex woke up from his six-month sleep completely hairless. Not even his eyelashes remained. Naturally, Baseball was clueless how this happened, but thoughtfully suggested that Alex change shampoo.

Baseball was also the chief suspect behind a virtual adversary that Alex faced after the itchy thumb incident. Ready for mortal combat, Alex ordered SADI to bring up the AD 410 Visigoth sack of Rome program, but instead of a deadly battleground, an AD 1970 South Bronx bingo hall appeared instead.

———————————

Everyone in the hall stopped and stared at the heavily armed young man.

"Dirty Gerdie," came the call.

Alex grinned sheepishly and walked toward the front of the hall. "Ma'am?"

"Have you paid your fee yet, dumbass?" demanded the caller, a nearly blind ninety-year-old lady in a wheelchair with a nasty disposition and a potty mouth.

His jaw dropped as his brows rose, and he stammered, "Um, fee?"

"You have to pay to waste my time, shithead," she spat at him.

Somewhat amused, Alex chuckled as he approached the little old lady, but when he got within range, she whacked him in the crotch with her white cane and let out a profanity-laced assault that would have made CPO Khaki proud.

Upon inquiry, SADI disavowed any knowledge or complicity in the program alteration. Still smarting from the crotch shot, and no longer amused, Alex ordered SADI to bring up the pirate-ship program centering on the Caribbean port of Tortuga in approximately AD 1750. The old lady, complete with white cane and wheelchair, was escorted off a plank and into shark-infested waters. She theorized on the nature of Alex's parentage all the way down before the splash silenced her tirade.

Alex had six months to plan his revenge, and it wasn't going to be pretty.

Waking up from an induced four-year-long sleep was not pleasant, and crew members often needed help reorienting themselves for the first seventy-two hours before they could resume normal duties. Immediately upon waking, they usually experienced nausea, cold chills, and dizziness that kept them close to their bunks and toilets for the first couple days. As a result, only four of the sixty-two sleeping crew members were initially woken up, so that Alex wouldn't have his hands full with more than just a few sick crewmates.

The first to be woken was the ship's commander, Captain Richard Jennings, followed by the ship's doctor, Lieutenant Commander Bogdan Prata, one of the medics, and the ship's chief petty officer, Romeo Arturo "Khaki" Martinez. After four years, Alex finally had someone other than a computer to talk to.

It took more than two weeks to wake the entire crew and get them back to normal duties. In the course of a fortnight, the character of the *Endeavor* changed from one of quiet isolation to the constant hubbub of human activity.

Baseball was more than a little perturbed with Alex after finding, upon waking, a tattoo of a single letter on the top of each finger that spelled out the words: WANT DICK. Naturally Alex vehemently protested his innocence, but he casually suggested that Baseball keep his hands in his pockets around the captain whose abbreviated name was, coincidentally, Dick.

Baseball glared at his fingers and fumed, "How exactly does one go about saluting his superior officer with his hands in his pockets?"

"Oh gosh, you're absolutely right, Baseball," Alex said sympathetically. "Perhaps you should accessorize your uniform with some gloves. I think Rox might lend you a pair of hers."

"Thanks a lot, buddy. Just a thought, but perhaps you should be really careful with your virtual combat opponents from now on. Your lack of respect for the elderly is legendary, and next time she might show up packing an ancient blunderbuss scattergun, which she'll need, of course. Being blind and all. Just saying."

In spite of their constant potshots at each other, Alex and Baseball were not only best friends, but inseparable. Their years at the IFC Academy had cemented their friendship. As a reward for all of Basil's unwavering loyalty, Alex had given him his undying friendship and hung the moniker of Baseball on him, which promptly became permanent. Anyone who ever met Basil thereafter immediately adopted this name.

Only Alex knew the truth behind the nickname's origin, and he never even came close to telling anyone. It was during their third year at the academy that Basil Jonathan Hartley, after striking out with yet another female cadet, became forever known as Baseball, solely due to the fact, as observed by Alex, that Basil could never get past first base.

The two friends were also the primary pilots for the two shuttlecrafts. These had more powerful fusion engines than the OVALs they'd used in training, and they could carry more weight. At fifteen meters long, the shuttlecrafts' primary role was transiting crew and cargo from an orbiting starship to a planet surface, and back again. These sleek craft had the ability to easily maneuver in a planet's atmosphere at high speeds, and their hardened heat shield deflectors enabled them to engage in repeated rapid atmospheric reentry.

Baseball piloted one OVAL with an extremely talented and attractive copilot, Second Lieutenant Luna Lucía Rocha, or Rox, as everyone called her. Hailing from the Nuequen Enclave at the foot of the Andes in old Argentina, she had long silky black hair, deep blue eyes, and a sharp tongue. It was common for Baseball to tell her, "You rock, Rox!"

Which never failed to elicit a blank look from her, and a perfunctory "Aye, sir."

Alex had a lot more success engaging his copilot, one Second Lieutenant Denish Velleraj, known in the mess room as the Raj of Kathmandu. Slight of build with sable skin, black hair, and almost black eyes, Raj was young and impressionable but handled the right seat as efficiently as anyone Alex had ever flown with.

CHAPTER 22

FAIRY-TALE SHIP
IFC ENDEAVOR—MISSION DAY 1528

Three days from their objective, Captain Jennings called an assemblage of the entire crew to the mess hall. It was the only place on the ship that could accommodate all sixty-two crew members in a comfortable, close-quarters environment.

The mood among the crew was buoyant with anticipation. Prior to launch, the rumor mill had been rife that this was to be a historic mission, but only a handful knew much more than that. The crew had just settled in when Captain Jennings entered the galley. Commander Zonta Eaglecreek, the ship's first mate, immediately jumped to attention and barked out over the hubbub of the assembly, "Captain on the deck!" All talk ceased, and the crew rose and stood at attention.

Captain Jennings walked to the front of the mess and took a calculated look at his crew. He liked what he saw. With deep brown eyes and graying temples, he stood a trim two meters and looked every bit the starship captain. "At ease, and please sit down."

As one, the crew sat and remained quiet.

Jennings waited a moment before continuing, "Is anyone still feeling ill effects from the suspended animation?"

A few glances shot around the galley, but no one spoke up.

"Good, but if some of you are still experiencing any ill effects, go see Doc Bogs, and I'm sure he'll fix you up." He paused momentarily to study his crew. Most sat at the twenty dining booths while the rest stood. "As you're all aware, we'll soon reach our mission objective. I want each department to begin preparation for orbit and surface observation. If we find anything of interest after the initial surface analysis, we'll send down the OVALs for a preliminary recon."

This caused a small ripple of quiet conversation through the crew.

Captain Jennings waited for the crew to quiet and then locked his gaze directly on Alex and Baseball. "And you two clowns need to make sure that both your boats are checked and double checked, and I don't mean pushing a button on the diagnostic program and watching the readouts. I mean check every system yourselves. I want these boats one hundred percent, and SADI?"

"Yes, Captain."

"Please give me a status report on their progress every hour."

"Yes, Captain."

Jennings turned his attention back to the rest of the crew. "I realize that few mission specifics were given out prior to launch, and that all of you are handpicked or volunteers. The time has come to let you know exactly what it is we were sent out here to do."

No one uttered a sound.

"As I'm sure you're all aware, our sister ship, the *IFC Monarch*, was lost in deep space nine years ago."

Not an eye blinked.

"Our destination is the last known position of the *Monarch* before she went missing."

Alex sat straight up in his seat and leaned forward. He glanced across the table at Baseball, who was trying to disguise a yawn. Alex frowned and looked back at the captain.

Jennings took a deep breath and ran a hand over his head. "The last communication from the *Monarch* was via the drone she sent back to Earth shortly after making orbit at Kepler 3211a. There was nothing that suggested anything was amiss. After that, nothing more has been heard from her." Relaxing slightly, he continued, "Incidentally, we'll send one of our drones back to Earth once we've completed the planetary survey.

"The *Monarch* was sent to our destination solar system to investigate a communication anomaly that had originated from there. The frequency picked up caused quite a stir when it was received and garnered the full attention of Fleet Command. This is because it was a type of deep-space technology not used for centuries, but an exact match used by human spacecraft one thousand years ago."

This final point rippled through the crew like a pebble dropped in a still pond, and more than a few furtive glances were exchanged. Jennings stopped for a moment to allow the crew to digest this bit of information before getting to the crux of his briefing. "It is believed by Fleet Command that this transmission came from the first starship thought to have ever used the Enhanced Magnetic Drive propulsion technology."

The furtive glances now became audible murmurs.

Captain Jennings held his hand up to silence the crew. "Every school kid for hundreds of years has heard the stories of this legendary starship. As you can probably guess, I'm speaking about none other than the *Magellan II*."

A chorus of *"what the hell"* and *"you gotta be kidding me"* emanated from the startled crew. The *Magellan II* was a ship of legend. Many even doubted its existence.

The captain saw that the *Endeavor's* chief security and weapons officer, Commander Gunnar Hammär, had raised his hand to speak. "Yes, Gunnar."

"Captain, tales of the *Magellan II* have been around forever, and to my knowledge no substantiated facts have ever been found. This isn't just the stuff of legend. With all due respect, sir, it's a borderline fairy tale. Why would Fleet Command even consider the possibility that a thousand-year-old communication transmission could actually be genuine?"

"Substantial proof was found, Gunnar, and the transmission wasn't one thousand years old. It was only a week old. Their ancient communication drone was recovered, and it checked out. The drone came from the *Magellan II* and the transmission exhibited knowledge that only the *Magellan II* could have known, which pointed directly at the Kepler 3211 star system. Look, folks, the complete mission directive has been deemed classified, and I can't discuss the details, but what was communicated on that one and only transmission was enough for the brass to send a starship to investigate, and, after the disappearance of the original mission, they deemed it important enough to send a follow-up mission. That means us."

Jennings sighed and sagged back against a countertop, dropped his head, and rubbed his temples. As he stared at the floor in front of him, the captain's voice suddenly dropped to an almost inaudible tone. "I know how you must be feeling right now. I share those feelings. We've been sent to investigate the loss of our sister ship, a ship that no one has the slightest clue what happened to, or what could possibly happen to us."

Jennings took another deep breath, pushed off the counter, stood up straight, and looked out at the crew with those piercing eyes that were so familiar to those who knew him. Whatever lapse in command demeanor that had taken place a moment before was gone. "Make no mistake, ladies and gentlemen, I intend to carry out our mission objectives. If there is any evidence of the *Monarch*, or what might have happened to her, I intend to find it. We will leave no stone unturned, and I expect every member of this crew to perform their duties with all due diligence.

"And, if we happen to find some evidence of Commander Hammär's fairy-tale ship, so much the better. But if I feel this ship is under threat, then I am not going to risk this command chasing ghosts. Is that understood?"

A strong "Aye, sir" echoed about the galley.

"Right. Are there any more questions?" He gave it a moment and, seeing none, he said, "Crew dismissed. Commander Eaglecreek, please assemble the senior officers in my stateroom thirty minutes from now."

His uniform blouse strained against a barrel chest and almost black raptor eyes over a hawklike nose, at 175 centimeters, Lieutenant Commander Zonta Eaglecreek stood ramrod straight. He glanced around the room at the officers in question before acknowledging him. "I'll handle it, sir. Is that all?"

"For now, Zonta. Carry on." Jennings stopped short as if in afterthought and locked onto his two young pilots who were among the last of the crew to leave the galley. "You two better come as well."

Keeping his eyes trained on Alex, Captain Jennings walked up to him, placed a large hand on his pilot's shoulder, and pulled him aside. "Lieutenant, it has come to my attention that during your six-month wake shifts, you regularly engaged in removing body parts off virtual combatants on the holographic deck."

"Well, I, um—"

"Now, I fully realize that these programs are not overtly dangerous to the human participant. That is not what concerns me. However, the psychological implication of my first pilot feeling the need to use a sword to slice body parts off folk, however imaginary, is a bit troubling. Therefore, your last lethal combat simulation is, in fact, your last lethal combat simulation. Do I make myself clear, Lieutenant?"

Still standing at attention and without betraying any emotion, Alex acknowledged his captain's order. "Absolutely clear, sir."

Satisfied, Jennings nodded, and exited the galley.

CHAPTER 23

GHOST SHIPS
IFC ENDEAVOR—MISSION DAY 1528

B aseball's usual carefree temperament turned broodingly silent as the two pilots made their way from the mess hall to the junior officers' ready room. He seemed more truculent than Alex had ever seen him before. "A bug crawl up your ass, Baseball?"

Baseball blew out an exasperated sigh. "Are you serious? This is one great big shit burger. So yeah, I'm feeling a tad put out, and so should you."

"Thanks, pal, but I prefer a bug-free ass."

"Look, the IFC sent the *Monarch* on a deep-space mission based on shaky evidence, and that brief didn't exactly fill me with confidence. Did you see the way the old man deflated when he started talking about the *Magellan II*?"

"What shaky evidence?" Alex asked. "What do you know?"

"Don't ask. You don't want to know, believe me. Anyway, the *Monarch* had the same mission destination as us, and vanished. We know this, but now they finally tell us that the *Monarch* was actually sent to chase a thousand-year-old ghost ship." Seeing Alex shrug, Baseball spoke through gritted teeth. "You just don't get the big picture, Alex. The IFC sent a starship on the farthest mission ever attempted based on a few seconds of a questionable communication."

"So?"

"So now we're chasing those same ghosts, except that we have the added mission of looking for the far more recent ghosts as well."

Alex flopped his head to one side and swiveled it toward Baseball. "Look, the only picture I'm interested in right now is why the old man wants us at his little get-together in a few minutes, and here's how I see this. We know the *Monarch* disappeared, and we know that it happened in the star system we're headed to. Beyond that, we know squat. But what little we do know is going to make the old man wary, and he's not going to take any undue chances with this command. I'm not saying that the *Monarch* took any chances, but they didn't have the benefit of hindsight that we have and didn't know everything that we now know." He gave Baseball a scrutinizing gaze. "So, perhaps they let their guard down, and it cost them big time. But until we make a thorough analysis of this planet, I'm not going to get too excited about it."

He stopped walking and looked his friend in the eye. "And frankly, Baseball, as my wingman I'd appreciate it if you didn't either. I need your ass free and clear of any and all bugs."

Baseball closed his eyes and took a deep breath. "Okay, Alex, I get it. I won't let you down. I know that if we head down to the planet's surface, both our asses will be hanging out."

"Good to know. Now, speaking of our asses, let's go get ours handed to us again."

Baseball shoved his hands deep in his pockets and followed Alex to the ready room.

Exactly thirty minutes after the general muster in the mess hall, *Endeavor*'s senior staff gathered in the captain's stateroom. While not plush, it was well appointed and the only cabin on the ship with more than one room. It consisted of the captain's personal cabin and an adjoining office. The office was much larger than his personal cabin, had a modest-sized desk at one end with two cushioned chairs facing it, and couches lining the walls on both sides. Data screens lined one wall, while the other had window ports with a view of deep space.

There were few personal effects on the captain's desk—a photograph of Jennings's two sons, an ancient-looking mariner's brass bell. And next to the bell sat a child's yellow rubber bath duck. There was endless speculation among the crew about what the rubber duck meant. Baseball held the perverse view that the duck was the ship's only reliable bellwether.

Unlike the earlier meeting in the mess room, the officers were slightly pensive, and there was no small talk as they waited for the captain. The nine senior officers seated inside the stateroom remained silent until Captain Jennings walked out of his cabin and sat down at his desk. Alex and Baseball remained standing.

"Relax, folks, this will be an informal meeting where everyone can freely discuss whatever is on their minds." He looked at the two junior officers standing like statues, grinned, and, with a slight shake of his head, added, "That goes for you two goobers as well." A small chortle skidded across the room. The goobers relaxed a little but remained at parade rest.

"Would anyone like something to drink? I know I would." Captain Jennings directed Alex to pour everyone a shot of 135-year-old Old Pulteney from a large decanter. Alex silently handed them out to the gathering, including himself and Baseball. Glancing around the room, he held the glass up, and then along with everyone else he waited for the captain.

After a moment Jennings stood up, held his glass at shoulder level, waited till the rest of the group did the same, and made a toast. "To you, ladies and gentlemen. Oh, and to you as well, Lieutenants." Another chuckle tittered through the room. "To our health and to the success of this mission. May we all get back home, safe and sound." The group knocked back the dram.

Captain Jennings sat down at his desk and took the measure of the officers. After a moment he spoke, not as their captain, but as their peer. "Okay, here's the deal. We really don't know a damn thing about what we're going to face once we make orbit around Keplar 3211a. I'm not going to blow smoke up your asses and tell you that this is simply a fact-finding bag-and-tag mission, and that once we find out what happened to the *Monarch*, or not, we all go home and live happily ever after. As for this *Magellan II* thing, all I can tell you is that the admiralty is convinced of the validity of the communication transmission that prompted the *Monarch* mission in the first place.

"Even though I can't go into specifics about that transmission, I can tell you this: the *Endeavor's* primary mission is to conduct an all-out effort to locate the *Monarch* and her crew, and finding any evidence of the *Magellan II* is secondary to that. Having said that, if something of interest crops up about the ancient starship, we will investigate."

The room went silent as Jennings paused a moment. Looking at each officer, Jennings settled on his large security officer, squirming like a three-year-old needing to go potty. "Gunnar, you look like you're about to burst at the seams. Please, everything gets tossed on the table here, and all opinions have merit—even yours. So, if you please, spit it out."

With wavy blond hair, Commander Hammär could stand eyeball to eyeball with Jennings, but outweighed his captain by twenty kilograms. He had a booming voice that was as big as his person, and his light gray eyes missed nothing. "Richard, with all due respect, sir, how the hell does Fleet Command expect us to react to orders that send us over a thousand light-years away from home on a nine-year mission in order to chase rainbows, and, oh, by the way, try to find our friends, colleagues, and even family members who just happened to disappear chasing those same rainbows?"

Murmurs of assent filled the room as Commander Hammär continued, "Can you please give us any and all available information we have about the *Magellan II*? Because all I've ever heard is that it supposedly launched right before the apocalypse."

Captain Jennings sat back in his chair. "Of course, Gunnar. I've already gone over all this with Zonta, and we decided to share what little we have with the senior staff. So watch the screens or follow along on your OC as SADI outlines what we do know about the history of the *Magellan II* and her mission. SADI, if you please, begin your presentation."

The soothing female voice of SADI took over, and most of the group switched on their optic computers. The screens flicked to life, and an image of a huge starship of an antiquated design came into focus. It was an elongated craft with a huge bulbous nose at one end. Connected to the other end by a long, slender, spine-like access causeway was an equally large rectangular-shaped aft compartment. An array of antennae and external sensor devices were scattered along the length of the craft.

SADI began. "Ladies and gentlemen, the image before you is believed to be that of the *Magellan II* and is a copy of the one and only known design reference in existence. The schematic was found at Olympus Mons where it had been sealed for centuries in their archives. It is believed that the *Magellan II* was the first starship to have used the Enhanced Magnetic Drive.

"As you can see, the ship had two main compartments. The forward compartment contained the life-support systems, command control, and crew quarters. The aft compartment contained the EMD, and the slender structure between the two was used for storage of water, food, oxygen, and other ship provisions.

"The *Magellan II* was approximately eleven kilometers long, and from the crew manifest included in her communication drone we know that she held over ten thousand passengers and crew. An exoskeleton was built around the slender causeway that provided access between the command module and the drive system. It also added structural strength, as well as containing control lines and life-support management systems between the two main compartments."

SADI briefly paused before continuing with her presentation. "The *Magellan II* was built in low orbit above Earth in a rare period of cooperation between the two main world powers of the time—the nation states of the United States of America and the Russian Federation. We believe that this occurred just prior to the year AD 2100. The population of Earth at that time had surpassed eleven billion people, and the ecology of the planet had reached its limits. A new habitable Class-M exoplanet was needed for colonization before Earth became permanently uninhabitable. There was no time to waste. A new home for humankind was needed, and the transformation of Earth's immediate neighbors, Venus and Mars, was not deemed a viable solution since those terraforming projects would take many generations to complete. Time was running out, and the Earth had, at most, only a few decades left.

"Almost a century of searching the relative proximity of Earth for possible habitable planets had resulted in only a few possible candidates, and none close enough for humans to make the journey using propellant-based rocket technology. Finally, a Class-M planet was discovered relatively close by, with strong evidence of an atmosphere of breathable oxygen, a temperate climate, and a mass proportionate to Earth's. Unfortunately, it was still too far away for rocket or fusion-driven technology to reach for thousands of years. This is Kepler 3211a.

"Transit beyond Earth's solar system was only made possible because in the decades before the advent of the *Magellan II*, the Enhanced

Magnetic Drive had been invented by an astrophysicist from Japan. For the first time in human history, a starship could make the transit from Earth to a point hundreds of light-years away within a human life span, a technological feat previously impossible.

"All available evidence points to the distinct probability that the *Magellan II* left Earth orbit sometime in early AD 2100 on its mission to colonize Kepler 3211a. However, humankind's first true starship was never heard from again, for reasons we will now discuss.

"Within a few months after the *Magellan II* launch, the assassination of the Russian president was blamed on Azerbaijani separatists who were seen by the new Russian government to be in the service of American interests. No one knows the specifics of what happened next, except, of course, that the most cataclysmic event in the history of humankind, a full-scale nuclear and space-based particle-beam weaponry exchange occurred between the competing spheres of political influence controlled by America and Russia.

"Only a few pockets of life remained, and these only survived because of the deep underground bunkers that had been built over the almost one hundred fifty years that the nuclear threat dominated human politics.

"Now, approximately one thousand years later, there is little specific information about the *Magellan II* mission, but Kepler 3211a, now known as Aqueous, has been confirmed by that ancient communication drone to have been its mission terminus. Aqueous was the *Monarch*'s mission destination. It is also ours."

At this point Captain Jennings stopped the presentation for a few moments to offer the group an intermission. "Does anyone need to take a break, or would you rather go on?" No one seemed inclined to pause, so Jennings pushed on. "SADI, please elaborate on our mission destination."

"Yes, Captain. We believe Kepler 3211a was named Aqueous because the planet's surface is made up primarily of liquid water. Whereas Earth's surface is seventy-two percent water, Aqueous is closer to eighty-five per-cent, and, unlike Earth, the polar regions on Aqueous are not covered with ice. This is, for all practical purposes, a warm planet, as the liquidity of its oceans substantiate."

CHAPTER 24

NO HUMAN LEFT ALIVE
THITH EMPIRE

L ike all Thith elite, the second most powerful member of the empire, Imperial Duchess Thorna, was hatched in the capital city of Saurinth on the southern continent. She had a long reptilian snout, golden scales, red eyes, and stood a head taller than the vast majority of her species. Since she came from such an elite and noble clutch-line, her tail was much shorter than the vast majority of belly crawling low-hatch Thith. The sight of their primitive tails was offensive to her, exposed the way they were. Her own tail could almost be hidden underneath the blue fine-spun floor-length robe robe that she wore. Yes, in every way Duchess Thorna was far superior to any Noble Lizard before her.

Soon she would prove it.

Admittedly, Thorna had struggled to learn the barbaric language of her enemy, but through hard work and a superior intellect she had become flawlessly fluent in English. Knowing the enemy's language had given her a tremendous advantage in planning their destruction, and since she couldn't trust any of those imbecile translators, Thorna had taught herself. Unlike the rest of the lazy, self-entitled aristocracy that had spawned her, Thorna had ambition, discipline, and unmatched intelligence. All these attributes would be a key element of her coming triumph. Thorna had an uncontrollable hunger to become the most powerful Thith Queen that ever lived, and this lust for power had led her to this precise moment in history, on the brink of immortal greatness.

She gazed across the calm waters of her naval base and reveled at the object of her glory: the largest war armada ever built by her empire. She was its master. She was now poised to exterminate the vermin that contaminated the northern continent. Once her war fleet was in place, she would fill it with millions of soldiers and sail it across the vast ocean to the lair of her enemy. She was mindful that all previous wars with the softskins had ended in disaster, but this time would be different. This time she was in charge, and she had an arrangement. Before the final attack, she would implement the plan that the human traitor had helped her devise. It was a good plan.

The traitor had been most helpful.

While watching the preparations take place at the naval base, her personal seat of power, she knew that not only would she personally destroy their enemy, but that she, Duchess Thorna, next in line for the throne, would succeed where all others had failed. By virtue of this magnificent triumph, she would become the next Imperial Queen and dispose of that doddering old lizard who now contaminated the Queen's chair. Thorna would have the ancient fool cooked to perfection.

Only then could she become the sole speaker to the Floating Gods.

Standing on the deck of her sleek flagship, the *Ocean Fang*, Thorna sucked in a deep breath of sea air. It was an exhilarating moment just to be alive, just to be her. Suddenly a shadow flickered at the edge of her pineal eye, and she blew out an irritated hiss.

With a skittering gait, the fleet's war admiral sidled up to Duchess Thorna. Bowing as low as possible, the admiral groveled at his master's clawed feet. "Your Excellency, in a few weeks the fleet of troop transports will be ready to sail," he said with a supplicating whine, "and the mission to destroy the filthy invaders will begin."

Duchess Thorna could barely deign to look down at this belly crawling long-tail incompetent, much less speak with him. Thorna ground her fangs at the fool as she shoved one jewel-encrusted claw underneath his repulsive chin. "Admiral Zidth, once our fleet has gathered and all our troops have boarded, you will leave at once."

"Yes, Duchess Thor—"

"Shut up, you slithering idiot," snapped Thorna, and shoved harder. A trickle of blood ran down her clawed finger. "Never interrupt me again. Am I understood? And tuck your filthy tail in. You're a disgrace!"

The admiral trembled, his fear palpable. Without making eye contact, the admiral vainly tried to tuck his offensive tail under his robe, and only managed to push her claw deeper into the soft scales under his chin. He gulped as the trickle became a stream.

With a satisfied sneer, Thorna pulled her hand back, flicked her forked tongue to lick his blood off her finger, and grinned at its taste.

Her eyes narrowed menacingly when she caught him looking wide-eyed at her. He quickly looked down, and after a moment she continued to give him his orders. "With my personal fleet of fast ships, I'll set sail before your lumbering transports. You will follow until you pass through the equator where you will hold station while I sail ahead to meet with the softskins. The success of my mission is already assured, whether I return or not," spittle flew from her forked tongue, "and I have every intention of returning," she reveled in her boast, "but if I don't, my bravery will not be in vain, and my glory will be celebrated forever. Be that as it may, your orders are to wait just north of the equatorial current until I return before you launch the invasion force."

She stepped in close to the cowering admiral. "But if I don't return in the requisite amount of time—one month—then you are to attack with the entire fleet and destroy every last one of them. After you've successfully destroyed their city, you are to take the fleet, proceed to the second objective, and repeat the slaughter. Leave no human alive. Is that understood?"

The admiral kept his eyes riveted on his blood pooled at their feet and groveled, "Y-yes, Duchess Thorna. No human left alive."

CHAPTER 25

HYPOTHESIZE
IFC ENDEAVOR—MISSION DAY 1533

As the *Endeavor* closed on the red dwarf system, she made preparations for braking out of her final electromagnetic hyper-jump. Since leaving Port Apollo, the starship had made multiple hyper-jumps, essentially tacking across the massive rivers of electromagnetic energy that ran like a web throughout the galaxy.

Braking from hyper speed was the reverse process of the jump sequence, but it was not simple. The ship's velocity increased after each hyper-jump, and it took years to reach maximum speed, but the braking sequence had to be completed in a matter of hours. This required a much stronger magnetic field to be in close proximity because of the immense energy required to decelerate. The strongest of these fields were only found in star systems, and the trajectory algorithms had to be precise, or the starship could miss its target magnetic field. And while the fusion drive engines could nudge its direction, they would take years to slow it down, much less stop it.

The greatest risk during braking was the tremendous g-forces exerted on the ship and crew. Reverse gravitational balance inside the ship had to be precisely synced with the deceleration rate or the crew would end up as greasy blood splats on a wall. As the EMD Control Officer, it fell to Commander Eaglecreek, working in conjunction with SADI, to maintain that balance.

Everyone in *Endeavor's* command, navigation, and flight crew were needed for the braking and orbiting sequence. The bridge began preparations for this crucial operation while the starship was still in its last hyper-jump, well outside the Kepler 3211 solar system. From that distance, the red dwarf was only a tiny speck of light on their longest-range view screen.

While Captain Jennings kept track of the navigation data on his optical computer, the ship's pilots, Alex and Baseball, prepared to engage the fusion drive that would take over from the jump system. It took time for the fusion drive to ramp up, and the two young helmsmen had to have their drive system ready long before it was needed. Once the fusion drive took over from the EMD, the two pilots would guide the starship into orbit.

While still three billion kilometers from the edge of the solar system, Captain Jennings tapped the ship's PA system and addressed the crew. "Attention all hands, we're about to engage in the braking sequences. Unless you're required at your stations, please remain in your bunk with your safety harness fastened until the completion of the operation. That will be all."

Jennings then addressed the ship's computer. "SADI, employ the long-range scanner and check for possible debris in our guide path that Gunnar can target practice on." He turned to his weapons chief and said, "Gunnar, you got your pop guns spooled up yet?"

"Ready, willing, and gimme something to shoot at, sir," came the casual response.

"Sir," SADI broke in to make her report, "our flight path is completely devoid of obstruction. In fact, the LRS isn't detecting any debris in the entire solar system. Except for the two planetary bodies, there is no other solid matter in this star system."

Jennings and his weapons officer exchanged a glance. It was just an accepted law of physics that when planets form they leave rocky junk behind that gets caught in their own solar orbit. The captain told his AI, "Keep the LRS at full power. I've never heard of a solar system without asteroidal debris, so let's not take a chance at missing something."

"Aye, sir."

"SADI, as soon as our EMD sensors register 250,000 nT in the star's nanotesla field, lock onto it and initiate the braking sequence."

"Aye, sir."

"What's the present nanotesla reading, and how soon will we be in range?"

The response from SADI was almost immediate. "Sir, there seems to be an anomaly concerning the star's magnetic field."

The two senior officers shot each other another uneasy glance. "What seems to be the issue, SADI?"

"Sir, there are only two bodies in this solar system: the star, and Aqueous. In all previous star systems, the strongest magnetic field has always belonged to the nucleus of the solar system, especially if it's a red dwarf, but in this system the reverse is true. Since the EMD is programmed to lock onto the strongest magnetic field, it has always been assumed that this would belong to the resident star."

Jennings sucked in a breath while running his fingers across his scalp. "So, what does this mean, SADI, and does it pose any threat to the ship?"

"Sir, there are no precedents for this, so I have no data with which to determine any type of threat, but the EMD should behave the same when locking onto Aqueous's magnetic field as it would that of the solar system's star."

"Should," Jennings softly repeated the word, "leaves a lot of room for interpretation. Is there anything significantly different between the two fields, or is it simply a matter of different field strengths?"

"Sir, the present nanotesla reading from the red dwarf is 43,063.9 nT. The reading from Aqueous is 131,592.4 nT, which is almost three times stronger than the star. The EMD has automatically locked onto the stronger field. We will be in range to begin the braking operation in thirty-six minutes and twenty-four seconds."

Jennings couldn't shake the feeling that this anomalous magnetic field was somehow tied to the reason they were here in the first place. Did this cosmic role reversal play a part in the disappearance of the *Monarch*? He decided to continue with the EMD lock onto Aqueous but pressed SADI for more information. "SADI, do you have any data that might suggest a reason for this anomaly?"

"No, sir. As I said earlier, this is unprecedented. However, Kepler 3211 has a magnetic field and radiation signature comparable to other red dwarf stars of her mass. The anomaly is in the extraordinarily high magnetic field emanating from Aqueous. This is the highest magnetic field, by a factor of six point four seven, that has ever been recorded for a terrestrial planet of this mass and circumference."

Lightly massaging his temples with his thumbs, Jennings considered the risk. He then asked a question he'd never considered asking a computer before. "I appreciate that you don't have any reference data, but could you hypothesize?"

"Hypothesize, sir?"

"Yes, SADI, I'd like to hear your opinion."

A slight electronic warbling emanated from the speakers throughout the bridge. Alex was very familiar with this sound.

"I'll try, sir. As you know, all magnetic fields are created through the motion of highly conductive molten metal fluids, which act as a self-exciting dynamo inside a planet's core. In all dynamos, electrically conducting material rotate through a magnetic field, which generates a current. Simply put, it's the motion of these molten metals that creates the dynamo effect, which in turn creates the geomagnetic field."

"I know all that, but how is it possible that a planet of this mass could have such a large magnetic signature?" asked Jennings.

"For a planet the size of Aqueous to have a geomagnetic field of this size, its core must have highly charged molten alloys moving at a tremendous rate. Although there is another possibility, sir."

"What possibility?"

"My hypothesis, sir."

Jennings's eyes narrowed imperceptibly. "Continue," he said.

"Yes, sir. Possibly, the planet's core has a yet undiscovered element that is somehow magnifying its magnetic strength."

Jennings pressed further, "What element could possibly do that?"

"Crystal, sir. Theoretically, a very dense crystal can produce a piezoelectric effect and increase the output of an electrical current."

"Is this what's happening at Aqueous?'

"Without further study, I cannot draw a more definitive conclusion."

The bridge crew all looked at Jennings, who lightly rubbed his jaw but seemed satisfied for the moment. "Thank you, SADI. I value your efforts and will take your opinion into consideration."

When the captain visibly relaxed, the mood on the bridge relaxed as well. "Ladies and gentlemen, in light of what little we know about this oddity, we will maintain a heightened state of readiness, especially during the approach phase, but we will continue on schedule. In other words, folks, stay tight, and keep your eyes peeled. Commander Eaglecreek, is the gravitational counterbalance ramped up?"

"Perfectly in sync, sir."

"In that case, folks, please make any adjustments to the navigation coordinates before the EMD begins the braking sequences, and prepare the navigation system to adjust our present heading to the proper trajectory."

The bridge crew answered back, "Aye, sir."

Jennings turned to his pilots. "Gentlemen, as soon as the EMD has completed its braking sequences, engage the fusion drive and guide us to our orbital plane."

CHAPTER 26

ORBIT
IFC ENDEAVOR—MISSION DAY 1533

A t 21:17, SADI's soothing voice addressed the bridge. "Sir, the planet's nanotesla reading has reached the earliest optimum strength. Engaging the EMD reverse polarization thrust in three seconds, two—braking sequence engaged. It will take three hundred two minutes of gradual deceleration before we drop below four percent of light speed and enable the fusion drive to take over as the ship's primary propulsion system."

Captain Jennings adjusted his monitor to track every facet of *Endeavor's* crucial gravitational counterbalance. "Thank you, SADI."

Five tense hours later, he turned to his pilots and reaffirmed his earlier command. "Time to dial in the fusion drive, gentlemen, and prepare to take over the helm on my command."

The two pilots double-checked their systems. "The fusion system is ready to take over now, sir," Alex reported.

Jennings turned to the EMD officer. "Zonta, if you please, coordinate our navigational presets with the helm and keep us on course for intersecting the target planet."

"Aye, sir."

Jennings again turned his attention to the ship's computer. "SADI, determine the optimum orbital eccentricity for maximum surface sensor efficiency, and relay those coordinates to the helm. I want to get as much data as we can on each pass."

While the fusion drive guided *Endeavor* to her orbital plane, SADI made the final calculations and relayed that information to the helm, where Alex and Baseball expertly placed the starship to within centimeters of her advised speed and altitude. After twenty-three minutes, Alex told the captain, "Sir, the *Endeavor* is now at an altitude of 837 kilometers, with a cruising speed of 28,056 kilometers per hour in a sun-synchronous orbit. We've arrived, sir."

For a moment, everyone maintained a tense vigilance at their stations. The entire bridge fell silent except for the occasional electronic chirp on various control panels. Instead of an order, Jennings just smiled and relaxed in the command chair. "Well done, everyone. But we're not standing down yet. I want at least one operations officer to remain at his or her station for six orbits. You pick who stays and who takes a break. Those on break are to take no more than four hours before relieving their station counterpart. Understood?"

"Aye, sir."

During the next few hours, the bridge crew were able to unwind in the galley or their bunks. Alex unwound in his usual manner on the holographic deck with a short half-hour sprint up Yerupajá in the Peruvian Andes.

After the sixth full orbit, during which no anomalies were detected, the bridge complement was reduced to a skeleton crew. Alex and Baseball were dismissed from helm duty as SADI took over the job as the helm's autopilot and maintained the constant monitoring of their orbital position.

During the seventh full orbit, Captain Jennings called the chief analytical officer, First Lieutenant Amil Malik, to the bridge. "Amil, we've got her in a pretty good spot for your team to begin surveying the planet's surface. It's time for your gang of peeping toms to start earning their pay. If you need any adjustments, don't hesitate to ask SADI. Do not, however, disturb me for the next eight hours. I'm hitting the rack, and unless you see space pirates attacking us, I expect to get a full and undisturbed eight."

At 187 centimeters, Lieutenant Malik carried a slight build on a relatively tall frame. He wore his jet-black hair at exactly regulation length. Dark brown eyes set over a thin aquiline nose looked straight forward as he rammed to attention, snapped out a crisp salute, and barked a parade ground "Aye, sir!"

Jennings inwardly groaned at his survey chief's awkward bridge formality. Lieutenant Malik never quite grasped the easy manner of Jennings's command style. The captain loosened the top button of his uniform and told the lieutenant, "That's good, Amil. You're now the watch commander. Try not to break my ship in the next eight hours."

Just as Jennings started to rise from his chair, he thought of something and hit the ship-wide intercom button. "Lieutenants Porter and Hartley, report to the bridge."

———————

At the captain's summons, both lieutenants were in the galley talking with their OVAL copilots. Upon hearing their names, they looked suspiciously at each other. Not seeing any guile in the other one, they just shrugged.

"What do you think this means?"

"I don't know, Baseball, but whatever it is, I'm pretty sure it's your fault."

Baseball gave a guttural grunt. "I find that highly unlikely since it's you who usually lands us in the shit house."

"Be that as it may, my friend, I dare say not this time. I noticed that you didn't heed my suggestion about accessorizing with a pair of Rox's gloves while on helm duty."

Rox's eyes turned hard as they darted between the two pilots. She finally locked on Baseball, glowered even harder at him, and then punched him in the arm.

Alex stifled a grin. "Perhaps the old man has taken exception to your new tattoos."

Rubbing his arm, Baseball grumbled, "Like I said."

Upon arrival on the bridge, the lieutenants came to attention and saluted as one. "Reporting as ordered, sir."

Jennings waved his hand in a dismissive fashion. "At ease, gentlemen. Thank you for your promptness. Before I hit the rack, I need to know; are both OVALs ready?"

Alex answered. "Yes sir, both craft are set to go. All systems have been checked and double-checked as directed, sir."

"Fine. No need to concern yourselves at the moment. It'll probably take Malik and his gang of spies a couple days before they come up with an anthill they want more closely inspected. In the meantime, I just wanted to know the status of your boats, and I wanted to see your smiling faces when you gave me that report. Fine job, boys. That will be all. Dismissed. Oh, one last thing—Lieutenant Hartley?"

"Sir?"

"Try to find some gloves next time you have helm duty." The captain strolled away.

Remaining at rigid attention, Baseball's usually pale complexion turned a splotchy red. Alex waited until the captain had left the bridge before he leaned in close and whispered in his friend's ear, "Told ya."

"Shut up, shit stain."

CHAPTER 27

THE ENHANCED BLOODLINE
OFOL'R—LOG'RFOLD

Jutting up from the ocean floor like the serrated fangs of some planet-sized monster, a jagged range of mountains ringed the entire circumference of Aqueous. With peaks of razor-sharp crystal shards, the mountains lay under four thousand crushing meters of seawater. At the foot of this submerged range a tectonic rip in the crust ran parallel to the mountains and dropped another thousand meters. This equatorial rift marked the boundary where the northern and southern hemispheres met. Like those underwater mountains, the trench encircled the entire equator, and had extensive and diverse bionomics. Deep-sea fish were hunted by large schools of predators, the most dangerous of which was a giant squid-like invertebrate called sq'raken by the Normad'r. These seven-meter-long killers roamed the deep trench feasting on the abundance of marine life found there.

But these native sea creatures weren't the only living beings that made their home in the dark waters of the abysmal ocean floor. Another being, intelligent but alien to Aqueous, also lived there. Although these beings had colonized Aqueous, a planet they named Log'rfold, hundreds of thousands of years before, they were not indigenous. Called the Normad'r, they had settled on Log'rfold for a single purpose: to mine the riches found only in abundance on this planet, riches that made this remote outpost the most important planet in their galaxy-wide empire.

To protect this essential resource, the Normad'r had created a planetwide defense system built to destroy all external threats, and from their underwater base at the bottom of the equatorial trench, another threat had just been detected.

Hovering within his large domed dwelling, the Supreme Mab'r of the Normad'r received the report within moments.

"A second human starship has achieved orbit," his minister of mines briefed him.

"Indeed, Dreng'r," replied Erland'r, "it is as expected. What are the details?"

"This new ship is an exact replica of their previous one," Dreng'r said. "It seems that their technology has not exceeded this design."

Erland'r opened his palm and fluttered three fingers. A holographic image of the starship appeared before him. "And the Rond'r," he inquired, "have the humans detected it?"

"No, Mab'r," Dreng'r said as he floated farther into the soft blue glow of his leader's dwelling. A translucent mist wafted up from a floor that had no substance, but there was no need; no Normad'r ever touched it. The mist barely rippled when Dreng'r passed over it as he approached Erland'r. The minister acknowledged the holographic image of the planet with a slight nod of his large head. "No detection has been made."

There weren't interior walls inside the ten-meter-wide dome, but thin membrane sheets provided both privacy and light. The floating sheets could be repositioned with a flick of a thin Normad'r wrist. "What about the Ramm'r crystal?" asked Erland'r as he waved a luminescent sheet aside.

"Their sensor technology is too primitive to penetrate our protective veil." Dreng'r paused for a moment before he related another aspect of the ship that concerned him. "Kanend'ra has informed me that there's an interesting development concerning a member of the human crew."

"A member from their enhanced bloodline is aboard," Erland'r accurately surmised.

Other than a soft blue glow pulsating from his body, no indication of surprise registered on the smooth blue face of Dreng'r. No emotion ever registered on the face of a Normad'r. No emotion could. "Yes, Mab'r, and more importantly, the bio-genetic scan Kanend'ra gave me has revealed that this particular family member is a seventh-generation male."

"An interesting development," acknowledged Erland'r. "Two seventh-generation males from this same bloodline, each originating on one of our bio-engineered planets; one born here, and one on Earth. And they are now both here on Log'rfold."

"Perhaps an even more interesting development," related Dreng'r, "is that his arrival coincides with the divination that same bloodline's Spak'rna wrote about one thousand years ago."

"Ah yes, I remember this female quite well. Until this generation, she had proved to be the strongest of that bloodline to have ever lived on Log'rfold, and yet, she too was born on Earth."

"It's fortuitous that Kanend'ra created this species to have such a short life span."

"True, Dreng'r," reflected Erland'r, "but the ultimate survival of this Earth-born male may not be in our best interest. I am undecided on this."

"Do you want the starship destroyed, Mab'r?"

"Not yet. Let us be patient for the moment," said Erland'r. "I have noticed that Kanend'ra does not have complete control over her project from this planet's bloodline."

"I do not understand, Mab'r."

"The youth has proved to be unstable," said Erland'r, "and instability is quite often unpredictable, which leads to unreliability. I simply do not trust him to carry out the agenda that Kanend'ra has programmed into him."

"How does this affect the new starship?"

"Given the capricious nature of Kanend'ra's project, we may need an alternative. There is a probability that we may have use for this Earthling to further our plan," Erland'r continued thoughtfully. "In the event that we do indeed need him, then we will allow the rest of the humans to trigger the Rond'r and be destroyed like their previous starship. This too works in our favor."

CHAPTER 28

LIZARD SHIPS AND DERELICTS
IFC ENDEAVOR—ORBIT DAY 03

A s the *Endeavor* shifted her flight path to a pole-to-pole orbit, Lieutenant Malik's team readied their surface analysis equipment. The first survey employed high-resolution analytical sensors, and since oceans covered the majority of the planet's surface, the Subsea Geographic System was needed to map and analyze the ocean floors. This was used in conjunction with the Acoustic Doppler Current Profiler that determined the temperatures, speed, and direction of the ocean currents. If the *Monarch*, or pieces of it, had crashed into the ocean, these instruments would find it.

Or so it was assumed.

The analytical team set up and tested its equipment, made small adjustments, and integrated their files into the mainframe. SADI acted as the data catalyst to receive, decipher, prioritize, and distribute as needed.

After two days of polar orbit only two continents were discovered; one surrounded each pole. Oddly, both landmasses were completely blanketed by a thick cloud cover, but very few clouds were found above the ocean in between. The survey of this massive ocean was completed within twenty orbits, but no trace of their sister ship was found.

The surveyors then turned their attention to the landmasses.

Using a basic thermal geomorphometry scan, they were able to map out the surface temperature and basic topography of each land-mass, but none of their other instruments seemed to work. While puzzling at first, the inability to use their most sophisticated analyti-cal equipment soon put the survey operation into hiatus. Without this data, the entire mission would be compromised.

The northernmost continent was by far the larger of the two. Dominating the continent's topography was a massive mountain range. Shaped like a giant spiral, it started as a ring around the north pole and continued outward in an ever-expanding coil until it reached the edge of the continent. The continent itself was shaped like a giant tadpole with the tail at the southernmost tip ending in a long, wide peninsula. The only noncircular mountain range on the continent split that penin-sula and ran its entire two-thousand-kilometer length.

Strangely, a perfectly shaped parabolic mountain sat at each pole's axis point. These two identical mountains were each exactly 9,006 meters tall. Unlike the northern continent, which was covered by huge mountains, the southern peak was the only mountain on the entire continent.

The temperature scans indicated that all mountain peaks were capped by snow and ice, but the lower elevations weren't frozen, and the rest of the landmass had a warm temperate climate. With its head-waters near the north pole, a huge river flowed down the forested valley that lay between the spiraled mountain range and emptied into the ocean next to the northern end of the peninsula.

The planetwide ocean between the continents was teeming with aquatic life, and, like the oceans on Earth, large schools of marine life migrated along the currents, both in the deep cold and in the warm shallow currents that flowed only in their respective halves of the planet. The strong ocean currents, moving in opposite directions in the northern and southern hemispheres, combined at the equator and produced massive rip waves that kept the two landmasses virtually isolated from each other.

Seven hours into orbit day three, the survey chief sent a junior officer to find Captain Jennings. The ensign found him in the engineering department speaking with CPO Khaki. The excited young officer burst into their conversation before he realized his faux pas, and then rammed to attention, saluted, and then quickly adopted an at ease stance.

The captain made a perfunctory salute in return and asked, "What can I do for you, Ensign?"

"Sir, Lieutenant Malik has sent me to find you, sir."

"Fair enough. You've found me."

The ensign went silent for a moment before he finally gathered himself enough to continue. "Sir, the uh—lieutenant has requested your immediate presence on the bridge."

Jennings offered raised eyebrows. "Enlighten me, Ensign, have we been attacked by space pirates?"

"N-no, sir. We—we've found evidence of uh—intelligent life—on the oceans."

Jennings managed to maintain his composure, but the hair on his arms stood straight up. "Elaborate, Robert."

The captain's use of the ensign's given name calmed the crew member enough for him to give his report without further stammering. "Sir, while studying infrared heat signatures very close to the southwest edge of the southern continent, we observed unusual heat-image fluctuations. When we zoomed in on these heat signatures, we recognized the obvious shape of ships."

"Ships," repeated Jennings, and then nodded to the ensign. "Good job, Robert. Let's head to the bridge."

"Aye, sir."

On the bridge, Jennings found the same state of excitement that the ensign had exhibited earlier. The exception was Lieutenant Malik, who, wearing old-fashioned glasses, hadn't even noticed his captain's arrival. His entire focus was locked onto a screen whose colors and shapes were unfamiliar to Jennings.

After a moment, Malik noticed the captain, pushed his glasses up to his forehead, and leaned back so that Jennings could see the screen. "Sir, as you can see, we've found what we believe to be an intelligent species capable of building oceangoing vessels." Malik dropped his glasses back into place, turned back to his screen, and adjusted the magnification. "Watch while I use thermal imaging to zoom in on this section of coastal waters. There, see that, sir?" He pointed to his screen. "On the water, but very close to the shore, right off this small point, there are three dark-brown signatures of an exact geometric shape. They all have the same elongated design and are the same size. They're ocean-going craft built by intelligent beings. And, sir?"

"You continue to have my undivided attention, Amil. Please go on."

"They're moving, sir. All with the same heading and speed." Malik bent close to the screen and used a stylus to point out more of the minute details. "These slender cross pieces above each deck, here and here, seem to indicate sails." He then pointed to some other slender parallel lines running perpendicular to the shapes. "And these are oars."

Malik again used his stylus to point out another detail. "If we zoom in even closer, we can see these cooler variations moving around on the decks of these vessels." He glanced over at his captain's face to see if he caught the implication. "Sir, due to the sun's heat absorption, the decks of the ships are close to 36°C, which means those small cool spots are the crew."

Captain Jennings was feeling almost as giddy as he studied the screen. "Well done, Amil. But now we need to find out conclusively just who or what is manning those boats." Jennings reached out and lightly gripped Lieutenant Malik's shoulder. "Amil, the identity of those beings is of the utmost importance. We might have just discovered the first intelligent species outside the human race, which has huge historical implications. Or frankly, more important to this mission, we may have just discovered the survivors from the *Monarch*."

Malik's grin faded as he moved closer to his captain. The glasses came off again as Malik lowered his voice so that only Jennings could hear. "Sir, those heat signatures couldn't possibly be human. They indicate body temperatures varying between approximately 22°C and 28°C. By contrast, our body temperatures are a very stable 37°C, which is close to the ambient temperature of the vessels."

"Meaning what exactly, Lieutenant?"

"Meaning, sir," Malik said with a less than enthusiastic tone, "that's a significant temperature differential."

Jennings tapped one finger on the console for a moment before asking, "Then what are we looking at?"

Turning back to his console, Malik pressed a control button, and the imagery zoomed in much closer. What they saw up close were humanoid type beings, but they weren't human. "Sir, without more study, I can't say conclusively."

"Lieutenant, just give me your gut feeling."

Lieutenant Malik looked back down at the monitor, took a deep breath, and then nervously glanced at the rest of his team. "Well, sir, it's been my experience that the first impression is often the correct one."

"Meaning?"

"Sir, my first instinct upon seeing these beings is that they're some type of reptilian species."

Jennings squinted down at the screen as if to see it better. "So, Amil, you're saying that intelligent lizards are manning those vessels."

"Possibly, sir. We need more study to draw a firm conclusion. But yes, in my experience, biological heat signatures like these have always proved to be of a reptilian nature. I'm running a DNA analysis now and should have a definitive answer soon."

Still taken aback, Jennings's command instincts took over. "Lieutenant, have SADI zero in on those boats with every whiz-bang instrument at your disposal, and conclusively identify the biology of those crews. Report back to me once you're absolutely sure, and I want regular status reports every twelve hours starting right now. I'll expect the next report at 07:00 tomorrow."

"Roger that, sir. We should have something substantial to report by the next watch."

"Very good. Carry on, Lieutenant. Oh, and Amil?"

"Yes, sir."

"You kicked ass here today, and my log will reflect that. You and your team are probably due a commendation at the very least, and quite possibly a paragraph in some future exobiology textbook."

CHAPTER 29

HIS DESTINY
CAMBRIA—AQUEOUS

G lazed in cold sweat, Bayne bolted awake and gasped for breath. For as far back as his disturbed memory allowed, the same nightmare had tormented him. Night after night he would fight off sleep, often for days, until finally, inevitably, he would succumb to its torture: chased through the vast empty halls of Drakon Rus. As he ran, he would wail in panic because he knew that his father pursued him. His terrified screams echoed off the high vaulted ceilings, but no one heard him. No one helped him. No one cared.

Bayne knew he was bad. All bastards were bad. *"You're a weak worthless little bastard,"* came his father's favorite accusation. Right before the fists rained down. So the little boy knew he deserved the punishment. Oh, but he was scared of the pain and the swollen eyes and the bloody lips and the broken bones.

He tried to hide, night after night he tried, running ever deeper into the bowels of the massive cavern city, but there was no escape. His scrawny legs always betrayed him, bogging him down as if he was running through water, and his father would always find him. Berate him. Beat him. Break him. So, the child in the nightmare, Bayne the weak bastard, sought refuge in the only safe place he could find—the deep recesses of his mind.

But even his mind wasn't safe. A demon lurked there, and she spoke to him. She called herself Normad'r—the Protector, but he knew who she really was, and what she really wanted.

She wanted him.

She wanted his power.

The Protector scared Bayne at first, because she floated like a ghost never touching the ground. But she was never cruel to him, and she praised him for his abilities. This made him happy. It was the only happiness Bayne the weak bastard ever knew. Then she showed him how to use those abilities, and whom to use them upon. He didn't want to at first, because what she wanted was bad, and he didn't want to be bad anymore, but she insisted.

Oh, how she insisted.

Every night she demanded more, and every night, as his father closed in, he escaped into his mind, and she would be there, waiting.

Waiting for him.

Finally, one night, long ago, he began listening to what she told him. He listened and learned, and the Protector freely gave her approval and he desperately craved her approval.

Any approval.

She extolled his progress, and lauded his performance, and gave him a new name.

A strong name.

She named him Count Darx.

Count Darx was strong and fearless, but best of all, he *was* feared.

Bayne the weak bastard was dead.

The Protector gave him so much more than Aunty Ox ever had. His beloved aunt had called it his Path. The Protector called it his destiny.

But tonight everything changed. For the first time ever it wasn't his father who hunted him. Tonight it was someone different—someone who looked exactly like him.

An evil twin?

How could this be unless this new tormentor was a ghost—Bayne's ghost? Count Darx was happy that Bayne the weak bastard was dead, but now this doppelgänger, this vile apparition, had come to hunt him—hurt him—take him.

Back to those dark empty halls.

Back to where Bayne the weak bastard's father waited for him.

Back to those angry fists.

But the Protector had shown Count Darx how to defend himself. She taught him how to use his talents to conquer those weaker than him, so he knew this ghost must be weak.

Bayne was a weak bastard.

As Count Darx pondered the weaklings he would soon rule, clarity struck him like a knife in the heart. He suddenly realized who this ghost was: an enemy sent to destroy him, and worse, that big fire-breathing bitch would help him. It had all been foretold; the Hope Prophecy was coming, but he couldn't allow that. Wouldn't. It would ruin everything. It had to be stopped, and there was only one way to stop it.

Kill the ghost.

Once their hope was dead, then he, Count Darx, would have no rivals.

He loved his new name. It would become the most feared name on the planet. The Count would become the Tsar—absolute monarch over the entire human civilization. It was his birthright to rule, and all who denied that birthright would die. And the best part, he could almost taste it, was the delicious revenge he'd inflict on those whose guilt was above all others: his family.

Them, he would kill personally.

CHAPTER 30

NO NATURAL PHENOMENON
*IFC ENDEAVOR—*ORBIT DAY 03

L ieutenant Malik's team resumed surveying the planet's surface with renewed zeal. But their enthusiasm was quickly tempered by the fact that none of their mission parameters had been met. Once the team shifted their analysis away from the oceans and concentrated on the landmasses, all their high-tech equipment began malfunctioning. Not only were their high-resolution cameras rendered ineffective, but their most advanced analytical survey instruments produced nothing but corrupted data.

With his patience at an end, Lieutenant Malik finally conferred with the ship's AI. "SADI, every time we test our equipment, it checks out fine. All the ocean surveys that used this same methodology delivered exemplary results."

"Could it be something on the ground that is causing the obstruction?" asked SADI.

"Perhaps," said Malik, "but I've never run into a disruption from a survey target." He placed a hand over his mouth and spoke through his fingers. "As crazy as this sounds, I'm beginning to think these clouds are the issue. I mean, they never change, never move. Even wind, or the typical temperature fluctuations between day and night don't affect them. I've never seen anything like it."

"I'll run a thorough diagnostic, Lieutenant, and get back with you," SADI responded.

Three hours and four orbits later, SADI hailed Captain Jennings to join Malik on the bridge and told him the moment he arrived, "Sir, I understand Lieutenant Malik's frustration, but I wanted to finish troubleshooting the analytical systems before presenting my conclusions."

"What have you found?" asked Jennings.

Lieutenant Malik's left foot beat out a staccato under the console. "SADI, is this an equipment or human error?"

"Neither, Lieutenant. There are unusual environmental conditions causing the data corruptions. Your equipment and your people are functioning properly. So, if we are to successfully gather the required survey data, we need to adjust our survey procedures."

Malik's foot tapping stopped.

"I think you should start at the very beginning, SADI," Jennings said. "Exactly what environmental conditions, and how can we rectify it?"

"Captain Jennings, there is an atmospheric anomaly over both continental landmasses that obstructs our most sophisticated survey equipment. I concur with Lieutenant Malik and believe this obstruction to be the cloud cover itself. We will need to survey below this cloud cover to confirm."

"Have you analyzed these clouds?" Jennings asked.

Malik cut in at this point. "We've tried, sir, but all our data comes back corrupted."

Ignoring the lieutenant's interruption, Jennings remained focused on the report. "You mentioned both continents, SADI. Are they both like this?"

"Yes, sir. Except for the topography and temperature scans, the rest of our survey sensors are completely obstructed over both continents."

Malik pushed his glasses up and rubbed his eyes. "But here's what I don't get: how can an atmospheric condition, dense cloud cover or whatever, obstruct my survey equipment? I've conducted analytical planetary surveys on countless planets, most with some kind of adverse atmospheric conditions, including extreme temperatures and pressure, often through dense cloud cover containing a wide range of toxic gases, and my equipment has never failed. The technology is sound."

Jennings rubbed his jaw, then looked over at the surveyor and nodded. "SADI, I have to agree with Lieutenant Malik. This just doesn't seem like a natural phenomenon."

Without hesitation, SADI finally came to the crux of her presentation. "Correct, Captain. This atmospheric phenomenon does not appear to be natural."

The bridge went deathly quiet while Jennings stared at the main view screen. When he finally spoke, his words were even and measured. "Are you saying there is some sort of artificial atmospheric defense screen? The indigenous inhabitants we've observed so far haven't advanced past wooden sailing ships."

"Sir, this is evidently an attempt to shield both landmasses from analytical surveys of the kind we are attempting," said SADI. "Even we don't have this level of technology."

Lieutenant Malik's shrill voice cut in. "Captain, if SADI is right, then there must be a more advanced race of beings protecting these two regions of the planet."

Given the nature of this information, and what Jennings already knew about the classified imputes of his mission directive, he had to agree, but didn't respond to Malik's comment.

SADI broke in with an even more ominous report from newly acquired data. "Sir, something has just been detected by our long-range scanners." The AI hesitated for a moment. "The LRS has just detected another planetary event of perhaps greater significance than the atmospheric defense screen below us."

"What do you mean by 'below us'?" Jennings's voice went ice cold.

"Sir, there seems to be another planetary event, not below, but above us."

Jennings sucked in a shallow breath. "Does this have anything to do with the matter at hand, SADI?" He began slowly pacing in front of the data screens.

"Probability models suggest that there is a possible correlation between the two, sir."

Jennings stopped pacing and stood next to his chair gripping the armrest. He looked up, exchanged a glance with his weapons officer, and said, "Let's have it, SADI. What's this new information?"

"Sir, the latest LRS finding indicates that there are hundreds of what appear to be derelict satellites situated in two planetary orbital planes high above us."

"Fuck a wildman," hissed Gunnar Hammär through his teeth.

The blood left Jennings's face. "What and where exactly are they, and why do you think they're derelict?" Again his eyes swept the bridge, and again they settled on Commander Hammär who was working his jaw muscles like a vise clamp.

SADI continued with her report. "There are exactly one thousand small, five-meter-wide spherical objects orbiting almost thirteen thousand kilometers above the planet's surface. There are five hundred orbiting pole-to-pole and five hundred in a retrograde equatorial orbit. I believe them to be derelict because there's zero energy radiating from them. They're not transmitting, nor can I detect any transmissions directed at them."

"How the hell did you—did the LRS miss a thousand satellites on our approach, SADI?" Jennings snapped at his AI.

"Sir, there are three possible explanations," offered SADI. "We could have experienced a system malfunction while making our approach. Also, the LRS was in the process of searching for space debris in our trajectory path during entry into the solar system."

"Doesn't one thousand satellites orbiting our mission destination count as debris?" Jennings asked harshly.

"Yes, sir, it does," the AI answered evenly. "Another explanation could be that they weren't there when we made our approach." At these words, the emotional level on the bridge approached critical mass. "Or they might have employed some sort of cloaking device."

In a low growl, Commander Hammär cut in on the discussion. "This just changed the whole scope of this mission. Remember why we're here in the first place." Gunnar's voice was neutral, but his face was etched with concern. "Richard, we need to make a reconnaissance of those satellites right now. And while we're at it, let's send down a drone to inspect those blasted clouds." Gunnar's tone was more of a demand than a recommendation. "We need to know exactly just what the hell we've got ourselves into."

"Hang on a second, Gunnar! Give me a moment," rebuked Jennings. He crossed his arms and stared at the screen. "SADI, bring up an image of the satellites."

"Yes, sir." An instant later a blurry image appeared on the screen.

"Is that the best you can do?" demanded Jennings.

"It is, sir. That's at maximum resolution on the nearest satellite," SADI responded.

Jennings nodded, and then turned to his security chief. "All right, Gunnar, send a drone up there and see what these things really are, but I want only benign sensor analysis used."

"Meaning what exactly, sir?" pressed Gunnar.

"Meaning, Commander, take photos of the damn things, and nothing else."

Gunnar's nostrils flared as he sucked in a deep breath through his nose, but he kept his voice neutral. "That means we'll have to get within spitting distance, and we need the LRS for guidance."

"I realize that, Gunnar," said Jennings, "but keep it on the lowest setting. I don't want any overt electronic scanning. Not yet anyway, and then use the same drone to make a drop and check out those clouds." The captain turned to the AI. "SADI, we need to find out what's just below this cloud cover, but we need to do it in an unobtrusive and non-threatening way. Blasting down gamma rays, GIS, and powerful radar beams may not be the best way forward."

Jennings turned to his survey chief. "Amil, your team has done a good job so far, but I need you to stand down until we know more about this latest wrinkle. Maybe it's nothing but an ancient protective shield left over by a much earlier civilization." Catching Gunnar's eye roll, Jennings frowned as he continued. "Or perhaps it was left by the same folk who left the high planetary orbit full of space junk. Until we know more, I don't want to take any provocative actions, or anything that can be construed as such. Our primary mission goes into hiatus until we have a clearer picture of what this all means. Understand?"

Lieutenant Malik slumped against his console, and softly answered, "Yes, sir."

In a more conciliatory tone, Jennings told the survey team, "I know this isn't what any of us want, but this'll give your team a chance to rest, and I absolutely need you to be ready to come back on line at a moment's notice."

With hands hung limply at his sides and his lips almost a pout, Malik mumbled, "Yes, sir. We'll be ready the moment you need us."

"This must be what the *Monarch* faced before her disappearance," Gunnar suggested to his captain.

Jennings squeezed his eyes shut and said, "I realize that, but we're going to find out. I knew the commander of the *Monarch*." He opened his eyes and stared at the view screen. "Admiral Mason ran a cautious and prudent command, but he didn't have the benefit of the hindsight that this command now has, and I'm not about to blindly forge ahead without using all my assets." He locked eyes with his weapons chief. "And that means I need to confer with the senior staff. See to it, Gunnar."

CHAPTER 31

STAR LIGHT STAR BRIGHT
AQUEOUS

Too many humans could get him killed, so like always, Count Darx chose to be the only one of his species to rendezvous with the Thith. He had done this many times before, and like before, he alone made his way through the trees to where the forest met the sand. Darx waited in the shadows of the tree line and watched the Thith drag their crude skiff onto the beach before he casually stepped out of the trees and approached the sworn enemy of mankind.

Even outnumbered, he had little to fear from these reptiles. Count Darx knew that they needed him as much as he needed them. It was a pact born of mutual ambition and barely concealed hate. Lasting for no more than an hour, this would also be the last meeting until the invasion.

Until his return to Drakon Rus.

Count Darx had met with the Thith several times over the past few years, always well away from Cambria. It was during these clandestine trips that he had learned to speak their hissing reptilian language. By doing so, he had gained a smattering of their trust.

But trust is an opportunist.

He'd made a pact with them; for his part, he taught them how to make a few crude improvements to their weapons technology, but only a little at a time. Too much military prowess among these stinking reptiles would not serve his best interests. But the most notable gift he gave them was the intelligence about where to build a staging port well out of the patrol range of Drakon Rus. He'd been a dragon rider before his exile and knew the extent of their patrols. Utilizing the intelligence he had given them, the Thith could land an army unseen, advance on the enemy's flank, and launch a surprise attack on cliff city itself.

He'd also made sure these little trips remained unknown. On the first two trips when a ship's crew returned to Cambria, they disappeared forever. They were expendable, and simply couldn't be trusted to keep their mouths shut past their first drink. These crews were hardened ruffians who were rarely missed by anyone except the whores who worked the waterfront, and when their regulars didn't come back, they quickly moved on to other customers.

But this present crew was different. They were greedy and ruthless enough to be trusted beyond just one voyage. Darx decided to keep them alive for now, at least until he no longer needed their little ship. Only then would their whores need to move on.

The rendezvous took place on a small beach far from human civilization—far from prying eyes. Except for that one human colony of unworthy cowards, only wild reptiles inhabited the main landmass of the northern continent. Humans rarely ventured this far away from their fortress city. It was just too dangerous.

Without so much as a greeting, the Thith officer approached Count Darx and said, "I am Officer Trath, the most trusted envoy of Her Most Excellent Highness. She requires to know if you have garnered the required steel."

"Is that a question?" asked Darx.

"It is *the* requirement, human," hissed Trath.

Count Darx knew every aspect of his being was scrutinized, his body language, his facial expressions, his words. While he didn't fear these lizards, he also didn't want to anger them. Not yet, anyway. "It will be made available at the previously agreed time."

"A guarantee is required."

"So many requirements," sighed Darx. "But I should warn you, my power is guarantee enough."

The Thith officer's forked tongue flicked spittle on Darx's shirt. A sneer twisted his reptilian face as he looked Darx up and down, and hissed, "You speak of power, but all I see is a fragile soft-skin." Trath moved uncomfortably close. "Give us a real guarantee, human."

Darx wiped the spittle off his chest and spoke evenly, "Ask your second if this is a real enough guarantee."

A loud crack punctuated by a painful scream suddenly filled the beach.

Trath spun around just in time to see his second in command fall to the ground clutching his right arm. His forearm had broken and folded all the way back until his knuckles touched his elbow.

The break had compounded, and the envoy sucked in a breath as he watched the thick blood seep into the sand. After a moment Trath looked up, disgust mixed with fear etched on his face. "I will explain your guarantee to the Duchess."

"I'm sure she'll understand," Bayne said haughtier than he meant to.

For several seconds the Trath glared at him with undisguised hate, then hissed something unintelligible before he made an impatient gesture at his whimpering second and stalked away.

Touchy touchy, thought Bayne as the gathering broke up without so much as a *by your leave*.

Intrigue makes for strange bedfellows, and while it was in their respective best interests to remain peaceful for the time being, they would have enjoyed nothing more than to rip each other apart.

That would come later.

The Thith vessel headed directly south into the oncoming gloom of night, while the human ship made its return voyage in sight of the coastline.

Darx stood at the forecastle and watched the coastline recede into the distance. After a few minutes he made his way to the tiller. "Captain, why are we so far out? We risk being seen by a Cambrian ship, and I assure you, that's not a good thing."

"Count Darx," the captain of the small vessel timidly explained to his boss, "these are uncharted waters, and I can't get us too close or we run the risk of foundering on rocks in the shallower water."

A cool wind snapped at the single sail and Darx flipped his wool coat's high collar to ward off its chill. He then turned to the captain.

"I see," Darx said. "And you feel confident that your river vessel can handle these ocean swells at night? We had no trouble getting here, and we were closer to shore where the risk of being seen is much less."

"Aye, master," stammered the nervous boat captain, "but that was in daylight. Now it's dark, and I feel it to be the lesser of two evils."

"Evils." Count Darx yawned the word in the captain's face and pulled his coat tighter. "Just what the hell are you on about?"

"Well, master, if we spent the night on shore, we'd more likely than not be attacked by God only knows what manner of monster. If we hug the shoreline, we could scuttle our ship on rocks," Captain Jersey explained. "So, I need to keep deep water under my keel, and starlight to guide me." He pressed his point. "And there's no cloud cover to block the starlight this far out, you understand."

Count Darx flashed an untrustworthy smile at the man. "I understand your situation, Captain." The smile disappeared. "So, I suggest you not allow us to be seen."

Count Darx gazed up at the night sky. *What a beautiful night to gaze up at the heavens. They shine over what will soon be my realm. All will be mine: the land, the sea, everything under all those gorgeous stars.* He snickered at the thought. *And maybe even beyond the stars. All is within my grasp.*

It seems so odd to be under a clear sky, away from those damn clouds, and actually see stars like this. There must be millions of them.

One in particular caught his attention.

The captain followed Darx's gaze, looked up, and saw it too. It was a big star, brighter than any of the others, and, most unusual of all, it moved rapidly across the sky. The captain's mouth fell open. "Stars don't move like that," he blurted.

"How observant of you," Darx offered languidly. He said nothing more and moved away from the man and the conversation. *But that idiot of a captain is right. In fact, nothing moves like that except*—a knowing smile crossed his lips as he watched the bright light fade into the distance—*that's it, a starship!* Aunty Ox had told him tales about them when he was a child, and at first he feared what it meant. But then the thought hit him, and he smiled at its significance. *This can only mean one thing: the ghost has finally arrived, just in time to die so far from his home.*

Yes, it was a good night for stargazing.

CHAPTER 32

TRAP BY DESIGN
IFC ENDEAVOR—ORBIT DAY 06

Alone in his cabin, Captain Jennings leaned on the small stainless-steel sink in his personal head and stared at the mirror, trying to get a measure of the man staring back. He saw the usual face of a confident commanding officer, but he also saw something else, something unfamiliar: a trace of doubt etched in the lines below his brown eyes. He'd never seen those lines before.

A soft electronic warble was followed by SADI's voice. "Captain Jennings, all the requested officers have arrived. They await your presence, sir."

"Thank you, SADI, Are Lieutenants Porter and Hartley present?"

"They are, Captain."

"Fine, I'll be with them shortly." Jennings pushed away from the sink, ran a comb through his dark brown, service-length hair, took a deep breath, and entered the stateroom.

The group of officers rose to their feet and stood at ease. They remained so until he sat at his desk, looked around the room, and addressed them formally. "Ladies and gentlemen, please take your scats. A download of the meeting's agenda has been sent to everyone's OC. Are there any questions before we get started?"

Commander Gunnar Hammär wasted no time firing the first shot.

"Richard, before we get started, allow me this one question: is this ship in danger?"

"Frankly, Gunnar, I just don't know yet, but the primary mission directive is suspended until I do know more. And that's what we're here to discuss."

Captain Jennings took a deep breath, stood up from his desk, walked around to the front, leaned back, and folded his arms. "I'm going to tell you what I know, what I feel, and then let SADI give you the hard facts. Afterward we'll talk it out, and everyone will be given a chance to voice their opinion. This is not a democracy, and I will make the final decisions, but I want to hear your input before I do. Fair enough?"

An uneasy, "Aye, sir," answered him back.

Maintaining his casual position, Captain Jennings said, "As you're all aware, we've been surveying the planet's surface for any signs of the *Monarch* and her crew. We've made several redundant survey passes over both landmasses, staying in the same orbital plane each time in our attempt to locate anything of use to the mission. And as some of you have already heard, almost our entire array of analytical survey sensors have been thwarted by the perpetual cloud cover over both continents.

"The only survey instruments that seem to work through this cloud cover are basic topography, and some thermal mapping. In other words, we know the geographical contours, and a narrow view of their temperatures. After that, we can only guess. The survey team, SADI, and I have reason to believe that this cloud cover is not only blocking our survey sensors but is not of natural origin. We believe it to be developed by an advanced technology for reasons that seem defensive in nature."

Sitting in the chair next to the captain's desk, Gunnar leaned forward with his big hands clenching his knees, and like a bull ready to charge, his nostrils flared with each breath. Several of the other officers darted their eyes back and forth between their captain and the commander.

Jennings's voice remained steady. "Our instruments can't determine the geological makeup of the mountains or the chemical composition of the rivers. Nor can we detect anything biological on either landmass. The oceans, however, are in full view of our sensors, and they are full of life. Naturally, this leads us to believe that the landmasses are as well.

"As you're already aware, we've observed wooden ocean-going craft manned by what seems to be an intelligent race of reptilian beings, and they've been observed in a number of places around the southern continent, so we're certain that this species has some form of civilization living on this continent and are constructing these craft from trees that must also be found there. Unfortunately, we cannot, as yet, detect them.

"In fact, a large fleet of forty of these craft has been spotted sailing from the southern continent and is, at present, on a northerly heading, landing them somewhere on the large peninsula of the northern continent in a few weeks' time.

"In addition to the impenetrable cloud cover, we've recently discovered evidence of another puzzling yet potential hazard to our mission."

At this point, Commander Hammär's knuckles turned white. The military decorum that had hitherto been maintained was about to be shoved out an airlock.

The captain continued to ignore him and went on. "Two bands of seemingly derelict satellites, five hundred each, have been detected in orbit about eleven thousand kilometers above our present position. Their orbits are perpendicular to each other."

Commander Hammär couldn't contain himself any longer. "Captain, if I may?"

"As if I could stop you, Gunnar," muttered Jennings.

"Sir, I have the results from our reconnaissance of those satellites," Gunnar reported with an unusually neutral tone, "and it's no real surprise that no real questions were answered, or that we found nothing conclusive."

"Finding nothing conclusive, real or not, Commander, doesn't mean that you don't have a conclusion. Mind sharing it with us?"

"Except for the LRS, and the comm link, none of the other scanners were activated." Gunnar became more animated as he continued. "All drones have a similar LRS as that carried by the ship, and as ordered the settings were at the lowest possible strength. But the drone's LRS couldn't detect anything until they were only twenty-two kilometers away. That's practically in their lap." His voice rose perceptibly. "Even at these low settings, they should have been able to pick up their signatures the moment they left the *Endeavor*, but not these 'dead' satellites." Everyone jumped when his big fist slammed the tabletop to drive home his point. "Oh no, these 'dead' satellites are definitely cloaked and definitely not the benign derelicts we've so conveniently labeled them."

"And the clouds," Jennings asked evenly. "What were those results?"

"Oh, that. Well now, Captain, it just keeps getting better and better." His voice dropped to a husky growl. "Again, as ordered, we kept everything but the comm link off during the drop and approach. And all the way down to those lovely clouds, everything came up puppy dogs and pretty girls."

"Commander," warned Jennings.

"Fine," Gunnar continued. "We had full comm link contact right up to the point of target insertion, but when it penetrated the target, we lost signal within seconds." His voice began to rise. "And its final seconds of transmission sounded like the electronics got ripped out by a sadistic rat." He was practically hyperventilating as he made this last point.

The two young pilots stood straight-faced at the back of the stateroom, and without moving his lips Baseball lightly nudged Alex with an elbow and whispered, "Puppy dogs."

Alex responded out the side of his mouth, "And pretty rats."

"Thank you for that engaging report, Gunnar," sighed Jennings. "Do you have any other concerns?"

"Concerns?" Gunnar's voice betrayed his incredulity as he loudly repeated the word a second time. "Concerns?"

"Yes, Commander." The conversation was about two heartbeats from going supernova, but Jennings and Hammär had been down this road before. The captain locked eyes with the commander and said, "Constructive concerns that will help this command with a way forward."

The commander inwardly groaned, and relaxed so slightly that only his captain could tell. He took a deep breath. "Sir, as I see it, we now have two unexplained, unnatural, and potentially threatening planetary events. Events that, I might add, had to have been built by a technologically advanced species and not by lizards in rowboats. Furthermore, sir, we are basically surrounded by these purposely built, planetary defensive mechanisms. I don't mean to sound alarmist, Richard, but we are now in a classic pincer position, and I for one am more than just a little *concerned*."

"As am I, Gunnar." Jennings unfolded his arms and stood up straight as he continued, "Which is why I called this emergency meeting of the senior staff. Before we get to SADI's presentation, I have one last thought to leave you with. We've been sent almost twelve hundred light-years to find and, if possible, rescue our sister ship, but now it seems we've reached an impasse. In light of these two planetary events, we have two choices: give up and go home"—this remark elicited several shocked expressions among the staff—"or, we can change our survey tactics and continue with our mission."

Jennings took note that almost every officer looked relieved at those words.

The lone voice of concern was Hammär's. "Sir, excuse my impudence—"

"Nonsense, Gunnar, I value your impudence."

Commander Hammär's next words sounded like two granite bricks being ground together. "Sir, changing our present survey tactics means that we have to survey the planet's surface from a much lower altitude, which means we have to get below this damn cloud cover, doesn't it?"

Captain Jennings turned to his survey officer. "Amil, I believe Gunnar is correct?"

Unused to public speaking, especially in front of a room full of distressed superior officers, Lieutenant Malik just nodded.

Jennings took a gentle approach with his diffident lieutenant. "Amil, please speak up so that everyone in the room can hear."

"Sir, yes sir, Captain. Commander Hammär is correct, sir."

"That's about what I would expect from a desk pilot," Gunnar muttered, and then in a volume and tone normally reserved for ratings and other lower life forms, he growled, "Thanks for that resounding confirmation, Malik." The commander was getting louder with each word. "So, in that case, in order to get below this blasted cloud cover, we've got to send down the OVALs loaded with survey equipment."

This got the two straight-faced pilots' rapt attention.

"Then, via low-altitude passes with the OVALs," Gunnar directed his tirade at the timid survey officer, "we'll finally be able to obtain all that critical information that has eluded us so far. Is this a fair assumption? A simple yes or no will suffice, Malik."

"Y-yes, sir."

"Close enough, Malik!" Hammär practically shouted.

Captain Jennings loudly cleared his throat and raised his eyebrows. "Gunnar, we're all in the same boat here, including Lieutenant Malik. I'm sure your point is just about to make its appearance."

The commander grunted and lowered his voice. "Sir, my point is this: if we send manned craft down to the planet's surface below this cloud cover and start using overt electronic means to analyze the planet's surface, then might that be construed by whoever, or whatever, built that defensive cloud-screen and all those 'derelict' satellites as a hostile act? And, Captain, if that's the case, wouldn't they be expected to react accordingly?"

"Yes, Gunnar," agreed Jennings, "I believe that to be a distinct possibility."

"Then, sir," responded Hammär, "with all due respect to our mission directive, shouldn't we be preparing for a fight?"

CHAPTER 33

SOFTSKIN BLOOD
DEEP OCEAN—AQUEOUS

W ith increasing ferocity, the angry blue horizon dove from view
only to reappear seconds later in a frothy spray that drenched
the bow as it plowed through yet another white-capped swell.
As the small armada of sleek warships closed in on the planet's merid-
ian, they could move forward only under the brute power of oar, and
even that took a grueling effort. While the red sun beat mercilessly
down on the cloudless sea, thousands of galley slaves labored below the
pitching deck and tried to make headway through the strong equatorial
current. But the Imperial Duchess was impassive to her fleet's misery.
All that mattered was that each sunrise brought her ever closer to realizing her dream.

With clawed feet firmly gripping the rolling deck, Duchess
Thorna watched the first stage of her invasion force crawl inexorably
northward, and with a reptilian grin that was more of a snarl, she sent
out word ordering all the fleet's captains to join her aboard the *Ocean
Fang*. She was ready to launch the second phase of her three-part plan.

By the time the red sun slipped below the waves, a small three-
ship flotilla would split off from the main force and head to an isolated bay on the northern continent's mainland. These three ships
carried a thousand soldiers and tons of crude engineering material,

and they were tasked with building a staging base at a deep-water bay protected by thick forest on one side and a tall rocky promontory on the other. Located on a remote stretch of coastline, it would be used to land her massive war armada and destroy the softskin slime once and for all. From this new base, a flank attack would be launched on the second human stronghold high in the northernmost mountains. But first Cambria and its entire human population must be destroyed.

A malevolent hiss escaped the Duchess's throat as she fantasized about killing the hated enemy. This time it would be softskin blood that darkened the Bay of Misery. Under a flag of truce, her expedition would meet those parasitical humans at their fortress city and demand their surrender, which she fully expected them to reject. In fact, she was counting on it.

Punishment for refusing her generous offer was death.

But first things first, and Thorna's upcoming meeting with the aliens would be just one element in their overall plan. A plan that depended on the traitor whom she had been meeting, and who'd been feeding her information for the past few years.

These vermin, they were so predictable. Promise them power, and they would slaughter their own to get it.

It took hours for most of the fleet captains to comply with their Duchess's command to join her aboard her flagship. Their fragile little skiffs had to fight their way through the raging sea, and six of them foundered, drowning all aboard. Thorna watched their deaths indifferently and then turned to the assemblage of shivering captains who had managed to comply with her order.

Hissing displeasure at the incompetence of those delinquent captains, dead or not, she turned to one of those who had survived the crossing. "Captain Droth," commanded Duchess Thorna, "it's time for your rendezvous with Trath. Follow him with your flotilla and make your way to the new staging area. "

"I hear and obey, my Duchess," groveled the captain. "I will have the designated bay ready to receive our glorious fleet once they've conquered and destroyed the softskins on the peninsula."

Thorna approached the captain so that only the two could hear what was said. "See that you do, Captain," she warned, "and push your soldiers like their lives, and your own, depend on it." She turned to leave, and then stopped and hissed over her shoulder, "Because it does."

"Duchess Thorna," whimpered the captain, "what if the dragon riders spot us and attack before we have the defenses built?"

"Then use our secret new crossbows, and kill them," she sneered. "Do not fail me."

CHAPTER 34

THE LAST HUMAN STARSHIP
OFOL'R—LOG'RFOLD

N o sunlight ever penetrated the two thousand fathoms of seawater that covered the multi-domed base of Ofol'r. In the total darkness of the abyss, their base had gone unobserved for hundreds of thousands of years. Populated by only a few dozen Normad'r, Ofol'r had always performed its essential task flawlessly well. From their underwater base they protected their charge and made sure no outside interference ever posed a threat to the dominion they held over this watery planet. A planet that was thousands of light-years from their home world of Hof'rust, the capital of the Normad'r Empire—an empire that controlled millions of support planets. But this planet was unique and held the most valuable asset in their galaxy-wide empire.

It held the Ramm'r crystal.

The three-meter-tall, blue-skinned Normad'r lived for tens of thousands of years, but they were a fragile species. Instead of liquid blood, their cardiovascular system pumped a carbon-based lighter-than-air gas, and this enabled them to float wherever they went. The key to the Normad'r longevity lay in their highly advanced technology, especially bioengineering. And because of their fragility, the Normad'r had cultivated countless civilizations throughout the galaxy for millions of years, which included the original life on Log'rfold. Each bioengineered species provided the Normad'r with an essential service, and eventually, over the eons, their engineered slave races performed all physical tasks required by the empire. This included a relatively primitive but sentient life form that originated on another blue planet.

A planet called Earth.

By design, that young species had arrived on Log'rfold one thousand years before, but now more of them had come, and their arrival meant that the multi-millennial Normad'r plan would soon come to fruition.

"Mab'r," reported Dreng'r, "the Earthlings will soon begin conducting surveys beneath the Glugg'ra screen utilizing their small, manned craft."

"Is it possible they could discover Ofol'r?" asked Erland'r.

"No, Mab'r. They've finished conducting surveys of the ocean and found nothing."

"And yet they discovered the outer Rond'r defense network," Erland'r reminded him, "and subsequently sent an unmanned craft to investigate."

"While accurate, Mab'r," conceded Dreng'r, "the Rond'r does not have the layers of shielding that Ofol'r has. They will not discover our base."

"In that assessment, I share your confidence. However, they are a highly motivated species, and logic dictates that these humans must suspect that someone other than the Thith control this planet. Hence, they must assume that a base exists somewhere on Log'rfold."

"That is a sound premise, Mab'r." A dull yellow glow emanated from Dreng'r. "Do you want them destroyed?"

"Not as of yet," said the Mab'r as he floated to his planetwide observation orb, and with a wave of his slender hand a holographic image of the *Endeavor* appeared before him. "If we remain undiscovered, then we will wait for the inevitability that one of their small craft lands on the planet surface and triggers the Rond'r."

"As did the last human starship," added Dreng'r.

Erland'r wiggled two of his three fingers, and the starship's image disappeared. "In which case the operation will go forward as planned. The loss of another ship will result in another investigation resulting in them sending more starships. The plan calls for a war fleet this time, and one armed much better than those they've sent so far."

CHAPTER 35

NOT ALONE IN THE UNIVERSE
IFC ENDEAVOR—ORBIT DAY 07

The room went quiet once Commander Hammär had finished his impassioned speech. Captain Jennings broke the silence. "Ladies and gentlemen, we've all got a lot to mull over, but for the time being I'm going to hand over the next portion of this briefing to SADI. Please engage your optic computers and use them to follow her visual presentation."

Jennings locked eyes with Gunnar and added, "If any of you have questions or need clarification on a particular point, please use decorum, and you will have your say. Any questions so far?"

Commander Hammär remained tight-lipped.

"Fine, then, with no further ado, SADI, if you please, give us a rundown on what we've discovered about Aqueous so far."

A soft electronic warbling filled the stateroom. "Thank you, Captain Jennings. The most threatening aspects of any sortie below the cloud cover are encountering a communication blackout, adverse weather, and possible dangerous life forms.

"As reported, we cannot detect anything beyond elevation and temperature, but we are able to make a detailed analysis of the oceans. We've detected a large number of these wooden sailing craft almost exclusively found around the edge of the southern continent. I say, 'almost exclusively' because that fleet of forty wooden craft previously discussed is sailing on a heading that, if maintained, will see it reach land on the tip of the northern continent's peninsula in three weeks and two days. They are presently struggling through the extreme currents found around the equator. Yesterday evening a group of three ships split off from the main body, and this small flotilla is now on a heading that will place them about three thousand kilometers from the peninsula."

The high-resolution camera zoomed in on the fleet of sail-and-oar-powered wooden vessels sailing north in a tight formation. There were audible exclamations of surprise and wonderment from many of the officers gathered in the stateroom. When the camera zoomed even closer, the detailed visages of the reptilian crews became evident, and, for the first time—other than the captain and a few of the surveyors—human beings were seeing the first intelligent beings other than *Homo sapiens* that had ever been discovered. The moment was not lost on most of the group, and many of the senior staff were moved to more displays of emotion, including the usually stoic Commander Hammär. More than a few laughed and even clapped.

Mankind was not alone in the universe.

"As you can see, there seems to be a significant indigenous population grouped exclusively on the southern continent. At present, we've no way of determining their population density, but logic dictates that there must be a sizable population to justify this rather large seagoing segment. We have also observed hundreds of wooden vessels in various sizes. They range from close coastal fishing craft to larger cargo vessels and military craft. These forty oar-and-sail-powered vessels are approximately sixty meters in length, the fastest observed so far, and since we can see crude weapons aboard, we must assume that this is a military squadron: a rapid naval force."

A few in the group smirked at the thought of a wooden warship manned by lizards. Commander Hammär was not among those smirking.

"We haven't been able to undertake any meaningful surveys of the landmasses, but we've made extensive analysis of the oceans, and if you'll please watch your screens, you'll see some interesting graphs that illustrate a few oddities."

The screen changed from a bird's-eye view of the indigenous vessels to one of colored graphs. The officers followed on their OC screens as SADI explained each one.

"Here on Aqueous, many elements that are normally found in oceans are almost completely absent. In short, gentlemen, this is the first freshwater ocean ever encountered on a Class-M planet."

─────────────────

After another hour of listening to SADI cite all the scientific data amassed so far, Captain Jennings stood, giving everyone in the room a cue to do the same. Some stretched, some yawned, but everyone paid attention as he told them, "Ladies and gentlemen, that pretty well sums it up, and is a lot to digest. Now I want your feedback, but not today. When I do get it, I need your opinions to be pragmatic and well thought out. So, I want you all to think about what we've heard here tonight. We'll reconvene here in twenty-four hours.

"If any of you want to give me your opinions at an earlier time, based on a legitimate rationale, then I'm all ears. Until then, go get some rest, decompress, and thank you all for your patience and attention. Dismissed."

CHAPTER 36

AN UNUSUAL DAY
IFC ENDEAVOR—ORBIT DAY 07

S everal hours after the staff meeting, Gunnar sat in the galley drinking a cup of coffee. He sat at his usual seat and, as usual, he sat alone. There were no assigned seats in the galley, but sailors are, for the most part, creatures of habit, and Gunnar was as habitual as most. Born and raised in the Køngsberg Enclave near the southern coast of Norway, Gunnar had grown up with straight talk and strict obedience, two virtues that were often at odds with each other. Navigating between the two had never proved easy for him, as his lack of career advancement bore out, and the prime reason why it was an unusual day when he didn't sit alone in the galley.

Gunnar felt someone approach and looked up as *Endeavor*'s junior weapons officer, a Marine first lieutenant with short brown hair, large brown eyes, and a nose that had been broken a time or two, stopped at his table. She stood in front of him for a moment and politely waited for him to say something. When nothing was forthcoming, she waited until he took a sip and then plunked her coffee cup down opposite him.

"Mind if I join you, Commander?" She sat down before he had a chance to answer.

"Why, of course not, Becky, why bother asking?"

"It's Rebecca."

"Please, take a seat, Rebecca."

As though she hadn't heard, Lieutenant Rebecca Laurent launched into a conversation as if they had been sitting around shooting the shit for hours. "Only my dad gets to call me Becky, but since he's the one who named me, it's tolerated."

Gunnar leaned over and conspiratorially whispered to his coffee companion, "I wouldn't let it get out that you actually tolerate something, Rebecca. It'll destroy that whole Valkyrie, hell-for-leather image that has the entire crew shitting themselves at the mere thought of reaping your displeasure."

She matched his forward lean. "Actually, Commander, since you're now the only member of this crew who knows that personal little tidbit, I feel relatively safe. But be advised: should I happen to find that small glimmer of information scrawled in, say, a toilet stall in the officers' head, I'll know exactly where to reap my displeasure." She took a sip of coffee.

After considering her for a moment, the 201-centimeter and 120-kilogram stature of Commander Gunnar Hammär recoiled in feigned terror at the prospect of the 154-centimeter, 55-kilogram lieutenant hunting him down to dispense displeasure. "Come now, Laurent, you wouldn't really hurt an old man, would you?"

Setting her cup down, Lieutenant Laurent looked her hulking boss square in the eye. "You do realize, Commander, that only Lieutenant Porter scores higher ratings than I do in the hand-to-hand combat training simulations?"

"Remind me to make sure both of you are on my side in our next bar fight."

"Commander, I'm here for a reason, and I'm pretty sure you already know that."

Gunnar jested, "Well, thank God it's not to kick my ass, because the galley staff would already be mopping my blood off the floor." His grin lessened as his eyes narrowed. "So, what *does* bring you to my table, Lieutenant?"

She stared at her cup for a moment, and then slowly, resolutely, raised her face until her eyes met his. "Commander, I've been asked to speak with you about your position in tomorrow's staff meeting."

All the levity left Gunnar's voice as he met her steel gaze with one of his own. "Asked by whom?"

"Asked by the majority of the other officers."

Gunnar's thumb tapped the side of his cup. "Why did they choose *you* to come and pick my brain?"

Irritation crept into her voice. "Because I'm expendable, because I'm the smallest member of the crew, because you and I work in the same department. What difference does it make?" She stopped for a moment and gathered her composure. "Look, I volunteered, okay? Everyone knows that you and the captain went through the academy together, that you're family of sorts, and that, for some unfathomable reason, he listens to you more than any other member of the crew."

One side of her mouth edged up when his brows furrowed, and she pushed on. "He respects your opinion, and we would just like an idea of what the outcome of tomorrow's meeting will be. That's it, pure and simple."

Gunnar sat dead still for a moment, and then spoke with carefully measured words. "I won't be part of any coalition against the captain, Laurent."

"I wasn't—"

"And furthermore, he'll see right through one if it rears its ugly head. Do I make myself clear, Lieutenant *Rebecca* Laurent?"

"You miss my point, Commander. I'm not—we're not trying to form an alliance against him. Good God, that man has more respect from this crew, especially the officers, than I have ever seen for any captain on any starship ever."

She glanced down at the tabletop for a moment, and when she looked back up some of the steel had left her eyes. "But there's concern, Gunnar. Hell, they're scared. I'm scared. We're at a bare minimum of four years away from any kind of help, which means we're out here on our own with our asses hanging out. The rest of the officers just want to know how the cards lie. That's it. That's all I came to say." She grabbed her mug and stood up. "I sincerely apologize if you got the wrong impression about my motive for coming to see you."

"Fair enough, Rebecca," Gunnar told her, "and since you asked, my position is as follows: I'll voice my opinions loud enough to settle any confusion as to their nature, and then, regardless of what those orders are, I'll follow them to the letter."

Laurent nodded, and said, "Of course." She turned to leave.

As she started to walk away, Gunnar spoke with the least domineering voice that anyone had ever heard come out of him. "For what it's worth, Rebecca, I'm scared too."

She turned to face him and opened her mouth to speak, but she shut it when she saw him place a finger across his lips.

It took a moment before he dropped it. When he did, it was as if someone totally unfamiliar was speaking. "I have no idea what Richard's going to say tomorrow, but there's one thing I can tell you about the man, and it's something you probably already know. He'll do his duty and expect every crew member aboard this ship to do the same. He'll also take every precaution he can to safeguard this ship and her crew. Beyond that, Rebecca, I have no answer for you. I guess we'll find out together."

With that, Gunnar picked up his mug, walked past the lieutenant, and left her alone with a cold cup of coffee. After he was gone, Laurent dropped her head and whispered, "Yes, I believe we will."

CHAPTER 37

ISLAND FORTRESS
IFC ENDEAVOR—ORBIT DAY 08

An hour before the senior staff meeting, Captain Jennings sat alone at his desk, drinking his own cup of freshly brewed coffee. He stared at an old photo of his ex-wife and their two boys standing on the beach at Skaha Lake near his boyhood home of the Penticton Enclave. The photo was ten years old. Aside from his sister, and her bearlike husband, they were the only family he had. A family he hadn't seen in over five years. Nor were they really his anymore.

As he sipped his coffee, he closed his eyes and reflected on the last conversation he'd had with the woman who had bore his two children and endured twenty years of being married to a man who was home cumulatively only six of those.

The vivid memory of that conversation still smoldered. She'd bravely informed him that she'd had enough of being the mother, the father, the disciplinarian, the only parent who ever attended their sporting events, the only one to attend their birthdays, their skinned knees, their broken hearts, and all just to crawl into bed night after night, year after year, and sleep alone.

Her words still tore at his heart like they were spoken yesterday.

He never blamed her for finding another man. She was entitled to the happiness that comes from a loving, caring companion; a companion who wouldn't disappear a few days after yet another set of orders took him away. The new man in her life—oh hell, he reminded himself, it had been ten years now—was good to her, and to her boys—his boys. This knowledge carried a bittersweet realization with it. One that he normally kept locked away in the baggage that followed him across the galaxy.

Starship captains could not afford to trot out their baggage for public display. Regardless of who the real man was on the inside, a good captain's public persona was not afforded the luxury of emotional exposure.

A ship's captain had to be an island fortress whose strength was all that stood in the way of any assault that threatened his command. Storms had to harmlessly dash themselves against those fortress walls and keep safe all those inside. Those walls could never be breached because once they were, then the captain had lost the legitimacy of command. And an emotional weakness was the quickest way for cracks to appear in those fortress walls.

Today was the first time since leaving Port Apollo over four years ago that he'd thought about the family that was no longer his. It was a memory that, for the time being, he needed to bury. He had a crucial decision to make regarding the safety of his command: a decision that could very well destroy his career as a starship captain, or, worse still, destroy his ship and all those who looked to him to maintain the strength of those fortress walls.

Jennings was not a captain who ruled tyrannically, as some starship captains did. His was a levelheaded command; the emotional executive outbursts that frequented other starships were never seen aboard the *Endeavor*. He was approachable and personable, but not a pushover. Once he had weighed all the information and had made up his mind, he would issue orders accordingly, and brook no insubordination.

Punishment details were rare aboard his commands because a simple look of displeasure from their captain was enough to settle any confusion about where the responsibility really lay.

Jennings inwardly smiled when he looked down at his desk and saw the little yellow rubber duck that his eldest son had given him when he was just five years old. It was one of the fondest memories of his life. He'd been giving his son a bath and got thoroughly soaked by the little boy who was more interested in playing than bathing. After drenching his laughing daddy yet again, the boy stopped all play, looked at his dripping dad, and in a serious tone, informed his him that since the duck had always floated upright while being splashed around, he wanted his dad to have it so that his ship would always float upright. The duck had been Jennings's constant companion since that day. He knew the mysterious duck was a topic of discussion for his crew, but it was one mystery that would remain his and his alone.

CHAPTER 38

DECISION
IFC ENDEAVOR—ORBIT DAY 08

A t 18:58 SADI informed the captain that the senior officers were
on their way to the stateroom. By 19:00 everyone was once again
seated where they'd sat during the past two meetings. Captain
Jennings was seated at his desk when they filed in. This in itself was an
unusual state of affairs. The captain was almost always the last participant to enter the stateroom, but today he was the first.

Once everyone was seated, the captain sat quietly for a minute
looking from officer to officer. Most officers have the unique ability to
hide their true feelings behind the mask of unobstructed authority, but
Jennings knew these men and women well enough to be able to read each
one. In fact, he had handpicked almost all of them, a fact unknown to his
two young pilots.

Finally, he stood, patted the air with his hands, and everyone
remained seated. As before, he walked to the front of the desk, leaned back
against it, and folded his arms in front of him in a casual yet commanding
posture. "Thank you all, once again, for your promptness. I trust that
you have all given a good deal of thought to the matter at hand and are
ready to voice your opinions and concerns." This was a statement, not a
request. "As usual, this is an informal meeting and seniority protocols will
not be considered." Looking directly at the two lieutenants, he continued,

"Seniority or rank mean nothing for however long it takes to hear everyone out. So, who wants to start this party?"

There was an uncomfortable pause as not a single officer volunteered to go first. After about thirty seconds of silence, the captain had heard enough, so to speak, frowned, and told the bashful group, "Look, folks, this isn't a middle school dance where no one has the balls to ask for the first dance."

Gunnar slowly stood up and cleared his throat.

"Somehow, I knew you would find a way to overcome your legendary shyness and ask for the first dance, Gunnar."

Several grins and a couple of audible guffaws broke the officers' silence. Commander Hammär acted as if he was unaware of any levity leveled his way.

"Richard, we, uh—that is to say I, um—do uh—"

With his eyes locked on the commander, Jennings decided it was time to rescue his normally bellicose security chief. "Aw, Gunnar, for crying out loud, man, spit it out. I promise to keep the number of flogging strokes down to a minimum this time."

This finally broke the tension, and the entire room, including Hammär, had a good chuckle.

"Richard, I believe that Becky—ah—I mean Rebecca—would like to speak first."

Seated behind him, an ice-cold glare from the Marine lieutenant stabbed the hulking security officer through the back of his head. Gunnar didn't seem inclined to turn around, and gladly released the floor to her as he sat down.

Jennings narrowed his eyes and said in an irritated tone, "Just what the hell is going on here? I wanted your opinions, but I'm getting stonewalled instead. I'm not sure of the reasons, but someone in this room better fess up, and fess up fast."

As if an electric charge had been applied to her chair, Lieutenant Laurent jumped to her feet and stood at rigid attention. "Sir, if I may?"

Jennings softened his tone a bit and directed his attention at the only officer so far willing to address the topic. "Rebecca, or is it Becky?" While Captain Jennings waited for her to respond, Lieutenant Laurent glowered at Gunnar, who stared straight ahead. "Please, Rebecca, I really want to hear what you have to say, but for the love of God, at ease."

Lieutenant Laurent adopted the at-ease position.

"Captain—"

"Richard, please, Rebecca. As I've attempted to make plain, this is an informal meeting."

"Yes, sir, Captain Richard."

"Close enough, Rebecca. Carry on."

"Yes, sir. The fact is, sir, that we have a consensus. We have discussed this mission among ourselves and, to an officer, we have arrived at said consensus, sir."

One of Captain Jennings's eyebrows rose as he addressed Laurent. "For a weapons officer you seem to be having some difficulty firing your guns, Lieutenant. Just what the hell are you stumbling around in the dark trying to tell me? If you please, Rebecca, get to the point."

"Sir, yes sir, I've been informally chosen to convey the following message to you."

Maintaining a blank look but opting to keep his mouth shut, Jennings waited patiently for her to get to the point, which he was pretty sure would be achieved by the end of the second watch.

"Sir, we the senior officers of the IFC *Endeavor* fully agree with any and all decisions that you deem appropriate, and furthermore, sir, we will support you in the entirety of said decision without preamble and without reservation, sir!" At this she sat down, head up, back straight, and drilled holes in the back of Gunnar's head.

The commander didn't seem inclined to even twitch.

The corner of Captain Jennings's mouth curved slightly upward. "My guess is, based on Rebecca's speech, that there's no one else in this room who wants to voice a concern, and that you have all abdicated the opportunity to present your opinions. And, furthermore, you have all decided, via said consensus, that no matter what I decide to do, I will hear absolutely no whining about it from my senior staff. Does that about sum it up? Gunnar, find your balls, man, and give me an answer this time."

"Sir! I know exactly where my balls are," protested Gunnar.

Captain Jennings's irritation subsided a little, but he couldn't help needling his friend a little more as he walked back to his chair and sat down. "Perhaps for now, Gunnar, but I'm pretty sure that once the lieutenant is finished with you, that may not be the case."

Gunnar stood up and made an audible gulp. "Be that as it may, but your assumption about Rebecca's speech is correct. Look, Richard, everyone in this room knows the score. We really have no idea of what could be waiting for us out there, but we also know that an entire starship crew, some of whom are friends and family of this command—" Gunnar stopped for a moment and breathed deeply through his nose, "—are lost, and we were given the task to find them. That is our mission directive, and if that's what you decide to do, then you will have the unequivocal support of this ship's officers."

"And if I decide to turn tail and run back home?"

Somehow Gunnar managed a simultaneous frown and grin. "Aw, come on, Richard, everyone on this ship knows that we're gonna keep looking for the *Monarch*."

Captain Jennings cocked his head to the side and threw his hands up. Feeling some of the irritation return, he pointed out, "Folks, you seem to know a lot considering that I haven't told you my decision yet."

Commander Eaglecreek stood and cleared his throat. "Then just what are your orders, Richard?"

"Well, Zonta, since I have everyone's blessing to go off and do whatever my little heart desires, and in spite of the planetary events that we're all well aware of, I've decided to continue to look for the *Monarch* and her crew." He looked out at the grinning faces and added, "Any objections?"

The grinners remained silent, and even Rebecca had a satisfied glint in her eyes.

"In that case, ladies and gentlemen, the mission directive stands as is, and the discussion is now closed. Carry on. Dismissed. Gunnar, you stay."

"Yes, sir."

Once the rest of the officers had left the stateroom and they were alone, Jennings walked over to the cabinet and poured two shots of an ancient single-malt Scotch from the ancient Scottish port of Wick. He set them on his desk and raised an eyebrow. "Is there something going on between you and Lieutenant Laurent that I should know about?"

In genuine dismay Gunnar vigorously shook his head. "Are you serious, Richard? No! Hell no! What the hell are you thinking?"

"Methinks the lady doth protest too much."

Gunnar slapped his forehead and let out a theatrical sigh. "Aw shit, Dick."

Jennings's smile faded somewhat. He looked at his friend and said, "Tomorrow, Gunnar, we, as in you and I, will come up with a game plan. I need to know exactly how this planetary survey is going to be conducted, what the survey protocols are, what the rules of engagement are, if any." Gunnar raised his eyebrows at that, but Jennings continued. "And just how much leash we give our two hotshot pilots."

At the words "rules of engagement," Gunnar quickly assumed his security-and-weapons-chief demeanor. "I've already got a few things worked out. And as for our two hotshots, frankly, I think they both have enough creativeness to think their way out of most unexpected situations that might arise under that damn cloud cover."

"What makes you say that, Gunnar?"

"Did you read SADI's report on the pranks they pulled during their wake shifts?"

"Just the overview," admitted Jennings. "Although I have noticed that Lieutenant Hartley keeps his hands wedged in his pockets a lot. What's your point?"

Gunnar tut-tutted. "But you *do* remember the psychological cognitive study that Fleet made after *our* first deep space-mission to Epsilon Indi?"

"Somewhat," said Jennings, "but where are you going with this?"

"The study that made the correlation between the ingenuity of wake shift pranks and career advancement?"

"Oh, that one," acknowledged Jennings. "How do they come up with crap like this?"

"Hell if I know," said Gunnar, "but stats are stats, and you know how those Fleet weenies love stats."

Jennings grumbled, "Yeah, well, it came too late for me. I still got a reprimand for that tattoo on your ass." He poked his friend in the chest. "By the way, is it still there?"

Gunnar crossed his big arms and growled. "Yeah, and it still says 'Dick was here.' Anyway, all I'm saying is that those two clowns will probably make admiral before we do."

Nodding their heads, both men looked at each other for a moment and grinned before Jennings pushed on. "Then we're in agreement about rules of engagement for the boys?"

"Right: they get a choke chain at the end of a very short leash."

"Ha! Why am I not surprised? Fair enough." He handed Gunnar a shot glass and raised his own. "To short leashes."

"And rude tattoos."

The two old friends knocked back their drams of single-malt scotch.

"See you tomorrow, Gunnar."

"See you then." Gunnar walked to the door, opened it, hesitated, and then turned around. "Look, there's something I need to get off my chest before I go."

"Well?"

"Just so you'll know, I've got issues with those two damn mountains."

Jennings frowned. "Really? You had your chance earlier."

"I know, Richard; it's just that I didn't want the meeting to go off the rails."

"Figures," sighed Jennings. "Let's visit this again tomorrow."

"Right, tomorrow then." Gunnar shut the door, leaving Jennings alone once more with his thoughts and his memories.

Unconsciously staring at the rubber duck, Jennings hit his private intercom. "SADI?"

"Yes, sir?"

"Schedule a briefing on the bridge for 10:00 hours. I want Commander Hammär, Lieutenants Malik, Porter, and Hartley, Chief Petty Officer Khaki, and, of course Lieutenant Commander Eaglecreek."

"Consider it done, sir."

"Thank you, SADI. Your input is going to be essential as well, but we'll get into all that tomorrow. I'm going to go get a few hours kip. Wake me if needed."

CHAPTER 39

I'LL BE WAITING
THE SPINE—AQUEOUS

Alex gasped for air, but gagged instead, and sucked in a mouthful of putrid mud. Lying prone, he'd been jolted awake to find an enormous weight on his back, and quickly found he was powerless to shake it off. His face had been shoved into a puddle of filth, and shallow as it was, he still couldn't breathe. Then suddenly something gripped the back of his head and rammed his face down over and over until he heard a wet crunch. Blood gushed from his broken nose, and it felt like his face was being ripped off. He gagged again and swallowed a mouthful of bloody corruption. What the hell was happening? Alex didn't know where he was, how he got here, and no idea who or what had so easily done this to him. And mud? There was no mud on the starship.

"Die, ghost," screamed his assailant as Alex's head slammed down again.

Face down, and unable to turn over, Alex's hands flailed helplessly above his head in a feeble attempt to get a hold of whoever had pinned him to the ground. A set of powerful hands had a vise-like grip on his head; meat-hook-like thumbs dug into the back of his neck. Alex bucked and thrashed in a desperate effort to dislodge his attacker, but it was useless. Those brutal fingers dug so deep into his throat that Alex soon felt something snap as his trachea collapsed and all air to his lungs was choked off.

As his vision failed, he heard someone laughing, but the voice seemed far away. It was a man's voice, and he was saying something, but the blood pounding in Alex's ears made it impossible to make out the words. Suddenly those cruel fingers released his throat, and the pressure on his back disappeared. Alex gagged again, and fought for breath, but the pain was excruciating. Finally able to draw a breath, it felt like fire as he gulped air down his ruined throat and into his starving lungs.

Alex retched, curled his knees up, and rolled onto his side. In the corner of his eye he saw his attacker, but the light was dim, and the man's face was steeped in shadow.

The shadow man bent over him and whispered in his ear, "I've been waiting—but not for much longer—don't make me wait too long—ghost."

Alex tried to speak, but a gargled sound was all that came out of his mangled larynx. The shadow man snickered, stomped his boot's hard sole down on Alex's shoulder and violently shoved him onto his back. As the man did so, his face moved out of the shadow.

Both men drew in a sharp breath.

"Y-you're the ghost?" stammered the shadow man, before quickly composing himself. "Well, so be it then, but only one of us will live to rule this planet, and it won't be you. I'm coming back, and next time I finish the job!"

Everything went black.

Alex bolted upright in his bed, panting for breath, and quickly drew in a deep lung full of air. His hand flew to his throat and found it sore to the touch. He slid out of bed, staggered to the sink, and turned the light on. When he looked in the mirror, he stopped breathing. There was blood streaming out of his nostrils. Alex closed his eyes and splashed cold water on his face. A low groan escaped his throat as he placed a towel over his face and held it tightly. After a minute the blood-stained towel landed in the sink. He reached up to turn out the light but his hand stalled, and the light stayed on. Alex shuffled back to bed, pulled the covers over his head, and stared at the inside of the sheet.

CHAPTER 40

DRAGON RUN
IFC ENDEAVOR—ORBIT DAY 10

T he nightmare had rattled Alex more than anything in recent memory, and sleep abandoned him for the rest of the night. After tossing and turning for a couple of hours, he finally gave up and dragged himself out of bed. Since the pre-survey planning meeting wasn't scheduled until 10:00, he had a few hours to kill, so he grabbed his running shoes and drank a cup of coffee to get the cobwebs out.

As of late it had been more and more difficult to have control over his astral projections during a run, and the nightmare only reinforced Alex's unease. Normally he could focus on a subject, set a furious pace, and then let his mind remove itself from the pain and slip into the astral plane of his choosing. Then things started to change. Soon after establishing orbit around Aqueous, he'd noticed a lack of control over where his mind took him. He was now going to places—like the planet's surface—that he wasn't familiar with. Was that nightmarish mud puddle on the planet, and was it somehow connected to his lack of control over his astral projecting?

Before last night Alex had assumed this new lack of mental discipline was due to the fact that he was now sharing the ship with the entire crew as opposed to the four years of virtual isolation. Back then he had no one to talk to but a sometimes recalcitrant, mommy-knows-best computer, but the bloody towel in his sink suggested something different.

Something down on that planet.

As Alex made his way to the holographic deck, he focused on the coming run, and began to feel like his old self again. *It was just a nightmare,* he told himself. *Everybody has them, so I guess I'm due.* Once he'd reached the locker room, all negativity had vanished, and he was more than ready for both his run and his daily test of wills with SADI.

"Good morning, Alex. How are you today?" came the chipper feminine voice.

As usual, he wanted to concentrate on his stretch routine, and as usual his answers were laconic. "Good thanks, SADI. How're things with you?"

"Well, during your run I'm going to jettison all your uniforms out an airlock."

"That's nice."

"Then I'm going to back up the toilet in your cabin."

"For about an hour."

"Right before I plunge the ship into the red dwarf."

"Same as last time."

The electronic warbling became a high-pitched whine. "Seriously, Lieutenant Porter, you should try paying attention once in a while."

"No more battle programs. Captain's orders."

The warbling became a screech and went silent. A small smile found Alex's face for the first time that morning and stayed on his face while he continued to warm up. Ten minutes later, during the final stages of his deep-breathing exercises, SADI attempted talking to him again. "Where would you like to run to today, Alex?"

"I believe that a run up the Devils Postpile in the eastern Sierra Nevadas would be perfect today."

"Very good choice, Alex. Might I suggest a night run during a volcanic eruption?"

"Good idea, SADI, but not today, thanks."

"So, why *are* you choosing such an easy run?"

"True, it's not the most difficult," Alex explained while leaning against a bulkhead to stretch his calves, "but I don't want an exhausting run today. I need to have complete possession of my faculties for today's survey planning session."

"Are you sure that's wise, Alex? If you have complete possession of your faculties, no one will recognize you." A small electronic warble followed that observation.

Narrowing his eyes, Alex suspected a devious hand at work here. "Has Lieutenant Hartley been tweaking your levity program again, SADI? I believe you almost made a funny joke that time."

"You didn't find that funny?"

"I said 'almost.'"

The electronic warbling stopped. "Your running trail is booting up now. Have a nice run, and if you trip and break a leg, I'm pretty sure I'll be busy elsewhere."

Alex stepped into the dimly lit spherical room just as a reddish amber mist spewed out from each projector. The mist began to swirl as the colors transitioned into green, then blue indigo, and finally violet. Within seconds this misty coalition of colors morphed into a beautiful blanket of evergreens as the holographic deck transformed into a warm Sierra Nevada day. Off in the distance, Alex could see the exotic shapes of the twenty-meter-tall columnar basalt formations.

A light breeze filled his nostrils with the heady aroma of a healthy late spring forest. Bird song and the gurgle of a nearby brook added to the tranquility.

For a moment, Alex basked in the warm sun and soaked in the scenery. He raised his hands above his head and took a couple deep-diaphragm, lung-filling breaths before starting out on his run. As usual, the first hundred meters were taken at a relatively slow pace. As soon as he was satisfied that his legs were warmed up, he increased his pace to what would be an almost all-out sprint for most people. This was his normal cruising speed of approximately twenty-two kilometers per hour. It was the pace he needed to entice the pain and shift his mind into the trancelike state required for the out-of-body experience he sought on his runs.

After about two kilometers, he began to feel that state of being when he was just about to slip the boundaries of physicality and enter into the realm of projected consciousness. His labored breathing became hypnotic, and the leg pain disappeared as he shifted into the familiar state of duality.

The last conscious thought he had before relinquishing his being to the cosmos was of the nightmarish assault and that blood-stained towel.

And then his mind and body separated.

At the speed of thought, Alex suddenly looked down at his sweat-sheened body as it pounded across the mountain trail. Within moments that astral projected state vanished as he unexpectedly found himself inside his OVAL cockpit racing through the planet's atmosphere with the familiar feel of the yoke in his grip. All of a sudden there was a bright flash in the windscreen, and he felt something slam into the OVAL. He instantly lost hundreds of meters in altitude as his shuttle spun out of control. Instinctively he fought the yoke, but that only lasted a moment before his reality abruptly changed again.

Alex still flew above the planet's surface, but he was no longer inside a crashing OVAL. He now sat outside of some kind of craft.

Icy wind stung his eyes. He looked down and was stunned to find that it wasn't a craft at all, but a giant golden-winged creature, and he was riding on its back.

As the frigid air whipped past his face, Alex saw jagged ice-capped crystal-peaked mountains pass only a few dozen meters away. He was strapped in, with some sort of primitive leather harness, to a saddle apparatus, and he was slightly amused to see that he held a set of reins, but less so when he realized that those reins had no control over the flying beast. On top of all that, he wasn't wearing his normal high-tech flight suit, but something else, something different. It was a heavy handmade suit with fur-lined sleeves, surrounded by protective armor made from hardened leather, complete with a fur-lined helmet and gloves. Alex felt the familiar press of the baldric that held his katana, and as he'd done thousands of times, he reached behind his head to grab the sword's familiar tightly woven grip.

The instant his hand wrapped around the hilt, an electric jolt surged into him. He'd only experienced this once before: the moment his mother died. But this time was different. Alex felt sudden elation and a sense of invincibility. Nothing in his life had ever come close to eliciting this type of euphoria. It was as if he was a different person altogether.

That sense of well-being ended abruptly when the beast took an unexpected nosedive straight toward the ground. Alex jerked on the reins like he would his OVAL's yoke, but nothing happened. He had no control to stop this reckless plunge. He squeezed his eyes shut and yelled as the g-forces crushed him against the harness straps holding him on the beast. After a moment he opened them again, but he was no longer riding the golden creature. He was back inside the cockpit of his OVAL, wearing his normal flight suit, and he was still hurtling toward the planet's surface. Instead of land, he now plummeted straight toward the ocean at tremendous velocity.

Alex was shocked at the sight, and knew he had to pull out of this dive or the OVAL would slam into the water with such force that it would be torn to shreds. He hit his nose thrusters and pulled back on the yoke with every ounce of his strength. The OVAL began an unsteady vibration, but slowly, reluctantly the nose edged upward. It finally achieved full trim the instant the small craft's belly slammed against the water.

The jarring impact snapped Alex's head forward, and he bit through his tongue. As he fought to gain control, the craft skipped across the swells like a rock on a pond, and whatever was wrong began to get worse. The vibration reverberated throughout the OVAL, making his grasp on the yoke useless as the cockpit filled with smoke. His tongue flared with pain as a coppery taste filled his mouth.

It was the second time that he'd tasted his own blood in the past few hours.

Without any warning an agonizing scream filled the cockpit. Alex jerked his head around to see who it was, and for the first time realized he was not alone in the craft. He saw two people strapped in their seats, but through the smoky haze that had filled the cabin he couldn't tell who it was, or who had screamed. Turning back toward the windscreen, his body tensed in fear; the coastline rapidly approached as the OVAL continued to pound across the white-capped waves. Each impact increased the shuttering vibration and reduced what little control he did have. The thought that this couldn't be real crossed his mind because he knew that he was still on a run in the ship's holographic deck, but no matter what he told himself, every slam against the water felt real, and the vise-like grip he had on the yoke didn't lessen.

Alex heard another scream as warm liquid splashed into his open visor and entered his mouth. It took a second to realize that this sticky substance was more blood, but it wasn't his this time. He spit it out and looked up just in time to see that they had almost reached the rocky coastline. There were huge crystal columns jutting out of the surface of the water, and his unmanageable shuttle was closing at tremendous speed.

He knew that if he stayed with the shuttle he'd die.

Alex had only one instinctive, coherent thought—eject. He yelled something to that effect and yanked the ejection lever between his legs. There was a bright flash, followed by intense g-forces, and then he blacked out.

The OVAL exploded the instant he cleared the cockpit.

The explosion obliterated the craft and sent a shock wave of razor-sharp shrapnel that ripped into the tumbling ejection seat and sliced through his seat harness. His unconscious body was thrown free of the spinning seat where it continued to carom across the waves with his arms and legs flailing like a rag doll.

Alex regained consciousness the instant he forcefully slammed into those surf-pounded columns shattering multiple bones. His broken body, now splayed against the jagged rocks, was no more than a meter above the roaring sea. Searing pain overpowered all his senses, and he was barely able to hang on as powerful waves tried to rip him off and drag him down. He desperately clung on with every fiber of his strength.

But that strength was failing.

Somewhere deep in his mind, Alex kept trying to make sense of all this. He must find a way to take his consciousness back to his reality, back to where his body, his real body, was running on a starship's holographic deck. But the pounding surf was as real as anything he had ever experienced. He could taste the water as it pelted his face through the visor of his shattered helmet.

Even in his shocked state, he was conscious that nearby, burning pieces from his destroyed craft sizzled as they disappeared beneath the white-capped waves, but his mind just couldn't grasp the logic of any of it.

Nothing made sense.

Alex briefly considered just letting go and let come what may, but he couldn't will his body to do so. He instinctively knew that he had to hang on, but he was being defeated, wave by crushing wave.

For a fleeting moment, the angry face of his nightmare assailant flashed through his mind. That image evaporated and was quickly followed by the notion that maybe Baseball had made some gross error in SADI's replication program and that this was all just part of a program alteration gone horribly wrong. But deep down all his senses told him that he really was in mortal danger. He'd fought many lethal battles with virtual warriors, and been wounded many times, but they were nothing like this. With each passing breath, his debilitation only intensified. Alex finally passed out from the pain. As his mind lost consciousness, his strength faltered, and he lost grip on the surf-pounded rock.

Alex's eyes fluttered open; he struggled to focus. At first, he was elated, because the raging surf no longer pummeled him. He felt sure he was back where he belonged—on the holographic deck aboard the *Endeavor*. Then, as his vision cleared, he became aware that instead of the *Endeavor*, he lay on warm wet sand as gentle swash washed over him. He could still hear the roar of the surf as it crashed nearby, but those angry waves no longer tried to kill him. He was weak, weaker than at any time in his life, and every breath felt like being stabbed in the chest, but he was alive.

For the first time he was able to glance down, and his spine chilled at what he saw. The tip of his katana stuck out of his chest.

It had somehow pierced his body, and its bloody tip had skewered something on his chest. Stuck fast on its tip and anchored in place was the family medallion that he'd worn since he was a boy. With a gnawing dread, he realized his two most prized possessions were now killing him.

His right lung quickly filled, and soon he would drown in his own blood. He had little time left. Warm liquid flooded into his throat, causing him to choke on the bloody mix that bubbled up from his ruined lung.

His vision suddenly dimmed as a shadow fell across him and a rhythmic thumping sound beat the air above him. Alex felt a heavy impact on the sand close by, and whatever it was began to approach. With the last vestige of strength he looked up. In his close-to-death state, he must have hallucinated, because towering over him stood a creature ripped from the depths of his no-longer-lucid mind. It straddled him with a massive leg on each side of his ravaged body. Its huge, clawed feet were buried deep in the wet sand.

His vision faded, and his eyes closed. An image drifted into his consciousness, and he sensed a feminine presence—perhaps his mother. Yes, it must be her. He reached out to the vibrant strength of her spirit, and as he desperately embraced this ethereal visage his despair vanished. He would see her soon—just a few moments longer. As he began to spiral into dementia, Alex accepted the inevitable. Suddenly the fondest memory of his life flooded into his mind, and he was back at that meadow near his childhood home in Koryak on his tenth birthday. The day his mother had given him the medallion, the medallion now skewered by his sword.

It was now killing him.

He could hear her voice as they sat together on a log near a small stream, but he couldn't see her. She said something, but he couldn't understand what she meant. Mother? *Yes, Mother, I'm here.* Then she said something more, but it didn't make sense—what message?

Why would she say that?

With extreme effort Alex willed himself to see. Light drifted back into his vision and as he regained focus saw that the creature still towered over him. It had extended its huge neck eight or nine meters above him and roared louder than anything Alex had ever heard in his life. It was a primeval roar from an age that had disappeared from Earth millions of years before.

But not on Aqueous.

The roar subsided, and within seconds the creature's muscular breast expanded as it took another huge breath. It extended its throat skyward once again, only this time, instead of just a roar from that impossible beast, a jet of white-hot flame shot up a dozen meters into the air.

The roaring flame lasted for several seconds. When it finished, the beast snorted and lowered its giant head. Smoke wafted from its nostrils as its huge intelligent green-and-gold-flaked eyes locked onto Alex's broken body. When the viper-like head came within a meter of the dying human, its mouth closed around him. Resigned to his fate, Alex had no fight left in him. He only had a few ragged breaths of life left, and he was beyond anything except the most basic instincts, breathing and vision. Now, those two bodily functions had almost failed. Just as his vision began to darken forever, the beast's mouth engulfed him.

Alex managed to suck in a final shallow breath when an acrid odor penetrated his nasal cavity. An extremely volatile set of alien molecules ignited his olfactory senses, forcing his brain alert. His vision cleared, and he saw some kind of thick steamy liquid drip down from razor-sharp teeth. Viscous red goo completely drenched his body and seeped into the bloody hole in his chest.

A feeling of euphoria swept over him as his chest wound began to burn. Alex felt his bones knit back together. Everything in his vision turned a greenish color, and he was able to breathe normally. Within moments he slipped into unconsciousness again. But this time it wasn't death he succumbed to, but life itself. An instant before everything went black, the burning sensation in his chest intensified, and Alex's last thought was of that strong feminine presence.

She protected him.

CHAPTER 41

NOT SO DEAD
IFC ENDEAVOR—ORBIT DAY 10

Perhaps seconds, perhaps hours later, Alex heard the electronically strained voice of SADI as she frantically hailed him. "Alex! Lieutenant Porter! Alexander Preston Porter! Wake up! Medic, come to the holographic room, stat! Bring a stretcher, stat! Alex! Wake up, Alex!"

The next thing he knew, he was being tussled aboard a gurney and taken somewhere. When his eyes fluttered opened, he saw the concerned face of the ship's surgeon, Dr. Bogdan Prata, holding his wrist and taking his pulse, and, on the other side of the gurney, the ashen face of his best friend, Baseball, the program tweaker.

When Alex finally spoke, his voice was strong and lucid. "What the hell did you do to SADI's programs? It could have killed me."

With an emotionally constricted squeal, Baseball pleaded, "Nothing, Alex, I swear to you. I haven't altered her holographic programs since the old lady in the wheelchair."

Then Alex heard another familiar, authoritative, but concerned voice. "What old lady in a wheelchair, Lieutenant Hartley?"

Dr. Prata irritably interjected. "Captain Jennings, can we please dispense with all conversation until I'm done with the initial examination of the patient? I need zero distraction right now so I can listen to his vitals. Please!"

The captain practically whispered his reply. "Of course, Doctor. My apologies. Please keep me updated on the lieutenant's condition. Baseball, you come with me."

Prata accepted his captain's apology with a grunt, looked down at Alex, and asked with his barely discernable eastern European accent, "Just what is wrong with you, Lieutenant?"

Slightly confused, but realizing that the pain, or rather the hole in his chest was gone, Alex looked up at the doctor and shrugged. "I feel fine, Dr. Prata. What's all the fuss about?"

They had reached the infirmary by then, and Alex was moved to an examining table. Before answering Alex's question, Dr. Prata arranged analytical instruments to get a better look at the patient. He glanced down at Alex with a puzzled expression. "Lieutenant, a few minutes ago you were found crumpled on the floor of the holographic deck, clutching at your chest, and then suddenly you stopped all movement." The doctor scanned Alex's vitals as he continued. "And the first aid diagnostic instruments indicated that you had vital stats not consistent with those of a living, breathing human. You were, to be technical, dead."

"And now, Doctor?"

"Not so dead. Now, if you'll lie still and let me do my job, I'll tell you more when I'm done." As the oldest member of the crew, the slim doctor had a full head of salt-and-pepper hair, and light brown eyes that studied his patient for any sign of injury. Prata strapped a series of diagnostic devices to Alex in a manner that seemed to indicate that his intense concern of a few minutes ago was dissipating. Prata's attention was drawn to an egg-shaped rash on Alex's chest that seemed to disappear before his eyes.

As the doctor silently worked, Alex's out-of-body ordeal seeped back into his memory. How did his run turn from a benign astral projection into something so deadly? He'd made these mental forays while running hundreds of times. What was so different this time? He remembered every moment of his experience as if it was a real event. He didn't know how, but he felt that what had happened to him was absolutely real. But if it was real, how did it happen, and how was he fully recovered?

The questions racing through his mind brought no answers. Had it been a vision? He wasn't really sure that he could accept that, but how else could he explain it? Was it somehow related to that nightmare he'd had only a few hours before the run? Perhaps he had just gone too far, pushing his body and mind to the breaking point. That was the only logical explanation, but it didn't ring true. What had happened to him was real, and deep down he knew it.

After an hour of examination, Dr. Prata declared Alex to be of sound body. His mind, on the other hand, couldn't be vouched for at this time.

Alex found it mildly surprising that upon exiting the infirmary he found waiting for him not only Baseball, whom he had expected, but Captain Jennings as well.

As Alex stepped into the corridor, the captain placed his hand on Alex's shoulder and looked him straight in the eye. "Alex, Doc Bogs says you're fine. He says that he found absolutely nothing wrong with you. He says that you are, and I quote, 'the most fit human being I have ever examined.'"

Alex gave a small shrug.

The captain's eyes didn't leave his lieutenant's as he closely scrutinized his pilot. "However, something happened to you on the holographic deck, and I'd like to know what. Do you have an explanation, Lieutenant?"

Alex opened his mouth to answer, closed it again, frowned, and then finally said, "No, sir. Not really. I don't know what happened. Perhaps I pushed the physical-mental envelope too hard, and it just shut down."

Captain Jennings removed his hand from Alex's shoulder and, in a confidential tone, told him, "I need you, Alex—you, and your partner in crime here." He nodded at Baseball. "In fact, I need you both for this survey operation, and I need you both physically and mentally able to perform tasks that, to the best of my knowledge, have never been done before."

"Yes, sir."

With a sigh of resignation, Captain Jennings adopted the air of starship captain. "With that said, I think that for the time being you should stop your running. In fact, I'd feel better if you stayed away from the holographic deck altogether. Just until we get this survey business behind us. Agreed?"

Alex had no reason to object, but still struggled to keep disappointment from his voice. "Yes, sir. I understand. I'll steer clear of the holographic deck until granted permission to do so again."

"Don't take it too hard, Lieutenant. You'll be back to shoving wheelchair-bound little old ladies into shark-infested waters again before you know it. Oh, and our little planning meeting is now scheduled for 14:00. Just for your benefit, Lieutenant Porter. Be prompt. Carry on, boys." With that said, the captain headed to the bridge.

The two young pilots stood quietly for a second before Alex finally broke the silence. "Did you get in trouble for the old lady?"

"Naw. Once he heard what that was all about, he said that imagination beats bucking for promotion any day, and kind of dropped it."

"What's that supposed to mean?"

Baseball grimaced and scratched behind an ear. "Dunno exactly, but he said we set the bar pretty high on our wake shifts."

"Oh, think that'll be the end of it?"

"Probably not," said Baseball. "I think he'll drag it out from time to time just to yank our chains with."

"Your chain deserves the harder yank."

"I'm not the one who made her walk the plank."

"Neither did I. She was in a wheelchair," corrected Alex. "Remember?"

"Whatever." Baseball waved his hand, and the two were silent a moment before he blurted, "What the hell happened in there, Alex? They said you were dead, as in dead. You know, not breathing, rigor mortis locking your muscles up, decomposing, gas bloating, stinking the place up, dead! And I gotta tell ya, buddy, from where I was standing an hour ago, it kind of sucked."

Alex started to walk away, saying, "I guess I had a vision, Baseball, a vision that almost killed me."

Baseball caught up and put his hand on Alex's chest. "A vision. Great. That really helps to explain you dying. I need more than that, Alex, and I'm going to get it."

Alex shrugged. "I really don't know much more than that."

"Well, I'm not buying it, Alex. You know more. You had a vision, then you died, and now you're fine. Oh, you know more all right. Why can't you just level with me? Why can't you trust my friendship, my discretion?" Baseball was practically pleading.

Alex sighed through his nose, looked down the hall as if to make sure that they were alone, and said quietly, "Baseball, there's something down on that planet, and that something reached out to me. I was aboard the *Endeavor*, but at the same time, I wasn't. I know how that must sound, but it's the only way to explain it. Anyway, whatever reached out to me wasn't what almost killed me, and, frankly, that part's got me troubled, but I can tell you this: whatever reached out saved my life."

Baseball demanded, "And just what was it that saved you?"

Alex gave his friend a blank look, then turned to walk away.

"Alex! For fuck's sake!" Baseball begged. "What was it that reached out and saved you?"

Alex stopped, but didn't turn around, and when he finally spoke, it was with utmost sincerity, "A fire-breathing dragon—"

So, the boy has moxie, Rodinya thought while flying patrol along the eastern edge of the Spine. *Good, he'll need it if he's to survive the next few months. I don't think he'll forget that episode anytime soon. But how did he end up in a twisted vision like that?* Suddenly a thought came to her with vivid clarity. *Bayne—that little bastard. He must realize that the Earthman is here, and somehow orchestrated that scene.* Another even more harrowing realization struck her: *Bayne's trying to stop the prophecy's progression. How did he know to do this? Unless his abilities are much stronger than I thought.* She snorted in anger. *It's a good thing I was able to insert myself into the boy's subconscious; he might actually have died. If Bayne kills the Earthman, then the prophecy dies with him.*

Her attention was diverted when she spotted a pack of colossal bears ten kilometers away that had a small herd of Montana elk trapped two hundred meters below the ridgeline. They had ripped into the herbivores in a merciless feeding frenzy.

Oh look. How nice of my smelly friends to catch my meals for me. She adjusted her heading and silently glided down toward the unsuspecting bears. Coming in only meters above their heads, the ancient dragon let out a deafening roar. The bears knew this roar well and knew what it meant. It meant death. They scattered for their lives and quickly disappeared into the trees below the ridgeline.

All but one, and he was not about to give up this meal without a fight.

You big ignorant turd, I hope you enjoyed what little you got to eat, because it was your last meal. She banked tightly and made a second pass, incinerated the stubborn bear and cooked the fresh elk meat. Her mouth watered as she landed next to the still-burning bear, kicked it out of the way, and began to consume today's lunch.

While she ate her meal, Rodinya couldn't shake the feeling that for the first time in her long life, events had spun out of her control.

CHAPTER 42

SEAT OF YOUR PANTS
IFC ENDEAVOR—ORBIT DAY 10

At 14:00 hours the planetary survey-planning group met on the bridge to develop the new survey strategy. They gathered around the two main view screens in front of the helm console. Captain Jennings cleared his voice, and all small talk stopped.

"We need to get this show on the road as soon as possible. While we are not necessarily on a critical timeline, time may not be on our side." The captain's eyes bore down on his young pilot. "How are you feeling, Alex? Are you ready to fly?"

Alex gave a small shrug but answered with an upbeat tone. "I feel great, sir. No effects and no reservations. I'm one hundred percent ready to go."

For several uncomfortable seconds, Jennings sat motionless in his command chair as he considered his first pilot. After a moment he said, "Good to hear, Alex, because I need you and your crew at one hundred percent." He shifted his focus over to his security chief. "Gunnar, I need you to level with me. Are you good with continuing to this next phase of the planetary survey?"

Gunnar set his jaw and stared down his captain. "You know I have reservations about those damn mountains, Richard." His eyes then took in the rest of the group. "How do we protect both the survey craft and the *Endeavor* from any external threat? As we are all fully aware, this ship has minimal defensive capabilities. This was never considered a military mission, and whatever weaponry we do have, I strongly suggest we keep on board the *Endeavor*."

"You're recommending we send the OVALs down defenseless?" asked Eaglecreek.

"Yeah, Zonta, I am," Gunnar explained. "I've given it a lot of thought, and I believe that taking armament away from the *Endeavor* is inviting trouble."

Jennings nodded. "So, what you're saying, Gunnar, is that the OVALs will penetrate the planetary atmosphere, but without any weaponry. Is that correct?"

The security chief made sure his opinion was clear. "There just aren't any good options, Richard. But I think it's in our best interest to keep as much firepower as possible on board the *Endeavor*. The shuttles are fast craft with highly maneuverable aeronautics inside an atmosphere. I believe their best defense is their ability to cut and run against any threat. I've gone over both Lieutenant Hartley's and Porter's flight records. They're both highly qualified atmospheric pilots, and can fly the OVALs out of any tight spot they might find themselves in." He paused for effect. "In any given situation."

"Agreed, Gunnar. Does anyone else have an opinion about the ability of the two pilots or feel the need to equip the shuttles with a defensive capability?" Jennings glanced around the bridge. He saw no overt concern, but noticed Lieutenant Malik's tight-lipped expression. "Amil, is there a concern you'd like to share with us?"

The survey chief snapped his head up. "Um, no sir. In fact, I completely concur with Commander Hammär's recommendation that the OVALs remain unarmed."

Gunnar snorted with indifference.

"Why?" Jennings wanted to know.

"Weapons take up space and create weight issues. It would be better to equip the shuttles with survey equipment and any technicians needed to operate and service it. Having a technician on board will eliminate the need to return to the *Endeavor* in the event of some technical glitch."

"Fair enough, Lieutenant. You'll have all the space you need for your equipment. Now, do you have any geographical priorities?"

A frown flitted across Lieutenant Malik's face while his hands twitched at his side. "Uh—why, of course, sir. Since there's only one landmass on which we have observed any semblance of civilization, it would be logical to start at the southern continent."

Commander Eaglecreek rubbed his jaw and questioned the survey chief. "Lieutenant Malik, what makes you think any sign of the *Monarch* would be found where there is a concentration of civilization rather than where there doesn't seem to be any?"

Jennings nodded at his first mate's comment but addressed the survey chief. "It's a valid question, Amil."

Malik cleared his throat. "Sirs, I believe the *Monarch* would have run into the same atmospheric interference as we have and would have also discovered the indigenous vessels clustered around the southern continent. It makes sense to me that they would have educed the same as us about where intelligent life is concentrated. Therefore, I hypothesize that she would have explored the southern continent first, and that their survey team might have left some evidence behind."

"Educed," snickered Baseball as he nudged Alex.

"What's that supposed to mean?" Alex nudged back.

"Dumbass."

"I don't think it means that," replied Alex.

"Lieutenants," rumbled Eaglecreek from across the bridge. "Do either of you two have a question or a contribution?"

Both pilots gave a quick shake of their heads.

"Then shut your airlocks."

Jennings studied his air group for a moment before turning his attention back to the survey chief. "Fair enough, Amil. One more question: Can we take all the survey equipment aboard the OVALs, or do we need to make multiple runs in order to conduct the full analytical sweep?" For the first time Jennings looked over at his chief petty officer, who, along with the survey team, would be in charge of loading and setting up the survey equipment. "Khaki, have you already conferred with Lieutenant Malik about logistical issues and what equipment needs to be loaded?"

CPO Khaki, with his gray crew cut, gray mustache, gray eyes, and deeply lined face, had a habitually nonchalant laid-back demeanor. He looked at the captain, said nothing, glanced over at the survey chief who was trying to remain unnoticeable against the navigation console, frowned, and then turned his gaze back to Jennings. After stretching out the moment to consider his answer, he said in his deep west-Texan drawl, "Yep, Captain. Lieutenant Malik and I have concurred—"

"Conferred," corrected Eaglecreek.

"Right, that too, and we pretty much reckon that all his gear will fit right as rain. A course we gotta use both boats at adverse times—"

"Do you mean reverse times, Chief Petty Officer?" demanded Eaglecreek.

"Mmm, could be," reflected Khaki. "Now where was I? Oh yeah, and a course there's fuel, and crew fatigue concern. Did I say that right, Commander?" He glanced over at the *Endeavor*'s CAG, received a cold stare, and then continued. "Thank you, sir. Anyways, like I was a saying, we kin load all that gear aboard the boats, but the only real unknown is the altitude that they'll need to drop down to before Lieutenant Malik's gear actually starts work'n like it's s'posed to."

Eaglecreek, a little stung by the CPO's complete lack of eloquence, latched onto this latest piece of news. "Just what are you driving at, Khaki?"

The CPO continued as before. "Well now, Commander, here's the way I see it. The lower the OVALs drop in the atmosphere, the thicker the air gits, and the thicker the air gits, the more fuel it takes to keep'm flying, and since we need'm to keep on flying to keep on surveying an' all, then I reckon we need to figure how much fuel they're gonna be burning up. So's they don't crash and bust up all that fancy gear an' all we drug halfway cross the galaxy. Y'all git my meaning?" He gave Eaglecreek an almost imperceptible wink.

In a tight-lipped response, the CAG barely held his temper. "Yes, Khaki, we've got it. Thank you for your colorful discourse."

"My what color, sir?" Khaki grinned from ear to ear.

Before Eaglecreek had a chance to snap back, Jennings stepped in. "SADI, with full fuel tanks, how much time will each survey craft have to do their jobs in the atmosphere? Give me the worst-case scenario."

"With the extra weight of the survey equipment, and the need to be able to enter and exit the planetary gravitational pull, I calculate that time on station within the atmosphere, where, as CPO Khaki pointed out, it will be the densest, each craft will have enough fuel for a flight time of nine point six hours, given that they maintain an average speed of 1,420 kilometers per hour. That's what Lieutenant Malik and I have discussed as the optimum speed for peak equipment efficiency. Naturally, a higher altitude means less fuel consumption, as well as a larger survey footprint on each pass."

"Lieutenants Hartley and Porter, do these flight parameters work for you?" asked the captain.

The two pilots glanced at each other, and by a silent consensus Alex answered for both of them. "Sir, almost ten hours is a long flight time in any atmosphere. Even with the pilots and copilots relieving each other every couple hours or so, there's no real rest until the craft is docked back aboard. Crew fatigue is a genuine concern. Not to mention that we really don't know what the flying conditions are going to be once we're below the cloud cover."

Jennings nodded in acknowledgment and looked thoughtfully at his pilot. "Good points, Alex. Are flight times of four hours apiece doable for you and your crews?"

"Yes, sir, more than doable."

"Good. Ladies and gentlemen," Jennings told the group, "as I stated earlier, we need to start this operation as soon as possible. However, I see no reason to put either flight crew or their OVAL into a situation where fatigue becomes a factor. Let me make this clear: there will not be an incident due to flight-crew fatigue. Understood?"

Jennings then turned his attention to the two large view screens, which presently had the beautiful blue curvature of Aqueous slowly turning below them. The cloud cover of the northern continent was barely visible at the top of the screen. "Zonta, the floor is yours."

Eaglecreek instructed SADI to adjust the view screens. "SADI, please bring up the two continents, and superimpose the topography on each one." Scale images of each continent flickered to life on the screens, complete with colored elevation maps and black contour lines. Eaglecreek turned to the maps and began his presentation.

"As you can see, the southern landmass is roughly half the size of the northern one, and it is almost perfectly round, whereas the northern continent has a more natural egg shape with a few large bays, large mountain ranges, rivers, and a large, two-thousand-kilometer-long peninsula protruding from the main body of land to almost 55° latitude. One curious thing about the continents is that they both have perfectly formed, conical-shaped mountains with small calderas sitting exactly atop their respective poles."

Gunnar grunted loudly.

Commander Eaglecreek paused while his eyes darted between Captain Jennings and Commander Hammär and then went on. "The southern continental coastline is 73° latitude at all points. It does have a few small rivers, but the rest of the terrain is virtually flat except for that conical-shaped mountain that I spoke of a moment ago. The coincidence of two seemingly volcanic mountains sitting exactly atop their respective poles is, to say the least, more than a little puzzling."

Gunnar raised a palm up and took a step forward. "With all due respect, Richard, can we please take a step back and at least discuss Zonta's mountain puzzle? The more we learn about this planet, the more it becomes obvious that we may be walking into a trap."

"All right," Jennings sighed, "I said we'd visit this. So, what are your concerns?"

"Sir, nothing in nature is as perfectly situated as these two polar mountains. Coupled with what we already know about the other unnatural anomalies on this planet, this latest information is more evidence that the threat is genuine." Gunnar's voice had dropped to a growl.

Jennings kept his voice neutral, but his eyes narrowed as he spoke. "In spite of all these anomalies, Gunnar, we've encountered no overt threat so far. As in nothing, and as I've clearly stated we need to get started. The survey mission will begin as planned. You had your chance to bring these concerns up at yesterday's meeting."

"I tried last night." Gunnar's face turned hard as he fumed, "Your decision to blindly continue with the mission without investigating these twin mountains leaves me no choice but to lodge a formal Joint Safe Action declaration regarding our mission directive and present course of action."

Maintaining his composure, Captain Jennings told Gunnar, "Fine, Commander. I'll sign any JSA you deem appropriate, but this briefing moves forward as planned. What I need to know, and know right now: Will this deter you from performing your full duty as security and weapons chief?"

Gunnar's back stiffened as he shook his head. "No, sir! Nothing will affect my duty to fully carry out any orders as directed by my commanding officer!"

Jennings gritted his teeth as his voice dropped a few decibels. "Fine, we'll deal with this later then. In the meantime, if no one else has any objections, let's bring this to a close. Zonta, do you have any further information?"

Eaglecreek replied evenly, "Yes, sir, I do, but I'll wrap it up quickly."

Jennings sat in his command chair and nodded at his navigation chief. "Fine. Wrap it up, and let's take a break."

"Roger that." Eaglecreek turned back to the screens, and, using a laser pointer, he pointed out the optimum points of entry for the survey crafts. "For entry and exit positions on the southern continent, we can pretty much use the position nearest to the *Endeavor*'s orbital position at that particular time. For efficiency's sake I suggest that this should be situated far enough away from the cloud cover in order to determine the cloud ceiling. We can then adjust our altitude accordingly, thus making our feet-dry approach over the landmass well beneath the cloud cover. We don't know the altitude of the cloud ceiling, so we need to make sure we give the OVALs every opportunity to make a gentle descent in case the cloud ceiling is very close to the planet's surface.

"I realize the OVALs are extremely aerodynamic and highly maneuverable, but they will be loaded with far more weight than normal, and if the cloud ceiling is low, I don't want them to have to make too rapid a descent. In no case are they to fly directly into the cloud mass.

"This next bit will be the most demanding for the flight crew—exiting the atmosphere. It's imperative that each crew keep track of its exact coordinates in order to calculate its location relative to the *Endeavor* at any given moment. This is so that the extraction point will place the OVAL in the optimum feet-wet exit trajectory for intercepting and docking with the *Endeavor*.

"This is not going to be a routine atmospheric ascent. You simply can't point the nose up and punch out of the atmosphere. We have to assume, since almost all our most technical instruments are unable to penetrate this cloud clover, that our communication systems won't work either. In other words, kids, once below the cloud cover, you're on your own. Not only can we not track you, we won't even be able to communicate with you."

Alex's brows slightly rose, while Baseball scratched a spot next to his nose.

"Gentlemen, this will be seat-of-your-pants flying, and you will be in pucker-factor mode from the moment you go feet dry. If you stray from the preassigned flight plan, we won't know where you are. Even though the *Endeavor* will have the space distress system engaged at all times, we don't expect any return signatures. We'll be as blind to your position as you are to us. So, in closing, I want to stress the following." Zonta locked his raptor-like gaze onto the two pilots. "Once feet-dry you're on your own, so do not expect any angels, and, for fuck's sake, stick to the flight plan."

The CAG glanced over at his captain and gave him a nod of finality.

Jennings didn't bother getting up from his command chair. He absentmindedly fiddled with a control knob and addressed the survey team without looking up. "Thank you all for your contributions." He then raised his head with a glint of purpose in his eyes. "Folks, I realize that we are in a less than optimum situation, but with careful planning, due diligence, and strict adherence to the set protocols, we can and will get this job done, complete our mission, and get everyone home safely. Is there anything else that needs to be discussed at this time?"

No one even blinked an eye.

"Fine. Dismissed. Carry on."

Gunnar was the first to leave the bridge.

CHAPTER 43

THE ENCOUNTER
CAMBRIA—AQUEOUS

The heel of one shoe was missing, and her light blue dress was torn and splattered with mud, but Lorraine noticed none of that as she limped toward the entrance to the monolithic ten-story Magellan Medical Center. The nurse at the front desk took one look at her mussed red hair and smudged face, and scowled disapproval. "Dr. Lawson is in prep," the nurse answered curtly when the disheveled young woman asked for her sister's whereabouts. When Lorraine hurried off in that direction the nurse called out, "But, Dr. Lawson, I don't think you should go in there right now."

Lorraine paid her no heed and kept walking. Like the nurse said, she found her sister in the scrub room, so she burst through the door. With her own red hair tucked into a surgical cap, Britt wore her greens and an annoyed set to her jaw. She stopped her prep wash and glared at her twin. "Thanks, Lori, you just compromised my scrub." Britt dried off her hands and began the process again. "I hope your good reason for this also explains why you came into a scrub room looking like that?" she snapped.

Lorraine steadied herself against the towel rack. "I just saw Bayne."

Britt froze, the scrub forgotten. "What? Where?"

"I was near the old abandoned warehouse behind the metal depository, and when I walked around a corner of the warehouse he was standing no more than ten meters away."

"What the hell were you doing in that part of town?" Britt put the towel down and folded her arms.

"The orphanage had a runaway, and I had a report that he was seen near the warehouse, so I went down to investigate and try to talk him back. Instead of the boy, I found Bayne."

Britt took her sister's shaking hands in hers. "Did he say anything to you? Do anything?"

Lorraine squeezed her eyes shut as she recalled the encounter. "When I asked, 'How are you, Bayne?' he jerked his head back like I'd slapped him and told me Bayne was dead."

"That's just crazy, what did he mean by that?"

"I have no idea, but then he told me not to come any closer, that he always liked me, and didn't want to see me hurt. Then he wagged his finger as a warning." Her voice broke as she recalled what happened next. "As soon as I stopped, the warehouse wall next to me started to shake, and then it just crashed to the ground no more than two meters away. I stumbled backwards and fell. Had I not stopped when I did, I would have been crushed to death. It barely missed me. When the dust cleared, he was gone." She looked imploringly at her sister and shook her head. "He saved me."

"Or he caused it to happen as a warning to stay away from him," Britt said. "You know his motivations can never be trusted."

"Maybe—"

"Maybe nothing," Britt insisted. "You know what our half-brother's capable of, and now it seems that he has gone mad. Did you find the boy?"

"No. I fled and came straight here."

Britt pursed her lips. "Then Bayne probably has him."

"Why would you say that?"

"Logic," Britt replied, "the boy was last seen exactly where you found Bayne. Do the math. But for what end, I can only guess." She gave her sister a concerned look. "Don't go back there, Lorraine. I feel bad for the boy, but don't do that again."

CHAPTER 44

COFFEE CONFESSIONS
IFC ENDEAVOR—ORBIT: DAY 10

An hour after the planning meeting ended, Jennings again stared at the man in the mirror. He wondered if others dreaded the face staring back at them as much as he had come to dread his own. After a few minutes he tapped the button on his private line to SADI.

"SADI, where is Commander Hammär at the moment?"

"He's sitting in the galley, sir."

"Is he alone?"

"He is, sir; no one has approached him since he left the bridge."

The captain walked into the galley, poured a cup of coffee, and went over to where his security chief sat alone staring at his own cup. Jennings stood directly in front of him. Gunnar didn't look up, didn't acknowledge his presence, and didn't move a muscle. The cup remained the sole object of his attention.

Everyone else who'd been in the galley when the captain walked in suddenly realized they had something else to do and left the two senior officers to their privacy.

Word travels fast in the small confines of a starship.

After about thirty seconds of uncomfortable silence, during which both men remained motionless, Jennings broke the ice. "How's the coffee, Commander?"

"Sucks as usual, Captain." Other than his lips, Gunnar still hadn't moved a muscle.

Jennings sat down across from Hammär and took a sip of his own coffee before attempting to continue. "And the company?"

"Jury's still out—sir."

"You're right, this coffee does suck. Who the hell made it?"

"The galley hand, sir, and I've already tossed him out an airlock for it." A small wrinkle appeared at the corner of Gunnar's eyes, as did an even smaller one at the edge of his mouth. "If the catering budget had been a bit bigger, then we might be able to drink a decent cup of coffee and that galley hand would still be alive to screw something else up, sir."

"If memory serves me correct, Gunnar, you were the requisitions officer." Jennings leaned back in his galley chair and flashed a smug grin.

Looking back down at his coffee cup, Gunnar shrugged. "Guess it just proves, once again, that I always end up crapping in my own coffee—sir."

Jennings pursed his lips and looked straight at his friend. "You've never been known for your tact, Gunnar, even with your commanding officers. Which may explain why you're a terminal dyed-in-the-wool commander and don't have a starship of your own. Oh, and by the way, drop the 'sir' crap."

"Aw hell, Richard, and here all this time I thought it was because the IFC couldn't find a captain's full-dress cap to fit my oversized head." A grim smile found its way to Gunnar's face.

Jennings set his cup down. "Just what the hell happened on the bridge, Gunnar? I have a right to know. Not just because I'm your commanding officer, but also because I'm your best friend." Jennings took a deep breath and tapped the side of his mug. "So, did you write your JSA, that I now need to acknowledge and sign?"

Gunnar nodded and glanced to the side. The captain followed his eyes as they drifted over to the next table. On it sat a galley plate containing recently burned ash. The two men studied the plate for a moment and moved on.

"Richard, you're my only friend, but what happened on the bridge had to be said. If you think you'd come in here and get me to apologize for saying it, then you have another think coming. It had to be said, and I was the only one in that room who could say it."

The mug tapping stopped as Jennings tightened his jaw muscles. "Fair enough, Gunnar, but did you have to shit all over your commanding officer in front of the crew? Friendship or not, we simply don't do that to each other. I sure as hell didn't deserve it, and you sure as hell didn't need to be seen by the other members of the crew as once again being a boorish malcontent."

"I know that, Richard. It just blurted out before I could stop myself, and why I didn't bring it up at last night's meeting."

"What? Are you six years old? You're a goddamn IFC officer, for crying out loud, and the best goddamn weapons officer in the fleet, and I need your goddamn help, not your goddamn undermining of my authority! So now the only question is: what's it going to be, help or hindrance?"

Gunnar sank down in his chair. "Richard, there'll be no more outbursts from me. Either when we're alone or in front of the crew. I'm still your security chief, unless, of course, you fire me, and still your friend even if you do. So, listen up, brother, and chisel this in stone: I'll die supporting you. Mountains or no mountains."

Jennings set his cup down and leaned back in his chair. "It's not going to come to that, Gunnar. We're going to complete this mission and go home in one piece. Together."

Gunnar looked back at his friend with bloodshot eyes, and in a slow but steady tone said, "No, Richard, we're not. The *Endeavor* is going to suffer the same fate as the *Monarch*, and no man or woman aboard this vessel will ever see Earth again."

As if a frozen hand had just gripped the exposed fiber of his soul, Jennings's mouth gaped as he huffed a couple ragged breaths before responding with a hoarse whisper. "Why the hell would you say something like that?"

"Because, Richard, that planet is going to kill us, just like it killed the *Monarch*, and it killed every soul aboard that ship except for one, and that one, I killed." Gunnar stopped short; his eyes began to glisten.

"Oh stop it, Gunnar. You didn't kill her. We don't even know what happened out here, so how the hell can you blame yourself for a death that hasn't even been confirmed? She made that decision herself. This self-flagellation is beneath you, and I won't hear it."

"Really, Richard? Maybe it's time you finally did hear the real truth. Maybe it's time you finally saw the real truth about the man who loved and married your sister and then sent her to her death." The glisten in Gunnar's eyes finally spilled over as a single drop found its way down his cheek.

"I loved her too, Gunnar. She was—is—my kid sister. But I'll never accept this self-obsessed guilt of yours."

But Gunnar's confession had just begun. "Do you know what actually happened, Richard? Do you? I don't think you do. So, give me a minute, and I'll explain it all. Then all your fraternal feelings, all our bonds of friendship, are going to be put to a real test. Then we'll see if you can still continue to profess my innocence."

Jennings waved a hand for Gunnar to stop.

Gunnar ignored his friend's silent plea and continued. "The day Patti found out that she'd been chosen as a pilot for the *Monarch*, she came home to me and expressed her steadfast reservations against it. She wasn't at all keen on being away from me for the nine years that this mission required, and, as you well know, I wasn't even being considered for this mission due to that lack of tact you mentioned earlier.

"Her resolve to turn down that position was absolute, and she couldn't wait to tell me. Except that I wasn't hearing any of it. I couldn't believe that anyone, even my wife—oh hell, especially my wife—could turn down a mission like that, an opportunity that would never come again."

Jennings just sat and stared at the tabletop.

Gunnar took a deep breath, gripped his coffee mug almost to the point of crushing it, and finished his confession. "I told her to go, Richard. She didn't want to, but I made her. You know she could never deny me anything, not when I really set my mind to something, and I was relentless with this. We had a big fight that night, and I slept on the couch. The next morning, she came in, sat next to me, and reluctantly agreed to go."

Jennings finally found his voice. "Gunnar, look—"

"I'm not done yet, Richard. You need to let me finish. *I* need you to let me finish. When she agreed to go, I was elated. It was almost like redemption for me, and my many career failures. But it was never about her, Richard; it was about me. I continually talked the mission up and continually praised her decision, but she was never enthusiastic about it." He looked at his captain with swollen red eyes. "Remember how she looked when we all said our goodbyes at Port Apollo? I'll never forget those accusing eyes. Ironically, it was the same bay where you and I embarked on this mission, the mission to go find her.

"I never saw her again, Richard. No one has ever seen her again." Gunnar stopped momentarily and heaved in another deep breath before he gathered enough courage to continue. "I sent her to her death, because I know in the deepest reaches of my worn-out soul that this planet took her. Just like I know it's going to take me. Frankly, as far as I'm concerned, that's justice. But what's not justice, what I cannot, will not reconcile, is that it's going to take every other member of this crew as well. I know it with absolute certainty. All those seemingly inactive, benign defense mechanisms will lure us in and kill us, just like they killed the *Monarch*."

"We don't know that, Gunnar." Jennings tried to stand up, tried to leave this conversation, leave this torment, but Gunnar reached across the table, grabbed his friend by the forearm, and, with a powerful vise-like grip, forced Jennings back into his seat. Jennings seemed to not even notice, and, like a limp doll, just let it happen.

"Richard, only one man on this ship deserves the fate that's waiting for him on this planet, and right now you're having a shitty cup of coffee with him." Gunnar looked at his coffee and made a face. "I'm sorry. I know you must think I've gone crazy as a shithouse rat, but my fate was sealed the moment we made orbit around this planet.

"That's why I acted like an asshole on the bridge. That goddamn planet scares the hell out of me. But, honestly, it's not me I'm really worried about. For what it's worth, it's this ship, this crew, and my only friend in the galaxy that I'm scared for." He stopped for a moment before going on. "I just thought you needed to know."

CHAPTER 45

RULES OF ENGAGEMENT
IFC ENDEAVOR—ORBIT DAY 11

The next morning both flight crews, the survey team, and CPO Khaki were in the thirty-meter-wide shuttle bay preparing for the first survey mission. Aside from the two OVALs, the bay held an array of maintenance equipment and, for this mission, the onboard survey devices and their external sensors. Even though the hangar deck was large, it seemed cramped with all the survey gear and extra personnel. Crew members stumbled over each other as they loaded the shuttles, tied in power supplies, and connected data feeds.

Lieutenant Malik was here, there, and everywhere, dictating every facet of the setup operation and generally getting under everyone's skin. So much so that Khaki confided to Baseball that he reckoned the survey chief was fast becoming a prime candidate for the first human to freefall through the planet's sinister cloud cover. "Just to test the atmospheric terminal velocity, you understand, and a course, see what falls out the other side." With a mischievous glint in his eye, Khaki flashed a broken-toothed grin at Baseball and then left to go inspect the power feeds.

Baseball glanced at Khaki and noticed him looking back at him. Khaki lost the grin as he turned around to vent at the surveyors, shouting some almost unintelligible orders at one of their crew about how to secure some power cables to the docking rails. "Jest keep the dang thang from dangl'n, you turd bird, or it's gonna git pinched, short out, and then it'll be your dick in the dirt!"

The survey technician muttered under his breath and then left to get more tie-downs.

"Some of these here survey boys act about nine kinds of stupid sometimes. It gits right vexing, it does," said the CPO as he made his way back over to Baseball.

"Speaking of acts, Khaki," observed Baseball, "why do you talk to almost everyone like a hillbilly when you and I both know you're anything but?"

The grin returned to Khaki's face, and he glanced around to see if anybody was in hearing distance. "Because, Baseball, most of the people I have to talk to are officers, and if officers don't think you're smart enough to do a job, they'll find someone else to do it."

"You *do* realize that I'm an officer."

With a look of mock surprise, Khaki told his new confidant, "Baseball, everybody on this ship knows that you and your buddy Alex aren't total assholes."

"So, Alex knows about you too?"

"Of course he does. He's known since before we left Mars. And here all this time I thought you were the smart one," chuckled Khaki. He then turned and yelled some roughneck profanity and marched off to take a chunk out of some poor ensign's ass.

Before the initial sortie, the command group met with the flight crew who were going to make the first penetration into Aqueous's atmosphere and begin the planetary survey.

Captain Jennings approached the three who were standing at ease next to their OVAL. The flight crew was dressed in standard form-fitting flight suits with their helmets under their right arms and their eyes locked forward.

The captain first approached the only survey member of the crew. "Lieutenant Malik, I'd like to commend your decision to be the first of your survey crew to make a flight into what could possibly be hostile airspace. Are you confident that all your equipment is up to scratch and ready to go?"

"Yes, sir, everything is in optimum condition and will do its job, sir. And thank you, sir. I felt it my duty to be the first surveyor, sir." The lieutenant couldn't keep the pride out of his voice.

"Nevertheless, Amil, it was an admirable decision. Good luck, Lieutenant." Malik snapped out a rigid, parade ground salute.

The captain proceeded to his flight crew and appraised them and their craft.

"Alex, it looks as if everything is in order. I know both you and Raj have been thoroughly briefed umpteen times, but Gunnar has a few words of wisdom to pass on to you before you depart. Please extend him the courtesy of remaining awake while he has his say."

"Yes, sir."

"Bravo Zulu, gentlemen."

Gunnar strode up to the flight crew with less formality than the captain. His permanent scowl seemed slightly less threatening than usual, but that didn't fool anyone. Lieutenant Malik looked like a gazelle ready to bolt from a watering hole. "Relax, gentlemen. I just need a word with you about a couple of things. Malik, you can go find a hole to crawl into if you want."

The surveyor's eyes darted around the room, but couldn't find a hole, so he stayed put.

The big security chief locked on Alex and spoke as if they were the only two people on the flight deck. "Lieutenant Porter, other than flying Malik's gear around the planet's surface, you're going to be responsible for bringing your craft and crew back to the *Endeavor* in one piece."

"Yes, s—"

"Don't interrupt, Alex." It was the first time the commander had ever called him anything other than Lieutenant or some other less flattering term. If Alex noticed, he showed no sign of it. "Since this craft is going into possible hostile airspace without much more than a slingshot, you need to be extra vigilant. I want you to be half rabbit and half hawk. Keep your eyes sharp and run like hell if anything even looks hostile. Are we clear?"

"Yes, sir. Absolutely, sir."

"Good. I've seen to it that you've been given three pulse rifles and enough ordnance to basically piss off an opponent of any strength but not much else. These small arms, if for some catastrophic reason you have to put down somewhere on the planet's surface, are to be used only to fight your way out. Are you still with me, Alex?"

"I am, sir, but do you know something I should be aware of?"

"No, Alex, I'm just trying to give you the tools you might need to survive in case of a shitstorm. None of us knows what you're going to find once you're under those damn clouds, and, in my experience, it's better to be prepared for a shitstorm than a sunny day."

"I understand, sir."

"In that case listen up and listen good, Lieutenant. Like I said, I'm giving you three pulse rifles. Keep the settings on low. The lower the settings, the more shots you have. You may not need to kill anything, but a low setting will still ruin someone's day, which may be enough to give you and your team time to extract. Again, do I make myself clear?"

"It's starting to sink in, Commander."

"That's good, Alex, real good. By the way, from now on it's Gunnar. We're now on the same team and the same page. You get my drift, soldier?" Gunnar's voice softened a little.

"I do, Gunnar."

"Good. Oh, and by the way, don't give Malik a pulse rifle. He'll just waste ordnance shooting his foot. I need men down there who can handle themselves in a fight, not ones who crap their pants every time they speak to superior officers. We're on the same page here as well, aren't we, Alex?" Gunnar grinned, but then hardened his voice again for his last set of instructions. "Did you happen to bring that pig sticker of yours?"

"No, sir! I did, however, bring my katana."

Gunnar narrowed his eyes ever so slightly at the young pilot. "Good. Keep it handy, soldier. I mean it. You never know."

Instead of the traditional step back and salute, Gunnar simply placed his big hand on Alex's shoulder, leaned close so that no one could hear, and told him, "There's no other man I would trust to get his team back in one piece, Alex—except of course, me. Kick ass and take names, Lieutenant." Commander Hammär stepped back and stood next to his captain.

The last member of the command team, Lieutenant Commander Zonta Eaglecreek, stepped up to Alex and briefly reiterated his final instructions. "Lieutenant, if something happens while feet dry, and you know you can't keep the boat in the air, then point her nose towards the coast, get as much altitude as possible, then dead stick it as long as you can before punching out." His raptor gaze had lost none of its intensity. "Keep your crew together if possible, but you only have one option." The CAG broke his gaze from Alex and took in all three of the flight crew. "You all have only one option—head to the coast. If the *Endeavor* hasn't heard from you by the time you should have reported in from a feet-wet position, we'll know you're in the shit. All we can do at that point is wait for a signal, and that signal can only come if you're out to sea. Commandeer a boat. Use any means, I repeat, any means necessary to get a boat, put to sea, get away from the landmass, and out from under the cloud cover. This is the only way to get a signal out. Is that fully understood, Lieutenant?"

"Yes, sir. Punch out, head to the nearest coastline, commandeer a boat by whatever means available, get out from under the cloud cover, and hope like hell you can pick up my transmission. Yes, sir, I fully comprehend, sir."

For a moment it seemed to Alex that the CAG's raptor gaze softened a little, but a second later he resumed his predator-like bearing. "See that you do, Lieutenant Porter. That is all. Mount up, gentlemen, and good hunting."

CHAPTER 46

STINKING MESS
IFC ENDEAVOR—ORBIT DAY 11

O nce the flight crew had climbed into the tight confines of the OVAL cabin and settled into their respective positions, Malik remarked, "That seemed a bit over the top, didn't it?"

Raj rolled his eyes and tapped his intercom. "You might have a different opinion if we have to take their advice. I, for one, hope like hell you paid attention in there because it might just save your ass and mine."

Alex interrupted them to begin his preflight checklist. "Raj, if you two are finished measuring your dicks, initiate the tie-in integration programs with SADI and coordinate the launch sequence. As soon as the flight deck is clear and battened down, relay our presets for launch, and let's get this show on the road."

Alex's copilot was young but capable and would follow Alex to the ends of the galaxy and beyond. He punched in the tie-in codes that integrated everything aboard the OVAL with the *Endeavor*'s AI system.

Raj tapped his link with SADI to confirm. "The flight deck is green on this end."

SADI's response was almost instantaneous. "The *Endeavor* bulk-head is green as well, gentlemen. We have a go. I'm depressurizing the flight deck now. Once complete, the bay doors will be opened. Please stand by."

The docking station had two overlapping bay doors, an inner and an outer door, as redundant sealing systems in the event of a pressure leak in either one.

The inner bay doors began to open, splitting vertically. Once again SADI's voice sounded inside the OVAL. "Inner bay door open. Preparing the outer door."

The outer door split horizontally, exposing the dark nothingness of space.

This time Alex communicated with SADI. "We've got a go here, SADI. Extend the docking rails."

"Initiating cantilever docking rails," SADI reported, "and releasing control lines."

All launches and landings aboard the *Endeavor* were conducted by two large, telescoping rails that held the nine-meter-wide OVAL inside the flight deck. The control lines fed new program instructions into the OVAL computers and downloaded all flight records from their data bank. SADI could not be aboard the small ship. The two craft could completely interface while connected with the umbilical control line, but SADI could not be separated from herself. Her operating base was strictly the *Endeavor*.

While the OVAL pilots had an onboard computer assisting their fly-by-wire control, the computer was not an AI system, and, for all practical purposes, especially in this coming set of sorties, they were flying by the seat of their pants.

The docking rails slowly ferried the sleek fourteen-meter-long craft outside the hangar deck where it floated free of the rails the instant the docking dogs were released and zero gravity took over. The three crew members were held in place by their flight harnesses.

Raj toggled his mic and said to the survey chief, "Malik, if you feel the need to puke, put your helmet on first, so it doesn't get all over the place in zero g."

Lieutenant Malik frowned in disgust.

Alex keyed his mic and said over his shoulder, "Just use an airsick bag, Amil. They're in the left-hand pocket of your g-seat." He frowned over at Raj and added, "I seem to recall some skinny little dude puking his guts out the first time he went zero g. In fact, if memory serves me correctly, he spewed up far more mass than was physically possible for someone his size. He then spent the next two days with a scrub brush in his hand and the CAG's boot up his ass. Do you recall anything like that, Raj?"

Raj's innocent shrug failed miserably. "Nope, don't think I recall that incident." Raj then initiated the craft's fusion drive engines that would propel them for the next four hours. "The fusion drive is online and ready for engagement, sir."

Alex took control of the yoke as Raj gently applied the overhead throttle control. The shuttle leapt forward under her own power for the first time. While Alex steered them toward their prearranged entry coordinates, he instructed Raj about their velocity requirements. "Give us Mach ten until we see how bumpy this thermosphere is going to get. I'll control the yaw damper and keep an eye on the altitude direction indicator. If the pitch and roll are livable, then stand by and adjust the throttle as per my command."

From the backseat came a panicked squeak. "What do you mean by 'livable'?"

The two pilots exchanged knowing glances. Raj's eyes crinkled as he explained. "He means that *if* we don't burn up on entry into the atmosphere, I can kick this baby in the ass. But don't worry, Lieutenant. *If* we do burn up, it happens pretty fast. You shouldn't feel a thing after the first four or five minutes or so. Before you turn too crispy to scream, that is. Say, you're looking kind of pasty pale back there, LT. Better keep that helmet handy."

Lieutenant Malik closed his eyes and scrunched down as much as his harness would allow.

A self-satisfied grin split Raj's face as he turned back to the control panel and began reducing the shuttle's speed as they approached the upper atmosphere.

The OVAL had delta wing avionics that were fully retracted while docked and during atmospheric entry. Less surface area meant less friction. Less friction meant less heat, and less heat meant that Malik just might survive the drop. Raj kept that glimmer of information to himself.

When they hit the upper reaches of the thermosphere, the craft encountered severe turbulence and the drop turned into a bruising bump fest for the crew. Alex and Raj tightened their harnesses, but their passenger was in an almost debilitating state of panic and just grabbed the edges of his seat.

In spite of the turbulence, Alex kept their descent at a consistent 42° while Raj monitored the external sensors. "How's our drop parameters looking, Raj?"

"Holding steady at Mach eight, Alex, and we've reached 1600° and still climbing. Hey LT, just in case you're taking notes back there, that's enough to melt steel."

"What are all those sparks?" spluttered Malik. His eyes were glued to the windscreen. "Are we burning up?"

Alex answered before Raj had a chance. "No, Amil, that's just superheated plasma from our pressure wave." Raj frowned and took his hand off his toggle. "It happens every drop."

A violent impact suddenly rocked the small craft, causing an instant shift in the yaw just as gravity returned. "Wh-what was that?" screeched Malik.

"Don't," ordered Alex just as Raj was about to tap his intercom again. He tapped his own instead. "We just hit an eddy at the top of a jet stream, Amil. Hang on a few more seconds. We're almost through." At that moment they hit smooth air and two minutes later were racing through the atmosphere at an altitude of less than one thousand meters above sea level.

Both pilots wrinkled their noses at the same time and turned around to see their passenger holding an upturned helmet in his lap, with globs of bile that had floated out while they were still in zero g staining both his flight suit and seat. Alex just glared at Raj and turned back to the windscreen. "That damn well better clean up, or someone sitting on my right is going to lick that crap up and like it."

In an octave higher than normal, Raj declared, "He's a first lieutenant and the survey crew chief, for crying out loud. How was I to know he's also an imbecile?"

"From where I'm sitting, I don't see much difference. You better hope to hell that whatever he had for breakfast this morning is compatible with your delicate stomach. Now get back there and show him where to get some water and towels, and get that stinking mess cleaned up and stowed away!"

Raj crawled into the back and guided the still-pallid-looking Malik back to the tiny head.

Alex yelled over his shoulder, "And don't take all day. I need a navigator, and I need him soon!"

"Right away, sir," came the chastened answer.

Alex hit the ship-to-ship communication toggle harder than he meant to, and made his initial atmospheric call-in. "*Endeavor, OVAL Porter.* Come in, *Endeavor.*"

The response was almost immediate. It was the voice of Captain Jennings. "*OVAL Porter, Endeavor.* How was your drop, *OP*?"

If Alex was surprised to hear the captain's voice instead of his CAG's, he didn't let on. "The drop went fine, sir. Although it seems that our passenger should ease up on the biscuits and gravy before his next drop, sir."

"Roger that, *OP*. Although I believe Commander Hammär will be shocked to hear about this. We've got your feet wet at 71.67° on the screen, and your heading is dead on. At this rate you'll be feet dry in twelve minutes. Do you see anything out of the ordinary?"

Alex's voice was even as he answered, "Nothing but water and air so far, sir. However, I can see a dark thin smear on the distant horizon."

"Roger that, *OP*. Give us a heads up before you go feet dry, and let us know what the cloud ceiling is. *Endeavor* out."

"Roger that, sir. Will do. *OP* out."

CHAPTER 47

BY THE SEAT OF HIS PANTS
OVAL PORTER—ORBIT DAY 11

Alex set his cruising speed at the survey optimum of Mach one point one as they approached the coast. The closer they got to land, the more of those wooden vessels they saw, and the thin dark smear became progressively thicker. Raj had returned to his seat after helping Malik clean up and stow the smelly towels in the survey equipment locker.

After getting strapped back in, Raj shot a wary glance over at his pilot, and then reported, "We're fifty-two kilometers from feet dry. The instruments still aren't picking up any solid readings about the cloud ceiling, sir."

"Drop the 'sir' crap, Raj, and talk normal." Alex was back to his old self and didn't want any pilot-to-pilot stress.

"Yes, sir. I mean, okay, Alex."

Alex kept his eyes on the thick, dark cloud that quickly approached. He tapped his mic and asked the survey chief, "Amil, have you got all your equipment fired up and ready to start your voodoo dance? We'll be feet dry in about two minutes, and I want to start surveying the moment we pass over the first rocks. Is that a roger?"

The distracted voice that answered was more of a rambling mumble. "Yeah, Alex. I'm getting the final calibrations for this atmospheric density. I'm actually ready now, but I want everything perfect when we engage the instruments."

"Good to hear, Amil. I'll rattle your cage right before you need to fire up." Alex's personal radar was also on high alert, and his eyes constantly shifted from his instruments to the windscreen, and then back to the instruments in a constant cycle. His optic computer gave him an over-the-horizon view of the fast-approaching coastline, but so far nothing seemed threatening.

At ten kilometers, Raj excitedly pointed out the windscreen. "Alex, that cloud ceiling is almost exactly a thousand meters in altitude. It looks constant, and it's clear sailing below that elevation."

Alex toggled the ship-to-ship communication mic to relay his status. "*Endeavor, OP.* Come in, *Endeavor.*"

Once again Captain Jennings's voice answered back, "*OP, Endeavor.* You're coming in scratchy, *OP.* What have you got, Alex?"

"Sir, we're about ten seconds from feet dry and have determined the cloud ceiling. It's 1,007 meters, sir. Repeat, cloud ceiling is 1,007 meters. Do you copy, *Endeavor?*"

"Roger that, *OP.* We read you as ha—"

At that moment *OVAL Porter* passed under the cloud cover, and all communication between the shuttle and the starship went dead. No further attempts by either crew were successful in reacquiring comms.

Alex turned and told his small crew, "Gentlemen, we're now completely autonomous, and we'll stick to the survey grid as per the flight plan. Raj, I need you to keep your head down and your ass up. I want constant coordinate calculations. Let me know if anything changes as per the flight plan. Got it?"

"Roger that, Alex, I'll keep us on the straight and narrow." Raj had his head down with a handheld calculator, and his optic computer was imaging the holographic flight grid.

Alex turned to Malik. "Amil, are we in business?"

"Roger that, Alex. We've been on the payroll for the past sixty-five seconds," reported Malik, "and everything is switched on and working perfectly. We're finally getting all the data we couldn't get from the *Endeavor*. Of course, from an altitude of a thousand meters, our survey footprint is very small."

"Meaning?"

"Meaning that you're going to rack up a lot of air hours," Malik replied stoically, as he turned his attention back to his instruments.

OVAL Porter continued to fly over the southern continent at an altitude of 890 meters, or 117 meters below the well-defined and curiously consistent cloud ceiling. The two pilots could clearly see the ground from this altitude, and once Alex engaged the ground enhancement sensor on his optical computer, he saw details not possible with the naked eye. Almost as soon as the *OP* became feet dry, it became obvious that not only was there a race of intelligent reptiles living on the southern continent, but there was a huge civilization of them. Many times, individuals looked up at them and pointed. Some were armed with spears, and some with bows and arrows. There was no concern about being observed from the ground or of any reaction to the sonic boom by the indigenous species. These were not going to be clandestine flights, and if the locals actually reacted to hearing them, the threat was considered nonexistent.

They could easily make out a crude road network connecting the largest of the cities and the few major ports of this lizard civilization. It also became obvious that the technological level of this species was much lower than they had originally calculated when the first seagoing vessels were spotted from the *Endeavor*. It was apparent that these crude boats were the pinnacle of their technology.

The dark underbelly of the cloud allowed most of the sunshine to filter through, and the continent was not abnormally dark. Enough light made the ground visible, but only the fact that they were flying so low enabled the crew to make visual observations of details with their naked eyes. Several times they flew through rainsqualls, and even a couple of storms, complete with strong barometric fluctuations, lightning, wind, and, in a few cases, almost zero visibility. But at no time did the elevation of the strange cloud ceiling change, even when they encountered increased wind speeds.

When Alex asked Malik about these unusual climatic phenomena, all he got in response from the survey chief was a mumble, a shake of the head, and a shoulder shrug.

At no time did they get a visual on the strange conical mountain sitting directly atop the southern polar axis. Their flight plan didn't put them close enough.

Within seconds of its flight schedule and less than a meter off its flight plan, *OVAL Porter* went feet wet with clear sky above them, and Alex made the first contact they'd had with the *Endeavor* since she had lost comms hours earlier.

Alex hit the ship-to-ship toggle, and as soon as he keyed the mic, he heard the voice of Captain Jennings. He was almost shrill. "*OP, Endeavor!* Where are you? Oh wait, we can see you now. You're spot on where you should be, and—" The communication went dead again, and after several moments of silence passed, Alex flipped the toggle on and off several times. Jennings's upbeat voice suddenly came back on amid a lot of background chatter. "Sorry, *OP*, I couldn't hear anything for all the cheering that's going on in here."

"Cheering, sir?"

"Yes, Lieutenant, cheering." The captain's voice had lost all its previous stress. "I'll tell you all about it when we shake hands on the flight deck. How did it go, Alex?"

"Boring, sir. Although I believe Lieutenant Malik's got a plate full of tasty data for SADI to chew on."

Amid all the noise came the unmistakable gravelly voice of Gunnar Hammär. "Get your skinny ass back to this ship, Lieutenant. There's not a swinging dick—um—person on this boat who doesn't want to see you three clowns! Yeah, and that means you too, Amil. *Endeavor* out."

CHAPTER 48

FIRST DATA
IFC ENDEAVOR—ORBIT DAY 13

The moment *OVAL Porter* touched down on the extended cantilever rails, the docking dogs clanked into place and the control lines reconnected. Gravity returned to the shuttle once it was back in the bay, and as soon as the bay doors shut, the flight deck pressurized. Raj looked through the windscreen, grinned at the crowd in the launch ready room, grinned over at Alex, glanced back at Malik, and the grin faded. He turned back to Alex and observed, "Judging by the reception committee, it looks like we're heroes, boss."

"Well, I know one hero who's going to finish cleaning puke off my boat before standing down. Catch my drift, Raj?"

"Yes, sir," moaned Raj, "I'll get it done right after the After Action Review."

"Good thinking, Raj," Alex told him as he unbuckled his flight harness and stretched. He turned to the survey chief. "Okay, Amil, I believe there's a lot more folk waiting for you than there are for me. Shall we go in and not disappoint them?" Alex gathered up his personal effects but left the katana on board.

The same group who had been there to send them off hours earlier met them on the flight deck. This time all the preflight stress was gone.

"*OVAL Porter* survey team reporting for debriefing, sir," announced Alex as soon as he stepped out of the shuttle.

Captain Jennings walked over, shook Alex's hand, and held onto it. He leaned forward and said quietly, "Alex, you have no idea the amount of hair pulling and gnashing of teeth that's been going on up here since you disappeared under that blasted cloud cover. Frankly, no one knew what you'd find under there, or, more to the point, what would find you." He let go of Alex's hand and motioned him toward the other two senior officers.

Wearing an unreadable visage, the CAG waited for Alex to come to him, and with his usual unsmiling, no-nonsense voice, commented, "I don't see what all the fuss is about, Lieutenant. That's a boat, you're a pilot, and you flew a sortie that was already planned out for you. All you had to do was follow a flight plan and not break my boat. You didn't break my boat, did you, Lieutenant?" His eyes narrowed at his pilot.

"Not that I'm aware of, Commander Eaglecreek. However, there is a small matter of previously eaten stomach contents that a certain copilot will be cleaning up right after the AAR."

"You mean to tell me that one of my copilots couldn't hold his lunch in the air?" demanded the CAG irritably.

"No, sir, the contents of the stomach in question were not his, although he was partly responsible for their making an appearance."

Standing nearby, Gunnar turned and grunted, "I knew that pencil pusher would puke on his boots the moment he hit a little rough water. That about right, Porter?"

"Almost, sir. He puked in his helmet." All three senior officers just grimaced.

Gunnar wasn't quite finished. "Good thing you didn't have to EVA, or our survey chief might have drowned in his own puke, and

I, for one, wouldn't want to be the poor bastard to write *that* incident report." Even though his voice was gruff as ever, his eyes twinkled.

Jennings cleared his throat and asked, "Alex, what did you see down there? I realize that SADI has probably already downloaded all the survey data, but what are your impressions? We can talk while we head to the AAR ready room."

Alex frowned slightly. "Sir, the landmass is teeming with inhabitants. They're that same reptilian species that we've observed on the sailing ships. There seems to be multiple millions of them, probably hundreds of millions of them. We overflew massive cities, crude road networks, and a large working port. Keep in mind, sir, that we only saw one survey grid."

"What else, Lieutenant?"

"Just that, sir. I'll make some notes after the meeting."

They reached the After Action Review ready room and filed in to hear both the pilot's report and, hopefully, some useful data garnered from the survey equipment. In attendance were the crew of *OVAL Porter*, Baseball and Rox, Malik, and his entire survey crew. Captain Jennings, Commander Hammär, and the CAG were the top officers. Also present was the ship's doctor, Bogdan Prata, who also doubled as the science officer.

Once all the seats around the rectangular conference table were filled with the primary AAR attendees, the rest leaned against the wall, and the big video screen at the far end of the room was switched on. Captain Jennings stood up and made the opening remarks. "The initial review will be on the screens. After that you can follow along on your OC, but let's get this thing started."

The screens flickered to life, and a view of the OVAL's drop was replayed.

"First of all, I'd like to congratulate the survey team for an exemplary job well done," he said enthusiastically. "That they did so in an unknown and potentially hostile environment speaks highly of their professionalism. Apparently, they paid a little attention during preflight." Some of the attendees chuckled while Alex just grinned into his knuckles.

Like everything else that had happened since their arrival back aboard the *Endeavor*, this too was highly unusual, because an AAR was normally a no-nonsense, get-to-the-facts-with-little-fanfare meeting. Normally only the flight crew, CAG, and possibly one or two other operation officers whose interests were included in the flight attended.

This time it was standing room only.

Jennings continued once the room went silent again. "This first flight has set the bar high, and all future survey flights will use this as a precedent. I realize that the elevation of the cloud ceiling will keep the survey footprint to a minimum, and that this will mean more flights than we had originally envisioned. Therefore, we will alter our mission durations to six hours per flight, but we will also increase the downtime after each craft has flown two sorties. These new shutdown periods will be twelve hours. Even though the flying conditions on this first mission were less than feared, we still don't know what the future holds. Therefore, all previous rules of engagement remain in place. I now hand over the briefing to Lieutenant Malik, who made this initial survey run and got his equipment to work as intended." The captain stepped back from the podium and gestured to the survey chief. "Lieutenant Malik, if you please. The floor is yours."

The timidity that the survey chief had previously displayed while speaking to superior officers had disappeared. Although his body language indicated a little discomfort at the podium, Malik's eyes were confident. "Thank you, Captain Jennings. Welcome everyone to this initial After Action Review. As the captain indicated, all the survey equipment worked perfectly. As anticipated, all the instrument distortions previously experienced were totally absent once we were below the clouds.

"SADI has successfully downloaded all the data. However, it will be some time before a clear picture emerges. I will, for the most part, remain aboard the *Endeavor* and work closely with SADI to aid in the interpretation of that data. The other members of my survey crew are perfectly qualified to accompany the flight crews on their sorties to the planet's surface."

Gunnar's low rumble briefly interrupted the lieutenant. "Will they be puking in their helmets too?" Several of the attendees groaned. Jennings went tight-lipped as his eyes bored into his security chief.

Lieutenant Malik turned bright red before continuing. "Since it will take some time to interpret and present the survey results, I'll now give you my impressions gained from monitoring the survey equipment during this initial flight. I couldn't see all the data, but much of it was apparent to me." He turned to the video screen and addressed the AI computer.

"If everyone will please engage their optic computers, we'll reconstruct this initial survey grid. SADI, please bring up the survey map that we made on this initial run."

"Yes, sir. Coming on visual now."

A map of the southern continent appeared on everyone's OC. Most of the map was obscured colorations with no definition. However, a very detailed strip of the survey footprint appeared as a hockey stick shape, moving from one edge of the landmass until it reached a point on the far side, made a sweeping 45° turn, and then continued in a straight line until it reached the far edge of the coastline where the OVAL had left the continent and returned to the *Endeavor*.

"Thank you, SADI. As you can see, the survey footprint is very well defined. We now have data on almost every scientific subject matter within the survey footprint. This includes biological, geological, elemental, and environmental. We even have interpretation programs for species social and interspecies interactions. From each of these analytical disciplines, we'll be able to interpret much of their historical evolution.

"Let me reiterate, most of the data is still being processed, and will be available later. If you give me your priority criteria, then we will have this data analyzed first and present it at the earliest opportunity."

Captain Jennings interrupted. "Lieutenant Malik, our mission directive dictates that we find the *Monarch* and her crew as soon as possible. Therefore, whatever data you have that would aid us with that objective *is* the absolute top priority."

Lieutenant Malik stood thoughtfully for a moment before addressing the captain's comment. "Yes, sir. Then I believe what we want to see first is any evidence of either the ship or the crew." Both Jennings and Hammär nodded. "That being the case, we will need to focus on any biological readings that indicate human DNA. We also need to concentrate on any metallic components that have the same combination of alloys and synthetic coatings used in the construction of the ship's outer hull."

Jennings broke in. "The *Monarch* and the *Endeavor* are sister ships, Lieutenant. They were built about the same time using the same design and, most important of all for our mission, they used the same materials in construction. They are, in effect, identical."

The survey chief nodded. "Actually, this simplifies our job considerably, as does one other strange piece of data that became clearly evident to me during the survey run, and I believe further analysis will bear me out.

From what I could see, and from what little of the planet's surface we were able to definitively analyze, I saw zero evidence of any type of ore needed to create metal of any kind. None at all, sir." Malik paused when Jennings held up a hand.

"Please elaborate, Lieutenant."

"Sir, we barely surveyed a fraction of the continent's surface, but on this initial survey grid, there was nothing. The surface geology is devoid of ore. In fact, I was able to compile a table based on the elements that appeared within our survey footprint."

Jennings brought SADI into the discussion. "SADI, what can you tell us to corroborate Lieutenant Malik's report?"

"Sir, as we already know, on mission day 1885 the LRS found one thousand seemingly derelict satellites orbiting Aqueous at an altitude of 12,930 kilometers, well above our present orbit. These satellites are constructed out of highly advanced metal alloys unlike anything we've ever encountered. Based on the survey results, the ores required for their construction don't exist on Aqueous."

"At least not in the survey grid," Malik pointed out.

Commander Hammär's eyes darted back and forth between Malik and his captain. Finally he jumped up and looked around the room, then blurted, "In case any of you might have missed the main point about these 'derelict satellites,' let me sum it up. They weren't built by lizards who aren't even in the Bronze Age yet, nor were they built on Aqueous." He looked directly at his captain as he continued. "They were built by some as-yet-unknown race as a planetary defense system, and, although they are presently dormant, they sure as hell weren't dormant when we entered this solar system." He maintained eye contact with Jennings. "Their very presence, along with the unnatural cloud cover obstructing our most sophisticated survey technology, dictates that this damn planet is under some form of protection. Protection that we, and probably the *Monarch* as well, have stumbled into." His eyes never left the captain's until he finished and sat back down.

From his seat Gunnar raised another issue. "Anyway, Lieutenant, what does the absence of metallic ores on the surface of the planet have to do with our search for the *Monarch* and her crew?"

For the first time ever, Malik looked the surly security chief straight in the eye and said, "Because, Commander, since the *Monarch* is made almost entirely out of one alloy combination or another, and since we've so far found zero evidence of metal on the planet's surface, then any we do find will stand out like a beacon in the dark. The absence of metal ores could quite possibly lead us directly to the *Monarch*. Instead of looking for a needle in a haystack, we'll be looking for a shiny chrome dagger on a flat black surface."

Gunnar softened his gaze. "I apologize, Lieutenant Malik. The logic of your position is, of course, infallible. Thanks for explaining it to me."

"There's one other, rather unusual item that we might need to explore more thoroughly," continued Malik as he brought up a close-up image of one of the cities they flew over. "What I'm about to show you in this one city is a phenomenon that the instruments found in each large urban area we overflew. Unseeable to the naked eye, but evident to the interferometer scanner, is a labyrinth of horizontal underground tunnels beneath each city." Malik pointed to the weblike lines that spread out from a central point. "These lines are shallow tunnels, and they all connect to a central point at each city center."

"So, this species lives above and beneath the surface," commented Dr. Prata, and then asked, "What's so unusual about that? They're reptiles."

Malik zoomed the image even closer to the central point. "The unusual thing is this central tunnel—it's vertical."

"So, it's the central access point for the other tunnels," Prata pressed, "but I still don't get your point."

Malik looked out at the group as he made his final summation. "The vertical tunnel is thousands of meters deep. Their geometry and extreme depth are normally indicative of a mine shaft. A shaft that should be extremely difficult, if not impossible, for a primitive species, such as the Lizard People, to dig themselves."

"Did you analyze what's in those tunnels, Lieutenant?" Jennings cut in.

"To a certain depth, Captain, but even our technology has limitations."

"I understand, Malik, but what did you find?"

"Our bio-diversification scan of the shallower tunnel systems indicated zero trace of human DNA." Malik pointed at the screen. "All we found were the Lizard People. Hundreds of thousands of them inside the tunnels."

The room went completely quiet. Malik paused a moment and then explained further. "If any remains of the *Monarch*'s crew are too deep in the warren of tunnels, then maybe our instruments can't pick them up. Even more perplexing is how can we investigate further without direct contact with the indigenous species?"

Malik stopped speaking as he gazed at the attendees.

Dr. Prata seized the lull in the conversation. "Lieutenant, it's now obvious that the landmass is inhabited by the same intelligent species of reptiles that we've observed sailing around its edges. Do you have any hard data on this species yet?"

Malik gave a little sigh and folded his arms. "Yes, Dr. Prata, somewhat. However, I need more time to study the data further, but from what little I could see on the bio-diversification scan, this species seems to consist of four different subspecies. Races, if you will, and it seems that each race has a specific purpose. There is a clear distinction between the two main races. I believe the largest to be the labor force, while the other one seems to be military in nature. I'm not sure about the other two, but I assume that the smallest one must be the ruling class. Be that as it may, this division of ethnicity suggests that their evolution has taken a very long time, possibly hundreds of thousands of generations. From what I have observed so far, they seem to exhibit more eusociality traits than what humans do."

"Eusocial," repeated Dr. Prata. "You mean like an ant or bee colony?"

"Sort of," replied Malik.

"This seems odd for a reptilian species," commented Prata, "but if so, then their political system could be matriarchal, dominated by a queen, or a series of them."

"Perhaps, Doctor," reflected Malik, "however, this species does seem to present a great evolutionary leap from reptiles found on Earth or other planets where we've discovered a similar type of life form. We have simply not found any species that exhibited this level of intelligence before. Which leads me to think that their species hierarchy is probably more sophisticated than that of an ant colony."

"But it *is* possible," stressed Prata. "They are rather primitive."

"Yes, it's possible, and their level of technology suggests that they are still in an early developmental stage; but ruled by a queen bee? That would mean strict instinctive obedience, and in my opinion, that's a stretch for any sentient species, even a primitive one."

"How primitive?" asked Jennings.

"Well, sir, since there seem to be no metallic ores, they're basically still in their Stone Age, and may never even reach a Bronze Age." Malik's eyes briefly found Gunnar. The big officer frowned and looked away.

"While they obviously live in densely populated cities of a sort, those cities, for lack of a better term, have almost none of the accoutrements that even the most ancient cities of humankind had during periods of similar development. These lizard cities are completely made up of residential dwellings." Malik nodded at Prata. "And they do seem to resemble a beehive or an anthill more than a city as we think of them. A more detailed biological analysis from the residual DNA scan will give us a far better species profile. Please keep in mind that it's difficult to make a determination based on what I could deduce during real-time surveying. I simply need more time to study the data."

Dr. Prata pressed Malik a little further. "I understand that without an in-depth analysis of the data, it'll be difficult to draw any definitive conclusions, but what are your initial impressions of this intelligent species?"

Lieutenant Malik opened his mouth, and then closed it again. He opened it again, frowned, shrugged, and said nothing. Alex stood up. "Dr. Prata, I observed the Lizard People closely for hours while Lieutenant Malik was otherwise occupied with his survey instruments. If you'll allow me, I'll give you my impression. Keep in mind that I'm just a simple pilot and not an anthropologist."

Malik stepped back from the podium and gestured for the pilot to take over. Alex moved to the podium. "First of all, I can tell you that there are hundreds of millions of them. Their cities are teeming masses where they live in such close proximity to each other that it's difficult to get a sense of any individuality. They live in dwellings, but these are crude mud-and-grass huts that are all kind of just stuck together. They sort of reminded me of a wasp's nest. I only saw a few that had more than one story."

Alex's face took on a more contemplative look. "There was something else that took me a while to figure out. We were traveling too fast to observe much with the naked eye, but because we were so low over their cities, I had a chance to observe them relatively close, and something stood out. I never saw any form of commerce. I mean, every town, every city, whether contemporary or in the ancient history books, always had a town center revolving around some form of commerce or market. I didn't see anything resembling this in their cities. After a while, I began looking for something that might indicate some form of market, but I saw nothing but dwellings. Entire cities with millions of inhabitants that seemingly had no buildings devoted to anything other than habitation." Alex stopped for a moment; his gaze seemed to wander off as he went on. "Also, there was something not quite right about the land in between the massive cities."

"What do you mean?" inquired Dr. Prata.

The doc's question snapped Alex's focus back to the meeting. "The land itself, Doc. There was nothing but grassland. That's it. No forests, no agriculture, no parks, nothing but a few places where some small, shrub-like trees were growing. My first gut feeling, and what has stayed with me ever since, is that something is wrong with the ecology. I can't really put my finger on it, but something just seemed out of order."

"Can you be more specific, Lieutenant?" pressed the doctor.

"Not really, but it just seemed odd to me that the cities were so full that the inhabitants were literally crawling over one another, but in the uninhabited grasslands, there was nobody."

"And your point, Lieutenant?" asked Prata.

"Sir, it just seems to me that the lack of anything resembling commerce and the total lack of any type of food production in the vast empty areas between cities carries an inherent contradiction." Alex shrugged, and asked no one in particular, "How do such massive populations feed themselves?"

He looked around the room, but no one said anything, so he continued. "There was one more oddity that I noticed just as we were leaving the continent: I saw one of the largest cities with several million inhabitants, only this city was next to a large port, and the inhabitants weren't like the rest. This population was obviously military—millions of lizard soldiers."

"It sounds like you overflew a military base," suggested the doctor.

Alex reflected for a moment, and said, "I know, sir, but it seemed like it was mobilizing."

CHAPTER 49

HE WILL BECOME POWERFUL
OFOL'R—LOG'RFOLD

The Normad'r minister of biogenetic engineering was in the chamber of interposition interfacing with her prime subject when the summons came from the Mab'r. Like all those of her race, she was blue-skinned, three meters tall, thousands of years old, and floated everywhere she went. Endemic to all Normad'r, her lower appendages ended at the bottom of her long legs like fleshy spikes. The Normad'r hadn't had feet in millions of years, but there was no need for them. The lighter-than-air gases that made up their cardiovascular system enabled the gravitational control that had been engineered into them eons ago.

Kanend'ra's thin, white dress shimmered in the soft light of Ofol'r as its sheer fabric floated out behind her like a wisp of vapor. She silently glided to her Mab'r's dwelling, stopping just inside his dwelling's entrance.

Erland'r emitted a faint amber glow as he felt her approach. "I have concerns about the abilities of your human prototype," he wasted no time in saying. "The young human male has become very powerful, and his abilities are growing. Are you confident that you can maintain control over him?"

Her large, yellow eyes blinked once as a light blue glow briefly glimmered inside her thin torso. "Since he reached puberty, I've tapped into his subconscious during sleep periods," she explained, "and have taught him how to maximize his abilities."

Erland'r had observed this particular being on several occasions and what he had seen made him uneasy. "I'm aware of this, but the specimen seems unstable, and your ability to manipulate him might fail if he proves uncontrollable. That would not be in our best interest."

"What is your command, Mab'r?" she asked. "Do you want to stop the implanting?"

"Not just yet, but you need to be careful with this one." Erland'r ruminated. "All I need is for him to act as liaison once the humans have sent their war fleet, and they must believe he is the human leader here on Log'rfold. However, if he proves uncontrollable, then it could destroy everything. The fate of our empire depends on your ability to keep control of him. Show him no more of his powers."

"I understand, Mab'r," she told him. "Lately I have implanted a sense of superiority into him and promised him strength. From now on, I'll emphasize fear instead."

"If he becomes intractable, you must explore the possibility of recruiting the Earthling."

"It will be as you command, Mab'r. However, I must make you aware that I'm not sure what proficiency the Earthling possesses with regards to his powers," she admitted. "The traits that I implanted into his bloodline hundreds of generations ago have grown in strength, and like the subject born here, this Earthling is a direct descendant of their ancient one. Therefore his abilities must be powerful, but it seems that he has little knowledge and limited access to them."

"That will come," Erland'r assured her, "once the divination of his ancestor, their Spak'rna, manifests itself. He will become powerful."

CHAPTER 50

SEA OF GRASS
IFC ENDEAVOR—ORBIT DAY 31

The next three weeks brought a mind-numbing routine for the flight crews as they rigidly maintained their flight plans and stuck to the grid coordinates. Slowly but surely, a complete analysis of the southern continent began to take shape. After each sortie the new data was downloaded to SADI, who sorted, categorized, and presented the information to the survey chief and the senior staff.

The only deviation from the normal flight routines was the operation to investigate the labyrinth of tunnels beneath the lizard cities. For over a week, both survey shuttles buzzed one lizard city after another and launched a series of recon drones deep into the tunnel systems. At less than ninety centimeters in circumference, these small propeller-driven drones were launched from the OVALs and dropped into the cities. They had limited flight time, narrow sensor parameters, and few returned. Expectations of success were low, but it was the only option that didn't include an EVA and probable human contact with the indigenous.

After most of the drones were lost and none of the mission directive had been achieved, the operation was called off. The only accomplishment was the confirmation of what Malik had already hypothesized: the deep shafts were mines. Other than the Lizard People, the only thing identified was what was being mined: an unusual form of crystal.

The operation was deemed another dead end.

The dominant indigenous species was by far the Lizard People, as the crew of the *Endeavor* had named them. A closer DNA analysis of this species indicated that there was some distant link, thousands of generations in the past, to that of a non-reptilian primate. Dr. Prada compiled all the anthropology data and theorized that this ancient DNA link accounted for the Lizard People evolving far above any other reptile species that had ever been discovered on any of the planets found to support life. The Lizard People were bipedal, had an increased cranial capacity, and an intrinsic set of phonatory muscles that equipped their larynx with the ability to establish complex vocal patterns that eventually evolved into speech.

Other than the Lizard People, there were few other animal species living on the southern continent. The only other species found that lived there in any substantial numbers was a small reptile quadruped, which lived in huge underground warrens in the grassy plains between the cities. There were also a few different types of reptilian birdlike creatures, who lived almost exclusively in the coastal regions and only in the areas dominated by steep cliffs. The popular theory proposed by Dr. Prata was that the lack of animal species was due to the huge urban populations, which, he theorized, had by virtue of sheer volume consumed most of the resources needed to support the other species.

One subject, however, had never been settled and was directly related to the comment that Alex had made during the initial AAR. It was about the lack of commerce as well as the lack of any obvious type of food production, coupled with the now-popular theory about the Lizard People eating all the other species on the continent: what exactly did the Lizard People eat?

As the survey missions continued and more and more of the landmass was intricately analyzed, it became clear that there was nothing to indicate any type of agriculture or any type of domesticated herd animals. There was speculation that much of their food must come from the oceans, but Lieutenant Malik, using a social-consumption, mass-balance program, calculated that the sheer population size, prevailing technology, and the proportion of the population living far from the oceans meant that only a small fraction of the population could actually live off of what was caught in the seas. There was no easy answer, and all the prevailing theories had at least one serious theoretical flaw. All except one: cannibalism.

Over the next couple weeks both survey crews overflew the massive naval base that Alex had discovered on that first sortie. Both pilots took note that not only did it have millions of soldiers, but that the soldier population was growing. Proportionate with the growth in numbers of the soldiers was the increase in numbers of the crude barge-like naval vessels that began massing in and around the large port. It was obvious to some of the more astute military minds aboard the *Endeavor* that some sort of invasion was being prepared, but there didn't seem to be anything on the rest of the continent worth invading.

The two pilots were having a meal together during one of their few mutual down times. Baseball was in the middle of eating the second helping of his favorite dish, something yellow that sort of smelled like mac and cheese, when he offhandedly said, "You ever notice that we fly through rain squalls that average exactly 4.7 centimeters an hour?"

Alex let out a green tea burp. "You mean to tell me that you actually calculated that?" He took another sip.

"Of course. What else do I have to do for hours on end?"

"Oh golly, I dunno, fly your boat?"

Undeterred, Baseball forged ahead. "So, given that we consistently fly through exactly the same precipitation rate, it stands to reason that this is the same rate of precipitation over the continent as a whole. Follow me?"

Alex answered with an indifferent, "Mm-hmm."

"That's a shitload of rain, Alex. Think about it. Any M-class planet that we've ever encountered where the precipitation rate came even close to what we see on this continent has always been covered by a rainforest."

"I know you're leading to some major conclusion," said Alex between sips, "but all this posturing is sort of getting in the way of it."

"For crying out loud, this is potentially important. Try to pay attention, and I'll get to the nut cutting, okay?"

"Whose nuts are you talking about?"

"For fuck's sake, Alex, just listen. Like I said, this precipitation rate is uniform. I've never even heard of a planet that has a uniform rainfall rate. There are always microclimates that dictate different rainfall, but not on the southern continent. Here it's all the same, and to me, this smacks of outside control."

Alex set his cup down and furrowed his brow. "Outside control? Really?"

"As in weather manipulation, as in outside interference, as in this mysterious planetary defense network, as in we may not be the only folks flying around up here, as in perhaps we need to be looking over our shoulder a lot more than we're doing now."

"As in a little paranoid perhaps?" suggested Alex.

Baseball blinked hard, swallowed a spoonful of yellow stuff, and pushed on. "As we are all so patently aware, this cloud cover can't be penetrated by any of our sophisticated analytical equipment."

Alex gave him a blank look.

"Look, I had an in-depth analytical discussion with a few of our survey team, and they all say the same thing."

"Like what exactly, Mr. Smarty Pants?"

"Alex, please, I'm trying to make a point here. Even though our high-tech survey stuff is completely thwarted by this cloud cover, it's perpetually light on the ground. Meaning that everything needed for plant growth makes it through, and yet our survey instruments cannot."

Alex yawned and looked at the time. "Okay, Baseball, you have my undivided attention for the next few seconds, but I'm flying the next sortie, and I gotta go pee, so you better make this fast."

"Fair enough, Alex, but bear with me for a couple more minutes, okay?"

Alex drummed his fingers on the tabletop.

"Sunlight fuels plant growth through photosynthesis, which converts light into food. Leaves on a single plant grow and change in response to the different light levels they receive. To maximize photosynthesis and light-absorbing chlorophyll, the leaves change in structure and thickness. Red and blue waves facilitate plant growth. Chlorophyll reflects mostly green light, making leaves appear green."

Alex shifted in his seat and began gathering up his trash. "Good to know," he said as he picked up his tray. "But golly gee winkles, look at the time."

"You're gonna want to make time for this," insisted Baseball.

"Look," Alex said impatiently, "I have no doubt that you're about to get to a valid point in this high school botany lecture, so just get to it already."

"Fine, here's my point," came Baseball's muffled mouthful response. "All the requisite sun rays needed for plants to grow, seed, and propagate are present despite the dense cloud cover."

"Meaning?"

"Meaning that even though our most sophisticated analytical equipment is unable to pass through this strange cloud cover, the sun's energy that all plants require for life is fully present. Do you see what I'm driving at?"

Alex drew his brows together, set the tray back down, and pushed it aside. "So this cloud cover, which can screen out prying eyes, still allows the all-important sun rays needed to sustain life on the planet's surface. Is that what you're driving at?"

"Exactly," agreed Baseball, "but all we see is a sea of grass. Grass, Alex! There's something very wrong with this picture. There's enough rain and sunlight to produce massive forests, and yet there are none."

Alex nodded, and admitted, "I have to agree with your rainfall versus environment hypothesis, Baseball, but now the only question remaining is—why?"

"A couple of things seem pretty obvious to me. Millions of lizard troops are massing, along with thousands of wooden ships to transport them." He stopped for a moment.

"I think I know where you're going with this," Alex said, "because I've had similar thoughts every time I fly over that massive naval base, but first I want to hear your ideas."

"About time," muttered Baseball. "Right, then here it is. The Lizard People have cut down all the forests that must have once covered this continent in order to build that huge fleet of warships." Baseball stopped talking, set his spoon down, and crossed his arms.

"Agreed, Baseball. Building thousands of ships would take a tremendous amount of wood, but—and here's what just doesn't add up—it wouldn't take an entire continent of lumber to build that fleet, even as large as it is. It would only take a fraction of the forests that according to your theory should be growing there."

With his arms still folded, Baseball drummed the fingers of his right hand against his left bicep. "It seems to me that there are two constants that are directly related to the events taking place at that port right now."

"Just get to it already, Baseball."

"Right, so here's the crux of the issue." He unfolded his arms and placed his elbows on the table. "This can't have been the first time. For whatever reason, they have built these gigantic wooden naval forces time and time again, perhaps for hundreds of years, and thus, for whatever reason, over time they have completely denuded the continent of all her trees and never replanted them."

"Yeah, I can see that too, Baseball, and as you and I have personally witnessed, there are hardly any trees left."

Baseball smiled. "Exactly, my friend. So, whatever their military objective might be, it has to be taken this time around, because there are no trees left with which to build another giant armada. What we're witnessing is a now-or-never scenario."

"Okay, but it still doesn't quite make sense. If they're building this massive invasion force, then they plan on using it. But who the hell are they going to invade? I mean, we've been over almost every centimeter of this continent, and there's nothing worth taking. Nothing! There is zero sign of conflict between any of the regions here. So, just where are they going to send their huge fleet?"

Baseball gave his friend a smug look, locked eyes with him, and said, "The only place they can: the northern continent."

CHAPTER 51

HER GLORY
DEEP OCEAN—AQUEOUS

F ar out to sea, under a cobalt blue sky, Duchess Thorna stood on the deck of her sleek flagship and stared at the northern horizon. She knew that her war armada, the bulk of her force, was almost ready to launch the invasion. Her small fleet of fast ships had boldly pushed through the turbulent waters of the equatorial region weeks ago and was in the northern hemisphere rapidly closing in on her ultimate goal, her glory.

Long before this glorious operation began, Duchess Thorna had been given overall command of the empire's armed forces, but it was a landlocked army with only a handful of naval vessels. To Thorna's way of thinking, it had no real purpose. That all changed when one of her spy ships came in contact with the human who was willing to betray his species. After personally traveling to the northern continent and meeting with this traitor, a plan was forged, and Thorna's destiny assured. Soon after she returned, Thorna marched her army on the empire's capital city of Saurinth, surrounded it, and made her demands. It only took two days to convince that old fool, the Imperial Queen, and her lackey central council that the last of the forests should be cut down to build the fleet that would finally destroy the softskin invaders.

Since first contact one thousand years before, the Thith elite had been obsessed with destroying the aliens. The Floating Gods had commanded it, and an edict in the holy book of the Saurinti confirmed it: the aliens were evil, and a threat to the sacred Ramm'r crystal. For a millennium, in war after war, the Thith had been thwarted in this quest; but this time, with millions of troops at her disposal and the fleet to transport them, she would succeed where other, less competent queens had failed.

But this would only be the beginning of Duchess Thorna's ultimate triumph. As queen, she would become the sole speaker to the Floating Gods. She alone would translate their words, their commands down to her species. It had always been thus, but this time would be different. This time she would demand of the Gods recompense for all the sacrifice her race had suffered at the hands of the softskins. Naturally, she had zero intention of elevating her species. They would remain as they had always been: enslaved to the Queen. Only Her Most Sacred self would benefit from her demands to the Gods.

She would demand to become a God herself.

Yes, this would be her right of destiny. And adding to her confidence was the value of the help she had. Help to create newer weapons, better weapons, and the all-important intelligence about her enemy that no other duchess in history had ever had. Yes, she, Duchess Thorna had done all that was needed for ultimate victory, and once that victory was achieved, she would rule the Thith Empire, which meant that she would rule the world. It was a position that she so deserved, a position that she so craved, a position she would exterminate an entire species to attain.

No one and nothing could now deter her from this goal. As Thorna watched her fleet approach the northern continent, she knew that with each oar stroke she was moving ever closer to immortal glory. It was now within her grasp, and soon her unstoppable army would launch the final battle to rid the planet of its most invasive parasite.

Nothing could stop her now.

CHAPTER 52

SHORT-LIVED SPECIES
OFOL'R—LOG'RFOLD

Erland'r, the Being Superior of Ofol'r, hadn't left the semitransparent, domed garrison in hundreds of years. Time meant little to the long-lived Normad'r, and everything the Mab'r needed was available to him within the protective confines of his base.

Erland'r watched with interest as the small craft returned to its mother ship. He waved the image away and stared into the abyss as luminescent deep-sea creatures swam past the energy field that held the ocean's crushing pressure at bay. But his large, yellow eyes weren't seeing that life. His mind was troubled, and he wanted a detailed report. "Dreng'r, did the humans find anything?"

"They've made multiple flights over the Thith Empire, Mab'r," answered his subordinate, "but found nothing of their lost ship. They have, however, found the Ramm'r mines, and investigated, but their drones have primitive sensor technology and provided little information."

"You feel confident that it is safe?" asked Erland'r.

"Yes, Mab'r, for now," said Dreng'r. "Any of their drones that ventured too deep were destroyed, and the others compiled no such data as to expose the true purpose of the mines. Few were allowed to return."

"Good, the O'rmsliki did their job well," said the Mab'r as he floated across his transparent floor. His long, silky hair was a translucent white, but there were no wrinkles on his twenty-six-thousand-year-old face. His body hadn't degenerated his entire life and wouldn't for at least another ten thousand years. The Normad'r lived for multiple millennia, and barring any accident, they suffered none of the maladies that affected the creations they had seeded on thousands of planets. That two of their seedlings had met on this planet was a first. In the millions of years of planet development, interaction between engineered species had never happened before.

"Dismissed, Dreng'r."

So much about this fragile, short-lived species was troubling. They were programmed to be self-destructive—a millennium before they had destroyed their home world—but here on Log'rfold they had exhibited none of those traits. This troubled Erland'r. He knew that the enhanced bloodline was accelerating human evolution, but was this program ultimately a mistake? Could humanity evolve to a point that they were no longer controllable? Kanend'ra's project here on Log'rfold had become the catalyst for that concern. If this one enhanced human proved unmanageable, then perhaps it could spread to others, or worse, be genetically passed down. That would be disastrous. Even though the genetic projection models indicated that this could never happen, Erland'r was well aware that it had happened once before. He also knew that the Normad'r Empire could not allow another genetically engineered species to successfully break free of Normad'r control. Especially another warrior race, because the one species that had won their independence was now a threat to Normad'r dominance over the entire galaxy. The threat from that species was the sole reason the enhanced human bloodline was developed in the first place.

Now the Normad'r depended on the warrior race from Earth to save their empire.

CHAPTER 53

LAST STONE
IFC ENDEAVOR—ORBIT DAY 33

After twenty-nine days, the survey of the southern continent had almost been completed, and there was a perceptible fall in morale among the *Endeavor*'s crew, especially the flight crews, senior staff, and the surveyors. They had found zero evidence of any piece, be it ever so small, of the *Monarch* or her crew. There was not so much as a shred of human DNA that had been found by the highly sensitive biological analytical instruments.

At no time did any of the missions penetrate the cloud cover, nor did they attempt sending any signals through it. The last region of the southern continent to be surveyed was the unusual mountain sitting atop the southern polar axis. It had been approached to within twenty-five kilometers on four of the sorties, but at no time did a flight plan include surveying this specific target area.

One side, championed by the survey chief Lieutenant Malik, argued that without a proper survey of the mountain, their entire mission would be incomplete. The other school of thought, led by Commander Hammär, stressed that overflying this mountain was akin to blasting Pandora's box into fragments with a pulse rifle.

As always, the decision fell into Captain Jennings's lap. After much deliberation, in which he more than agreed with his security chief, Jennings knew that he could not leave any stone unturned, and that last stone was the mountain. It was therefore decided, with no fanfare this time, that a survey mission of the mountain would be made and that all the survey safeguards were to remain in place.

Alex's flight crew drew the short straw for this final sortie. As on that first survey mission, the captain, security chief, and his CAG met the flight crew on the flight deck.

Captain Jennings remained conspicuously silent while his security chief and CAG laid down the flight protocols. Commander Hammär did not adopt his usual domineering demeanor with Alex.

"Alex, I realize that you already appreciate that there's genuine concern about this polar mountain, but I just want to reiterate that you're to heed every self-preservation instinct you have." Gunnar stressed this point more than any other.

"Yes, sir."

Gunnar dropped his voice and said in a confidential tone, "Like that damn cloud cover, and the thousand dead satellites, I'm concerned that this mountain is a trip wire. One that we have so far been lucky to avoid stumbling over." He moved closer to his pilot. "Alex, you need to take extreme caution while making this overflight. If you see any abnormalities while in close proximity, then you are to bug out ASAP. Capisce?"

"Yes, sir. I understand the concern and that I'm to be extra vigilant."

Gunnar's voice remained steady. "Alex, it could be a trigger. We just don't know, but we absolutely do not want to push its buttons. That's it in a nutshell. We don't know, and we don't want to find out." Hammär stepped back.

Eaglecreek stepped forward to address the flight crew. The CAG wore his usual scowl, but directed almost all his attention to Alex. "You've done an exemplary job on all your flights so far. Somehow, you've managed to stick to the flight plans and parameters given to you and provided all the data we've needed to analyze the planet's surface. You've also brought your boat and your crew back safely."

"Thank you, Commander Eaglecreek. We were just following orders."

"I fully realize that, Commander, and just want to leave you with this last bit of wisdom."

"Sir?"

"Don't fuck it up on the southern continent's last mission. That is all. Carry on, Commander Porter."

During the CAG's usual highly starched mission brief, Alex almost missed what had just happened. Eventually the words registered, and he finally caught on. He couldn't help the protocol breach that suddenly blurted out of his mouth. "Commander? What?"

For the first time during this preflight briefing, Captain Jennings stepped up to his pilot and, with a tight grin on his face, began unfastening Alex's lieutenant bars while he nonchalantly mentioned what was now obvious.

"Oh, I guess we forgot to mention it to you earlier. You've been promoted, Lieutenant Commander Porter. And just so you'll know, Lieutenant Hartley's is on the docket. Please keep that between us," the captain told the new commander. Once the lieutenant bars were off, the captain intimated to the young officer, "Even though you are now the junior commander aboard this ship, you are no longer a lieutenant, which means that once you get back to Earth, your accrued mission pay will be a bit more. Spend it wisely, Commander."

Alex was stunned to silence.

The captain affixed the bronze oak leaves to Alex's blouse, stepped back, and gave him a crisp salute, as did the other two senior officers on the flight deck. A rather shocked Lieutenant Commander Porter snapped one back.

Commander Hammär then boomed out loud enough for the entire galaxy to hear, "And don't think this means I'll be taking any crap from some wet-behind-the-ears, soft-tail, hotshot pilot, especially from just a lieutenant commander!" He then winked at Alex, and the three senior officers left the flight deck, leaving Alex and his flight crew to ready themselves for their last mission over the southern continent.

CHAPTER 54

DRAGON MOUNTAIN
OVAL PORTER—ORBIT DAY 34

O*VAL Porter* made the drop to cruising altitude, and just before going feet dry, it flew over the massive port complex. It had been over a week since he'd overflown the naval base, and what the newly promoted lieutenant commander saw this time got his full attention.

The base was almost empty, and one thing was certain—the mobilization was complete, and an invasion imminent. The sea of grass conversation he'd had with Baseball came to mind as he watched the stragglers from the huge fleet head north.

As he did on the first survey sortie, Lieutenant Malik accompanied *OVAL Porter*. But, unlike the first mission, the survey chief had skipped breakfast and showed no ill effects during the bumpy ride down.

As they passed over the practically empty port, Raj also noticed and quizzed Alex. "What do you think is going on down there, Lieutenant Commander Porter?"

While Alex still glowed from his recent promotion, he admonished his copilot. "Raj, I understand your enthusiasm about flying with a commander as your pilot, but even if I were an admiral, you'd still be required to call me Alex and leave all that military stuff behind once we shut the airlock. Got it?"

"Yes, sir, Lieutenant Commander Alex. We should be at target in thirty-seven minutes. Hey, Lieutenant Malik, do you need an extra helmet back there?"

The survey chief huffed into his mic and fired back at the cocky copilot, "Only to shove up your ass, Second Lieutenant!"

Alex grinned, and without looking at his rightseater, asked, "Think it'll fit, Raj?"

Conversation was subdued until the polar mountain came into visual range, and by that time all three members of the flight crew were busy with their respective tasks.

As soon as they were within ten kilometers, Alex tapped his mic. "Amil, looks like you'll be back on the books in about thirty seconds. Is everything spooled up? My mission parameters say that we make our passes on opposite sides, get the itinerant surveys, and then get our tails back home, which means no loitering and no redundant passes. I know you've already been briefed on this, but I wanted to reiterate that before we go survey hot."

"Roger that, Alex. I'm all set to go now."

"Then let's get this show on the road," said Alex and set the throttle to survey speed.

When he brought the OVAL to within one kilometer of the mountain, he saw details on its surface that had not been visible before. He frowned and switched on his OC zoom. Confusion quickly turned to shock.

While Alex stared at one of the most disturbing sights of his life, he heard Lieutenant Malik's shrill voice yelling at him through the intercom. "Alex, you're not going to believe what I'm seeing on my data screen right now!"

"Trust me, Amil, if it's anything like what I'm looking at through my windscreen, then I'll believe you."

"The biological analysis of this mountain shows that it's alive," reported Malik. "I mean, the entire mountain is alive!"

Raj, who'd had his head down calculating flight-plan coordinates, finally looked up, and dropped his jaw. "Oh, holy mother of God, what the hell is that thing?" His voice constricted to a throaty whisper and his breaths started coming in short bursts.

Alex stared unblinking through his windscreen. The entire mountain, all that they could see of it before it disappeared up into the cloud cover, was a seething mass of red reptiles. At less than five hundred meters, Alex engaged his docking thrusters and slowed to a hover to get a better look.

"What're you doing?" squeaked Raj.

Alex nodded slightly and said, "Good point. I think we've seen enough."

Suddenly all movement on the mountain became highly agitated right before the entire spectacle exploded in front of the three humans. Without warning, hundreds—thousands—of winged reptiles, about five meters long, took to the air.

The strange mountain that those reptilian creatures had blanketed only seconds ago, now discharged those creatures en masse. It looked like a violent red cloud was headed straight for them.

The winged creatures rapidly closed with the hovering shuttle. In seconds, the gap had decreased to less than one hundred meters. "Of all the stupid—" growled Alex as he hit the throttle and juked into a power roll to avoid a collision with their leading edge, but the creatures accelerated into a hard bank, and intercepted his shuttle.

The crew felt a hard impact as something large hit them, then another, and another.

"Shit!" Alex swore and tried to punch his way out of the swarm, but something was wrong—he had no thrust. The shuttle was practically dead in the air.

They were only able to achieve minimal speed, and Alex had almost no control in the yoke as he tried to maneuver away from his attackers. They felt several more impacts as more of the creatures caught up and threw themselves against the shuttle. Alex glanced at the altimeter, and felt a cold shiver go down his spine. He tore his eyes free and fought the yoke in an effort to climb, or even just maintain altitude.

"Raj! Flip your optic computer to the external cameras and put them on the main cluster screen!" shouted Alex. When the screens came on, all of them were dark except two, both under the wings.

With shoulders set, Alex clenched his jaw, and then ordered, "Raj, grab the yoke and keep us in the air. Direct all power to the dynamic thrusters, and keep trying to gain throttle response, but not too much till I tell you. Have you got all that?"

"Yeah, Alex, I got it, but where are you going?" the petrified copilot squealed as Alex released his seat harness and climbed toward the rear, working his way through the survey equipment.

"I'm going to throw these damn things off my boat! Now keep us in the air!" Alex looked over at the panicking survey chief and ordered him, "Come with me, Amil. I need you to give me a hand." When Malik didn't move, Alex grabbed him by the scruff of his collar, jerked him to his feet so they were face-to-face, and warned him, "If you don't help me right now, we're going down hard, which means that more than likely we're all going to die, and it'll happen soon. Now get a grip and give me a hand." Alex released him and made his way to the hatch.

Malik snapped out of his paralysis. "Just what do you want me to do?"

"Do what I say, when I say it!" Alex yelled back. "Now grab that lanyard over by the airlock and clip it to the back of my flight harness."

Malik moved quickly and did what he was told. By the time he got back to Alex, his pilot held a pulse rifle, and slung diagonally across his body was a baldric. Attached to it was a sword scabbard. Malik looked wild-eyed at Alex and squeaked, "Seriously, you're taking a sword? Are you crazy?"

Alex ignored the question, handed him a pulse rifle, and told him, "When Raj pops the hatch, I'm going outside to blow these things the hell off my boat. Keep that hatch open and shoot anything that sticks its head in but me. Do your best not to shoot me. You've got to do this, Amil. No arguments. Just do it!"

Alex stood next to the airlock and looked over at Malik. "You ready?" Malik gave him a weak nod, and Alex yelled into his intercom, "Pop the hatch, Raj!"

As soon as the hatch blew open, Alex tucked the pulse rifle under an arm, climbed out of the OVAL, and hung onto the recessed hand-hold by the side of the hatch. He then leapt out and swung up to the wing using the lanyard. This freed up his arms to work the pulse rifle, which he wasted no time in using. He set the impact force at maximum, giving him twenty shots before it ran out of juice. He hoped it wouldn't take that long to blow these things off his craft.

The closest beast was only a couple meters away, and once he'd gained his balance, he brought the pulse rifle to bear. As Alex looked down the barrel, he saw why they couldn't maneuver or use velocity control—the creatures had used their dexterous, finger-like claws and their large, powerful feet to latch onto and render the ailerons inoperable. Each of the fusion engine nozzle thrusters had a creature covering it with its body, and more had done the same thing with the inlet ports. *These fuckers know what they're doing and are committing suicide to bring us down. Well,* he thought, *if they want to kill themselves, then who am I to stand in their way.* He fired his first shot, blowing half the head off his first target.

Alex swung the pulse rifle around and began blasting away. As each hit from the pulse rifle blew chunks off the creatures, they screeched in angry pain and fell away, but almost as soon as he blew one away, another took its place.

Hundreds of the creatures circled the overwhelmed OVAL and soon turned their attention to Alex. Screeching in anger, they attacked him from all sides. The first one hurled itself into him with outstretched talons and an open mouth, but at the last instant Alex thrust the rifle past its razor-sharp fangs and pumped the trigger. The creature's head exploded in a wet sticky mist that drenched his sleeve. Its headless body tumbled away, but an instant later another screamed in. Its deadly talons were only meters from snatching Alex when a pulse rifle blast blew its wing off. Alex jerked his head around and saw Lieutenant Malik hanging out of the hatch using one hand for stability and the other to pull the trigger. From this position the surveyor blew several of the flying beasts out of the sky.

Alex twisted around and faced the beasts still attached to his craft. He swung his pulse rifle into position and pulled the trigger.

Nothing happened.

Alex dropped the empty rifle, yanked the katana from its scabbard, and dove off the wing. Alex swung in a looping arc toward one of the creatures, and with a powerful slash the sword severed one of its muscular front legs just as he landed on the wing. The creature let out an ear-piercing shriek as it fell.

The OVAL suddenly lurched forward when Raj regained throttle control, but he punched it too hard and flung Alex off the wing.

"Crap!" yelped Alex. He free-fell four meters until the lanyard jerked tight snapping his head painfully forward. It knocked the wind out of him, but somehow, he held onto the sword. Stunned, he dangled for several moments below the accelerating craft before he lifted his head and saw that there was still one more creature furiously tearing into his boat. Helplessly trailing behind the shuttle, Alex was out of reach of the beast.

Suddenly something banged into his shoulder, causing him to practically jump out of his skin. It was a pulse rifle that Malik had tied to another lanyard and swung to within his reach. It took a few seconds for Alex to regain balance, re-sheath the katana, and gain enough dexterity to aim the rifle. The head of the last creature exploded in a flash of sparks and red gore.

Alex looked around for any more attackers, but Raj had outdistanced the pursuing scorch of dragons. Hand over hand he climbed up the lanyard and pulled himself halfway into the hatch. Malik had already retrieved the pulse rifle and helped pull Alex the rest of the way in.

The moment Alex was back inside, Raj shut the hatch, made a bat-turn, and punched the throttle up to Mach three leaving the mountain far behind. The OVAL gained even more speed up as they headed for the coast.

"Back off the throttle, Raj," ordered Alex. "I don't want to burn up leaving the atmosphere. How would that look?"

"We could actually do that?" sputtered Malik.

"Roger that, Alex," mumbled Raj and reduced speed until they went feet wet, and then pointed the nose straight up and blasted out of the atmosphere.

Alex looked back at Lieutenant Malik and exhaled a deep breath. "We'll be fine, Amil, and thanks for saving my ass out there. Twice." His adrenalin-fueled pulse rate was already coming back down when he grinned and said, "I hope you got some worthwhile data."

CHAPTER 55

THE TROUBLE WITH DRAGONS
DRAKON RUS—AQUEOUS

The riot began just as Colonel Moroz settled down to have dinner in the senior officers' mess. He turned a questioning frown toward his tablemates, dropped his cutlery, and bolted out the door. The other officers were hard on his heels. They raced into the stockade where one entire wing, half the dragon army, was quartered. Every dragon was ransacking its pen, screeching at the top of its lungs, and tearing at the bars to get out. The pandemonium made it almost impossible to communicate.

The colonel grabbed one of the stock masters who had just run past, and yelled in his ear. "What the hell's going on? What's happened to them?"

The stable master shrugged and yelled back, "I have no idea, sir. They just started going berserk a minute ago. I can't see any reason for it."

"Find out what the problem is and report back to me at once," yelled Moroz. "Now go!" An officer from the other wing's stockade ran up out of breath.

The officer stopped in front of the colonel, caught her wind, and said, "I see Dragon Rage is in the same state as Dragon Fury, Colonel."

"This chaos is happening with your wing as well, Captain?"

"Yes, sir. As soon as it started I came to report what was happening, and I see that it's not just our wing." The captain had to yell even louder because the unruly dragons had suddenly become savage and turned on the dragons in the next pen. "I've never seen anything like it before. I hope those cages hold."

Colonel Moroz turned to his adjutant and ordered, "Have all riders try to calm their mounts, and I want the stable hands to start inspecting all the cages, but for God's sake, make sure they don't get too close." He turned to the captain from the other wing and told her, "Go do the same there as well. If any break free, kill them."

A dragon riot had only happened once before in the colonel's memory, and that was about the time the old Tsar had died. Then it hit him. It was only a couple days before the Earth woman had been found. He sprinted toward the Tsarina's quarters.

The colonel didn't bother to slow down as he flew through the old steward's office and burst into her personal chambers. The steward followed him in wearing an angry frown.

Anya rushed in from the terrace. Her face twisted in anxiety, but when she saw her steward she calmed and said, "It's all right, Sergei, the colonel has important business to discuss." She turned to her cousin. "Don't you, Vlad?"

"Book business," growled her cousin as he strode past her.

"He still should've observed protocol, Tsarina," protested the elderly steward. He gave them a curt nod and turned to leave, muttering, "No one pay attention to Sergei. Just old man, Sergei."

"What's happened, Vlad?" Anya demanded the moment the door shut. "From my balcony I just saw a patrol suddenly turn on each other. The riders couldn't control their dragons. All of them perished."

"Something's happening with the dragons, Anya. They've all gone berserk. Both stockades are in a state of pandemonium. And there's more." He walked over and placed both hands on her shoulders. "This happened once before: a few days before the Earth woman arrived."

"But how could what's happening now be related to her arrival?" Then she too saw the parallel and gasped in shock. "Do you think this means that—that?" The word stuck in her throat as she looked up at her cousin with wide eyes.

"Perhaps, Anya," he told her. "But even though they've been domesticated for a thousand years, these are still dangerous animals, and I've never believed that all their feral instincts were bred out of them when our ancestors removed them from the mountain."

"Then do you think that they instinctively sense something?"

Moroz clenched his jaw and gave a solemn nod.

"So, he's here now," she said resolutely, "on Aqueous, and somehow his arrival has caused the trouble with dragons."

Moroz narrowed his gaze and asked, "What does your book say about this?"

Her long, black tresses gently swayed as Anya shook her head. "Nothing. The only dragon it mentions is Rodinya, and how she will bring him here—to me."

"Great, I can't wait," grumped Moroz, then noticed the troubled shadow that darkened his cousin's face. He looked away and asked, "And then?"

"And then," she echoed his words. "Then I must fulfill my—obligation. You already know all this, Vlad. Must we discuss it again?"

"I will never allow you to be hurt," he promised as he slipped a protective arm around her slender shoulders. "You do believe me, don't you?"

She ignored his question. "And if it turns out that he is a good man?"

"Then I will love and protect him as a brother."

CHAPTER 56

SCRATCHED PAINT
IFC ENDEAVOR—ORBIT DAY 34

Less than twenty minutes after the dragon attack, and moving at Mach ten, *OVAL Porter* approached *Endeavor*'s orbital plane. But this was an unscheduled extraction, and the starship wouldn't be in her rendezvous position. They had to make a long-range intercept.

Alex engaged the LRS and contacted his starship. "*Endeavor, OP. Come in!*"

The CAG's voice responded quickly. This was the first time that a sortie hadn't called in exactly on schedule. "*OP, Endeavor,* we have your position and are now tracking you. What's your status, Commander Porter," asked Zonta, "and why did you mission abort?"

Alex tried to maintain a professionally neutral tone, but the tightness in his voice still bled through. "Commander, we were unable to conduct the survey as per flight plan, and I need to report in ASAP."

The CAG heard his pilot's angst but answered back in an even tone. "All right, Commander, I got that. I'll hail the captain and get him on the line ASAP. What's your crew status?"

"No injuries, sir, but I bent your boat."

"Understood, Commander. Stand by." The comms went silent for three minutes before it crackled back to life. "*OP, Endeavor,* do you copy?" asked Commander Eaglecreek.

"Copy. Sir, we had an issue at the mountain that resulted in the mission abort and subsequent return to base."

Alex could hear Captain Jennings in the background. "I'm finding out now, sir," the CAG responded first to the captain, and then turned his attention back to Alex. "Commander, we'll have our usual AAR upon your return, but I want something now. What the hell happened down there?"

"Sir, as we came within visual range of the mountain, we observed thousands of a previously undiscovered reptilian species literally covering its entire surface. These creatures were big, sir, and they could fly as well. As soon as they saw us, they attacked en masse and several managed to attach themselves to the hull." Alex paused a moment before he continued. "They came close to disabling our flight capability. We had to literally blow these creatures off the hull in order to regain control of the OVAL. They were determined to bring us down, which is why I ordered the abort."

The captain came on the comm. "Good God, Alex! They physically attacked and almost brought you down? Helluva first mission after your promotion, huh? Good job and we'll see you in a few. We'll want to jump on this as soon as you dock. *Endeavor* out."

———————————

Thirty minutes later, the AAR group had assembled, and without the usual preamble, Jennings launched into the briefing.

"Alex, I just want to reaffirm what I told you in our initial communication after the abort. Well done for not losing your ship." He turned to Lieutenant Malik to set the record straight. "Amil, I realize you didn't get much data this time, but we're just going to have to live with what you did get. We are not returning to that mountain."

"No argument there, sir."

"SADI, please bring up *OP*'s approach on the survey objective."

"Right away. *OVAL Porter*'s video feed is coming up now, sir."

The screen flickered to life, and the shuttle's external video came up. The initial view was of the mountain from a distance of fifty-two kilometers. There was no hint of what was about to happen. The closer the approach, the clearer movement on the mountain's slope became. At a distance of three kilometers, the movement on the mountain became more definitive. It seethed with agitation. Then the zoom on Alex's OC flashed across the screen, and there was a collective gasp in the AAR.

Then suddenly, as soon as the shuttle came within five hundred meters of the mountain, almost the entire mass of creatures launched themselves into the air on an intercept course with the shuttle. Most of the external cameras went dark as the first of the winged beasts caught up and swarmed the OVAL.

The cockpit voice recorder captured the entire conversation of the crew during their engagement. The AAR room was shocked into silence by the new commander's effort to dislodge these attackers. Many of the officers who watched the battle could barely believe their eyes. No one had ever seen or heard of anything like it before. Commander Hammär pulled Alex aside and quietly told him, "It's a damn good thing you brought that pig sticker of yours." Gunnar snorted and then added, "It should probably be standard issue from now on."

After the video finished, the captain blew a heavy breath through his teeth and asked, "I guess the only real question now is: How much data was actually gathered before the abort?"

Jennings looked over at the survey chief, who just gave a slight shrug of his shoulders and said, "A fair amount, sir. The survey instruments had been switched on for about a minute before the attack, and at the initial distance some of our more sensitive analytical equipment wasn't close enough or didn't have enough time to gather data. They were, however, left running during the attack, and I believe we did get some useful data even during the battle."

"Like what exactly, Lieutenant?" asked Gunnar.

"Sir, the creatures had every square meter of the mountain's surface covered with their bodies. Shrouded like that, they acted like the cloud cover, in that our instruments couldn't penetrate past them. Almost all we know for sure is that this mountain is the sole habitat of these large, aggressive flying reptiles."

"Almost? But what about once the dragons had left their perch and exposed the mountain?" asked Dr. Prata.

"Terrific," Alex muttered to himself, "dragons."

Lieutenant Malik nodded at Alex and continued with his report. "Once the creatures—uh, dragons latched on to us, they managed to disable our flight control systems."

"Yeah, we got that part, Lieutenant," commented Gunnar.

"As I was saying," continued Malik, "while we were in a steady, if perilous position, for the few moments it took to dislodge the attackers, the instruments were able to make a lock. Once we broke free and resumed a steady flight pattern, the survey equipment lost that lock and was unable to get much more, if any, reliable data."

"So, you did get some data. Is that correct, Lieutenant?" Dr. Prata persisted.

"Yes, Doctor. The equipment did collect some hard data while the OVAL was stationary. Ironically, it seems as though the dragons did us a favor by rendering us temporarily immobile."

Captain Jennings gripped the sides of his chair, and snapped, "Lieutenant Malik, for crying out loud! Get to the point."

The lieutenant barely nodded his impassive face and said, "All right, Captain. The inside of that mountain is a four-meter thick, perfectly shaped parabolic sheath of some kind of steel-nickel alloy. Layered directly on the outside of this is a solid coat of tetragonal crystal."

The AAR went quiet as a tomb.

Captain Jennings sat back in his seat and stared at the survey chief for a few heartbeats. "Do you think these vicious flying creatures were actually guarding the only source of metal on the planet?"

"Maybe, sir. I can't scientifically draw that conclusion, nor can I say it's the only source of metal, but it's the only metal we've found so far."

"Fuck scientific data!" swore Gunnar. "What does your gut tell you about these creatures who attacked your ship?"

Malik cocked his head and paused a moment. He finally shrugged and said to the group, "My gut instincts tell me that, yes, the dragons are there to guard it."

After the AAR broke up, the CAG approached Alex shaking his head. "That was one helluva thing you did down there, Commander."

Alex tried to brush it off. "Sir, it took the whole crew, even Lieutenant Malik, to save the boat. In fact, the lieutenant saved my life, which probably saved all three of us as well as the OVAL."

The CAG smiled and spoke his next words softly. "I understand all that, Commander, and appreciate you giving him credit, but it was you who pulled your asses out of the fire with that crazy lanyard-swordfight stunt. But I do have one bone to pick with you, Commander Porter." He stepped up almost nose to nose with Alex. "You scratched the paint on my boat."

CHAPTER 57

ALWAYS WITH THE DRAGONS
IFC ENDEAVOR—ORBIT DAY 35

The next day, Baseball found Alex back in an almost deserted galley having some breakfast. He got a cup of coffee and sat down across from him. "I have a couple theories I'm going to pass by you, and I'd like your input."

"What, no mac and cheese?" mused Alex as he took a bite.

"The galley's run out. So, are you good with this?"

"Hmm—my mouth is full."

"Even better. Just sit there and listen. I'll try to make this simple."

"Well, that's a relief."

Baseball stirred the cream in his coffee. "Here's my take. We just let our dog shit all over a well-manicured lawn, and the owner of the house has been watching us from the attic window."

"That's pretty deep, even for you," Alex managed between bites. "So, what's the dog's name?"

Baseball scowled across the table and muttered, "Asshole."

"That's not nice. Don't you like the dog?"

"You know, sometimes I'd never get tired of slapping you."

"Better me than the dog, I suppose," offered Alex just as a pained look found his face. "Say, you don't still beat your dog, do you?"

"Stop it."

Alex shrugged innocently, glanced down at the remains of his food, frowned, and then turned his attention to his friend. "Fine, so what's this other observation you need to simplify for me?"

"Just a couple of things I need to trot past you."

Alex pushed his plate back.

"Right, then, here's my take. The *Monarch* was lured here by some obscure message sent from an ancient starship and then disappeared."

Alex yawned.

"Now we show up, with you aboard, to look for the aforementioned *Monarch*." Baseball stopped. "You still with me?"

Alex tilted his head back as his eyes fluttered.

"I'll take that as a yes. So, here we are orbiting the same planet that the ancient message drone originated from, and where the *Monarch* disappeared—"

"You said that already."

"I'm making a point here, Alex," Baseball stressed. "Now, we show up with a guy—that being you—who has visions about dragons, almost dies in the process, then, coincidently, has a life-or-death battle with them." Baseball scanned his friend's face for a reaction.

"Dragons," Alex said dispassionately. "Wonderful. Always with the dragons."

"Word around the ship has it that you charged into a pack of man-eating dragons with your sword in one hand and a practically empty pulse rifle in the other."

"You start believing everything you hear all of a sudden, Mr. Skeptical?" Alex looked at the remainder of his toast, decided against it, and drank some juice instead.

Baseball gave his tablemate a satisfied smirk, and then forged ahead. "Well, considering your recent associations with dragon hallucinations, that green-eyed dragon eye medallion that you never take off—" He shot Alex a sly glance. "Which, coincidently, is almost an exact match for the Dragon Eye Nebula that was referenced in that oh-so-secret *Magellan II* transmission that started this whole parade. And now, with your new penchant for slicing body parts off of the local dragon population with that big-ass razor you've got, I'm giving this rumor a definite possible oh hell yes."

Alex threw up his hands. "Why can't anybody call my katana by its proper name? And just who the hell is saying those were dragons that attacked the ship yesterday? Not me. And not only that, but how do you even know about my medallion? I've never shown it to anyone. And for that matter, how the do you even know about what was on the *Magellan II* transmission? Only the captain was given access to its content, and, in case you've forgotten, it's classified."

Baseball rolled his eyes and sighed like he was talking to a five-year-old. "Why, you called them dragons, and I'm not going to insult either of our intelligences by answering your question about the medallion."

"And the 'oh-so-classified' transmission?"

"Alex, I spent six months at a time with nothing to do but pick my nose, write those virtual combat programs that you enjoy so much," Baseball winked at his tablemate, "and of course, hack into the IFC's 'oh-so-classified' files."

"Whatever, but I never once called those things that attacked us 'dragons.' How do you come up with stuff like this?"

"Remember when you described the vision that almost killed you and then confided to me what actually saved you was, in fact, a golden-skinned, fire-breathing dragon?"

Alex retorted with more harshness than he'd ever used with his friend before. "I remember everything I said," he growled, "but these creatures weren't gold, they were a dark red, and they didn't breathe fire.

Not to mention that they were maybe a quarter the size of the one in my vision, and they sure as hell weren't trying to save me."

"So, yesterday, what you actually found was a smaller, redder, meaner species of the big dragon that spit goo all over you. Am I right?"

"Maybe," conceded Alex with much less venom than a second ago.

"Maybe my ass, Alex. Here's my main point. The original message from the *Magellan II* wasn't sent under command authority. Someone named Yanbeyeva sent it clandestinely. Ring a bell, brother?" Alex's jaw dropped. "Thought so. It wasn't sent to lure the *Monarch* here, or subsequently lure the *Endeavor* here either. No, that message was meant to get you here." Baseball leaned forward and locked eyes with Alex. "Because for whatever reason, this planet wants you, my friend. The rest of us are just the supporting cast waiting for our cue."

Alex's mouth opened to speak, but nothing came out.

Baseball sat back in his chair placing his hands behind his head and said, "Tell me you haven't thought the same thing in the last twenty-four hours."

Alex shut his mouth and continued to look at his friend with a blank stare.

"Okay, we both know that when you sport that glazed look and refuse to answer, it's because I'm right, and you just don't want to admit it. Right again, aren't I?"

The stare continued.

"All right, Alex, you've forced my hand here. So, here's what I'm willing to do just to get you to open up and admit what's really going on behind that vacant look attached to your face. I'll grant you any request—*any*—if you come clean and just admit that I'm right about this whole dragon-planet-getting-you-here-for-some-kind-of-ultimate-destiny-thing."

Baseball leaned back and waited.

While his expression didn't change, Alex said flatly, "Yes."

Baseball's smug expression evaporated. "Yes! Yes, what? Yes, I'm right? Yes, you'll answer me? Yes, the coffee sucks. Yes, what the fuck?"

"Yes, you're absolutely right." Alex's tone was barely audible as he admitted, "Yes, I've thought about the similarities between the dragon in the vision and the creatures that attacked us yesterday. Yes, I've endlessly dwelt on my family's role, with their green-eyed dragon crest, their generations of selective breeding that seem to have centered on me, and how all this is somehow predestined to play out down on that planet. Happy now?"

Baseball beamed like a kid with a new toy.

"I just have one major concern," Alex went on. "Not about your theory, because its plausibility is almost undeniable." Alex frowned at the smirk on his friend's face. "It's just—why did the IFC send a practically unarmed *Monarch* to a planet where they *knew* there was a possible threat, and then, when it disappeared, why did they send us with the exact same armament?"

"Exactly!" Baseball snapped his fingers. "When I hacked the IFC mission directive, I also managed to get in and read personal communications between the IFC top brass."

"That's a court-martial offense. You *do* realize that, right?"

"Yeah, whatever. Shut up and listen, because this is crucial."

Alex grimaced and asked, "More crucial than a court-martial?"

"The IFC believes that there's a human colony on Aqueous, and they think that it's under threat of an invasion by hostile natives, who, as you and I have already seen for ourselves, are mobilized and heading north as we speak, but here's the really important thing. They also believe that there's an advanced race of aliens, not the Lizard People, who actually control this planet and have a far more advanced technology than we do."

Alex slowly brought his hand to his forehead. "So, they sent in two basically unarmed ships that could never pose a threat to these advanced aliens." His voice grew taut with frustration. "Two ships that never had the firepower to start a fight, or worse, defend themselves in one." Alex's eyes widened as a thought struck him. "That means the captain has known about this all along. Imagine the stress of knowing that you're outgunned before you ever walk into a gunfight."

"I see you do get it after all," declared Baseball. "And since I'm a man of his word, what wish do you want me to grant you?"

"Call my sword by its real name."

"You named your sword?"

CHAPTER 58

QUESTIONS FIRST, SHOOT LATER
IFC ENDEAVOR—ORBIT DAY 35

D ragon Mountain changed everything.

When *OVAL Porter* was closely inspected for damage, it was discovered that the avionics, the aerothermodynamic inlet ducts, and the fusion nozzles had been the dragons' main targets. This discovery caused considerable debate about just how intelligent these flying lizards really were.

These vulnerable target points bore deep gouges where the dragons' talons had dug into the extraordinarily strong high-tech composite steel alloys. Only something stronger than the skin of the OVAL, which could withstand the extreme heat of repeated atmospheric entries, could cause these deep gouges. Dr. Prata presented a theory on how this was possible. He argued that the dragons must be able to excrete some kind of corrosive chemical from glands within their talons that could embrittle even the hardened alloy skin of an OVAL.

A qualitative-mass spectrometry analysis verified the doctor's theory. After all the data had been finalized, the command authorities' quick acceptance of this turned the dragons from just an aggressive animal into a formidable weapons system, and one not to be overlooked from now on.

Gunnar sat transfixed. He barely breathed, barely moved a muscle as he stared at his virtual monitor, stared at only one number. A feral growl emanated from deep within his throat as he balled both big hands into white-knuckled fists. After several moments, he blew out a long-held breath and relaxed his fists. He then used his thumb to tap the ring server on his left hand, blinked his left eye, and sat back as his OC screen closed. Without turning to face his captain, he muttered, "Twenty-nine hull perforations." He rubbed his eyes and asked no one in particular. "How the hell did they even make it back?" He finally looked over at Jennings and said, "I've changed my mind about keeping all the pulse cannons aboard the *Endeavor*."

Jennings blinked off his own OC and tilted his head toward the commander. "Care to expound on that, Gunnar?"

"Arm one of the OVALs," answered Gunnar, "preferably Porter's, and send them down in tandem."

"Agreed," said Jennings, "and we're done with the southern continent. Until further notice I'm ordering a cessation of all operations there." He glanced at Gunnar, who nodded his head, and added, "From now on we concentrate on solely the northern continent, and all sorties will fly in teams of two. *OVAL Hartley* remains equipped as is, and once Khaki's repaired *OVAL Porter*, we'll fit it with the weaponry."

Gunnar grunted something that sounded like approval.

Jennings stood up, stretched, and asked, "Is that what you had in mind?"

Another grunt and the matter was settled.

Though the *Endeavor* would not be completely stripped of her weapons system, half of it would now be used to protect the survey team.

One thing was for sure: there would be no more close contact with these dragons. All measures were taken to avoid them. If unavoidable, the dragons would be blown out of the sky without hesitation by the armed escort OVAL.

The thought that any intelligent, or even semi-intelligent, being was willing to die in order to protect their lair caused considerable concern and disagreement among the senior staff. During one particularly heated meeting, Baseball pointed out that perhaps the reason the dragons targeted these specific vital points was because they had faced these craft before. The debate ended at once.

An entirely new survey flight criterion would be in place from now on.

After conferring with Lieutenant Malik, Captain Jennings decided to begin surveying the northern continent from the tip of the peninsula, and then work the sorties up to the mountainous region that made up the bulk of the landmass. Except for the peninsula, a linear flight plan wouldn't be possible because of the extreme elevations of the mountains. Each survey within the continental interior would have to be intricately preplanned, and each flight plan would be mission specific. It also meant that most of the sorties could only be flown up the spiraling valley in order to remain below the critical altitude. It was assumed that there were a few places in the mountains that were low enough for them to pass through, and these were determined to be the crucial valley-to-valley extraction points. If a shuttle found that it couldn't safely fly through any of the mountain passes, it would have to turn around and return by the same route that it had taken up the valley.

As the chief weapons officer, Commander Gunnar Hammär ordered that *OVAL Porter* be fitted with two of the pulse cannons removed from the *Endeavor*'s hull. These could fire at a rapid rate and packed enough punch to blow a dragon to pieces. The cannons were mounted to hard points beneath the wings.

So far, throughout all of man's exploration of the stars, these weapons systems had never been fired in anger, and very few members of the IFC were trained in their use.

There had never been the need until now.

Commander Gunnar Hammär and Marine weapons specialist First Lieutenant Rebecca Laurent worked closely with CPO Khaki to install the swiveling pulse cannons. They tested their range of movement by hoisting the OVAL off the docking rails. While the installation crew was trying to decipher Khaki's profanity-laced instructions, Alex and Raj were inside the craft familiarizing themselves with the weapons control system. Neither pilot had ever fired a pulse cannon outside a simulator at the academy. Few pilots had. Gunnar, however, had fired them many times, always at practice targets, but he was an expert marksman, and only he and Lieutenant Laurent knew how these weapons would perform under flight conditions. After giving Rebecca some final instructions, Gunnar climbed into the cockpit with Alex and Raj.

With his usual louder-than-everybody-in-the-room voice, he gave the two pilots a few insights into how to operate the weapons. "Gentlemen, these puppies are not at all like the small-arms pulse rifles. One good shot at the maximum settings can damage a starship if fired outside an atmosphere. A few good shots can disable, maybe even destroy one." He looked at his two young pilots to see if they were on the same page before continuing. "However, it's damned near impossible for a human operator to make those kinds of shots on his own, even with the targeting sights that'll come up on your optic computers. Therefore, I strongly suggest you keep your hands off the gun controls at all times and allow the Marine gunner to operate them. Any questions so far?"

Raj wouldn't have asked Gunnar Hammär a question if his life depended on it, so he kept his mouth shut, but Alex had a few questions. "Gunnar, if we happen to land in the shit and find ourselves with thousands of bandits, like we encountered at Dragon Mountain, how close do I have to be before the atmosphere degrades the plasma?"

"If you can see them with the naked eye, then that's close enough," answered Gunnar.

"That's good to know," continued Alex, "but how much of the ship's power can I use for the cannons while still leaving the engines with enough energy to hit escape velocity, if it comes to that?"

"Alex, if you run into a target-rich environment, then you are to cover the survey shuttle until it makes good his escape, then get your ass the hell out of there. Do not stand and fight! Is that clear, Commander?"

"Absolutely, sir, but is there a point when I need to either stop firing the cannons, or slow down, in order to maintain an overwhelming suppression fire?"

Scratching the bridge his of his nose, Gunnar paused a moment before answering. "Alex, there's no way for me to answer that. You'll just have to make the decision on the spot. Look, every engagement is going to be different. There's no handbook on what to do in every possible scenario. You'll just have to choose an option at the time and hope like hell you picked the right one."

"I understand, sir. I'll maintain position so that Lieutenant Laurent can lock onto those big flying bastards and blow them to hell before they can close. We'll be fine, sir."

When Alex and Raj finally crawled out of the cockpit, Raj looked at the pulse cannons and asked, "What do you think, boss? Are we going to have to light those big candles up?"

"I sure hope not, Raj, but if we do, we're going to do exactly like Commander Hammär suggested." He slapped his copilot on the back. "We'll be good because we'll be ready this time. At Dragon Mountain we got too close out of ignorance. That won't happen again."

The next morning the two flight crews met with Captain Jennings, Commander Hammär, and CAG Eaglecreek on the flight deck. Joining them was the Marine weapons officer, Lieutenant Rebecca Laurent. Lieutenant Malik had joined the survey team on Baseball's OVAL.

As usual, Captain Jennings led the briefing. "Ladies and gentlemen, this initial survey run will only last four hours. It's not a lengthy mission, but we want to evaluate how flying the OVALs in tandem will work out. If all goes well, as I expect it will, then we'll lengthen the mission duration up to six hours, and possibly eight." His gaze took in every member the sortie teams before giving up the floor. "I'll now turn over the mission briefing to the CAG. Good luck, gentlemen."

CAG Eaglecreek launched into his usual, no-nonsense, get-to-the-point, watch-your-ass, and don't-break-my-boat briefing. "The escort, *OVAL Porter,* will be first to enter the atmosphere. Commander Porter, you are to be extra diligent during your drop. Your weapon system will be worthless if you burn the damn things up entering the atmosphere. Are we clear here, Commander?"

"We are, sir," replied Alex.

Eaglecreek narrowed his eyes at the new commander and said, "See that you are." He addressed Baseball next. "*OVAL Hartley,* you will wait until *OP* is safely within the atmosphere and standing to at station before making your drop. In the event that Commander Porter was, in fact, clear with his instructions, and manages to make his rendezvous position intact, then he will cover the survey shuttle's drop. At this point both craft will advance feet wet in a staggered formation. Once feet dry, and under the cloud cover, you will continue as per your preset flight plans.

"Here's the deal, gentlemen. As you're aware, this is a totally different terrain from what we encountered on the southern continent. Instead of endless flatland and few rivers, you'll encounter huge mountain ranges with peaks well into the 7500-meter range with large rivers and their deep valleys. We have to assume that we can't go over most of these mountains because of the cloud ceiling." The CAG paused and locked eyes with each member of his flight crews before continuing, "We will, however, be traversing multiple valleys. Often more than once per sortie, but if you find that you can't cross through a low altitude pass before your flight time has run out, then you're to turn back and extract the way you came in.

"You already know the initial mission parameters, but it bears repeating: for today's flight, you will begin at the southern end of the peninsula and work your way up the western edge. By the time you get to the northern end of the peninsula, your mission time is over. Wrap it up, head to the edge of the cloud cover, return to orbit and rendezvous with the *Endeavor*." Eaglecreek placed his hands behind his back and methodically walked up and down the line as he spoke. "The survey shuttle will conduct their mission parameters exactly as before. The armed escort will be the hawk watching over the dove from above. This will give you a height advantage in case of any engagement."

He stopped his pacing and took a small step forward. "If *any* bandit is encountered and contact is unavoidable, the survey shuttle is to immediately leave the engagement area while the escort covers. Once the survey shuttle has safely removed itself from the theater, the escort will disengage and do the same." His eagle-like gaze then locked onto

Alex's eyes. "There will be no stand and fight. Is that fully understood, Commander Porter?"

"Roger that," replied the junior commander.

"Good to hear, Commander. Because as impressed as we all were with your last sortie, I want zero bent boats that we have to send back to the taxpayer. I want you, your crew, and my boats back in the basement safe and sound." The CAG took a stiff step back and said, "That will be all. Carry on. Oh, and if I haven't mentioned it before, bring my boats back unbent! DEAL?" His final word echoed in the flight bay.

"Aye, sir," the flight crew resounded in unison.

The preboard broke up, and the two crews headed for their respective OVALs. Alex and Baseball had a brief conversation on the flight deck before mounting up.

"Baseball, in the immortal words of Khaki, 'don't y'all fret none you sombitch, cuz I gots yer back, Bubba.' You'll get your survey, *and* I'll get the CAG's boat back unbent. Promise."

"That's really reassuring, Alex," said Baseball, "and if it was anybody else up there I might be worried, but I'm pretty sure that you couldn't shoot me down even if you tried. So, I'm feeling pretty safe." They bumped fists, turned, and made their way over to their own shuttles. Standing at his OVAL's hatch waiting for his crew to enter, Baseball turned and yelled over at his friend, "Just remember the order of engagement: questions first, shoot later. Okay?"

"I'll pass that onto my gunner," Alex shot back, "but she might have other ideas."

"Don't worry, gentlemen," Lieutenant Laurent assured them as she ducked her head to enter the hatch, "I'll kill anything with leather wings."

"They've got scales," Malik corrected from the other hatchway right before Rox shoved him inside.

"Right, those are dead too," Laurent said confidently and disappeared into the shuttle.

Baseball cocked his head to one side and silently mouthed over to Alex, "Yikes." The two pilots grinned at each other, turned, and followed their crews into their boats.

CHAPTER 59

THE NORTHERN CONTINENT
IFC ENDEAVOR—ORBIT DAY 36

O*VAL Porter* made its drop over the ocean, stood off at 11,000 meters and reconnoitered the point of entry. Once he determined that there weren't any threats, Alex gave Baseball the all clear. "*OH, OP,* do you copy?"

Baseball responded immediately, "Copy, *OP.*"

"*OH,* the entry point is an all clear. Repeat, entry point is an all clear. Come on down, Baseball, the water's fine," quipped Alex while keeping his optic computer tied in with the scanner.

Within five minutes both crews were at their feet-wet rendezvous position and headed toward the southern tip of the long peninsula at a leisurely Mach one point five.

While they were still hundreds of kilometers from the coastline, Lieutenant Malik made a startling discovery and immediately informed his pilot. "Lieutenant Baseball, I'm getting some interesting readings concerning the cloud ceiling."

"*OP, OH.* Alex, Amil's getting a cloud ceiling reading here that's completely different from what we had over the southern continent. It's over 8,000 meters high."

"Roger that, Baseball. But as good as this news is, we maintain the flight plan until otherwise informed. I'll let the *Endeavor*

349

know, but until our orders change, we stick to the original descent schedule."

"*Endeavor, OVAL Porter*, do you copy?"

"*OVAL Porter, Endeavor*, what's your copy, Alex?" answered the CAG.

"*Endeavor, OP*. Commander Eaglecreek, I need to speak with the captain ASAP. *OVAL Hartley*'s LRS is showing the cloud ceiling at 8,300 meters. Repeat, cloud ceiling is much higher than before. *OP* out."

Within a minute Captain Jennings came on the comm. "*OP, Endeavor*, the CAG has told me that *OH* is registering a cloud ceiling of 8,300 meters. Is that correct?"

"That's a roger, Captain. We'll have visual confirmation within four minutes, but even from here it looks much higher than before." Alex couldn't help but grin at this prospect.

The captain sounded cautious. "*OP, Endeavor*. Alex, remain on your present descent schedule until I've had a chance to confer with the CAG. Do you copy?"

"Roger that. Sticking to the original flight plan until otherwise informed," Alex quickly confirmed. "Sir? We'll become feet dry pretty quick. May I suggest we maintain a holding pattern about one hundred kilometers off the coast until I hear back from you?"

"Good thinking. Hold station until I get back to you. I'm sure it won't take very long. Keep an eye on the cloud ceiling. *Endeavor* out."

Alex relayed the new orders to Baseball, and both shuttles began a fifty-kilometer-wide loop while still over the ocean about one hundred kilometers from the southern tip of the peninsula. *OVAL Hartley* maintained the lower altitude at 850 meters while Alex kept his at 890. At these low altitudes, they could clearly see anything on the surface of the water, and what they saw looked familiar.

"Alex, are you seeing what I'm seeing? About 30° off our six?" Baseball made a bat-turn to get a better visual. It was still early morning at this latitude and the red star's light reflected off the listless sea, turning the horizon's aurora into a deep magenta.

"Roger that, Baseball. We got ourselves a fleet of those lizard boats on a northernly heading. Looks like about thirty or forty of them," Alex said.

"There's actually thirty-eight of them," Baseball rectified.

"But there should only be thirty-seven," mentioned Malik.

"How so?" asked Alex.

"Remember? There were forty, then three split off," answered the surveyor. "Now there's one extra. And I think I know which one."

"And?"

"There's a ship being towed, and it's unlike any of the others," Malik told Baseball. "It's got a completely different design; far more advanced, and its wood is a completely different species."

"What about the crew?" asked Baseball. When no answer came, he pressed the survey chief. "Malik, the crew?"

"I can't tell, Lieutenant," mumbled Malik. His eyes riveted on the scanner. "There's no one on board, but I'm picking up blood trails on the starboard aft."

"Whose blood?" Alex's voice came over the intercom.

"I can't tell, Commander. It's too diluted with seawater."

"Understood. Baseball, go take a look, but not too low. Rebecca's tracking you, but keep a safe distance."

"Just keep those fingers off the trigger," Baseball muttered and turned toward the small fleet.

"That's no fun," commented Rebecca as she made target acquisition on the fleet.

Baseball banked tightly over the ships. "I see it, and Malik's right; there's no one on the deck of what looks to me like some sort of schooner."

"It's a sloop," corrected Malik. "I used to sail when I was a kid."

"What's it doing with the Lizard People?" wondered Alex.

"Maybe it was captured by the war fleet." The two OVALs went quiet for a moment as Malik's answer sunk in.

"Are you thinking what I'm thinking, Baseball?"

"Yeah, Alex," answered Baseball, "I am. If so, then it probably belongs to the folk they're going to invade, and if that's the case then it's gonna happen soon. Because at this rate they should make landfall in about a day."

"We'll let *Endeavor* know, and it looks like your invasion theory was spot on," said Alex. "I also remember that naval base. There were several thousand huge, barge-like, galley-looking war craft, and millions of troops there. This fleet is made up of much sleeker and faster ships. I wonder if this is the advance guard of that invasion?"

A chaotic panic swept the deck of the *Ocean Fang*. The frightened crew screeched, pointed at the sky, and scrambled for cover. When the rhythm drums missed a couple beats and her flagship lurched to port, Duchess Thorna let out an angry hiss at the coxswain and screamed at the terrified crew, "Get back to your posts, you craven belly crawlers, or I'll have you cooked alive!"

Another sound, different from the cowardly cacophony that had taken over her ship, suddenly screamed overhead. Thorna looked up and went rigid. A huge silver bird, or maybe some new species of dragon, roared directly over her ship, and then just as quick, disappeared from view. Thorna searched the sky but saw nothing more. Her eyes turned molten and swept the ship to find the officer of the watch. Finally finding him quivering at the aft, she jabbed at the deck in front of her. The lizard deferentially scrambled forward and fell to his knees. Thorna hissed her angry order, "Double the lookouts, and inform me if that thing returns, but I'm sure that the sight of my glorious fleet scared it off."

The officer bowed and scurried away, but before he could take three steps, his Duchess master added to the orders. "And go tell that miserable cook that I want those softskins served bloody rare. Now move it, I'm ravenous."

Five minutes after their last communication, Captain Jennings came back on the comm with the command decision: "*OVAL Porter, Endeavor.* Do you copy?"

"Copy, sir."

"Alex, the mission parameters remain in place for now. Proceed on the survey grid as per the original plan until we've had a chance to crunch the numbers." The comms went dead for twenty seconds before Jennings came back on line. "We'll have a plan soon. SADI will transmit it to you as per the following schedule: at 09:30 you are to temporarily suspend operations and both crews are to head to the nearest feet-wet point. It looks like that's at 16° latitude. Once you've become feet wet, rattle our cage, and we'll send you the new survey grid. Is that a copy?"

"Roger that, sir. We copy and will call you the moment we leave the cloud cover at 16° latitude." Alex liked this plan, but suddenly the bee in his chest began its irritating buzz. "Just one more thing, sir. We've spotted a fleet of those lizard boats on a heading toward the southern tip of the peninsula. Probably the bay, and it looks like they've taken a boat prisoner."

"We've seen them too, Commander. However, this fleet is inconsequential to our mission directive. There will be no communication between the indigenous population and us."

Jennings finished up his transmission with one final thought. "This altitude change really works in our favor, gentlemen. The survey time has been reduced by over eighty percent. We should have this wrapped up in seventy-two hours. Is all this a copy?"

"Roger that, sir. We copy. *OP* out," said Alex evenly, but the buzzing in his chest became more insistent.

———————

After receiving their new flight parameters, both crews turned inland. They were quickly feet dry, and the first major surprise manifested itself within seconds of crossing the coastline.

As Baseball began heading up the peninsula, an excited Lieutenant Malik yelled in his mic, "BASEBALL! I've got a huge electronic signature coming up in 52 kilometers! It looks like a power grid of a major modern city!" He began to adjust his analytical equipment to better focus on this new survey target. "And their harbor is filled with boats just like that captive one we spotted earlier."

Baseball went on full alert. Using his OC, he was able to zoom in on what had Malik so worked up. "Good job, Amil. Stay focused on it, but for fuck's sake don't scream in my ear again."

"Uh, okay. Now I'm picking up hundreds of thousands of biological units!" Malik had calmed somewhat but was still amped up. "I'm getting a read on them now. Coming up—holy shit! This is really weird."

"Amil, can you be a little more specific than 'holy shit this is really weird'?"

"Baseball, this city is inhabited by people."

"People, Lieutenant? Again, more specifics?"

"Absolutely," reported Malik, "people, as in human beings, as in *Homo sapiens*, as in hundreds of thousands of them."

Rox had so far stayed out of the guys' conversation, but their present discussion broke her silence. She frowned over at her pilot, and then keyed her intercom. "Lieutenant Malik, you'd better be one hundred percent on this. If we report we've found a human civilization, and it turns out to be something else, we're all going to look like idiots. You catch my drift, Lieutenant?"

Undeterred, Lieutenant Malik responded with complete conviction. "I understand, but I've dialed in the bio-diversification analytical unit, and it's coming back with a 99.98 percent DNA match. These are human beings! I'm also picking up tens of thousands more in the region surrounding this city. This is a sizable population. There could be half a million people down there. Maybe more. There's too much mountainous terrain to get an accurate body count. Be that as it may, this is a significantly sized civilization."

Baseball instantly made the connection and told his copilot, "Rox, these must be the descendants from the *Magellan II*. So that means that boat must've had a human crew. That mysterious message must have originated from their ancestors. The IFC brass got that part right anyway."

"What 'mysterious message,' Baseball?" she asked suspiciously. "Is this the same message that the captain made plain to the entire crew as strictly classified?"

"Oh, um, I guess I forgot to tell you," Baseball angled away from his hack job. "I, er, might have accidently read a communication between

IFC and the captain, and it may have mentioned something like that."

"I'm pretty sure I don't want to know any more," declared Rox, shaking her head. "Do I?"

"Yeah—um, probably not," Baseball mumbled and quickly shifted his attention to his escort. "*OP, OH*. Alex, we've got some extraordinary data coming in here. Are you sitting down? Our data is showing that we're presently approaching a highly technological city, complete with an electrical system, and get this: it has about half a million human inhabitants. Do you copy?" Baseball smiled over at his copilot.

Alex's response was immediate. "Did I copy right?" he asked. "Repeat your last transmission. Did you say human inhabitants?"

"That's a roger, Alex. Amil has double-checked his bio-diversification toys, and their DNA is a match. They're *Homo sapiens*, Alex. Folk like us."

"That's a copy, but how did this—Baseball, this only makes sense if these are the descendants of the *Magellan II*. If that's the case, as extraordinary as that sounds, then we've probably just achieved one of our mission objectives. This is huge, but as big as this is, we need to keep it tight until we reach the extraction point. This city isn't going anywhere, but as soon as we get feet wet I think we'll blow the *Magellan II* fable right out of the water."

"Roger that, *OP*. Maintaining original flight plan as per orders. I'll keep you abreast of any further developments. Just a thought, but we've found more in the first ten minutes surveying this continent than we did in all the weeks spent in the south."

"Look at that city, Baseball," exclaimed Rox as they cruised directly over it. "It's perfect. Beautiful tree-lined boulevards, and all the buildings look like they're made out of crystal. It even has a gorgeous river running right through it, and look, there's more of those boats on the river."

"They've used the same wood anyway," confirmed Malik.

"Seems to me that these 99.98 percent humans have done pretty well for themselves. It's got everything," mused Rox.

"Including those perfect giant walls that surround it," observed Baseball. "My take is that they're gonna need those in the not-too-distant future."

Malik got on the mic. "Lieutenant Baseball, there's something else significantly different on this continent."

"Let me guess, Amil," replied Baseball, "you've found metal, right?"

"Well yes," affirmed Malik. He slid a finger across his screen and increased the sensor's resolution. His mouth went slightly agape at the enhanced data. He finally tore his eyes away from the screen, looked at the back of his pilot's head, and asked, "How did you know that?"

"You don't want to go there, Malik," warned Rox.

"Gosh, let me think," Baseball said thoughtfully.

"Told ya."

"Please, Rox," Baseball said, "I'm struggling to come up with an answer here."

"Of course you are," she said from the side of her mouth. "Is it too late to request a transfer?"

"I've told you before: only if you take me with you," offered Baseball.

"Are you missing the point on purpose?"

"Probably," Baseball admitted, "but be that as it may, request denied." He turned his attention back to Lieutenant Malik and told him, "Amil, I'm gonna take a wild stab at this and say that perhaps you found metal in that city's power grid."

"Yeah, but not simple ores. There are a variety of manufactured alloys with a metal matrix similar to our own. I'm running an MAS now."

"A what?" asked Rox.

"The Molecular Aging Scan," Malik mumbled while studying his instruments, "and the scan shows that all these alloys are at least a thousand years old."

CHAPTER 60

A FRIEND
CAMBRIA—AQUEOUS

S prawling over eight hectares, Troy University took up more land than any other single institution within the protective walls of Cambria. Housed on its grounds were the schools of science, engineering, medicine, and the cradle for all the knowledge that humanity possessed: the University Library.

When Cambria was first built, the original colonists created huge swathes of parkland on both sides of the Crystal River and planted thousands of bur oak trees with seeds they had brought with them from Earth. A thousand years later, these majestic trees still towered over the Park of the River Woods. The slow-moving river flowed past the university's northern boundary. Its grassy banks were planted with wildflowers under low-hanging willow trees. The park itself provided students and faculty with easy access to the myriad of garden pathways, small creeks, and footbridges that interlaced through the ancient trees. No building was closer to the park than the library.

It had been five years since Patti Hammär had been dumped in Cambria by the dragon riders of Drakon Rus. Five years of living and working at the library. Five years of filling in the thousand-year gap in human history. She'd written books, taught classes, conducted seminars, and given up all hope that her life was ever going to be anything different from what it had become since being stranded on this planet.

Admittedly, it hadn't been a bad life. The Cambrians, for their part, had treated her well, and she was a respected member of the faculty, but it wasn't the life she would have chosen for herself. Her life was somewhere in the stars. Stars she hadn't even seen in five years. Except for the park's hiking trails, Patti rarely left the university grounds. Her comfortable apartment was there, and her office had a large window overlooking the tranquility of the tree-filled park. It was her favorite escape, and it was right outside her window.

While on her daily sojourn away from the confines of the library, Patti took a walk on a particularly secluded trail. After several minutes, she was deep in the woods when she heard a sound that sent a chill down her spine. It was as familiar to her as her own voice, but it was a sound that she hadn't heard since the day she became stranded on Aqueous. Patti heard the unmistakable whine of fusion engines as they flew overhead. It sounded like two craft, and they sounded close, no more than a thousand meters above her. She began running, trying to get to the riverbank and open skies. She was desperate to get a glimpse, hoping beyond hope that they were OVALs. But by the time she got to the river the sound was gone, and the sky was clear: nothing but those damn clouds. Patti put her hands over her ears and let out a wailing shriek.

"Hurts, don't it?"

Patti whipped around at the sound of the oddly familiar voice. "You," she said to the man standing in the shadows. "W-what hurts?"

He stepped out from behind a giant oak tree, so she could see him clearly. He had filled out since the last time she had seen him. His voice had become manlier, and his face had lost all trace of youthful innocence.

"Being so close to your heart's desire that you can almost taste it," he said sympathetically, "only to have it disappear in the blink of an eye."

Her eyes darted to the sky and then back down. "Yes, it does."

"I understand completely." He closed the distance and put a hand on her arm.

Patti pulled away. "What is it you want, Bayne?"

"Bayne is dead," he told her. "I am Count Darx, and I have come to inform you that I have forgiven you."

She frowned and took a small step back. "Right. Well, see ya."

"Don't you want to know why?"

"Some other time maybe," she said and started walking away, but only managed two steps before a painful cramp seized both her calf muscles. Patti squealed in pain, stumbled, and fell to her knees.

"Now would probably be best," said Count Darx. "I'll stop the pain if you promise to listen to me."

Grimacing, Patti squinted up at him and barely managed to croak, "Okay, I-I'll listen." The pain stopped.

"So nice to hear," he said casually, and extended a hand to help her off the ground. "I've forgiven you for telling Major Garcia all those nasty things about me." He smiled down at her. "Now that that ugly business is out of the way, I'll also tell why I've sought you out."

"Y-you've looked for me?" she said, ignoring his hand.

"Of course I have, Patricia. I need a friend."

She curled her legs underneath her and said, "We haven't seen each other for five years, and then only briefly."

"True, but things have changed, my lady. We now have a mutual need."

"What are you talking about?"

"As I believe you're already aware, those craft that just flew overhead are from Earth." He smiled at her reaction to the mention of Earth. "I have it on good authority that one or more of the craft will land soon."

"Whose authority?"

"I'm not at liberty to say, but when it happens I'll need introductions, and I believe that you are uniquely qualified to provide those."

Patti gasped. "T-that means—"

"Yes, Patricia," he told her kindly, "it means that your time here on Aqueous could soon be coming to an end. So, are we agreed?" He offered his hand again.

Patti hesitated a moment, and then nodded. "All right," she said, and took it.

CHAPTER 61

EVIDENCE
IFC ENDEAVOR—ORBIT DAY 36

The mood in the OVALs became optimistic as the teams cruised up the peninsula. Just seeing the thriving human civilization gave the crews from Earth hope. It was also obvious that this continent supported a far greater diversification of life than did the southern landmass. For hundreds of kilometers just north of the city, much of the land had been cleared and a modern agricultural region was well established. Produce ranged from fruit orchards to wheat fields, vegetables, and even large cotton fields. Intermixed with these well-managed farms were large ranches full of domesticated herd animals. All the abundant farm animals had similar DNA profiles as their horse, cow, and hog cousins on Earth.

All of Malik's social physiology scans showed that this human civilization was well established and fully self-sufficient. It also seemed well balanced with the ecology. One oddity that had Malik checking and double-checking his sensors was that this seemingly modern civilization had no self-propelled vehicles. Transportation was either on horseback or riverboat. It just seemed an inherent contradiction. Nor were there any aircraft. Nothing was in the air but the OVALs and a wide variety of small flying creatures.

The large coastal plain on the western side of the mountain range was blanketed with a dense forest of huge twenty-meter-tall oak-type trees found up to the edge of the human frontier. Just beyond that frontier the coastal plain rose in elevation as the peninsula approached the main landmass, and the forests became more of a coniferous type with trees growing up to thirty meters.

The bio-diversification instruments also showed that, unlike the southern continent, most of the animal life on the southern half of the peninsula consisted of an assortment of mammals. These ranged from large herbivores to a huge bear-type omnivore that seemed to be the dominant predator species. The farther north they traveled up the peninsula, the fewer mammals and the more reptiles they encountered. So far, none of the intelligent species of reptile that dominated the southern landmass were present.

There was also a mix of birds in the southern portion of the peninsula, but as they made their way up the peninsula, they found more small flying reptiles. None of the dragon beasts that had attacked *OVAL Porter* were spotted, and nothing approaching even a twentieth their size was evident.

As they approached the scheduled extraction point, Lieutenant Malik began to pick up a faint reading on his over-the-horizon scanner that riveted him like nothing else before. As they drew closer, he focused the elemental diagnostic scanner on the reading. Fumbling with his intercom, Malik was barely able to speak. "Baseball, I've picked up something—"

Baseball and Rox heard the stress in their surveyor's voice and shared a quick glance as Baseball keyed his mic. "What've you got, Amil?"

Malik's gulp was audible through the intercom, "Ugh—"

"Relax, Malik," encouraged Rox. "Just take a deep breath and spit it the hell out."

Baseball pressed the survey chief, "So, what's got your attention? In four minutes we'll head back to *Endeavor*."

"I know, but I think I've just found part of the *Monarch*."

Baseball and Rox shared a quick glance before she tapped her intercom and demanded, "Just what are you on about back there?"

"I'm picking up a small craft, or the remains of one with a composite alloy skin. Guys, this is an exact metallurgical match for an OVAL. It must be from the *Monarch*." He couldn't hide his emotion, and Baseball found it difficult to hide his.

"Fantastic job, Amil!" Baseball exclaimed. "Keep trying to get data from it, and I'll get hold of *OVAL Porter*." Speaking twice as fast as he normally did, Baseball's voice was about two octaves higher as he tapped his ship-to-ship. "Alex, I really hope you're still sitting down this time, because we just blew the lid off this baby!"

"You didn't find more cows, did you?" asked Alex.

"That's a great big nooo, buddy. We just found the first evidence of the *Monarch*!"

A moment of silence followed before *OP* came back on line. "What exactly did you find?"

"We've found evidence of an OVAL on the northernmost ring of mountains," Baseball's voice cracked with excitement, "a-and it appears to have had a hard landing, but maybe it's intact enough to make a positive identification."

"That's huge," replied Alex. "Did you find any life or human remains in the wreckage?"

"No, not yet. Maybe it was evacuated either before or after setting down."

Malik's excited voice came over the comm system. "Baseball, I'm picking up an ident signature from the hull. It's from the long-range scanner, and it's not complete, but I think I can run with what I've got here." Malik's voice became steadier as he bent over his instruments and cross-referenced the information. "And it looks like this is—was, *OVAL Hammär*."

His voice grew circumspect. "I know I'll be asked, so my gut feeling is that this must be connected with our own Commander Hammär?"

If there was an error, Baseball wanted it to be on the side of caution. "Could be, Amil, but we'll find out for sure soon enough." Then to *OP*, he said, "Alex, did you hear any of that?"

"Yeah, I heard it all, Baseball, and this just changed the entire game. Let's get back to *Endeavor* and let the brass know."

CHAPTER 62

HER OBSESSION
THE SPINE—AQUEOUS

The two Dark Dragons had staged their patrols from the cave for three days. It was cold, hard, and smelled like stale dirt, but it was large enough to accommodate a dozen dragons and their riders. As of late, it housed only two. The cave was well concealed on the eastern slope of the Spine, and it was the perfect vantage point from which patrols could keep an eye on the Cambrian colony. Dragon riders had been using it for centuries.

"But she listens to you, Vlad." Daymi appealed to his colonel as he tightened the harness straps on his mount.

Moroz heaved his provision-laden saddlebag over the back of his fidgeting dragon, turned to the other rider, and told him, "Apparently you haven't heard the last several conversations we've had. If you had, then you'd know that the Tsarina has a mind of her own. Especially ever since she—hey! Stop that, damn it!" He swore and grabbed for the saddlebag dangling from his dragon's mouth.

After watching the ensuing tug-of-war for a moment, Daymi finished the other man's sentence. "You mean ever since she came back from the Sanctuary." He climbed into his saddle and strapped in.

"What I *meant*, Major," grumbled the colonel as he managed to wrench the bag free, "is that ever since Rodinya began meddling, the

Tsarina has become obsessed."

"Meddling with what?"

"This conversation has officially gotten old," Moroz growled irritably and climbed into his saddle. "We have a patrol to fly."

Daymi reached down and patted his mount on its neck. "So you say, but before my dragon breaks a sweat, I'd like to be reminded just what it is we're supposed to accomplish on these patrols, because I'm down to my last clean set of underwear, and the company's grown cranky." The major leaned back in his saddle, threw a leg across its pommel, and scratched underneath his flight helmet.

"Fine," Moroz groused, "be stubborn."

"Permission noted."

"Her meddling is why we're now sleeping in a cave, and not our own beds."

"So," surmised Daymi, "you're saying Rodinya ordered the two top officers of Drakon Rus to personally go on this patrol?"

"Are you trying to try my patience?"

"Pretty much."

Moroz threw his hands up in frustration. "Ever since Rodinya lured—"

"Lured, really?"

"Let me tell this," Moroz snapped, his face flushing red, "would you?"

Daymi shrugged.

"Yes, lured Anya to the Sanctuary—"

"Yeah, I know all that, Vlad. To get her prophecy book," interjected Daymi, "which, if memory serves me correctly, is pretty damn important to our civilization."

"Are you defending Rodinya?"

The junior officer shot right back. "No more than you're condemning her. Look, it seems to me, that dragon's the reason Anya has this obsession in the first place. And as far as I'm concerned, that's a good thing. If you ask me, your problem with Rodinya stems from the fact that she introduced Anya to her prophecy book. The tenets of which our Tsarina now regard as policy of state."

"I didn't hear anybody ask you."

"That's because I'm right."

Moroz sighed, and barely nodded his head. "Yeah maybe, but it still rankles me."

"Yeah, I get that too, but what I don't get," Daymi pushed, "is why Anya doesn't reach out to Cambria? I mean, if we normalized relations with them, then these damned patrols wouldn't be needed."

Moroz grumped his answer. "Anya's waiting for Rodinya." He pulled his goggles down. "We're all waiting for that damn dragon," he groused and launched his own.

It took a day to cross over to the west side of the Spine and fly past the mouth of the large bay at the end of the peninsula. They made camp on a tranquil beach only twenty meters from where powerful breakers slammed into a natural jetty. Moroz built a small fire while Daymi caught their dinner. As evening waned, the two patrolmen ate quietly and watched the sun turn from rusty red to a deep lavender as it sank below the ocean's horizon. Soon, twinkling stars filled the southern sky.

Moroz stared into the flames, and finally broke his daylong silence. "I'm here right now because Anya is convinced that the Hope Prophecy is imminent and feels the need to know what's happening in Cambria without alerting them to our—her obsession." The campfire's flicker obscured his strained features. "And she trusts no one else with this."

"Okay, so why am I here?"

"Because you're my oldest friend," Moroz confessed, "and there's no one I trust more."

Early the next morning they took off and flew back toward the Spine. An hour after launch, both dragons snarled and became agitated at the same time. The two riders automatically banked hard in opposite directions and dove below the treetops. By the time the dragons had touched down, both riders had their crossbows cocked and loaded. After landing, Moroz remained in the saddle and swiveled his head around to see what had caused all the fuss. Directly above them a flash of silver caught his attention. "Daymi!" he yelled and pointed up just as two metallic vehicles zipped overhead less than a kilometer away.

"What the hell are those?"

"Anya's obsession," muttered Moroz.

"Really?" snorted the junior officer, and offered a grin to his friend. "Then it looks like Rodinya was right all along?"

"Don't remind me, Daymi, and while you're not reminding me, fly back to Drakon Rus and report to Anya what we've seen."

"Aren't you coming?"

"No."

"You should reconsider," asserted Daymi. "It's too dangerous to be out here alone with a dragon that doesn't like you."

"There's no choice now," Moroz offered solemnly as he glanced back up at the sky. "I need to stay and find out if the final war really is upon us."

CHAPTER 63

THE SAME FATE
OFOL'R—LOG'RFOLD

Dreng'r floated into his supreme leader's dwelling to give the latest report. "Mab'r, the Earthlings have discovered the evidence they were meant to find."

Erland'r began emitting a soft green glow as he rotated toward Dreng'r. "Good. This means that they'll want to investigate, and in doing so they will set into motion the next phase." Erland'r thought for a moment before asking, "Was it exactly where we wanted it to be?"

"Yes, Mab'r, it was left where it crashed, near the northern axis projector, and any attempt to access its systems will destroy it. The Rond'r brought it down since we no longer have O'rmsliki protecting that projector," explained Dreng'r. His bodily gases flashed a brief but intense red. "Unlike on the southern projector. Recently the O'rmsliki there almost destroyed a similar type of this craft from this new starship."

"Understood," acknowledged the Mab'r as he began wafting back and forth in deep thought. "This is sooner than anticipated," he mused, "so the plan will need to be accelerated before implementation, but this might work out well for us, Dreng'r." He floated in place. "When they investigate the bait, they will need to touch down, and when they do, their starship will meet the same fate as its predecessor."

"Once their starship is under imminent threat from the Rond'r orbs, they will launch a communication drone back to Earth," Dreng'r theorized, "but what if they don't?"

"They will," the Mab'r replied confidently. "And once underway, I want it uploaded with the required data. Make sure the Rond'r leave their drone unscathed."

"And the starship, Mab'r?" asked Dreng'r.

"There is nothing to be done about that, but that drone is to reach Earth. They must have the technology we give them."

Dreng'r made a slight bow to his master, and reflected, "Once the drone reaches Earth, the humans will use our technology to build advanced weaponry and send a powerful war fleet next time."

"Yes, they will," Erland'r agreed. "I'm counting on it."

CHAPTER 64

EFFERVESCENT EFFECT
IFC ENDEAVOR—ORBIT DAY 37

Back on board the *Endeavor*, once the survey results of the northern continent had been downloaded, the emotional state became electric. An operations meeting was called by Captain Jennings to discuss the findings and reevaluate their previous mission parameters.

Jennings was convinced that their initial survey grid was now immaterial, and that they should concentrate on the OVAL crash site—an OVAL from the *Monarch*. Focusing their assets there was far more important to both Captain Jennings and Commander Hammär than anywhere else. The fact that it was empty meant there could have been survivors. For the first time in years, the two men dared to feel hope.

This was Patti's ship.

Jennings approached his brother-in-law, and for a moment they just grinned at each other. "Let's not get our hopes up too much, Gunnar. The shuttle was empty."

"Yeah, but you know as well as I do that that means the crew abandoned ship and could still be alive," the big man insisted. "I refuse to give up hope now. Patti was trained at survival and found some way to stay alive." Gunnar drew in a big gulp of air before going on. "She's down there, Richard. Remember, there's that human city the boys flew over, and if their theory holds water, and those lizard ships are closing in for an attack, then we need to step in soon."

"I see it the same way, but let's wait to see what the physical inspection comes up with," Jennings cautioned his friend. "If there's any sign of an evacuation, we'll search this planet until we find her, starting at that city."

"She's there, Richard," Gunnar said with more conviction than he had ever felt in his life. "I just know she's there. Looks like we got here just in time."

"Agreed, Gunnar, but I need to be absolutely sure before I take any martial action." Captain Jennings smiled as he looked at his security chief and couldn't help yanking the big man's chain. "And all that bit about the planet killing them and us? Did the IFC's famous pillar of stone, Commander Gunnar Hammär, just crack?"

Gunnar's eyes narrowed ever so slightly. "I still don't trust this planet, Richard. That *'bit'* hasn't changed, but perhaps there's hope that some of the crew did survive. If they did, and are in that city, then we need to be mindful of those warships headed straight for it."

An operations meeting was scheduled for 16:00, with the usual senior staff, the two pilots, and the survey team. There was a general feeling throughout the vessel that this was the moment they had all been waiting for. The mission's real goal was now within their grasp, and the ship's morale was as high as it had ever been. Everyone, it seemed, was certain of success—everyone except the newly promoted lieutenant commander.

Baseball grabbed Alex's arm and cornered him before entering the captain's stateroom. "Okay, out with it, Alex. What the hell's the matter with you? And don't give me any of your usual crap about how you don't know and that it's probably nothing. We've been down this road too many times for me to buy that bullshit."

Alex shook his head and told Baseball the truth. "Seriously, I really don't know. All I know is that I've got a very bad feeling about this whole thing." He took note of the tight-lipped scowl Baseball wore, and said, "Look, if I knew something, I'd level with you, but all I have is a gut feeling that tells me there's something not right here. Something none of us have control over. Somehow, your dog shit theory is beginning to make sense. That's it. That's all I've got."

"Something that involves more than just dragons, you mean?" Baseball pressed.

Alex folded his arms across his chest. "Look, if you want to stand here and try to force me into saying something, dragons or no dragons, then we'll be here all night, miss the meeting, and get our asses handed to us by the CAG. I'm going in before I'm late." He finally dropped his hands, put one on the door, and looked back at his friend. "You coming?"

Baseball frowned and then followed his friend into the stateroom.

The face that stared back from his cabin mirror was conflicted, and though the way forward was clear, the risks they entailed were anything but. The fact was that Captain Jennings was simply out of time. He had to act, and act soon. Jennings pushed away from the sink just as the gentle, electronic warbling of SADI broke him out of his reflections and informed him that all the senior staff was gathered in the stateroom. As was his usual wont, he was the last to walk into the meeting.

Captain Jennings strode to the front of his desk and saw hopeful expectations on the faces of his senior staff. "At ease, ladies and gentlemen."

Hope was infectious that night.

Captain Jennings finally broke the silence. "Well, folks, while it may be a bit premature, it's starting to look probable that we'll be able to discover the fate of the *Monarch*, if not actually find the ship and her crew." This news, while generally known throughout the ship, still had the effervescent effect the captain had hoped for.

The room went quiet once again, and Jennings filled them in on more details of the day's sorties. He then answered the question that was on everybody's mind. "The present survey plan has been scrapped for now. Our focus will be on investigating the crash site. Since its location is near the identical twin where *OVAL Porter* was attacked, the crews will continue to work together. *OVAL Hartley* will remain the survey shuttle while *OVAL Porter* will fly as armed escort." He looked over at Gunnar, nodded at his friend, and said, "But this mission will have a slightly different crew complement." Furtive glances swept the room as he continued, "Commander Hammär will now man the weapons system aboard *OVAL Porter.*"

Gunnar beamed like a kid with a new toy.

Captain Jennings looked over at his two pilots and, with a slight nod of his head, outlined the coming mission. "*OVAL Hartley* will land at the crash site, take samples, and attempt to either extract its computer, or if possible, download all available data. In addition to this, the survey team will try to determine what brought it down." Jennings looked over at Gunnar and asked, "Are there any questions so far?"

Commander Hammär hunched his big shoulders and muttered, "Why is everybody looking at me?" A few chuckles rippled across the room. "I got what I want."

Jennings grinned and went on. "Once we've extracted all the data from the crash site, we'll attempt to analyze what happened. We'll also retrieve any and all remains they find." It was more subdued this time, but once again there was a verbal murmur of agreement from the senior staff.

After a few more specifics about the latest survey, including the discovery of the human civilization, the captain wrapped up the meeting with a final thought. "We don't really know what we're going to find in the next few days, but I assure everyone in this room, we will not leave this planet until we get all the information that has so far eluded us. There are still some minor mission parameters to work out before tomorrow morning, but launch is set at 07:30. That is all. Dismissed."

Fresh enthusiasm spilled out of the stateroom. Baseball walked with Alex as they headed for their respective cabins. "Still got nothing to say, Alex? If you do, I'd really like to hear it." He gave his friend a penetrating look. "Now would be a fine time to talk."

"Baseball, I'd tell you if I could. All I can say is get a good night's sleep because we're really going to need it tomorrow. See you on the flight deck, buddy."

CHAPTER 65

HOLE IN THE SKY
IFC ENDEAVOR—ORBIT DAY 38

The next morning both flight crews were rested, briefed, and made ready for their mission. Except for the addition of Gunnar, the crew complement was the same.

As before, Captain Jennings gave his flight crews the final operations briefing. "Ladies and gentlemen, I just want to say how proud we all are of the job you've done so far and to let you know that we anticipate that you'll be able to provide us with the answers we need to discover the fate of the *Monarch*. We couldn't have gotten this far without your dedication and hard work. Carry on, team."

As Alex and Baseball were heading to their crafts, Alex yelled over to his friend, "Hey, Baseball, don't trip and break a leg when you're on the ground, because I'm pretty sure that Rox can't carry you back to the OVAL. She'll probably leave you there, get a promotion, and change the call sign to *OVAL Rox*."

This got a thumbs up from Baseball's beautiful copilot, who yelled across the hangar deck, "Damn straight, Porter."

Baseball smirked, rolled his eyes, and yelled a final, "Yeah, just keep that big-ass razor of yours handy. What's its name again?"

Just before ducking their heads at the hatches, the two pilots glanced over and nodded at each other. They then entered their crafts and prepared for the launch. As soon as Alex strapped in, the bee in his chest went wild, and he couldn't shake the overwhelming feeling that that was the last time he would ever see his friend.

The launch window was set for the approach to the northern continent before the *Endeavor* left the relatively low altitude and entered the high elliptical orbit over the northern continent. Both shuttles launched and made their way toward their drop point.

As the *Endeavor* reached the extreme height of its apogee, it increased its velocity in order to circle back around to the northern landmass as soon as possible. While crossing over the equator and heading into the southern hemisphere, SADI hailed the captain.

"Captain Jennings, I've observed that large fleet of those wooden sailing vessels that we observed with such regularity while surveying the southern continent."

"What exactly have you found, SADI?"

"Sir, there's a fleet of 3,057 of those naval vessels carrying 2,023,762 soldiers." SADI was always precise with her figures.

Jennings's eyes darted to the view screen. "What's their present heading, SADI?"

"Sir, this fleet is now 7,371 kilometers from their point of origin, and they seem to be struggling through the strong equatorial currents. However, if they maintain their present heading and speed, they will make landfall somewhere close to that human city near the southern tip of the peninsula. I calculate that they will reach this possible objective in about sixteen weeks."

"Why are they so much slower than the smaller fleet we saw recently?"

"Sir, these are much larger vessels, troop carriers with deep drafts, and not built for speed. They're oar-powered barges, whereas the smaller fleet was made up of sleek oar-and-wind-powered craft."

"Thank you, SADI. Four months buys us a lot of time. I expect our mission directive to be in the books by then. We'll definitely address this again."

SADI's next words stopped the captain in his tracks. "Sir, I've just picked up five of those human ships leaving the bay."

"What's their heading?" asked Commander Eaglecreek.

"They are on an intercept course with the reptilian rapid deployment force."

Jennings and Eaglecreek exchanged glances. "How soon until they engage?"

"Minutes, sir."

The captain turned to his weapons officer and asked, "Lieutenant Laurent, what kind of damage can you do from here?"

In her usual no-nonsense, get-to-the-point tone of voice, Laurent told the captain, "Depends on what you want, sir. I can definitely ruin their day from here, but if you want lizard soup, then we'll have to make a drop."

"Captain," Eaglecreek quickly interjected, "both our pilots are on the surface, and though I can drive the fusion engines, I'm not comfortable making a drop with the *Endeavor*."

Jennings wasted no time deliberating. "Neither am I, Zonta." He gave the order, "Lieutenant, take a shot off their bow. If they don't get that message, remove the bow."

Once both crews had entered the atmosphere, they dropped below the cloud ceiling and made their way toward the OVAL crash site. It was located at an elevation of 3,033 meters and situated on the northern face of the jagged mountains that formed a ring around the north pole. Upon approach, the crews could clearly see this strange mountain.

As they traversed the last ring of mountains, Lieutenant Malik began scanning for any sign of the aggressive flying reptiles. But the bio-diversification scan came back negative. There were none of the dragons on or near the cone-shaped mountain. The mountain itself was bare of all foliage and covered with a smooth crystalline exterior. Except for the absence of dragons, it was an exact duplicate of what they had found on the southern continent.

Once he was satisfied there wasn't a threat, Malik shifted his attention to the crash site itself. The debris trail was still clearly evident, and the wreck was quickly pinpointed. The OVALs set a direct course for the target area.

While *OVAL Porter* circled overhead, *OVAL Hartley* made a slow approach to the crash site. The wreckage had come to rest on a rugged boulder-strewn slope, and there wasn't a suitable landing spot close by. Finally, a 25-meter-wide shelf appeared 152 meters from the crash site. Baseball carefully set down on this spot. It was the first time any craft from the *Endeavor* had made landfall on Aqueous.

As soon as they landed, the survey crew donned their EVA gear, which included an open-face helmet, light-adapting goggles, and calf-high all-terrain boots. They then gathered up what equipment they could carry and opened the hatch. Rox carried the small portable computer and the hard line they would attach to the computer on the crashed OVAL, if it remained intact. Baseball lugged the portable battery while Lieutenant Malik carried an array of analytical devices.

As the crew moved toward the downed OVAL, the wind began to rise.

The crash site was strewn with debris stretching back for hundreds of meters. It quickly became obvious what had brought down the craft—a scorched hole about a half a meter wide had burned through the tail section and taken out both thrust nozzles.

What had caused that scorched hole was not evident.

All but one of the ejection seats was gone, and the sole remaining seat belonged to the pilot. No bodies were found.

They entered through the open airlock. Curiously, it had been blown open from the inside. The cockpit remained in a fair state with only minor damage, but the rest of the cabin was strewn with the detritus of a wrecked craft. Not unexpected at a crash site.

Baseball and Rox switched their goggles on, giving them clear visibility as they picked their way through the dark cabin and entered the cramped cockpit. Rox quickly found the computer and hooked the battery to power up some of the OVAL's vital systems. Malik took his helmet off to adjust his goggles.

It took over a minute for the computer to boot up. It soon became apparent that even though most of the data was corrupted, some of it was still of use. They began downloading everything they could.

Suddenly an ear-piercing distress signal wailed inside the cockpit. The team clamped their hands over their ears as the screaming alarm made talk difficult. Within seconds, the noxious smell of an electrical fire assaulted their noses and stung their eyes. The cabin filled with throat-gagging smoke just as crackling sparks spat out from the console.

Baseball's head whipped around. "Shit!" He yelled, "Everyone out now! Evacuate and find cover in the rocks."

Rox bolted out of the wreck yelling, "Move it, Malik."

"Why, what's happening?" squealed Malik.

"Get the fuck out, Amil!" Baseball shoved the surveyor toward the hatch, and once Malik had stumbled out of the cabin, Baseball quickly followed.

Baseball sprinted five meters and dove behind the large boulder where Rox already lay on the ground covering her head. Within seconds, the cockpit erupted in a flash of sparks and metal shards. "Keep your heads down," Baseball bellowed, "there's pulse cannon ordnance scattered around the rear of the cabin." He grabbed Rox's helmet and shoved her head down so hard that it was underneath his upper body.

"Ouch! Watch what you're doing? Get off me." Her voice was muffled underneath his chest as she tried to squirm out from underneath him.

"Stay put, this isn't over yet," he told her. A second later, what remained of the OVAL exploded in a massive fireball that sent a powerful shock wave out for hundreds of meters. The large boulder that shielded both Rox and Baseball shook, but it didn't dislodge. Lieutenant Malik had stumbled out of the wreck and dove for a boulder that was not much more than a rock. He curled up into a fetal position, and placed his arms over his helmetless head. After the first explosion he raised his head up and peeked over the top just as the second explosion detonated. His boulder was much smaller than the one Rox and Baseball had huddled behind. The explosion's massive shock wave blew the rock and the survey chief a dozen meters where they smashed into a pile of large boulders. His skull was crushed on impact.

Baseball heard Alex anxiously trying to call him as he jumped up and ran over to where Malik's broken, lifeless body lay. Baseball's ears were bloodied, and their ringing drowned out Alex's voice on his communicator. A bloodied but intact Rox came running up and stopped short when she saw Malik's mat of black hair slick with blood, bone, and brains.

Rox ripped off her helmet and fell to her knees as the rising wind painfully whipped her hair around her face.

"BASEBALL! COME IN, BASEBALL!" came Alex's repeated hail. "BASEBALL, DO YOU COPY?" *OVAL Porter* had descended to get a better view of the explosion site.

Baseball finally recovered enough to answer his friend. "Alex, something went horribly wrong. After we plugged in the battery, it shorted, and then ignited the electronics in the cockpit, which set off a whole battery of pulse cannon ammunition. The wreck was armed, Alex, and I didn't notice until it was too late. Lieutenant Malik—Malik's dead."

Within seconds of the explosion, the dense cloud cover over the mountain began to break up and started swirling around it. Within a couple of minutes, the cloud rotation had strengthened to over 100 kilometers an hour. SADI was the first to notice these simultaneously developing phenomena.

"Captain Jennings, there is an extreme atmospheric disturbance taking place over both poles. The cloud cover has begun to rotate at ever-increasing speeds. There are now hurricane-speed winds forming directly around both conical mountains."

"Hurricanes form over water, SADI," Jennings pointed out, "not land."

"I understand, sir," SADI responded, "and this doesn't seem natural."

"No," Jennings said dejectedly, "of course it doesn't." The cold hand of recognition gripped his spine as the captain realized that it was no coincidence that this had happened during the present sortie. Gunnar's paranoia was coming to fruition; they'd peeked inside Pandora's box.

By the time the *Endeavor* had left the northern hemisphere, both storm eyes were enormous. The hurricanes were now howling at over 350 kilometers an hour. Eaglecreek dispensed with any formalities. "What the hell is happening down there, Richard?"

Jennings's response was as succinct as it was ominous. "Zonta, the cloud covers over both poles have suddenly become raging vortexes. They've become holes in the sky."

CHAPTER 66

NO LONGER A MAN
THE SPINE—AQUEOUS

A scream welled up in Count Darx's constricted throat, but what came out his slack mouth was no more than a child's fearful whimper. Terrorized, he stumbled through the cavernous halls of Drakon Rus searching, hoping for a place to hide. It had happened again. The most feared man on the planet was nowhere to be found. There was only a scrawny, frightened little boy.

Bayne was back.

Other than his own pathetic mewling echoing throughout the empty halls of Drakon Rus, the only sound he heard was his bare feet as they slapped against the cold, hard tiles. But he sensed a presence and knew he wasn't alone. Someone came for him, someone who wanted to hurt him.

Someone always wanted to hurt him.

Bayne couldn't hear his pursuer, but every time his courage allowed, he glanced back and saw a figure moving in and out of the shadows. Coming ever closer. But it wasn't his father this time. It was that other hateful being. The one he had tried to throttle, and now it hunted him like an animal. It wanted to trap him. Hurt him. Kill him. Bayne wasn't brave enough to face this evil ghost. Bayne was a weak bastard.

He was no longer a man.

The frightened child fled in terror. He ran until he couldn't lift his legs any longer. They felt heavy, sluggish, and try as he might, Bayne couldn't take another step. He was trapped. Again. He knew his only escape was into the depths of his mind where his protectors waited. They'd always helped him before. But this time there was no one there. This time Bayne was truly alone, and he squeezed his eyes shut. Shut to the light, shut to the fear.

Finally, a sound.

An evil sound invaded Bayne's darkness. It frightened him even more.

Tink tink tink.

From the shadows it came—metallic, threatening. Fear drove the breath from his lungs, but he was too afraid to breathe. Too afraid to look. He squeezed his eyes tighter.

Tink tink tink.

It was closer now, close enough to touch. Bayne's chest tightened, pleading for air, but he dare not make a sound.

Screeaatch—the tapping became dragging, metal on stone. Bayne heard someone breathing, but the frightened child had yet to breathe. Someone stood next to him.

Someone who would hurt him.

Bayne's head felt clammy, cold, his pants warm and wet. Moaning with fear, his lungs ready to burst, he finally gulped in a breath and opened his eyes. Less than an arm's length away stood the ghost. Its face was a mere shadow, and even though it was obscured in the dark, Bayne saw that its arm was cocked back. It held a sword, a red sword, only millimeters from his throat. "Noooo—" whimpered Bayne. "Please let me live."

"No," it hissed harshly.

Bayne woke up screaming and kicked at the cold, damp sheets clinging to his legs.

CHAPTER 67

BODY BAG
IFC ENDEAVOR—ORBIT DAY 37

At the detonation site, Baseball stood immobile and stared at Malik's mangled corpse while Rox, now on all fours, took ragged breaths. The wind painfully whipped her hair about her face, but she didn't move. Couldn't. After a moment she dry retched and then threw up on her hands.

"Come on, Rox." Baseball gently touched her shoulder. His own breaths were coming in quick gulps. "We need to get moving," he said and held out his hand.

"I know." She hesitated a couple seconds and then took his extended hand and stood up. "Sorry," she whimpered, nodding at her puke smeared on his hand. "Now what?"

"We've got to get his body back to the OVAL," he said loud enough to be heard over the rising wind, then wiped his hand on a pant leg.

All OVALs carried an array of emergency medical equipment, and each crew member was trained in their use. None of it was needed except for one item—the body bag. The wind grew stronger as Rox headed back to the landing zone to retrieve it.

Baseball could barely bring himself to look at Malik's crushed skull. A pilot was responsible for the safety of his crew. He kept going over in his mind just what could have gone wrong.

But he knew.

The wreck had been loaded with pulse cannon ordnance and several rounds were strewn about the rear of the unlit cabin. That the interior was dark simply wasn't an excuse; it was a bomb just waiting for someone to do something stupid—like not making a thorough inspection upon entering. That it was extremely rare for an OVAL to be armed also meant nothing, because at that exact moment, his best friend was similarly armed and presently circling over his LZ trying to hail him.

By now the wind was howling, and when Rox got back with the body bag, she and Baseball could barely hear each other over the growing tempest. They struggled to put Malik's bloody corpse in the bag, and once it was done they began the arduous burden of carrying it back to their shuttle. It was a grim and demoralizing task, made all the more difficult by the rough terrain and gale-force winds.

Above them, Alex maintained a constant vigil of the surrounding region for any sign of an attack. His feeling of impending disaster had increased tenfold after the explosion, and he was absolutely sure that this wasn't the end to the bloodletting.

"Alex, what the hell happened down there?" demanded his new weapons officer.

"I'm not sure, Gunnar. All I know is that there was some kind of detonation at the crash site, and Lieutenant Malik was killed."

"Oh shit," groaned Gunnar. "Are you in contact with *OH*?"

"Baseball's last transmission was garbled, and now he either can't respond, or has his hands full." He turned and glanced back at Commander

Hammär. "Gunnar, I have my own hands full as well. The wind has reached critical levels, and it's all I can do to maintain trim. Please excuse me if I can't do much more than fly this boat right now."

"Roger that, Alex, I'll leave you to it." Gunnar dejectedly scrunched back in his seat and tightened his harness.

Alex struggled to maintain stability as the raging wind pummeled his craft. Raj helped him cope by maintaining a semblance of trim. The copilot had engaged his optic computer to extend his external data sensor, and it showed a huge storm brewing over the conical mountain about fifty kilometers away. Raj glanced up from the data screen and out the windscreen. What he saw sent a chill through his bones. "Alex, take a look at the clouds forming over that mountain. The instruments are saying that the wind speed there is now over a thousand kilometers per hour, and the residual effect of that wind is spreading toward us at an alarming rate."

"I see it too, Raj."

"Yeah, well, we've got maybe a minute before our thrust vector is no longer able to compensate for these rising wind speeds." Raj's voice turned shrill as he fought his yoke. "You see that too, right?"

Alex was alarmed at both his deteriorating situation and the obvious threat to his ground team. "Baseball! Get out of there! This wind is increasing exponentially, and we've got to leave before we're unable to stay in the air!" Alex's voice was strained, and his feeling of imminent disaster was growing as fast as the wind speed.

A response finally came in from Baseball. "Roger that, Alex. Rox and I are carrying Amil's body bag. We should be back at our LZ in about five minutes." Baseball's voice could barcly be heard over the howling wind.

Alex barked into his intercom. "Baseball, listen to me, you don't have five minutes. Drop the body bag and get you and Rox back to your OVAL right now! Run, for crying out loud. Launch the moment you touch your controls. That's a direct order!"

Baseball still wouldn't let go of the body bag until Rox yelled, "Look!" and pointed behind him at the storm raging over the polar mountain.

When he turned around his mouth fell open. "Drop him, Rox, and run like hell. We'll come back later, but if we don't get away from here there'll be three body bags from this crew. NOW RUN!" he screamed through the deafening wind.

Rox dropped her end and started sprinting toward their OVAL. She got ten meters when a powerful gust blew her to the ground. Baseball caught up to her, grabbed her by the elbow, and yanked her up just as an even stronger gust hammered them both off their feet.

Still maintaining their station, Alex found it almost impossible to fly in a circular pattern. Raj glanced from his data screen to the sky. "Alex, you'd better take a look at this. If we don't leave right now, it may be too late."

Alex saw that a giant dark vortex swirled around the top of the conical mountain at an alarming rate. The eye of the storm was centered directly over its summit, and the clouds around the eye had turned fiercely black. Monstrous lightning bolts suddenly blasted out from the mountain's summit in every direction; many violently hit the valley floor and caused fiery explosions. This voltaic conflagration was now more threatening than the wind and rapidly spreading out. It would engulf them in seconds.

Again Alex admonished his ground crew to get out of there without delay. "Baseball, we only have seconds before we all die here and now. I'm not leaving without you, so you've got to get out of there now. RIGHT NOW!" At that moment, a powerful bolt of lightning slammed into his shuttle like a hammer blow and threw her into a tailspin. Smoke filled the cabin as the pilots fought to gain any semblance of flight control. *OVAL Porter* went into a ragged spiral and plunged toward the ground.

CHAPTER 68

DEATH OF *ENDEAVOR*
IFC ENDEAVOR—ORBIT DAY 38

ieutenant Laurent set her plasma rounds to their highest setting and zeroed in on a point twenty meters off the bow of the leading lizard ship. Still focused on her target acquisition, she informed the captain, "The weapon system is ready, sir. Keep in mind that the atmosphere will degrade the plasma by sixty-five percent by the time it reaches sea level, but it will leave an impression, so to speak, on the target."

Jennings made a dry swallow and took a deep breath. He was about to become the first captain in IFC history to order a shot fired in anger. "SADI, how close is the human fleet from the target ships?"

"The humans are less than one kilometer distant, sir. The two fleets are closing at three point four meters per second. I calculate first contact in less than two minutes."

"They're outnumbered seven to one, Captain," Zonta pointed out. "It's a now-or-never scenario, sir."

The captain clenched his fists until his knuckles turned white, and then gave the order. "Engage, Lieutenant."

"Finally," whispered Laurent, and pressed the fire control button.

"Those softskin fools actually think they can challenge me," Duchess Thorna growled to herself, "and in sight of their precious bay. What will these slime do when I show no aggression, and meet them under a flag of truce?" A hissing sneer escaped her fang-laden mouth. "This is just too—"

The air between the two fleets began to hum. An instant later the hum became an intense crackle as an orange bolt of light erupted from the cloudless sky and, with a deafening crack, exploded directly in front of Thorna's lead ship. In a flash of phosphorus the shock wave coated the closest ships with boiling drops of seawater. Duchess Thorna screeched and jerked her head back when the blast of steam swept over her ship. Her clawed feet splintered the rough wood as she instinctively dug in. After a moment she stood immobile, breathing heavily out her long snout, but recovered quickly and angrily looked over at her fleet. Her eyes narrowed at the approaching human ships, the flag of truce all but forgotten. "Flank speed, you lazy lizards! Close with the softskins before they can fire that weapon again. Destroy them. Destroy them all. I want no enemy ship left afloat."

SADI immediately relayed the information. "Sir, the plasma round hit precisely on target, but the lizard fleet has increased their speed and will intercept the humans in twenty seconds." The bridge went stone-cold quiet as those implications set in.

Jennings's eyes darted to Commander Eaglecreek who asked, "Now what, sir?"

"If you will, Lieutenant Laurent," ordered Jennings, "take out that leading ship."

"Aye, sir."

Just as Laurent's finger reached for the fire button, SADI's voice broke in. "Captain, the storms over both poles have just intensified almost exponentially, and something's begun to happen inside the mountains."

Jennings hesitated a moment before snapping out of it and barked, "Belay that fire order, Lieutenant," but her finger had already released the weapon. The captain groaned inwardly as his eyes turned toward the view screen.

The plume of strange vapor still sizzled above the waves as it slowly dissipated. It stung the humans' eyes and skin as their five ships raced through it, but it was cover, and temporarily masked their movement as they sought to flank the enemy fleet by turning hard to port directly in front of the oncoming enemy fleet.

Twenty-two seconds after the last human ship passed through the lingering mist, the lead Thith vessel exploded amidships in a flash of sparks and fire. Only meters from the burning ship, the humans fired a salvo of titanium-tipped arrows that sliced into the reptilian crew as they plasma burned, but when the humans passed through the thick smoke every Thith ship in range counterfired with hundreds of crossbow bolts. It was the first time in Aquean history that humans had ever faced this weapon, and it caught them completely unprepared. The human crews were cut down with dozens killed or wounded. The little fleet went chaotically awry. Two of the human ships careened into each other, foundered, and lost all momentum. The Thith wasted no time in taking advantage of their crippled enemy and easily surrounded them. Hundreds of Thith soldiers swarmed over the disabled ships and butchered the remaining humans.

The bridge watched the slaughter with horror, but SADI's insistent reporting wrenched their attention back to the climatic pandemonium where their away teams carried out their mission. Torn between what he had just witnessed on the ocean and what might be happening beneath those roiling clouds, Jennings shifted his focus to the mission, and what he saw was shocking.

"Disengage, Lieutenant," came the reluctant order.

"Those humans still need our help, Captain," argued Laurent, "or they'll be wiped out. There could be crew from the *Monarch* on those boats."

"I have to agree with the Lieutenant," said Eaglecreek.

"And our OVAL crews?" snapped Jennings as he pointed at the screen focused on the storms over the poles. "They're human too and are presently carrying out our mission directive under that."

Laurent pointed at the other screen. "But—"

"Put a lid on it, Lieutenant," growled Eaglecreek. "We have our orders."

"Look, folks," Jennings said sharply, "no one likes what just happened, but we have priorities, and that means staying the course on our mission. A mission that is at present under severe threat." With less force he added, "After we've completed it, we'll come to the aid of that human city."

"Yes, sir," Laurent said solemnly.

No one uttered a sound on the bridge as everyone turned back to his or her respective tasks. Jennings didn't move a muscle as he watched the screen with growing alarm, because he was helpless to give them any aid. With *Endeavor's* view from orbit, every scrap of data could be monitored, and what he saw just wasn't making any sense.

Gripping the armrests of his captain's chair at the raised center of the bridge, Jennings finally broke the silence. "SADI, the eye of that vortex has cleared out the cloud cover enough that we can see the ground. Since it's visible, can any of our instruments penetrate to the surface? Specifically, can we contact our ground teams?"

"Sir, I've continually tried to hail them, but we still cannot establish communication. I will continue trying to get through to them."

"I need more information, SADI." The captain got up from his chair and stood in front of the view screen. "Can you tell me the origin of this storm?"

"Sir, I have little data, but I am detecting a highly unusual phenomenon that is affecting the entire planet, and this might be tied to the cause of these storms."

"Just tell me, SADI. I appreciate that you don't have all the answers, but just give me what you do know, whether you believe that it's related or not." Jennings paced up and down the bridge, his eyes darting from one data screen to another.

"Yes, sir. The planet's electromagnetic field is reversing polarity at an extraordinary rate. It began at the same time the storm started, and as the storms over both polar regions intensified, so too has the frequency of the polarity reversal. This fluctuation has reached 992 times per minute and is increasing."

The captain stopped in his tracks as his blood turned cold. He glanced over at Commander Eaglecreek who stared back at him. The planet was about to attack.

Gunnar had been right all along.

"Sir, it seems that these polarity reversals are connected to the two polar mountains. They seem to have created a tesla polyphase system on the entire planet." SADI paused for a moment. "Sir, the core temperatures of both conical mountains are rising at a very high rate. Before the storms began, they held at a steady 24°C, but since then, they have risen to their present temperature of 372°C. But the rate of temperature increase is accelerating and correlates exactly with the storms' intensity." SADI went silent for a moment. "Sir, I believe that all these planetary events are related, and that the planet is preparing for some kind of climactic event."

Step one has begun, but what's next? wondered Jennings as he read the data screen.

He limply walked over to his command chair, sat back down, placed his elbows on the cushioned armrests, and held his head in his hands as a cold sweat formed on his forehead. "Thank you, SADI, I've already come to the same conclusion. Please keep me informed of any other changes the moment they happen."

Zonta walked over to his captain and put his hand on Jennings's shoulder. "For what it's worth, Richard, we were never in control here, and, just like the *Monarch*, we didn't understand that until it was too late." He took his hand away and stepped to the side of the command chair.

"Gunnar understood," Jennings muttered to himself. "I just didn't listen."

"Sir!" SADI's voice broke the silence. "Sir, the core temperature inside the mountains has increased to 1,578°C. That's a higher temperature than the point at which iron becomes molten, and there seems to be some kind of opening at the calderas of each mountain."

"What do you mean by an 'opening'?" A cold revelation hit him like a slap in the face, *Step two has just begun. How much time do I—we—have?*

"Just that, sir. Each conical mountaintop has a small caldera, about twenty meters wide, and these have now opened."

Jennings and Eaglecreek moved to the thermal imaging data screen and silently watched the tremendous heat become more visible as the mountaintops opened to their full width. An intensely bright pulsating blaze appeared on the screen as the heat index went off scale.

"SADI, what's happened?" Jennings asked, without looking away from the screen.

"Sir, some kind of energy force is building within the mountain. This is not just pure heat but a radioactive pulsation of some kind. The intensity is phenomenal. We've never seen this type of energy before, not even on the hottest stars."

Suddenly a beam of white-hot light shot straight up from the top of each caldera and into space.

Step three is now in play. Jennings's guts twisted into knots; his breathing became rapid, as his heart pounded in his chest. "What the hell is that thing, SADI, and where is it aimed?" Jennings almost jumped back from the thermal screen and looked over at the planetary view screen.

"Sir, those are powerful energy beams, and each beam is aimed at one of the derelict satellites orbiting Aqueous."

Starting as a cold knot in Jennings's stomach, a wave of nausea exploded upward and filled his throat with gorge. He swallowed it back down, and unsteadily asked, "What's the status of the satellites, SADI?"

"Sir, the satellites receiving the energy have powered up and are now activated. They are also acting as catalysts and are redistributing energy to the satellite immediately next to it, and that satellite is doing the same, and so on. Simultaneously, the polar orbiting satellite closest to those orbiting the equator is now directing an energy beam and powering up those satellites as well. The energy beams from the two mountains are powering up both rings of derelict satellites." As SADI finished her commentary, silence momentarily gripped the bridge.

"I think we can stop referring to them as derelicts," Jennings said softly.

Zonta turned to his captain and quietly suggested what would have been unthinkable only a few minutes before. "Richard, let's get the *Endeavor* out of this orbit and well away from Aqueous. We can always come back once this defense system has gone dormant again." As he waited for Jennings's response, Zonta scrutinized the thermal imaging on the data screen. "We may not have much time left."

Did you stand and fight or try to run, Admiral Mason? Jennings wondered and then said to his second, "How can we leave without the OVAL teams back on board, Zonta? We'd be abandoning them to a death sentence."

"I don't like the idea of leaving anyone behind either, Richard," Eaglecreek said, "but if anyone can make it through this, it's Alex Porter. That man is better equipped to survive than anyone I've ever met."

It took less than three minutes for both rings of satellites to receive enough power to reactivate all their systems. As they began to reboot, they sent out a powerful scan that the *Endeavor* picked up on her defense-based systems. SADI announced, "Sir, we have just been scanned by the powered-up satellites."

"Which ones?"

"All of them, sir."

"Richard," cut in Zonta, "the *Endeavor* is unprepared for an engagement, might I suggest changing that?"

"Yes, of course," replied Jennings. *But prepare for what?*

SADI kept a running commentary on the satellites' status. "Sir, there is now movement from both satellite rings. They have begun to leave their orbits and are now grouping together in flights of twenty-five per group. This makes forty groups, sir, and all of them are accelerating on an intercept heading at an extremely high rate."

"SADI, launch a communication drone back to IFC immediately," Jennings ordered. "With a complete status report inclusion.

Update it to this moment."

The drone launched within seconds and was flung out into space where it flashed past the converging satellites, none of which reacted to its passing. "Captain," relayed SADI, "the drone is away, but it can't engage the onboard EMD until it's well out of the solar system, and that may take years."

"Understood, SADI." Captain Jennings turned to his weapons officer. "Laurent, what's the status of our defensive systems?"

The Marine lieutenant looked at her captain with a blank stare before answering. "Captain, we gave *OVAL Porter* half our defensive capability."

"I know that, and I don't care how much fire power we have," he said. "I want to know if you're prepared to repel an attack with what we do have."

"I've been trying, Captain, but my target acquisition system can't find a lock." She kept working the controls at her station. "They worked fine when I targeted the lizard ships, but not now. I think we're being jammed, sir."

"You mean to tell me that with a thousand targets you can't lock on any to shoot at?" he blazed at her.

After a moment she told him, "You do realize, Captain, that even *if* we had all four pulse cannons, and *if* our TA system could find a lock, which it can't, we still couldn't mount a defense against a thousand attackers. We only have one option: escape."

"Be that as it may, Lieutenant, switch to manual targeting, and fire every damn weapon at your disposal," ordered Jennings.

Laurent carried out her orders without any more delay, and began to manually rapid fire the pulse cannons at where she thought the enemy might be.

She hit nothing.

Undeterred by the wild fire coming from their prey, the forty groups of attacking satellites closed on the *Endeavor*, splitting up and surrounding the starship.

"Sir, all the satellites are now fanning out," SADI informed the captain. "They have formed an equidistant sphere around us at a distance of ten kilometers. Sir, our sensors have confirmed that all the satellites have achieved a firing solution on us."

In an even voice, Lieutenant Laurent made an ominous addendum to her report. "That's a can't-miss range, Captain."

"You seem to have no trouble missing, Lieutenant," Eaglecreek barked at her.

"We need to move in the next few seconds or we're all dead," she fired back.

Step four is now complete. I've led us into this trap, but perhaps we can escape. Jennings had finally made up his mind.

But it was already too late.

Jennings yelled over at his CAG, "Commander Eaglecreek, join me at the pilot's helm. I'm ordering *Endeavor* to immediately leave orbit, and possibly the solar system, for the time being. SADI, lock the EMD on the planet's magnetic field, calculate coordinates for an immediate hyper-jump for the far side of the red dwarf, and get us the hell out of here!" The captain had joined his CAG at the helm.

SADI's response brought dead silence to the bridge crew. "Sir, the EMD cannot lock onto the planet's magnetic field due to the fluctuating polarity."

He turned to the CAG. "Zonta, the fusion drive is partially ramped up. Finish spooling it up, and let's get moving! I know it takes some time to achieve fusion thrust, but let's get moving the second you've got enough power."

Commander Eaglecreek grimaced. "Yes, sir. It'll take a few seconds, but I can still do what needs to be done. I'll punch out the moment we have thrust, sir."

Captain Jennings ordered his weapons officer, "Laurent, engage the EMD anti-debris shield and make it ship-wide. Maybe we can provide some temporary protection from whatever they throw at us. Don't take any power away from the fusion drive, but put all available power into these shields."

Lieutenant Laurent began making adjustments on her console, turned to Jennings and reported, "All available EMD power is now allocated to the ADS, sir, but as I'm sure you're already aware, we're just pissing in the wind."

Glaring at his weapons officer, Jennings toggled the ship-wide address system and told the crew, "Prepare for immediate orbit departure." He turned back to the bridge and said, "All right then, let's get this show on the road—" Suddenly, hundreds of powerful energy beams rocked the *Endeavor.*

Jennings was determined to go down fighting and turned back to his weapons officer. "Keep up your fire! Shoot at something, Laurent! Anything!"

She never got the chance.

The ship was violently hit again, and SADI's voice came online. "Sir, we've just been hit by fifty percent of the satellites concentrating their fire at specific areas of the ship. They've targeted our defensive capabilities and life support systems. The pulse cannons are now destroyed. Several outer decks have been breached and are experiencing rapid depressurization. The loss of life is severe and growing rapidly. The ADS provided zero defense against their weapons, sir." The bridge erupted with warning lights and alarms, making verbal communication difficult.

Step five. Jennings wrenched his attention away from SADI and screamed at the helm, "Get that fusion drive online *now!*"

It was his final order.

Somewhere between the shrieking metal of his ship being torn apart and the screams of his crew as they died, Captain Jennings shared one final moment of eye contact with Commander Eaglecreek, who was still frantically trying to engage the fusion drive. The reactor had reached sixty-three percent of the power needed to move the ship, but another blast blew through the hull. An instant later the fusion drive system started fluctuating erratically and went offline. Zonta stared at his console for a moment, looked up at his captain, and shook his head in resignation. They grimly nodded a silent goodbye to each other. Jennings despondently sank back in his chair, closed his eyes, and accepted that he had just lost his command.

A second later another violent impact hurled the bridge crew across the command platform amid a shower of sizzling sparks. The ship's artificial gravitational system ceased operation as the bridge depressurized and went dark. In his mind's eye, Jennings pictured a little yellow rubber duck floating away from his desk, rolling end over end.

At that same moment, SADI gave her last ever status report. "Sir, all the satellites have now locked their targeting systems onto our fusion drive. If they all hit the reactor's core at the same instant and with the same intensity, it will implode; the result will be a nuclear reaction that will completely destr—"

At that instant one thousand powerful energy beams simultaneously tore through the *Endeavor*'s hull and hit the EMD core. The uranium isotopes imploded and ignited a hydrogen-based thermonuclear detonation of cataclysmic proportions. The massive radioactive blast was bright as a supernova, but, in the cold vacuum of space, the death of *Endeavor* was as silent as the grave itself.

EPILOGUE

THE WITNESSES
AQUEOUS—THE HOPE PROPHESY—DAY 01

"It is done, Mab'r," reported Dreng'r as he hovered just outside the entrance to his superior's dwelling. "The humans have triggered the Rond'r, resulting in the elimination of their starship."

"Did their communication drone launch?" Erland'r asked as he drifted over to his planetwide sensor. With a slight wave of his hand he witnessed *Endeavor*'s final moments. The image automatically dimmed when the fierce nuclear flash announced her demise. His large yellow eyes never blinked, never left the image, and never changed expression. "What of the technological data, and survivors?"

"The requisite data has been uploaded, and their drone was not interfered with. It is presently on a return trajectory back to Earth," Dreng'r answered. "As for survivors: there are five. They were on the two small craft that investigated the bait we left at the northern axis projector. One landed and triggered the storm. Both craft are, at present, trying to escape. One has been crippled, while the other is just now lifting off the planet surface. Escape will be futile."

"That is satisfactory," said the Mab'r. "See to it that the Rond'r finishes the operation," he ordered.

The subordinate flashed a dim glow of green as he accepted the order. "It will be as you command, Mab'r."

Dreng'r turned to leave but was stopped by Erland'r's final rumi-nation. "It seems that one of the surviving humans is the central figure from his ancestor's divination. I am as yet undecided about whether or not to mandate this prophecy. For the time being we will allow him to live, but he must never return to Earth."

"Yes, Mab'r, he will remain on Log'rfold for the rest of his life."

Somewhere off the southeast coast of the peninsula, a large pair of green viper-like pupils looked up at the flash in the sky. *At long last, Hope has finally arrived, and my watch is almost over.*

After the light faded away, the winds quickly diminished, and she was able to adjust her huge golden wings and change her heading. Rodinya flew toward the tip of the peninsula, where powerful ocean waves broke against a jagged wall of giant crystal shards. She knew that she would find a man there who had only moments left to live—a man she had waited a millennium to pluck from the sea—an Earthman foretold to lead the human race in their coming fight for survival.

End

PROLOGUE: *KATANA RED*

MONSTERS

Survival in the far reaches of the human frontier was wholly dependent on how wary one approached this remote and dangerous wilderness. Few ventured into the primeval forest that blanketed the far northern end of the peninsula, and not all that did returned to tell about it. For a thousand years the colony had been all but free of the reptilian carnivores that inhabited the vast northern continent, or the packs of huge bears that had been bioengineered as a counter to those giant reptiles. But occasionally one or more of these roving monsters would invade the frontier and hunt those that lived there.

The wilderness was sparsely populated by the humans who lived on the peninsula, and because of that, it was also far from prying eyes. Deep in this dense forest, another monster had appeared: a monster that walked on two legs, a monster whose agenda was far more insidious than simply raiding a few ranches and feeding on its inhabitants. This monster had a plan: a plan that promised power, was laced with vengeance, and bought with greed.

Where this monster tread, misery would follow.

It was in this remote region of the Cambrian frontier that two groups of men, amid the chirps of small reptiles and the rustle of dead leaves, approached each other from opposite directions. The rendezvous chosen was deep in the ancient forest and only four kilometers from the banks of the Crystal River, a large slow-moving river that meandered through the western lowlands of the Spine, making the human colony, and all life within it, possible.

Enslavement of that life. That was the sole purpose for the meeting.

There were a total of seven men present for the meeting. Four had made the eight-day ride from Cambria itself, while the other three had hiked through the forest from a small riverboat anchored at the river.

Three of the four riders reined in their horses at the edge of a small forest glade, opposite the three who had approached on foot. The fourth rider continued into the meadow to meet a man from the other group. That man had also left his companions at the edge of the clearing. Once the two were at the center of the secluded meadow, the rider dismounted and approached the other man. A private conversation between them was imperative.

"What have you heard from our friends, Bayne?" asked the portly man as he tried to stretch his soft legs, sore from the long ride.

"It's Count Darx, you fool!" snarled the younger man. "I've told you before to address me thusly, and that's the last time you'll have the benefit of a reminder. We've too much at stake if anyone hears some imbecile use that other name." An insane intensity took over the count's green eyes as they watched the blood drain from the other man's face. After a tense moment Count Darx calmed enough to answer the question. "The first element of the plan will manifest itself within days. You need to return to Cambria right away and see to your part of the bargain."

"Yes, well—about that," stammered the older man, whose fear rose with each heartbeat. "It may be more difficult than you realize to acquire the requested amount."

Darx stepped in uncomfortably close and hissed a warning through gritted teeth. "It wasn't a request. You are the metal depository guild director, are you not? I strongly suggest you make it happen as previously agreed." A glint of the earlier insanity returned as he jabbed his trembling companion in the chest and snapped his fingers in the man's pale face. "As you well know, spinelessness has its own reward."

A sickening snap, like the breaking of a small branch, filled the forest glade when the older man's right pinky finger broke and folded back across the top of his hand.

Never a brave or physically hardy man, the guild director squealed as he grabbed his broken finger, backed away from the younger man, and blubbered, "Removing a t-ton of steel from the depository won't be easy, even for m-me. It's closely watched with strict p-protocols in place." Self-preservation kept him from making eye contact with his tormentor as he whimpered his excuses, "If the t-theft is discovered then some unanswerable q-q-questions will be asked."

Unmoved by the fat man's pain, Darx scoffed, "It's not theft. Think of it more like an investment. An investment our friends require to prove our resolve to help them." He grinned with a passionless mien and pressed his deadly point. "So, abide by our agreement, Director, and your reward will be more power than you can imagine. Fail, and you'll find that all the bones in that blubber bubble you call a body can snap just as easily as a single finger. Imagine, if you will, the excruciating pain if they all broke at once. Well, like I said, I've no need to tell you." The insane presence briefly reappeared as Darx stepped in close and said in a confidential tone, "I'm sure you get the picture."

"Y-yes, I understand."

Darx dropped his head, but rolled his eyes up, locked onto his companion, and warned, "Keep in mind that I went easy on you this time." He left the rest unsaid as his malevolent demeanor vanished as quickly as it had appeared. He gave the whimpering man a small bow, a gracious smile, and walked away, casually calling out over his shoulder. "Be so kind as to hurry back to Cambria and remain true to our agreement. Don't forget. Bye now."

ACKNOWLEDGMENTS

My first editor once told me early on that no book is ever ready even after the first rewrite. I was determined to prove her wrong. I failed. Thank you, Sarah Kasman for showing me the way of the word. Given that, I want to acknowledge the indispensable contributions to this trilogy by the editor extraordinaire: Philip Newey. His kick-butt style of editing took this story from a lump of clay, cut out about fifty percent of the words, and turned them into a sculpture of a story. But most of all, I especially want to thank Brad Pauquette who turned the sculpture into something worth all the effort. A huge thank you goes to Doug Davis, whose interior work is an absolute thing of beauty. And finally, I want to thank Boyle & Dalton's visionary publisher, Emily Hitchcock, who took a chance on unknown, untested, and undeserving author and saw my story get to the light of day.

I would also like to acknowledge my beta readers: Steve and the Bison. Two of the most intelligent people I've ever known. One helped me get the science right (yeah, I get it: Einstein was right, and I was wrong), while the other casually suggested that I might want to consider altering sentences with seven commas and one period. Still dunno what he was on about …

ABOUT THE AUTHOR

Author Tobin Marks has masterfully created an alien watery world called Aqueous. Orbiting a Red Dwarf 1,187 light-years from Earth, Aqueous is teeming with dangerous reptilian life . . . and one long-forgotten human colony.

Marks is a world traveler who grew up in a household of rocket scientists. As a boy he had a front row seat observing many NASA and NOAA projects. Now, from his home in northwest Baja, he has written the trilogy: The Hope Prophecy. Book one, *Endeavor's Run*, is a blend of real science, science fiction, and fantasy. Book two, *Katana Red*, and book three, *Drakon Rus*, are exciting continuations of the series.

He has released the action-packed prequel, *Ark of the Apocalypse*, published by Boyle & Dalton, and is now working on the second trilogy, The Hope Progression.

www.ingramcontent.com/pod-product-compliance
Lightning Source LLC
Chambersburg PA
CBHW020502260626
47156CB00006B/1827